T0374475

TWO-ELEVEN

Dream Child

Joseph Browne

iUniverse, Inc.
New York   Bloomington

TWO-ELEVEN
Dream Child

Copyright © 2010 Joseph Browne

All rights reserved. No part of this book may be used or reproduced by any means, graphic, electronic, or mechanical, including photocopying, recording, taping or by any information storage retrieval system without the written permission of the publisher except in the case of brief quotations embodied in critical articles and reviews.

This is a work of fiction. All of the characters, names, incidents, organizations, and dialogue in this novel are either the products of the author's imagination or are used fictitiously.

iUniverse books may be ordered through booksellers or by contacting:

iUniverse
1663 Liberty Drive
Bloomington, IN 47403
www.iuniverse.com
1-800-Authors (1-800-288-4677)

Because of the dynamic nature of the Internet, any Web addresses or links contained in this book may have changed since publication and may no longer be valid. The views expressed in this work are solely those of the author and do not necessarily reflect the views of the publisher, and the publisher hereby disclaims any responsibility for them.

ISBN: 978-1-4502-2419-2 (sc)
ISBN: 978-1-4502-2420-8 (ebk)

Library of Congress Control Number: 2010905859

Printed in the United States of America

iUniverse rev. date: 04/23/2010

Two : Eleven
Dream Child

My name is Joseph Pratt; I am 38 years old, I work at the county prison as the supervising Lieutenant for the Special Management Inmates there. I just moved to a small town just outside of the prison near Buffalo New York. I wasn't looking to move, but one day I received a flier on a house for sale, a three story single home in a gated community. I knew there was no way I could afford it, but something inside me made me want go look at it. When I went to the open house, I was the only one to sign in. The realtor appeared to be scared, like she didn't want to be in the house. Before I could ask the selling price the realtor practically gave it away. There are only 8 houses on the inside, with a total of about 120 people in the whole surrounding town. The old saying, "If it sound to good to be true, it probably is." Kept running thru my head. But I had a felling in my gut that this was the house for me.

Several days after moving in an event started in the receiving room at the prison that would bring me together with all who live inside of the gates, and almost everyone else in town. It was a puzzle, a mind bender. It soon became a real life puzzle that I would find myself trying to solve. This puzzle at first was a nuisance, and then it started to affect my home life, and then my sanity. It got in my head and would not let go of me. I kept a log of the events that happened. Below is that log. I kept this log just in case anything should happen, in case I should die before solving the puzzle.

THE BEGINNING

10-28-97 / 7:10 am

I was late to work again this morning. It's like a disorder I have where I can't leave my house until I solved the puzzles in the morning paper. This mornings puzzle was a thinker and I almost found myself calling out sick just to solve it. If I had known what was waiting for me at work I would have.

A strange white man that was transferred from upstate was sitting in the receiving room when I finally reported to work. He was slightly overweight, dirty and had long brown hair that came down past his shoulders. He had a stare that at times went right thru you. He was to be assigned to a general population unit but he requested that he be put onto the Administrative Segregation Unit, my unit. In this unit the inmates are housed in one-man cells and are secured in those cells 23 hours a day. This unit has been under my supervision for about two years now. All the inmates that come to this unit are placed in leg irons and shackled with traveling belts whenever they are let out of their cells. The inmates that are housed here are the worst of the worst. This inmates name was Robert

Johnson, and he refused to leave the receiving room area unless I came down to speak with him. He would only sit in silence, refusing to speak with anyone but me. He never lifted his head to even see who it was that was speaking with him. When I arrived he would not respond, when I addressed him by his name Robert Johnson. He just continued to look down at the floor. Only after I told him I was leaving did he whisper, "My name is Sogod". To speed things up I went along with his request. When I addressed him as Sogod he asked without lifting his head, "Who are you?" I told him I was Lt Pratt, he then asked, "Lt Joseph Pratt?" When I answered yes, he stood up and proceeded to let the receiving room staff process him into the system. I stood in the receiving room and watched him as he watched me. Not once did he take his eyes off of me. I started to get creped out and went back up to my office. It wasn't until I sat down behind my desk that I realized he knew my first name.

I had not been in my officer for ten minutes when I received a call from the sergeant in the receiving room stating that a man called claiming to be Johnson's lawyer, he requested that Johnson have access to a phone 24 hours a day, and that he be allowed to wear a flowing white robe instead of the prison issued orange jumpsuit, he also stated that Johnson should be permitted to have his church followers and family members visit at any time of day or night. I instructed the sergeant to have his lawyer send us the court order on all of those request. Knowing from the start that all would be denied. He was secured in cell 11 at 8:30 am and he went right to sleep.

9:45 am

The touring officers called me to the unit at 9:45 am. Touring Officers Williams and McGee told me that they noticed that Johnson was somehow able to write on his cell walls. When I looked into the cell I observed that every inch of the cell was covered in some sort of gibberish, Officer Williams thought it was some sort of spell, or religious prayers, I even heard him say black magic. I didn't care if it was war and peace it had to come off the walls. I looked over at the bed and saw that Johnson was still asleep in the cell. Officer Williams stated that he was asleep the entire time. I asked both if Johnson was searched when he came up to the unit, Officer Williams told me they took everything, that Johnson was stripped down and only given his jumpsuit and bed sheets. Williams then said, "The only way he would have been able to sneak in a pencil was up his ass". I looked at Officer McGee who seemed to not want to get to close to the cell. I then asked both if either of them looked up his ass. Neither answered, McGee told me Johnson was asleep in his bunk every time he walked by, and then within 20 minutes all the writing appeared. I then called for the door to be unlocked and as soon as the door opened Johnson sat straight up on the bunk and gave me permission to enter. I told him that I didn't need his permission to enter his cell and that I would enter it whenever I wanted. I then told him to give me what ever he used to mark up my cell walls with. Johnson stated, "The walls were marked as I slept" I now knew I was dealing with a special inmate. I photographed the walls and held out a rag and some cleaning solution to Johnson and told him to clean the walls. Johnsons stare never left me as he said, "You will realize soon that I was sent here to help you." He then turned and laid down on his bunk with his back to me. I tossed the supplies on the floor and told him he had 1 hour to clean the walls, and if they were not clean when I returned he would lose his phone and commissary privileges. I left the area about 10:10 am

10:30 am

I checked Officer McGee's log and noticed an entry that said Inmate Johnson was asleep in his cell and was not making any effort to clean the cell walls. Officer McGee called to tell me he had just made a tour and when he approached Johnson's cell he heard several different voices coming from the cell, he said one of the voices appeared to be that of a child. He told me he tried to look in the cell but the cell was dark inside, even tho it was mid morning and the sun was shining from the other cells on that side of the unit. I then asked McGee if Johnson could have been talking on a cell phone, and if he checked the cell to see what Johnson was covering his window with. McGee didn't answer, I could feel his fear over the phone. I then told him to sit tight that I was on my way.

11:00 am

When I entered the Unit McGee met me at the door and told me that the entire unit was refusing to come out for their 1-hour exercise time. This was strange because the number one complaint I get from these inmates is that they are never allowed to come out. I looked over at cell 11 and noticed that it was the only cell without the sunlight shining thru the door window or from under the door. As I walked up to the cell I reached down on my belt for my flashlight, but when I reached the cell and looked up the sunlight was coming thru. I looked in the door window and saw Johnson standing in the center of the cell with his arms outstretched and reaching towards the ceiling. He appeared to be chanting. I looked at the walls and noticed that all the marking were now gone, the walls were cleaner then they have ever been. I tapped on the glass with my flashlight and said "Good job", I then noticed the cleaning supplies were where I left them, untouched. Without turning around Johnson said, "I didn't remove my words, I moved them." I said "What ever, as long as they are not on my walls." Johnson then lowered his arms letting his jumpsuit fall off his shoulders down to his waist. I had to shine my light in but it appeared that all the marking were now on his back.

I had Johnson shackled and removed from the cell, he was held face first up against the wall as Officer McGee and Williams did a full search of the cell and Johnson's body, they were looking for any type of writing instrument, Cell phone or anything that he could have used to block the sunlight from the window, but nothing was found, they even had Johnson bend over as they looked up his ass. Several inmates on the unit started banging on their cell doors and screaming at Johnson to shut up. I looked over at Johnson as he stood staring at the wall, he was silent the entire time. Johnson then stepped back from the wall, slowly turned his eyes towards me and whispered, "I am in your jail for a reason, you will save her." Johnson then stepped towards me and he was out of his handcuffs, he lifted his hands towards the sky and yelled, "She needs to be saved". Officer McGee then hit Johnson in the face with a stream of pepper spray. Johnson never blinked, he just slowly walked back into his cell dropping the still secured handcuffs on the floor by my feet, the spray had no effect on him at all.

12:00 pm

Medical was called to the area to decontaminate Johnson from the pepper spray use. He refused to let any medical personel near him. He stated, "You can't treat who is not here". Medical quickly referred Johnson to the Mental Health Department.

2:30 pm

Dr Gray from Mental Health came on the Unit and interviewed Inmate Johnson for about twenty minutes. Dr Gray reported to me that Johnson was delusional and that he thinks he is the mighty Lord Sogod, and that he claimed to be able to control not only the air and ground, but also thoughts and dreams, and thru dreams he will save her. When I asked him who her was? Dr Gray told me he asked Johnson that same question, and Johnson told him to ask me. Dr Gray also stated that Johnson claimed to be able to leave his cell at will and said, "All that there is must be stopped by 211". This guy is a big time nut job I thought, I then asked the doctor, "How was he able to write on his own back, can you explain how the officers heard several voices coming from the cell?" Dr Gray said split personalities and told me he felt Johnson was harmless, but that he should not be on this unit, Dr Gray told me he would see to it that Johnson was transferred to a better suited Unit.

3:20 pm

My shift ended twenty minutes ago and I was still in my office filling out paperwork when I heard a response call to the Ad/Seg Unit. I got up and responded and when I entered the unit I saw Johnson being dragged across the floor by several other inmates. They slammed him up against the wall and started to punch and kick him.

When the Response Team arrived on the unit all the assaulting inmates dropped to the floor and put their hands on their heads. Inmate Johnson just stood there, he stood there staring right at me. He was bleeding and his face was swelling up as I looked at him. Seeing this I knew he was hurt, but he appeared to not be in any pain at all. All involved inmates were re-secured in their cells and Johnson was taken down to Medical.

4:00 pm

I stayed to listen to the inmate statements on why they were attacking Inmate Johnson. I had a lot of questions for both them and the staff. Why were so many inmates out of their cells without restraints on? Why were they attacking an inmate that just arrived on the unit less then 8 hours ago? When asked, the officer's response was the inmates were banging on the cell doors and when they were questioned as to why they were doing this, they all said the same thing, that Johnson was in their heads telling them what to do. The officers then stated when the inmates refused orders to stop banging on the cell doors, the officers went to call for a supervisor. Then the cell doors all opened at the same time. Johnson walked out into the middle of the Unit as the other 6 inmates rushed out and started to attack him. The officers said that Johnson never even tried to protect himself. The inmates all claimed to have heard Johnsons voice in their dreams telling them to kill him. All six of the inmates were told to give detailed written statements by the Captain. I left and went home and took a hot shower and fell right to sleep. Not once did I hear Johnson voice in my dreams.

10-29-97 / 7:20 am

The puzzles in the paper this morning were quite easy to complete, so easy I arrived at the prison a few minutes early. Right after roll call I reported to medical. I wanted to speak with Johnson about yesterday's incident. Dr Gray met me and told me that he still will only answer to the name of Sogod and that I should address him that way, The doctor told me it may open him up if I was to address him by his made up alter ego. Johnson was strapped into the bed in four point restraints but he appeared to be at ease with himself. He was asleep but he had an eerie smile on his face, sort of the joker smile from the batman movies. I waited about five minutes and when he did not wake up I got up to leave. Johnson turned his head and said "211" I asked him what he meant by that, He stated "211 will be an obsession for you because you have been chosen, you will not fail her." I tried not to laugh but a smile came across my face. Johnson became

angry and he tried to break free from the restraints.
Dr Gray was then called out of the room. I then bent
down, I was almost nose-to-nose with Johnson, and I
asked him, "What's your problem, you can leave your
cell when ever you want, but you can't get out of leather
restraints?" This angered him more, "DON'T MOCK
ME" he yelled, "YOU WILL SAVE HER". I then told
him to start making sense, I told him that he talks all
types of gibberish no one understands and that he scares
the shit out of half the staff, and the other half just thinks
he is nuts. I then asked him, "What are you some sort of
street magician, are the other inmates in on your game?"
In a way they are he said now calm, "Read their memos
and count the words, do that and you will be closer to
understanding what 211 really means." I started to walk
out but turned around and asked, "Why don't you just
tell me what 211 is? Humor me you crazy motherfucker".
Johnson just slowly closed his eyes as he said, "You will
save her, your compulsion for solving every puzzle put in
front of you will see to that."

8:30 am

Against my better judgment I went and got copies of
the inmate's memos. There were only five because one
inmate refused to give a written statement. As I read the
memos I realized all of the inmates had changed their
stories from what they had told the captain yesterday. I

was thinking they came to their senses and didn't want to sound just as crazy as Johnson. They all wrote that the cell doors must of malfunction and when they exited the cells Johnson came at them. It was all bullshit, but it was the protocol for inmates not to help out in any type of prison investigation. I then counted the words and all five had a different amount of words. As I wrote down the numbers I caught myself thinking, why am I letting this guy get under my skin. It may just be because I can't let a puzzle go unsolved. I looked at the 5 different numbers, 32, 48, 47, 53, 31, they didn't mean a dam thing to me. Then I added the numbers up, it came to 211, creepy, but still no meaning.

10:00 am

I received news that Johnson was being sent to a Mental Hospital where he will be able to receive better treatment, and he would be observed by a trained mental health staff. I walked down to the receiving room to make sure he was being processed to leave and not giving the staff any problems. It was the other way around, Johnson was sitting in a holding cell shackled and waiting for transportation. There were several officers in the area and I watched as one officer walked by Johnson with a sheet wrapped around his head. He asked Johnson as he walked by if he liked his white flowing robe. Johnson just sat and stared right thru them. When he saw me walking towards him he stood up and walked to the front of the cell, before I could say anything Johnson said, "I know you counted up the words, there were two hundred and eleven of them, right?" Before I could answer he then said, "Those five double digit numbers will also have meaning". I told him I didn't bother, that I forgot all about it. He then became very angry and started yelling, "WHY ARE YOU LYING?" Officers responded to the cell and threatened him with pepper spray. I told them to ease up, that the spray doesn't affect him at all. I then turned back at Johnson and he was now on his toes and it appeared that he was about to lift up from the floor, his eyes were back in his head and all white, I heard giggles coming from the staff behind me. Johnson then said in a low whisper, "Count out the letters, every 21st letter circle it, then by using your alphabet take the letter to the left of the circled letter". Then he paused as he came down from his toes and his eyes returned. "It will help you, it will help you to understand 211". As Johnson sat down on the cell floor he said, "You will believe, I'll see you on the outside". I then noticed that several more officers had come to see what was going on. I then turned back to look at Johnson and said, "I doubt that, you will die in prison". Johnson looking at the ground looked up and said very slowly, "My name is SOGOD, and I have died a thousand times, but this time will be my last". I told Johnson that I could not make heads or tails of his rants. The officer with the sheet on his head again walked slowly past the cell. A smile came across my face. My smile seemed to anger Johnson, he said as he stared up at me, "I am disappointed in you Joe, you should take the high road and fire that officer, at least discipline him, but you appear to be a week leader, and the officer that has been disrespecting me, he will feel my touch because you refused to react to his actions, all of you will see my way." I turned and started to walk away, "Maybe I chosen the wrong man to save her". Was the last thing Johnson said before he spun his body around and sat back down on the cell floor with his back to me. I walked back to the cell gate, "How do you know my first name, did someone tell you it?" Without turning around he said, "I was sent to you, you will see soon" Again I had no idea what he was talking about.

2:00 pm

I went back to my office and I did what he said, I counted the letters, went to the letter to the left and there were eighteen letters, EVASDOGOSDESUBAYMA. This was nothing, but I put the note in my pocket anyway. As I was walking out of my office I was called over to Sogods old cell. Officer McGee was standing outside the cell like he was on guard duty. "What now?" I asked as I entered the unit. McGee just pointed over his shoulder into the cell. I looked in and it was pitch black, no light at all coming thru the window. I shined my light at the window and saw thousands and thousands of flies were covering it.

They were on the outside of the window, there were so many that even as they crawled over each other no light was able to come into the cell. I tapped my flashlight on the window and the flies all suddenly flew away, all of them except for a small group that seemed to stay in the shape of a cross, and as we looked at them the cross turned upside down. The sunlight filled the cell with light and on the sidewalls were unreadable writing. I pulled the note from my pocket and it was the same as the marking on the walls only on the walls it repeated itself over and over, and if you looked at the markings on an angle, it appeared to take the shape of a small child on their knees praying.

I then called to see if Johnson had left the Receiving Room yet. I was told he was in the van in the sally port. I ordered them to hold him up as I ran down to the van. I opened the door and grabbed Johnson and ripped open his jumpsuit, he no longer had the markings on his back. He did however have 1-1-2 carved into his upper back and it was bleeding. Johnson didn't make a sound the entire time I inspected him. When I went to pull his jumpsuit back up, a fly landed by the carved numbers. Then as I went to secure the van door Johnson said, " Sometimes you have to go from finish to start to understand a god like me".

3:00 pm

While driving home I could not understand what Johnson was trying to say, "From finish to start." Johnson was on his way out of the prison, out of my watch, why am I letting this asshole get to me? Then it hit me, 1-1-2 on Johnson's back is 2-1-1 backwards. My desire to solve every puzzle put in front of me keeps bringing me back to this nutcase. How does he know this about me? I know I should just drop this, he is gone, strapped down to a bed at the mental hospital. But I know in my heart I will not stop until I figure this out. I pulled over and parked the car on the shoulder of the highway, I got out the note and wrote the letters backwards, AMYABUSEDSOSODSAVE. Broken down there was only one saying, "Amy abused Sogod save". I thought, again, what the fuck? Is he just lucky, did he see the memos or did he tell the inmates what to write, maybe it is just a parlor trick? As I went to start my car back up, I saw three flies on the windshield directly in front of me. I then pulled back onto the highway, I could only think of one Amy. I hardly ever see her, and I have never spoken with her. She was my new neighbors kid.

10-30-97 / 2:11 am

I was driving down Broad Street, there was fine mist in the air and the street was starting to get wet. I pulled up to a stop sign at Broad and James Street. I saw a car coming down James Street and it was flying. I knew it was not going to be able to stop. It went right thru the stop sign and slammed into a tree across the intersection. I got out and ran over to the car. The impact of the accident was so violent that the driver went thru the windshield and was lying on the street in a mangled ball in front of the car. As I ran up I saw that it was Officer Anderson. Officer Anderson was the officer in the receiving room with the sheet on his head, the Officer that angered Johnson so much. I then noticed out of the corner of my eye that there was another person in the car sitting in the passenger seat. He didn't seem to be hurt. As I walked around to the passenger side door I could hear this person laughing and thought they must be in shock. I walked up to the

19

window and bent down to look in, I asked if everything was all right? Inmate Johnson then turned and looked at me from the passengers seat. I woke up to realize this was all a dream, a nightmare. I rolled over and looked at the clock, it was too early to get up. It was only 2:11 am.

6:40 am

I was being briefed in the roll call room for my upcoming tour of duty when Capt Harris came in and informed everyone that Officer Anderson was killed in an automobile accident last night. Before I could ask, the Captain stated he was killed when a drunk driver ran a stop sign at Broad and James at about 2 o'clock in the morning.

8:00 am

Northeastern Mental Hospital is one of the fastest growing Hospitals in the area, just ten years ago it was a single story Hospital with a two bed ER and a staff of 14, it now takes up a city block and employs over 2000 people, including over half of the 120 people that live in my town. The Hospital is fifty-five miles away from the prison and Inmate Johnson is refusing all medications and advice from all staff. Still insisting he is this god like leader Sogod, lord of all. When my neighbor, Nurse Danielle Williamson entered the room and asked Johnson how he was feeling, Johnson spoke for the first time since being admitted into the hospital, and he answered to the name Johnson. He looked Danielle straight in the eye and said, "I had a great nights sleep, I had to take a detour but my mission has started". Danielle then asked, "And what mission is that?" Johnson then replied, "To save you". Danielle said as she reached for his chart, "I don't need you to save me, I am doing fine." Danielle noted that Johnson seemed to go into some sort of self-induced trance at 1:55 am. Also noted was that staff could not shake him from this state. The final note stated that Johnson opened his eyes and laughed. The last note was written at 2:11 am

3:20 am

With the death of Officer Anderson and that creepy dream I was glad this day was almost over. As I was pulling into my driveway I noticed my neighbors kid Amy sitting on the curb. I walked over and stood behind her. She was a bit of a strange little girl, she was about eleven years old and I think she is home schooled. I don't think I ever seen her outside alone or talking to anyone other then her mother. I patted her on the head and asked her if she was okay, she just shrugged her shoulders. I then asked her what that meant. She turned and looked up at me her eyes appeared to be sunken into her face and she looked like she was frightened. I reached for her and told her she better get up before a car hits her. She smiled and grabbed my hand. Her mother Danielle the nurse from the Hospital pulled into their driveway. Amy pulled her hand from mine and ran to the front door of her house. I noticed that Amy had some bruising on her lower back and wrists. Danielle looked over at me with a look on her face like I was trying to steal her kid. So I waved, she put on a fake smile and waved back. She turned to see Amy sitting on their porch. It looked like Amy was trying to hide from her. Danielle walked towards her and asked her why she was outside, "Did your father drop you off early again?" Amy just shook her head no. I then told Danielle that Amy was sitting on the curb when I pulled up a couple of minutes ago. Danielle then walked over and leaned on the fence and said, "Her bum ass father, I hope he just dropped her off early, I would hate to think she sat out here all day. Her home schoolteacher quit and I'm looking for a new one. Fucking Dan is just going to have to watch her until I can do that. He is not working, and she is his daughter". Just then a beat up 92 blue Mustang pulled up to the curb. This little man about 5 foot tall all skin and bones with a lot of tattoos gets out. I was willing to bet the ink in his tattoos weighed more then him. He walked up to Danielle, looks at me and tells her he was sorry but he had to drop her off early. He then told Danielle to give the kid a house key. Danielle turns and yells at him, "My neighbor there came home and found her playing in the middle of the street". Dan looks back at me and says, "Maybe your nosey neighbor should mind his own bees-knees". I looked at this little turd and thought if I sneeze he would blow over, and he is talking shit to me. Dan then turned back to Danielle and told her that he is taking Amy to dinner. Amy then jumped up from the porch and ran over to her father and took his hand and started to pull him towards his car. Danielle yells at them to be back by 9 o'clock. Amy didn't seem to make any effort to say goodbye to her mother, nor did Danielle seem to care. Danielle still standing by the fence turns back to me and says, "Dan left us right after Amy was born and now he is attempting to become father of the fucking year. He didn't want anything to do with either of us until about 2 years ago when he showed up on my front steps asking for joint custody." I then asked, "Why didn't you try to fight it?" Danielle said she didn't have the time, energy or money to fight him. So she agreed with him, but he had to agree to stay clean, no booze and no drugs. It worked out for the best. She then says, "I just hate when he takes her overnight, she always comes back different." I don't know why, but I asked, "Different how?" Danielle now not looking at me says, "Just different", she then asks me if Amy ever spoke with me before, "Not much", I tell her, "Just Hi here and there". Danielle now looking back at me says "I hear her talking in her room at night and I swear sometimes I hear a mans voice". I didn't know if she was accusing me of being that mans voice she hears so I thought I'd walk away. I did want to ask about the burses, I thought I mind my own bees-knees.

10-31-97 / 2:11 am

I'm sitting on my porch, it's a bright sunny day. I am just sitting back relaxing drinking a soda. I look over and see Amy running and jumping over a sprinkler. She looks over at me and waves, when I waved back she smiles and runs over to me. She asks if she can have a soda. I reach into my cooler and grab her one, but when she put the bottle up to her mouth it wasn't a soda, it was a beer. I reach to take it from her. She pulls away and says, "It's okay, I drink beer all the time at my dads". Amy then tries to climb up onto my lap and I push her away, "What's the matter?" She asks, "Dad always wants me to sit on his lap". I tried to hold her away as I told her it was because her bathing suit was wet from the sprinkler and I didn't want to get my clothes wet. She then says "What clothes?" I look down and realize that I am naked, wrapped only in a bath towel. When I look up Amy was coming at me, she grabs my neck and her grasp is extremely strong and she pulls our faces together, just as our lips are about to touch she whispers in Johnson's voice "Save me". I wake up in a pool of sweat, another bad dream. I then hear some noise outside, it was Amy being dropped off by Dan. I didn't notice the flies that were covering the top of the window as I turned to look at the clock, it was 2:11 am

6:30 am

As I was driving to work I kept thinking about the dream, not just the one with Amy, but also the one in which I saw Officer Andersons accident. It made me think, did Amy's father get her drunk and abuse her? Was she trying to kiss me? Maybe I am at the start of a mental breakdown? As I pulled into the prison parking lot I was met by Captain Harris, he told me to report to Northeastern Hospital and take a statement from Johnson. It turned out he was talking about some sort of abuse at the prison, and the last thing the prison needs is a lawsuit involving abuse. Captain Harris told me that Johnson would only speak with me, that he was actually demanding that I be sent to him. Before I left I informed the Captain that Johnson was housed at the prison for less then 2 days, and the only abuse I seen was caused by him.

7:30 am

When I arrived at the hospital I was escorted back to the security wing and I was impressed as it was more secure then the prisons medical wing. Once buzzed inside, I was greeted by a Doctor, She told me that Johnson had requested that I be sent to speak with him, she also told me that the only Hospital staff member he speaks with is Nurse Williamson. "Danielle?" I asked. The doctor said yes, you know her? "She is my neighbor". Danielle then met us. She told me that Johnson told her about some sort of abuse at the prison, and he requested that I be sent over. I told her I heard he demanded that I be sent over.

We walked into Johnson's room, he was strapped down on the bed in four point restraints. When he saw us walk in, he asked Danielle to step out of the room, Danielle stated that she could not leave me in the room alone with him. Johnson then said that he has nothing to say. I asked him what abuse he was talking about at the prison? He just lay quietly on the bed staring straight up at the ceiling. I told him if he would not talk, that I had to leave. Johnson turned his head and said, "You will save her?" I turned and looked back at him and asked, "Who are you talking to, me or this pretty nurse?" Johnson laughed, and then said, "You call her pretty, but it was her daughter you tried to force yourself on last night". Danielle grabbed my arm and gently pulled me from the room. I stood outside the room as Danielle went back in. I could see her arguing with Johnson, but I could not hear what they were arguing about. When a Doctor came and went into the room, both stopped their arguing. Danielle came out as the Doctor examined Johnson. Danielle told me that she was sorry for having me come down to the hospital for nothing, she told me that Johnson was crazy, and not to worry about what he said about Amy. She leaned in and gave me a hug, it surprised me a little, it seemed unprofessional and when she let go she said she would see me after work.

Danielle then went back into Johnson's room. As the Doctor came out I kicked a doorstop in so the door wouldn't close all the way. As I stood to the side of the door I heard Danielle call Johnson an ass, and she told him if he doesn't stop all this nonsense she would have him sent back to the prison. Johnson than said that he was only looking out for Amy. This made Danielle even madder, she told Johnson to keep Amy's name out of his mouth, and then she told him to stop with his mind voodoo, she said she knows what she has to do and so will Amy. Danielle then turned to leave, but Johnson yelled, "What Amy needs is to go to school, she needs to live like every other child her age, you both need to get from behind those fucking gates" Danielle stopped and turned back towards Johnson. Nothing was said for several moments, then Danielle calmly said, "You know it is too late to start sending her to school, you know why she has been home schooled, now leave me alone, leave Amy alone, and leave my neighbor the fuck alone". I ducked around the corner as Danielle came out of the room. The doorstop was still in the door and I was able to enter after Danielle left. I kicked the doorstop away so

the door shut behind me. Johnson didn't acknowledge
me coming back into the room. I asked him if he knew
Danielle and Amy, Johnson just stared into space. I picked
up his chart, there was a note that said he went into
another self induced trance or coma. The time stamp
was from 1:00 am to 2:11 am. That was the time of my
dream about Amy, his first one was the time I had the
dream about Officer Anderson. I went to put the chart
back in its slot at the foot of the bed, and noticed that he
had several other episodes logged where he would go into
trances or self-induced comas. As I read the chart I did not
notice that Johnson was now sitting up in the bed, both
his arms were out of their restraints. He seemed larger
than life as he said, "You didn't see me last night, but I
saw you." He startled me as I almost screamed, I took a
step back and told him I didn't know what he was talking
about. He laughed and said, "I also know what she said to
you." Johnson then whispered as I turned to leave, "Save
her". When I turned back around to look at him, he was
once again laying down, all restraints tightly secured on
him. On the drive back to the prison my mind was going
a thousand miles a minute. Danielle and Johnson were
arguing like they knew each other. Danielle told him to
stop with his mind tricks. I was starting to believe that
Johnson requested to be put in my unit because of me,
and he had the other inmates beat him just so he could
be sent to Danielle at the hospital. I tried to put it out of
my head as I walked into the prison.

9:43 am

Danielle went back into Johnson room to give him his medications, even tho he refuses them she has to offer, hospital policy. After refusing his meds as Danielle wrote on his chart Johnson asked, "You mad at me?" Danielle never looking up from the chart didn't answer. Johnson then told her that he couldn't help it, that he just wants to make sure Amy will be safe. Johnson then tells Danielle, "When I first went to jail I believed that this was done, that you and Amy would be fine. Then I started having visions of what is going to happen to her if you let this happen. I understand that it was me who started this, at first my visions were of what I expected, I put myself here to protect you, but now I see what it is they want, I see the end, and it is not what any of us want. I have reached out to other people to try and stop it. I am now reaching out to you." Danielle looked up at Johnson for the first time and said, "Reaching out to me for what? Because you think Amy may be in danger, because you had a vision? You knew it wasn't over when you put her here." Johnson then says thru clenched teeth to keep his voice down, "She is in danger, you should know that more then anyone." All Danielle said back was "You are crazy." Then as she went to leave the room, she turned holding the door and said, "When you figure out why it is that Amy may get hurt, you know who to blame, mind fuck them". Johnson then softly said he would have to die to do that. Danielle then stormed out of the room. As the door shut Johnson still strapped to his bed whispered, "I will see you in your dreams"

10:45 am

Danielle was sitting in the nurse's lounge when Johnson is pushed in next to her in a wheelchair. Danielle starts to get up telling Johnson that she doesn't have time for his shit anymore. Johnson grabs her arm tight and calmly tells her to sit back down. Johnson then says, "I see Amy getting hurt, she is strong and she will handle the abuse in the beginning, even after awhile she will start to enjoy it". Danielle tries to pull from his grip, but Johnson holds on and says, "In my visions with her, I ask Amy to just runaway, Amy tells me that her mommy will be taken away if she doesn't do what she has to do. I am now almost able to see what is happening in her room, I can almost see who it is that is going to hurt her." Danielle stops struggling and asks him if it is Dan that hurts her? Johnson reveals that Dan is not there, Danielle starts to cry. Johnson then says, "You are there, so is your neighbor Joe, but there is someone else, but they never come out of the shadows." Danielle now talking thru tears asks, "If you can see us, why cant you see who is going to hurt Amy". Johnson starts to wheel away, he then turns and says, "I always get there after she is hurt, every one else is there when it happens." As he turns to wheel away he says, "There is a smell of blood and death in the room." Danielle gets up to go and grab Johnson's wheelchair, but bumps into a Doctor almost knocking him over as she stood up. The Doctor asks her if she is all right. Danielle pushes him away and says she needs to get Johnson. She reaches the wheelchair and spins it around. Its not Johnson in the wheelchair its an elderly woman who spilled her food when she was spun around. Danielle looks around the room, Johnson is nowhere to be seen. Danielle then almost falls to her knees with her face in her hands as she starts to cry. The Doctor catches her and holds her up and leads her from the room. Danielle looks up at him and says, "I know he was here, I was just talking to him, I felt him grab me" She lifts her arm and she can still see his hand print on her wrist. The Doctor tells her as he sits her back down in a chair, "Johnson hasn't been out of his room all day, he has been secured since he got here".

11:00 am

Back at the prison I am sitting at my desk looking at the numbers I got from the memos, I added them up again just to be sure they added up to 211. I could feel there was something there, Johnson the nut bag was trying to tell me something. The numbers themselves 32, 48, 47, 53, and 31 meant nothing to me. I lent back in my chair and closed my eyes. I soon found myself asleep, dreaming, the funny thing was that I knew I was dreaming. I was in an unfamiliar house, similar to my own so I figured I may be in Danielle's. I heard crying coming from upstairs. I walked up to the middle bedroom and slowly pushed the door open. I saw Amy in the bathroom doorway, she was being pushed up against the doorframe, she was talking to someone, but I could not see who. As I walked around to her side I could see there was no one in the bathroom with her, I could see she was sobbing uncontrollably. Most of what she was saying I could not understand because of the crying, I did hear her say, "I don't want to tell, everyone will be mad at me". Suddenly she yells, "Don't hurt me", as her whole body was jerked back against the doorframe making me think this is how she got the burses on her back. She is just about to be thrown up against the frame again when she yells through her tears, "I'LL TELL YOU, I'll tell everybody." A ringing telephone on my desk wakes me up. When I answer the phone I hear a voice tell me to make a call, to help her, that the numbers are right in front of me. The phone then goes dead. As I sit there rubbing my eyes I notice that the first three numbers I have written down are my area code, and the other seven may be a phone number. So I broke it down, area code 324, phone number 847-5331. What did I have to lose, I dialed it. A man answered it, he sounded like he just was woken up. He says "Hello, Hello, who is this, my caller ID says county prison, is this Danielle's nosey fucking neighbor?" I am in shock, what are the odds that it would be a number of someone I know. I don't answer, I just gently hang up. I have this feeling that I must tell someone, but who, who will believe me. Is it a sign that Dan may be the one that I have to save Amy and Danielle from? In my dream Amy told me he gives her beer, and always wants her to sit on his lap. All girls sit on their parents laps, what am I thinking, I know mental breakdown here I come, I hope I get Danielle as my nurse. Then I thought maybe Amy would tell me something. I am sure I'll see them tonight. It's Halloween.

6:10 pm

"Trick or Treat" Danielle yelled as I opened the front door. Danielle was standing in the doorway with Amy hiding behind her. Amy was wearing a blond wig and dressed in a cheerleader costume, I bent down and dropped a candy bar in her bag and I asked her who she was. Amy said in a very low whisper "I'm Clair from Heroes" Danielle said that's her favorite show on TV. I asked if Clair was the one with the powers that prevents her from getting hurt? Danielle said, "I don't watch it, you would have to ask Amy". Amy was at the end of my walkway waving for Danielle to hurry up. I pulled my door shut and asked, "Do you mind if I walk with you guys? I'm out of candy". Danielle jokingly replied, "Are you hitting on me neighbor?" I held her arm and escorted her down the walkway. As we walked I asked if she knew Johnson before he came into the hospital, I told her that her argument appeared to be between two people that had met before. Danielle told me that Johnson used to work at the hospital, then about 11 years ago he started to try and sort of recruit staff into a church he was starting, that is when he first started with the Sogod name. Then he started ranting about child abductions, the hospital was about to fire him. He got wind of it, and before they could fire him, he set the record room on fire, the fire destroyed all of the hospitals records and half the hospital, two interns died. That is what he was sent to prison for. She then told me that he was her assistant, she said she was shocked when he was brought onto the mental wing, and that he requested her as his nurse. Before I could ask any other questions, Amy ran up the walkway to an older man standing on his porch. The older guy bent down to one knee and embraced Amy as she ran up to him. I heard the man say as he embraced her, "Is this my little Amy girl?" Amy pulled her wig off and shook her head yes. I looked at Danielle and asked, "Her Grandfather?" Danielle laughed and said, "No, that is Dr Adams, he is Amy's shrink". Now I was shocked, what is an eleven year old child doing seeing a shrink. Danielle must of seen the puzzled look on my face, she said, "Amy kept going into fits, like little fits of rage when she didn't get her way, some of them turned violent, Dr Adams worked at the hospital with me and agreed to see her, that was about 6 months ago, Amy now sees him once a week." I asked Danielle if Amy ever tried to hurt her, Danielle said, "Ever since Dr Adams started seeing her, her outbursts have stopped. But the other day when she returned from a stay with Dan, I noticed some redness and swelling on her back, Dan said she threw herself up against the wall when he wanted to bring her home during Amy's Heroes show, Dan said he had to grab her by her wrists and calm her down". Amy then came running back down to Danielle. I thought that story could explain the marks I saw the other day, but Danielle did not answer my question. Dr Adams walked down and asked Danielle if he could speak with her, I took Amy's hand and started to walk to the next house. As we walked I asked her if she was having a good time, how she liked Halloween, and if she would share her candy with me, she looked up at me, smiled and answered yes to all of my questions except the sharing one. I then stopped walking and we turned and looked back at Dr Adams and Danielle, Amy pulled on my arm to keep me walking, I told her to wait for her mother, Amy then started to squeeze my hand, her grip was strong and pain shot thru my fingers. I yanked it away and told her we had to wait for her mother. Amy then looked up at me and said, "Sorry". I told her it was all right, that her mother would be done with the Doctor in a minute. That's when I noticed that Amy's face again appeared sullen, and sunk in, almost skull like, I was looking into the saddest eyes I have ever seen on a child. I then bent down to her level and asked her if her dad has ever hurt or touched her. Amy looked down at her feet and whispered "No". Amy then looked up and pointed towards Dr Adams.

7:40 pm

After returning from trick and treating, Amy ran right into her house to count her candy. I sat out on the porch with Danielle. She told me that Dr Adams wants to see Amy more, maybe up to three times a week. I wanted to tell Danielle that Amy pointed to the doctor when I asked her if anyone was hurting her, but I didn't. Danielle may want to know why I would even ask her that question. But for some stupid reason I asked Danielle if Amy was ever treated at the hospital for abuse. Danielle got a little angry, I guess I should have kept that question to myself also. Danielle was asking me what it was I was accusing her of. I told her nothing, I said Amy just appears to be withdrawn from other people, she only talks when she is with someone she knows. She hides behind you at every door you knock on, and the marks on her back and wrists that she got at her fathers, and you say she seems different every time she comes back from a visit with him. Danielle, still angry asks me if I think her fathers is abusing her. Before I could answer Amy came running out the door screaming, she ran up to me and grabbed my hair. Danielle had to pull her from me. I looked at Amy and asked her if she wanted me to leave. Amy just pointed at my house

11-1-97 / 2:11 am

I woke up on my sofa, I was wet with sweat, yet it was cold in the house. I looked over and saw my front door was open. I went over to shut it and I saw Amy sitting in the middle of the street. A car was approaching, I ran out and picked her up and sat down on the curb with her in my lap. I looked at her and asked her what the hell she was doing. She looked up and hugged me, and then in Johnson voice again said, "You are going in the right direction." I woke up in my bed, another bad dream. I looked at the clock, again it was 2:11 am

9:35 am

It was my day off, and I decided to go and see Johnson, I wasn't sure if I would even be allowed in to see him. Something wasn't right, I was able to walk into the secured area and right into his room. Johnson looked up and asked me where Danielle was. "I don't know" I then asked, "She is not here?" I told Johnson that I saw her last night. Johnson interrupted and asked me how the trick and treating went. Danielle then came into the room with Amy. I turned and quietly asked Danielle how she could bring Amy to see this guy. Danielle appeared more surprised that I was there. Johnson then answered for her as he said, "I told her to bring Amy here". Johnson then reached out and grabbed Amy's arm. As soon as he touched her, Johnson went into what could only be described as a seizure. Amy fell to the floor crying and Johnson flopped around in his restraints, but he continued to hold onto Amy's arm. Danielle appeared to be unfazed by all of this. Then just as quickly as it started, it stopped. Danielle got down on her knees and held a sobbing Amy. Johnson was lying face up on his bed, his eyes were back in his head, and he didn't make a sound. A Doctor came rushing into the room as Danielle picked up Amy and walked towards the door. As I went to go after them, Johnson called me over to his bed. He whispers as I bend down to here. "I was there Joe, I saw her die". I asked him, "Where were you, who did you see die?" Then right before the Doctor juiced him up he softly said, "With the man she will call daddy".

10:50 am

As Danielle and I were walking from the hospital, Amy appeared to have no effects from Johnson's touch in the hospital. I could not stop thinking that Johnson saw into Amy's future when he touched her. Did Amy see anything when they touched? I also wondered if this was why Danielle brought Amy to his room. Amy did become agitated when Danielle kept asking her if she was okay. Amy got into Danielle's car and slammed the door shut. Danielle turned and asked me what Johnson said to me after they left the room. I told her he just asked if everyone was okay. I then turned to walk to my car, Danielle grabs my arm and hands me an envelope. "What's this?" I asked her. She tells me she took Amy to a hospital out of state this morning to be examined for any signs of abuse. She then tells me the report shows that there were none. I ask why she went out of state, why not bring her here? Danielle said she felt funny. I handed her the envelope back, she asked me why I didn't want to read it. I told her she just gave me the results. Danielle looked away from me. She then said, "There is one thing, the doctor seems to think something, or someone is tormenting her, and she is holding it inside." I asked her if she thought it was Johnson. She said, "After today, I don't know". Danielle looked scared and I asked her why she brought Amy here. Danielle told me that she didn't know why, she said something inside her told her to bring her. I tried again to leave but Danielle again grabbed my wrist and asked, "Last night, did you have a person in mind that you thought may want to hurt Amy?" I told her it really don't matter now and pointed to the report. As I walked to my car I thought, Danielle asked if I knew someone that wants to hurt Amy, why didn't she ask me if I thought someone was hurting Amy.

2:00 pm

I ran into Dr Adams at the gas station, I waved and yelled how you doing when he looked over at me from the pumps. I could tell he had no idea who I was by the look on his face. I then yelled over, "I met you last night, I was trick and treating with Danielle and Amy". He then smiled and put the handle back in the pump, I thought he was going to leave, but he walked over to me, "I didn't recognize you Joe", he said as he approached. I was about to ask him how he knew my name, and then I thought that Danielle must have told him. He asked me what I thought of Amy. I told him she was a quiet kid, she seems a little shy. He then said its not shyness, I think she is terribly afraid of something, or someone. I told him that's the second time I heard that today. I knew he wanted more sessions, so I asked if he thought more session would help. He said that he is not getting paid, that he is seeing Amy as a favor to Danielle. I then finished pumping my gas, I thought to myself as I hung the pump up, Danielle did say he wanted to see Amy more, now he is crying about money. I then said to him, "Maybe she should take her to someone else". Dr. Adams then changed his tune, he even invited me to sit in on one of Amy's sessions. I told him it might be interesting to observe. He then asked me to do something strange, he asked that I don't tell Danielle.

11-2-97 / 2:11 am

Danielle was standing in Amy's bedroom, she could hear party noises downstairs. She is standing in a dark corner of the room. She was watching as Amy sleeps in her bed, Amy is covered only in a sheet. Her nightgown is torn and lying on the floor. There is someone standing at the foot of the bed, Danielle is unable to make out who it is. Danielle then notices that Johnson is now sitting on the bed, he is holding Amy's hand as he asks Amy who it is that is hurting her. Amy turns and looks into the dark corner where her mother is standing. Just as Amy starts to speak. The person at the foot of the bed plunges a knife into Amy's chest. Danielle wakes up. She sits up in the bed. She puts her head in her hands and starts sobbing. This can't happen again, I just don't know how to make it stop she cries.

41

8:47 am

I'm in my office and all I can think about is my session with Dr. Adams and Amy this evening. I then thought about the story Danielle told me about Johnson. I pulled his history up. Danielle story was correct. Johnson was arrested and charged with arson and manslaughter for the burning of the records room at the hospital. I then called the Warden of Clearfield State Prison, the last prison Johnson was at before being transferred here. Warden May informed me that Johnson was a model inmate at Clearfield when he was first brought in, and that Johnson was even hired to be an inmate worker in the prison mailroom. But he was caught opening the staff mail and locked in. His cell was searched and addresses and names of other institutions were found in a journal. Warden May said Johnson then became a loner, didn't talk to anyone, he even refused to bathe. In the ten years he spent at Clearfield he was assigned two cellmates, both hanged themselves in the cell while Johnson slept. Warden May then told me he would fax me a copy of his file. May then told me before he hung up that Johnson was feared by a lot of the population at Clearfield, even by some of the staff. It was like Christmas morning the day that crazy motherfucker was transferred out.

2:30 pm

I was just getting ready to leave when the fax machine came on. It was the Johnson file from Clearfield. I noticed as I took the pages from the fax that some of the pages were missing. What jumped out at me was my name in the journal he kept. Written next to my name was "Saveher". One word. Danielle's name was also in the journal, her name was circled about twenty times. Also included in the report was a note from the Mental Health Doctor that said Johnson claimed he didn't try to burn the hospital, but that he was trying to protect innocent people from burning in hell. It also included a statement that Johnson made to the Doctor, that statement was "I did it to save her, I did it to keep her safe, to keep her alive, but now they need her, she is in danger". Another thing that sort of made the hair on my neck stand up was that both of Johnson cellmates hung themselves at 2:11 am.

6:00 pm

Danielle and Amy walked into Dr Adams house. Danielle asked if she could speak with him before the session started. Dr Adams sent Amy into his office and closed the door. Danielle told the doctor about her dreams. She told the Doctor that the dreams started the day Johnson came back, and he was sent to her Hospital. She said they were always the same. Danielle says, "I am in Amy's bedroom and Johnson is sitting on the bed asking Amy who the person is at the foot of the bed. Amy attempts to answer, but I wake before she speaks, and now the dreams are becoming more graphic, I think the person at the foot of the bed is there to hurt Amy, maybe even kill her." Dr Adams asks Danielle why she would think the person might kill Amy? Danielle answers, "She is the last one, they don't want her to tell". Dr Adams asks why this mystery person was there to stop Amy. Danielle looked at the doctor with tears in her eyes and says, "I think he may be there to stop me, to stop me from letting this happen." Dr Adams then asks if she has told anyone else about her dreams. Danielle says no. Dr Adams then tells Danielle that he too is having the same dream, but in his dreams he is sitting on the bed asking Amy who is hurting her. He tells Danielle that his dreams are also progressing, and that in his last dream when he asked Amy who was hurting her, Amy pointed into a dark corner of the room, but when he looked into the corner he could not see anyone standing there, and in that last dream he felt a hand on his shoulder and someone whispered in his ear, Doctor Adams looked scared as he told Danielle that the sound was so lifelike, that he felt this person breath on his ear as he said, "You have one chance to make the right decision or die, you will never be able to walk away." Dr. Adams then said, "You may think I am crazy, but I think someone is trying to control our dreams, someone that wants us to find out what is actually going to happen to Amy". Danielle turns to leave, Dr Adams stops her and says, "Next time you dream try to control it, get up and walk over to the person at the foot of the bed, see who it is." Danielle wiping away tears looks back at the doctor and says as she leaves the room, "I don't know if I want to know."

6:45 pm

I was sitting in the other room waiting for Danielle to leave, I could see them talking but could not hear their conversation. I tried to get closer without Danielle seeing me, and I was able to hear them talking about their dreams, were they having the same dream I was? I did notice that Danielle started to cry before she left. I don't think Danielle knew I was there. When Danielle did leave I walked over to Dr Adams and was about to tell him about my dreams but I didn't, something inside me told me to wait, and I still felt like I could not trust him. We went into the office, Amy was lying on his sofa. Dr Adams asked her if it would be okay if I sat in on their session. Amy shrugged her shoulders, she seemed indifferent. I sat behind the couch, sort of out of site out of mind. Dr Adams started with a few simple questions, probably to calm her. He then appeared to be hypnotizing her. Amy suddenly fell limp. Dr Adams then stood up and told me to come around to the front of the couch, "Watch this". He said as Amy lay there silent for several moments, and then she suddenly started talking, she said, "I don't want to wait anymore, I just want to finish this and go away", then silence, "No, I haven't told anyone". Silence again, then in a terrified voice, "No I don't want to do that", She was lying on her back and had her arms outstretched towards the ceiling. It appeared like something or someone was pushing them in towards her body. Her arms then went limp, her legs spread, her head turned to the side, her eyes suddenly opened up and she stared directly at me as she said, "I just want you to stop this". I then realized that she appeared to be being pushed into the couch. Dr Adams then quickly woke her. Amy appeared to have no knowledge of what just happened. I asked the Doctor how this was not a sign of abuse. The Doctor told me after the first time he did this with Amy, he had a doctor examine her, and there was no sign of trauma, or any type of abuse. I then told him Danielle took her the other day, same results. I asked if he ever told Danielle of this. Dr Adams became very serious, he grabbed my arm and said, "I need this to be kept between us right now. If Danielle was to be informed, who knows who she would tell?"

8:30 pm

I left the Doctors house confused, my head was spinning, why would he want to keep this from Danielle, and who would she tell? Is Doctor Adams the one that is hurting her, abusing her, Amy did point to him on Halloween night, maybe she is being hurt when she is hypnotized. Amy did look at me when she was under and she asked me to stop this. But stop what? Stop hurting her, or stop the person that is hurting her. She could have been asking me to stop the Doctor from hypnotizing her. And how are all three of us sharing the same dreams. I needed a drink and walked up to Shorties Bar and Grill. Danielle and Dan were sitting at a booth, I sat as close as I could without being seen. Dan was upset, he was asking Danielle how she could hide something like that from him. Danielle said something I could not hear, Dan then slammed his drink down and stormed out of the bar. I waited several minutes before I walked up to Danielle, she didn't even realize I was standing there until I asked, "What's up?" Danielle said, "I just told Dan about Johnson, and these creepy dreams I've been having". I asked her to tell me about her dreams, she just called it stress and said she needed a vacation. I asked her if Dan thought she was nuts. She said, "No, he became real combative, and told me to keep my mouth shut, He asked if I told anyone else, and when I told him I told Dr Adams he became angry, he was the angriest I have ever seen him, and he doesn't even know who Dr Adams is." I sat down and put my arm around her shoulder and said, "They must be some serious dreams", as I thought that Dr. Adams might also be having the same dream. Danielle may have seen Dan in her dreams and that was why he got so upset when she told Dan that she shared this with Doctor Adams. I then told her that maybe Doctor Adams could help her understand why she is having these dreams. I didn't want her to know I was at Dr Adams tonight, neither did the Doctor. Danielle leaned over and cupped my face with both hands, she gently kissed my lips and said, "They are just dreams, thoughts you have while you are sleeping, it's not a big fucking deal". I held her hand and told her that she was right, that all dreams were not real, and maybe she should take a sleeping pill. She never told me that Dr Adams was having the same dreams, but I knew he was. I didn't tell her that I was also having dreams, or about my conversations with Johnson. She told me that Doctor Adams told her to control her dreams, she also stated she wasn't really sure if she wanted to know what the dreams meant. I told her she should not live her life being afraid of dreams, they are called nightmares for a reason. On the way back to Dr Adams, I thought out loud hoping Danielle would tell me something about her dreams, and I said, "Maybe Dan is upset because he is actually doing something he shouldn't be doing, and he is afraid that you might see it in a dream". Danielle didn't answer, she just kept walking. Dr Adams and Amy were sitting on the porch waiting for us. I was surprised when Dr Adams told Danielle that he had hypnotized Amy, because he was very clear when he told me not to mention it. Although he didn't tell her what Amy did or said while she was hypnotized, and for some odd reason, Danielle didn't ask.

10:15 pm

I called Dr Adams with an idea, I told him that when Johnson touched Amy the other day he was able to see her future, so I asked, "What if Johnson was to touch Amy while she was hypnotized, if this shit was real, Johnson may be able to see what is going on." I then told him the only problem was that Johnson was locked up in the security section of the hospital, and we would have to tell Danielle, she is the nurse on duty. Dr Adams said, "Maybe not, let me take care of it". Doctor Adams then grabbed my arm and said, "Even if we are able to pull this off, are we sure Johnson will tell us what he seen, or what he wants us to think he seen." I was almost sure he would, I told the Doctor that Johnson appears to really want to help Amy.

11-5-97 / 12:00 pm

D anielle was sitting at her desk when she received the fax stating that Johnson will be sent out to a medical center for further testing. The fax explained that the prison would provide all the transportation to and from the center. She then noticed that my name was listed as the person in charge. She called me to confirm this was actually going to happen, I wasn't sure if Dr Adams had told her of the plan, so I informed her this was normal operating procedure to take prisoners to other facilities for treatment, and that I would check into it. Then before she hung up she told me that Dr Adams has an office in that building, and he asked if Amy could be brought in at 12:00 pm the same day. Coincidence I told her. I called Dr Adams and told him everything was set. He then told me he felt like he has to tell Danielle. I told him I just got done talking to her, and that she questioned the timing that Amy would be there. I then told the Doctor that I would call Danielle back and let her know, but I didn't, I'd thought I would let her know later.

4:00 pm

I went over to Danielle who was raking leaves in the yard, I told her what was going on. She appeared upset and angry that Dr Adams didn't tell her. I had to let her know that not just Dr Adams, but I too had a part in this plan. She didn't understand why I would be involved, and I didn't offer an explanation. At first she strictly prohibited this from happening, she even threatened to call the police. I had to call Dr Adams down to convince her that Amy would be safe, and this may be the only way to see what might be getting ready to happen to her. Danielle remained upset, she was defiant in her stance. What struck me as odd was that she didn't question neither of us as to what could be happening to Amy. Dr Adams then took her into the kitchen and talked to her in private. Danielle then suddenly agreed to let this happen, she came into the living room and told me that if Amy appears to be in any distress at any time, the experiment is to be terminated. I stood up as I asked if she was allowing us to try it, she said, "Yes, but I have to let Dan know". When I walked back home I wondered if Doctor Adams knew I was also having dreams and if he told Danielle.

11-6-97 / 2:11 am

had another dream, Amy is on her bed, and both Dr Adams and Johnson are by her side. Neither are talking or moving, they are frozen in time. I see Dan walk out of the shadows as he walks right up to me. He then turns and walks up to the person at the foot of the bed, their face still hidden in the shadows. Dan slowly starts to turn this person around. Just before their face is revealed in the light a knife is stuck into Dan's chest. I wake up it is 2:11 am. Directly across the street Danielle had the same dream, she would later tell me she was unable to see who it was, but I could tell she was lying.

6:30 am

I met Danielle as I was leaving for work, Amy lagged behind struggling to carry an overstuffed backpack. "Going camping?" I joked. Danielle looks up and tells me that Amy is going to spend a couple days at her fathers. I ask Danielle about the session with Dr Adams tomorrow. Danielle tells me not to worry, that both she and Dan will be there. "So you told him?" I asked. "He is her father" Danielle snapped back. Before I left, Danielle asked how I slept last night, I told her like a baby, but I think she knew I was lying.

7:00 am

To many hands in this little experiment we are doing tomorrow. Not only will Dr Adams, Danielle, Dan and myself be there, but also what about the other medical people, plus there will have to be at least two escorting officers from the prison. I had to pick officers that would not question me when they were told to leave the room. I asked Officers Williams, and McGee to do it, they were already spooked by Johnson, and I'm sure they would welcome the chance to leave the room. I was surprised when they agreed.

8:30 am

Danielle dropped Amy off at Dan's trailer, she told him the details of what was going to happen, and what they thought would come of it. Dan appeared to be excited about the session. Danielle told him to make sure he was there on time. As Danielle walked to her car, she turned around and yelled back at Dan, "And don't forget to bring Amy". As soon as Danielle was out of site, Dan left Amy with his crackwhore girlfriend, he jumped into his car and sped off.

10:00 am

Danielle was sitting in the hospitals lunchroom staring at her half eaten sandwich, She watched as a fly circled the plate, just as the fly landed on the sandwich an announcement was made "CODE RED ROOM 15" That is Johnson's room. Danielle gets up carries her tray over to the trash, she stops flicked the fly off the bread and took one last bite, and then she proceeded towards room 15. When she enters the room several doctors, and nurses are already attending to Johnson. Moments later one of the doctors pronounce Johnson dead. Danielle watched as they pulled the sheet up over his face. She didn't notice the flies that were covering the bars outside his window.

I'm sitting at my desk watching a fly zoom around the room, never coming close enough so I could smash it. I then watched as it landed on the pest strip hanging from the ceiling. "Got you, you little fuck. Tell your friends." I then got up to crush it as it was stuck to the strip. Just as I reached for it, the fly walked calmly up the strip and flew towards the door just as Johnson walks in, I jumped back, and summoned for the officers to respond. I then noticed that all the lights outside of my office were out, there is no noise, and there is never no noise in the prison. I slowly sat back down behind my desk. Johnson walks over and sits down in front of my desk. Johnson never spoke, he just pulled out a folded paper cup from his pocket, he unfolds it and spills the contents onto my desk. It is what appears to be crushed up pills. He then stands and walks out. I look down and notice the logo on the cup was from Northeastern Hospital. I woke from this dream when my phone rang. I looked out and saw all the lights on, and the sounds of a busy prison were also present. I looked up at the pest strip still hanging pest free from the ceiling. I picked up the phone and received the message from Capt. Harris that Johnson was dead.

10:30 pm

I called Danielle and she told me that Johnson had died of cardiac arrest. She said he was fine when she went to lunch, but he went into cardiac arrest shortly after. By the time she was able to get back to the room he was already dead. Before I hung up Danielle said "I am standing in his room right now, his heart monitor still shows a heartbeat" I asked if she was sure he was dead. Danielle said yes as she held onto the unplugged monitor, that continued to show a pulse.

11-7-97 / 2:11 am

woke up, probably out of habit. I did not dream, I looked at the clock, even tho I knew what time it was. I rolled over and drifted back to sleep. I slept till my alarm went off at 5:00 am. I woke up refreshed for the first time since Johnson came into the receiving room at the prison. Maybe his death was also the death of all my dreams.

10:00 am

Dr Adams called and asked me where Johnson was, Dr Adams was unaware of his death. He told me that Amy and her father were in his office. When told the news of Johnson's death, Dan got up and left the office leaving Amy and his backpack behind. Danielle was in a meeting at the hospital covering the death of Johnson, she asked if I could go and pick Amy up.

10:50 am

When I picked up Amy at the Medical building Dr Adams threw Dans backpack to me, "What's this?" I asked, Amy grabbed my hand and pulled me towards the door. "That's my dads," she said. I noticed the pack was locked, and at close inspection it appeared that the lock was tampered with. On the way home I attempted to open the backpack, but the lock would not open, I pulled up to a red light and attempted again to force the lock open to no avail. When the light turned green I gave up and handed the bag to Amy. She sat in the passenger seat staring out the window, she was oddly quiet. When I pulled into my driveway Amy handed the pack to me with the lock open. There was nothing of importance in the pack, paper, his license, which stated his name was Daniel Williamson. There was a zippered compartment on the inside, when I unzipped it a packet of pills fell out, they were similar to the ones I saw in my dream. I was about to close the bag up when I saw a photograph, I turned it over, it was a photo of Amy, she was topless, the photo was taken from behind, Amy appeared scared as she was looking over her shoulder at who ever was taking the picture. I was going to ask Amy about the photo, but she was already out of the car and headed towards my house. I then saw Dan's cigarettes in the pack and grabbed one. I just sat in the car and smoked, I was looking at the photo of Amy, I don't know what it was, but there was something wrong with the photo. There was something about the photo that I could not see. Something about the photo that I could not figure out. Like when you enter a room and something is out of place but you cant figure out what it is. I was starting to zone out as I looked at the photo, suddenly Amy knocked on the window scaring me, causing me to drop my cigarette down between my legs. "Lets go it's fucking freezing out." She yelled as she ran back up towards my house. I stuck the photo in my pocket and got out of the car. I didn't realize until later that Amy cursed.

1:00 pm

As soon as I open my front door my phone rang, and on the other end was a man that told me he was a friend of Sogod, I said, "Excuse me, who is Sogod?" The man then told me that I would know him as Johnson. I then asked what it was he wanted. The man said that Sogod was murdered while at Northeastern Hospital, that he was murdered so an evil act against a child would be able to happen. I asked what evil act, against what child? There was a long silence, then in a voice I would have sworn to in court was Johnson's came on the line and said, "Now you are the only one that can stop it from happening, SAVE HER". The line then went dead, I checked my caller ID, but it said no calls.

3:10 pm

Amy was asleep on the floor in front of the TV. I turned it off and went to get her a blanket. When I returned she wasn't there. I looked all over, I checked the backyard, she wasn't anywhere I looked, and then I saw her in her bedroom window. I called for her, she looked down at me, and then she left the window. She didn't appear to have heard me. I went over and as I approached her bedroom I heard voices coming from the room. I stopped as I heard Amy say, "I was promised that I would not die in here". Then silence. I went to open the door but heard another voice, a man's voice say, "They are not lying, but they are not telling you the truth either, they are telling you what they believe will happen". I slowly pushed the door open, Amy was lying on the bed in a X-position that made it seem she was tied down to the bedposts. She appeared to be sleeping, there was no one else in the room. I sat down on the bed and gently shook her. Without opening her eyes she said, "If I don't do it, they will hurt my mommy". She then pulled her arms and legs up into her body and laid on the bed in a ball weeping.

5:15 pm

Danielle came in and was surprised to see that we were in her house, she thought we would be at my place until she got home. I told her Amy came over and wanted to lie in her own bed. I didn't tell her about the voices. I then gave her Dan's backpack and said he left it at the Doctors office. I told her there was a bag of pills in it. Danielle pulled the bag of pills out and threw the pack on the table and said, "I'm not surprised". I then told her that I had a dream where Johnson may have been killed with the same type of pills. Danielle then sat on the couch holding the bag of pills and asked. "Do you think Dan would do that?" I then handed her the photo and said, "Look at this". Danielle stared at the photo, suddenly tears started to run down her face. She just sat sobbing on the sofa, she didn't say a word. I then heard a car pulling into the driveway, I looked out the window and saw Dan walking towards the front door. As I turned back around Danielle was running towards the door. She swung it opened and attacked Dan on the porch. If I didn't pull her off of him she would have killed him. Dan stumbled to his feet, he had no idea of what just happened or why. Danielle then threw the photo at him. Dan bent down and picked it up, he didn't even try to say it wasn't his. He looked at the photo, then back at Danielle. She started yelling again, Dan yelled back, "Hold up you crazy bitch". This only made Danielle want to kill him more. Dan then said in a calm voice, "I took that picture, yes I did, I took it last week after Amy stayed for the weekend." Danielle swung and just missed Dan's face. "Just look at the photo and tell me what you see". Danielle yelled back, "I see a sick bastard". Dan still in a calm voice said, "There are no burses on her back." Danielle now getting even madder at the calmness in Dans voice, Screamed, "WHAT THE FUCK ARE YOU TALKING ABOUT?" Dan sat down on the porch step and said, "Every time I would bring Amy home you would accuse me of hurting her, saying she was coming home all bruised up. I took that photo right before I dropped her off, if you look at it you can see she is in the backseat of my car with your house in the background. The only reason I took it was to show you there are no burses on her back." Danielle then reaches down and grabs the photo from Dan's hands and yells, "IT'S DOCTORED, she had burses up and down her back when she came home that night". Dan staring at the ground said, "It's a Polaroid they can't be doctored". Amy came to the door and Danielle grabbed her, spun her around and lifted her shirt. Danielle yelled, "LOOK". I could see bruising from where her pants started to almost her neck. Danielle then told Amy to go up to her room. Danielle stared at Dan, she stared for a long time, like she was thinking, or restraining herself from killing him. She then looked at me and said, "He could have taken that picture before he abused her". Dan then stood up in an aggressive manor, "I would never hurt that girl, and I would never put her in harms way, you fucking hypocrite." Danielle crumbled up the photo and walked into the house.

Everyone calmed down and we were all now sitting in Danielle's kitchen. No one has said a word as we sat in silence for several minutes. Dan then asked where we got the photo. Danielle didn't answer. I told him I found it in his backpack he left at Dr Adams office. Dan looked up and asked me what gave me the right to go thru his stuff. I didn't get a chance to answer as Danielle said, "What right should a person get, one that abuses a child?" Dan keeping his cool, laughed and asked, "Maybe you should look at who put it in there". I looked over at Danielle. She had a look like Dan was right. Dan then said he took that picture to Dr Adams, Dan said the doctor asked him about the burses, so he took the photo to show him that there were none. Danielle snapped again that the picture could have been taken before he hurt her. I started to get the feeling Danielle was acting just a little too upset. Amy then came into the kitchen. Everybody watched her in silence as she took a box of juice out, then as she was attempting to put the straw in looked up at everyone and asked, "What?" I took the juice from her and stabbed the straw into the top, some juice squirted out and landed on Amy's shirt. Dan grabs a napkin off the table and went to wipe off Amy's shirt. Danielle screamed, "DON'T YOU FUCKING TOUCH HER" and pulled Amy away from him. Danielle then got on her knees and asked Amy if her dad had ever hurt her. Amy started to cry, Danielle shook her, "DID YOUR FATHER EVER HURT YOU" she yelled at Amy. Amy shook her head no. Dan stood up and said, "Are we done with this witch hunt?" Danielle then showed Amy the photo. Amy threw it on the ground and yelled for everyone to leave her alone. She then ran up to her bedroom. Dan grabbed his backpack and said, "No matter what I say, I'm guilty" as he went to leave I took the bag of pills from my pocket and tossed them to him, "Don't forget these". Dan caught them, looked down at them, and asked what they were. I told him they were also in his backpack. Dan threw them onto the table and said he never seen them before. Dan then walked to the back door. Before he left he turned around, Danielle would not look at him. Dan said, "I gave that picture to Dr Adams, he had it on his desk when I locked my pack up. Maybe you two private dicks should do your Colombo act on him. I sat and held Danielle, "He could be telling the truth", I told her. Danielle pushed me away and told me to leave. I got up as Danielle slumped in the chair, she was an angry mess. I said, "Maybe we should ask the doctor how that shit got back in his pack." Danielle then stood and screamed for me to leave. I didn't have the time to tell her that his backpack lock did appear tampered with, and I am sure she would not have believed me anyway.

9:35 pm

As I left Danielle's house, Dan walked up to me from behind a tree. He told me that I had to believe him, that he never seen those pills before. I then asked why he would take that photo. Dan again said that Danielle was always blaming him for Amy's injuries. He wanted a way to show that he was not the one doing it. I looked over Dan's shoulder at Danielle in her window watching us and said "Dan, like Danielle said, there is no way to show when the photo was taken". Dan lowered his head. "Joe" he said, "I really believe that Dr Adams put that shit in my bag". I looked at Dan and told him that the bag was locked when the Doctor gave it to me, I didn't tell him I thought the lock was tampered with. He said, "I know, I locked it". He then asked me how I got it opened. When I told him Amy opened it, he looked back at me and said, "If Amy was able to open it for you, what makes you think she didn't open it for the doctor?" I started to walk up to my front door. I left Dan standing on the sidewalk, he said, "Joe, do you believe Danielle is having dreams about Amy?" I shrugged and said, "Sure, but dreams are just that, Dreams". Dan then turned and said as he walked to his car, "Good, because I have been having them also, and if they were to be true we both should stay as far away from Danielle as possible." I looked back up at Danielle's window, she was no longer there.

11-8-97 / 2:11 am

I was jolted from a dreamless sleep again by the phone. I rubbed my eyes and looked at the clock, it was 2:11 am. The machine for some reason did not pick up and the phone continued to ring. When I picked it up there was no response at first. I then thought I was dreaming again and I would hear Johnson's voice on the line. Then just as I went to hang up, I heard a whisper, "Joe, this is Dan". I said, "It's two o'clock in the morning, what's wrong?" He said, "Joe I can't sleep, every time I close my eyes the dreams start again". I asked what dreams? "Old nightmares, before I dreamt about dying, now I dream about hurting Amy." I then ask what do you mean starting again? Dan tells me when Amy was about five years old, he started having dreams where a man in the shadows told him that Amy was not safe. I then asked him when the dreams stopped. Dan told me they never did, that he would have them off and on, that they would progress to the point where I wanted to kill myself, but I slipped into drugs and booze. Dan then said, "Probably the only time drugs and booze ever saved a person." I asked if Danielle was having the same dreams back then. Dan said, "I think so, I don't know, I'm not sure, she called me one night about this time of night. She told me if I ever tried to get custody of Amy, that Amy would be taken away from both of them. "Why would that make you think she was having dreams". Dan said, "Because that same night, right before she called, the man told me in a dream to take Amy away, that I had to take her away or she would be hurt". I then asked if the same man was now in his new dreams. Dan said, "Yes". There was then a long silence, I broke it when I asked Dan why he was telling me this. It sounded like Dan was starting to cry as he said, "The man on the news, the guy that died at the hospital". I asked "Johnson?" Dan said "Yes, that's the man in the shadows in my dreams, he came to me tonight, only now he wants me to kill her". I asked, "What happened, kill who? Tell me about your dream". Dan says he was standing outside Danielle's house, he could hear Amy crying in her bedroom. He tried to climb up to see what was wrong, but right before he reached the window, someone came into her room and turned the light on. Amy's crying stopped after the light came on, he could hear Amy asking if she could leave, she was asking someone to leave her alone, she sounded terrified. He kept climbing once he reached the window he was able to see Amy lying in the bed, there was someone else in the bed with her. He says Amy turned and looked over at him. Dan says he reached in thru the window as Amy reaches out to try and grab his hand. He asks Amy who is hurting her, Amys mouth is suddenly covered by a hand, Amy struggles but she cant get free from the hand, Amy bites down, she bit so hard that blood was running down her chin. Amy then screams, and Dan fell from the window landing on his back in the yard. Dan said when he looked up he saw Johnson standing over him. Johnson had a gun in his hand, Johnson says this will save Amy. Dan reaches for the gun, it goes off. Then Dan woke up. I ask Dan if Johnson wanted him to kill Amy or the other person in the room. Dan softly answered, "I think he wants me to kill myself." I tell Dan that it was just a dream, that it is not real. Before Dan hung up, I was able say, "Don't let these dreams control you, you have to control the dreams."

11-16-97 / 5:00 am

I haven't had a dream in days, not since the last time I spoke with Dan, I haven't heard from him or Danielle since then either. I think Danielle may be mad because I sort of believed Dans story about the picture. I think I may be starting to get my sanity back. I still needed to know what was going on, it was the compulsion of having to solve every problem that came my way. I tried to just let it go, I was just going to get ready for work and relax all day in my office. The relaxing didn't last long. After I got up for work I got into the shower and as soon as I was soaped up, I heard the phone ringing, I let the machine pick up. I pressed the message button as I was getting dressed. The call was from Dan, he said, "Joe, I just wanted to let you know that the dreams have stopped. I haven't had a dream since the last time we talked, I just called to say thanks I feel safe now". I hit the delete button. There was a loud banging at my door, it was Danielle and as soon as I opened the door she tells me that Dan had been arrested. "How, when, for what?" I asked. Danielle says she fell asleep last night and had a dream. In her dream she stated she hears Amy crying in her bedroom, and when she pushed the door open she saw Dan coming in thru the window shooting Amy. She then says she woke up in bed just as she was hanging up the phone. I asked her who she called. Danielle says she didn't remember dialing the phone, let alone talking to anyone. But she thinks she called the police and told them about the photograph, and the pills. I pulled her inside and asked, "You think you called the police?" Danielle then looks up to the sky and starts to cry and says, "I did this, this is all my fault, and he is going to be so pissed". I shake her, she looks at me with tears in her eyes as I ask, "When did he get arrested". She says around midnight. I then pulled her in for a hug, I told her everything will be all right. I was thinking did Dan call me from prison. Was that even Dan that called? I look at my machine and realize that I deleted his message.

1:00 pm

I stopped at the police station to talk to my old prison partner Johnny Downs. John transferred into the Police Department right after I was promoted to Lieutenant. I was hoping he could tell me what was going on with Dan. John was able to tell me they went to his trailer after a complaint, it was about midnight. John told me Dan said he was with his daughter all night the night before Johnson died. But his girlfriend, who is not a reliable witness, gave a statement that he left right after Amy was dropped off, and he didn't return to the trailer until early the next morning. John told me that Dan said the pills were found in his backpack, but he had left the pack at the Doctors office and his lock was broke when he got it back several hours later, anyone could have put those pills in the bag. The evidence was not strong enough and we weren't going to arrest him. We were going to have to investigate. But as Dan was being questioned, an officer knocked over a canister and naked photos of Amy fell out. Johnny then opened the box on his desk. Inside were about 10 photos of Amy, all the photos were of Amy in different stages of undress, there were even photos of her in the shower. "When we found these, that is when we arrested him." John asked how I knew Dan. I told him I was Danielle's neighbor. I then asked what Dan was being held on, "Possession of child pornography for now, depending what those pills are, more charges could be added." Just as John finished that statement his fax came to life. He received information on the pills, they were some sort of high-power diet pills. "He is a skinny mother fucker isn't he"? John said with a laugh, "Thank god, all I need is an homicide investigation". I got up and asked if Johnson's death was under investigation. John sitting still staring at the photos of Amy said, "No, it appears he had a heart attack."

5:00 pm

As I pulled into my driveway I saw Danielle and Amy walking up the street. For the first time in a long time Danielle appears to be smiling. Amy was skipping along beside her, she even looked like a different little girl. "How are you guys doing?" I asked. Danielle tells me its like a weight has been lifted off her shoulders. Danielle then grabbed me and gave me a hug, Amy wrapped herself around the both of us. I went to ask a question, Danielle put her finger over my mouth and said, "You don't need to apologize". That's not what I was going to do. When she took her hand away from my face, I saw what looked like a little bite mark on her hand.

12-5-97 / 6:30 pm

I was driving home from work and all I could think about is how it has been almost a month, and I have not had a single bad dream. I have received letters and E-mails for Johnson from the church of Sogod, all of which I have thrown into a box. Just in case any family members come to claim his belongings, I did notice that all the mail seemed to have been sent from Miami.

I have been happy, Danielle and I have started a relationship, but every time I try to get close she pulls away. Amy appears to be adapting to her dad being in jail, I don't think she misses him at all. Doctor Adams told us that Amy is making great strides in her therapy sessions. As I was sitting at a light, I saw Johnny Downs going into the neighborhood bar. So I decided to go and see what was up in the police world.

Johnny was sitting at the bar. So I walked up and took the stool next to him. After several drinks our conversation started to fizzle, then for some unknown reason I told him the story of Sogod, and the dreams I had. When I finished talking I really expected him to laugh, or at least think I was crazy. But he didn't, he sat there staring at me with his mouth open. The bartender who was listening to our conversation gave us another round and told us that there is a Sogod website, he told us he found it one night while surfing the web. John gave the bartender a stare, like he was pissed. I grabbed John's arm as I thought he was going to hit the bartender. The bartender tells us the drinks are on him and walks away. John looks back at me and asks me if we were talking to him. John then says that this Sogod clown sounds really out there. He then pushed his drink over to me and said he had to go. I asked if he was going to check out the website. John shrugged his shoulders and said, "I don't know if I care, and if you don't want them crazy dreams to start back up, maybe you shouldn't either." The bartender came back down after John left and told me that this website covers theories and stories about people who can control others thru mind games and dreams. As I got up to leave the bartender says, "You mentioned in your story the number 211, on this website there is a countdown clock that expires on 2-11-98". I give him a tip and excused myself. After I left the bar the barmaid who was washing out dirty glasses said without looking up at him, "You should not have told him that". The bartender watched me out the window, "He is all we have." He whispered to himself as he swatted at a fly with his bar rag.

12-6-97 / 10:15 am

could not get over the shit I was reading on this website. This guy wrote about how you can control someone's mind and thoughts, he explained how the same technique was used to get the terrorists to fly into the World Trade Center. What sent shivers down my spine was when I read about how he was going to die in the hospital, and that he welcomed it, writing that he must die to control the future. By the date, it was written the day before he died. How was he able to get on the Internet, when he was secured in a mental hospital? I paged down thru all the other shit this guy wrote. He actually believed he was some sort of profit. Sogod wrote about stories I remembered from past newscasts, stories of people running into burning buildings to save people, How poor people became rich overnight. Johnson took all the credit, writing he was able to control the people thru their dreams. I tried to find a name or address in any of the stories, I thought if I could contact anyone this has happened to, maybe I could get some answers. After about 4 hours on the computer my vision became blurry and I leaned back in my chair and rubbed my eyes. I was just about to shut the computer down when I noticed a blinking icon in the corner of the screen. I didn't remember ever seeing it their before. It was a little box with the words "SEE MORE". I clicked on it. A photo of Johnson, AKA Sogod appeared on the screen. He was standing in a dark hallway holding today's paper. He turns around and drops his robe off his shoulders, and as it falls to his waist, I saw scratched into his back, "Amy is not safe." He then turns and says, "She only thinks things are right, you must watch who you trust, there are a lot of people who don't want you to stop this." I turned to look at the clock, it was 2:11am. Was I dreaming? Sogod flexes and the wounds disappear from his body, they appeared to go into his body. He turns back around and looks at me thru the screen. Silence, the hair on the back of my neck starts to stand up. He then whispers, "Before 211". The screen returns to the original website. I look back at the clock, it is now 2:12 am. I turn off the computer and say to myself, "It's already too late".

2:00 pm

Officer Downs was in the receiving room dropping off some more criminals, I called him up to my office, I wanted to see if he looked at the website. He told me he didn't at first, but then admitted that he glanced at it. He called it all bullshit. I asked if he saw the blinking "SEE MORE" icon. He told me he saw it, but that he did not click on it because he thought it might cost money to view. I told him what I saw, I didn't tell him that Johnson spoke directly to me. He then tells me that anyone could have written what was on the site and that any photograph or video on the Internet these days can be doctored. "The photo was probably his head on someone else's body, probably one of the nut jobs that keep sending you shit to give to him." He said as he looked around my office. "What do you think about the writing on him"? I asked. Officer Downs appeared to be getting freaked out. I changed the subject and asked him, "You said that on the day Dan was arrested it was late that night." John shook his head yes. "I received a phone call from him the following morning around 6:00 am." John looked confused, "Impossible" he said. "He was in the police holding cell, even if we wanted to give him a call, the Inmate phones are turned off at 10:00 pm, they are not turned back on until 8:00 am". What about a cell phone I asked. He told me the holding cells are in the basement of the police station and there is no reception. He then asked if I was sure it was Dan that called. "Yes, I'm not crazy" I answered. "What was the call about" he asked. "I don't really know, he left a message on my machine, thanking me for something or the other". John then asked if I still had the message. I told him that I deleted it. John then changed the subject and asked me if Amy was okay now, and if Danielle and I were getting serious. I told him we were starting to get a little serious. John smiled, "Then concentrate on that, Fuck all this other shit. When was the last time you had one of those dreams?" he asked. "Haven't in a while". John then told me to stay off the goofy god website, and start enjoying my life. On the way out of my office John saw I had a photo of Danielle pinned on my bulletin board, He pulled the photo off and held it up, "She is nice," he said. "I can't believe you are now hitting that", I had to tell him we haven't gotten that far in our relationship, I told him she appears to not be interested in sex at all. "Sex" he says with a laugh, "Danielle is not interested in sex." John kept laughing as he pinned the photo back on the board, "It may be that she is just not interested in having sex with you".

8:00 pm

I had a great night with Danielle as we went to a nice little restaurant and went for a walk in the park afterwards. We were together the entire night, and not once did we talk about Johnson, Dreams or 211. We walked home hand in hand. I gave her a little kiss at her door. I then leaned in and tried to let her know how I really felt about her. She embraced the kiss, but suddenly stopped, she put her head on my chest, and said "I had a wonderful time tonight". She then went in, leaving me standing in pain on the porch.

12-07-97 / 2:11 am

I woke up to a banging on the front door, I quickly jumped up and ran down to the door. I looked out thru the peephole and saw that it was Danielle. I opened the door and she embraced me with one of the most passionate kisses I have ever received. She kicked the door shut and pushed me in towards the sofa. "I am an idiot", she said. "I need this, it's been so long." She reached inside my shorts and grabbed me. "Hold on, slow down" I said, I couldn't believe I was saying slow down, but I was. She grabbed my hand and led me up towards the bedroom. "We can slow down after". We fell onto the bed and went into a long hard kiss. I ran my hand up her thigh, and over her shirt. I reached for her breast, but there was no breast. She suddenly started to bite at my lip, I opened my eyes as I tried to push her off me. Except it wasn't Danielle, it was Amy. She sat up on me and started to laugh. I went to push her off and she locked her feet around me, she was freakishly strong. We then rolled off the bed and I was able to push her off of me. "What's wrong with you?" I yelled. She sat in the middle of the floor and put her hand down her pants, "I want you to show me how to touch myself?" I grabbed her hand and pulled her up. "Don't you love me anymore?" She asked. Hoping this was a dream, I remembered what Dr Adams said about controlling the dreams and said, "Amy, I will always love you, but you have to tell me who's hurting you". Her head dropped, and she started crying. "If I tell, you will be taken away from me," I then told her, "I promise, I will never leave you, I will always love you" I then grabbed her and demanded that she tell me who it is that is hurting her. Amy then pulled away from me, she stood up and pointed at me. I woke up, but not in a panic. What was all that about I thought? Then the hair, the hair was standing on end. The dreams were back, I laid back down and smiled.

12-08-97 / 9:00 am

I sat in the third row of the courthouse as Dan's trial was about to begin, Amy was seated next to me, and Danielle was sitting in the row in front of us. When Dan was brought in, Amy only took her eyes off him for a second when she looked over at Danielle. Dan looked at Amy, and said "I love you baby girl". I saw Amy mouth the words, "I love you daddy", back. No sound, but I could tell what she was saying. Danielle yelled for the guards to keep Dan from talking to Amy. The Judge seemed more interested in keeping Danielle quiet, he even threatened to have her removed from the courtroom. Amy became withdrawn and started to cry softly as she snuggled up to me on the hard wooden bench. The trial was long and drawn out, I thought it would be open and shut. The photos, the main piece of evidence were blown up so people in the last row could see them, Amy's' privates covered with yellow tape. They were on display at the front of the courtroom. Amy seemed unfazed by them. I whispered to her, "Did your daddy take those pictures". Amy's softly said, "I don't remember", as she wiped away the tears from her cheeks. Again the photos, there was something about them that seemed out of place. They were not on display for long, a sheet, only being lifted when the lawyers talked covered them. When the photo of Amy in the shower was shown, that's when I noticed something that I didn't see before. With the photo being blown up, I could see a mirror behind Amy. A little round shower mirror attached to the wall, the flash from the camera was reflecting off of it and I could see the person taking the photograph. I was sure it wasn't Dan. It looked like it might have been a woman, but the flash reflection covered who ever it was. I tapped Danielle on the shoulder and told her what I saw. She flagged me and continued to watch the trial. Several hours later the lawyers gave their final arguments and the case went to the jury. Amy was asleep on the bench next to me. She didn't see her father as he was led from the courtroom. I grabbed her arm to wake her. As soon as I touched her I was transferred into a tiny bathroom, I was standing in the shower. I looked at the little mirror behind me, a washcloth covered it. I pushed the cloth away and saw in the reflection that it wasn't me standing there in the shower, I saw Amys reflection looking back at me, I was seeing what Amy saw, just then I heard someone say "Smile" and as I turned around a flash went off. I was blinded for a second. As my sight came back I found myself being shook awake by Danielle, I was back in the courthouse. Danielle was yelling, "What's wrong with you? You scared Amy". I got back up on the bench and asked what happened? "You passed out", Danielle said, "Fell right on the floor". I looked over at Amy as she was standing behind her mother, frightened, looking at me, and when she saw me looking at her, she smiled.

4:00 pm

The verdict was in. Guilty of possession of child pornography, and related charges. Dan was never charged in the death of Johnson. The coroner listed the cause of death as heart failure. Dan was scheduled for sentencing on February 11th. On the ride home I was still puzzled about the reflection in the photograph. Danielle blew it off as an optical illusion. She refused to believe that someone else could have taken that picture. "What about his live in girlfriend" I asked. "If she did, it was for him" she rebutted. "Then she is just as guilty" I said. Danielle stared straight ahead and said, "Can we not talk, I just want to ride in quiet". As I drove all I thought about was that vision I had, but I decided to honor Danielle's wishes and I kept my mouth shut.

5:15 pm

We stopped to eat in a tiny dinner off the highway. While we were waiting for our food Danielles mood changed, she was now happy again, almost childlike. She was overjoyed at the verdict. She could not stop smiling. "Did we have a good day?" I asked her. She hugged Amy and said, "He can never take you away from me, and he is never going to hurt you again, ever again." Amy smiled and looked at her mother. Danielle released her hug and rubbed the top of Amy's head, "And we can do what ever we want". Amy's smile left her face as she sat back down in the booth. "Did he try to take Amy away from you", I asked. "Right before those photographs were discovered, he told me he wanted full custody". I was surprised, and asked "On what grounds?" Danielle whispered, "He was going to use my mental state, he said he would bring up Johnson, and the shit I told him". She appeared to be lying, "It would be his word against yours," I told her. "No" she said, "He was going to call you and Doctor Adams as witnesses". I sat in silence as the food came, thinking to myself that Dan, a drugged out loser would not have a leg to stand on if he tried to take Amy away from her. But any mention of this to Danielle would make her go crazy with far-fetched theories, and both of us could not have crazy theories. I left it alone, Danielle just wanted Amy to be safe. With Dan in jail, she feels like she got what she needed, or wanted.

9:00 pm

I was sitting with Danielle on her porch. "Its getting late" I said, "I m gonna head home". Danielle just stared into space. I stood behind her and started to rub her shoulders, this brought her back into focus. "Sorry" She said, "I must have zoned out" she tilted her head to look up at me, "It's over, isn't it?" She asked. "I think so," I said, we both knew that was a lie.

12-9-97 / 8:15 am

I thought I'd visit with Dan before he was sent back up state. I had the officers bring him up to my office. "How you doing?" I asked as they brought him in. I told him to sit, and excused the officers. Dan looked like he hadn't slept in days. "I didn't do it," he said. I looked him right in the eye, I could tell he was scared, I could tell he wasn't lying. I told him I believed him. "Why would I take those photos, I love her, I want to keep her safe." He put his face in his hands and started to cry. "Who else could have taken them?" I asked. "That's the problem", he sobbed, "There is no one else". "What about your girlfriend?" Dan looked up, "Judy" he said with a laugh. "That stupid bitch can't operate a toaster, no way she operates a camera". He then put his head down again, staring at his shoes as he said. "Amy is the last person she would try to hurt," I asked if he tried to get full custody of Amy. He just laughed and said "Danielle would kill me first." I then

85

asked if he was still having bad dreams. "Every night". He said, and then added, "At least I can't hurt Amy from inside here". I then asked why he called me the night he got arrested and told me the dreams had stopped. Dan looked up at me, "I never called you, and the dreams will never stop." I then asked him if the dreams still tell him to hurt Amy? A long pause, then he said without lifting his head, "I watch her die every time I fall asleep".

3:45 pm

I saw Judy, Dan's girlfriend leaving Danielle's as I pulled into my driveway. Danielle was apologizing, saying if she knew she was coming over she wouldn't have let Amy go to Dr Adams for her appointment. Judy appeared to be extremely upset. She walked to Dan's mustang, threw an envelope in thru the open window and then shouted back. "You can't keep her hidden away, I still have a right to see her", Judy saw me getting out of my car. She looked back at Danielle and whispered, "You promised." I walked up to Danielle and asked what that was all about. Danielle blew it off saying "Judy thinks just because she and Dan were together that she has a right to see Amy". I then saw Amy peeking from behind the door window. "She's not at Dr Adams, is she"? I said as I pointed to the top of her head peaking thru the window. Danielle laughed and said, "I hope she wasn't there the whole time, not that the crack whore would have noticed her." She then told Amy to get ready for Dr Adams appointment. Danielle stood there staring into space. "Something bothering you". I asked. She turned and looked at me, sort of looked straight thru me. "You think Judy could have taken that picture of Amy, you did say it appeared to be a woman behind the reflection". Before I could answer Amy came bouncing out the door the way any normal 11-year-old kid does. Amy grabbed Danielle's hand. Danielle appeared to be a little annoyed that she had to walk Amy down to Dr Adams house. So I told her I'd take her down, "I was going to take a walk anyway". Danielle seemed relived and stated, "I do have a few errands I have to take care of". Amy then took my hand and we walked down to Dr Adams house. Dr Adams was waiting on the porch, Amy let go of my hand and ran up to greet him. I kept walking as Danielle drove speeding by.

5:00 pm

I came back to Dr Adams and I was about to ring the bell when I heard Amy screaming, the door wasn't locked and I ran in. Dr Adams was sitting in a chair and Amy was on the sofa. She appeared to be in a hypnotized state. Dr Adams stood up and was about to bring her out of it. I grabbed him and said, "Hold on, I want to try something". As I reached down to touch Amy. Dr Adams was saying, "This is not right, I can't let you do" was all I heard. Because as soon as I touched Amy on the arm,

I was in her bedroom. I was standing in a dark corner. She was sitting on the bed pulling her legs up into her chest, she was screaming at the door. A chair that was wedged up against the handle blocking the door that was about to give way. Someone was trying to break in. I then went to walk over to Amy on the bed when the door suddenly burst open. It was me who was entering the room. I tried to grab myself but tripped and cut my leg open. I watched as myself rushed towards Amy on the bed. I grabbed hold of the dresser and pulled myself up. I then saw Amy lying on the bed holding her neck that had been cut, blood was running down her nightgown. I then saw myself on the floor with what looked like a bullet wound to my chest. Dr Adams slapped me back to my senses. He was holding a rag over a cut on my leg that he said just appeared. I jumped up and looked at Amy, I wanted to make sure there were no wounds to her neck. I then grabbed my chest, no bullet wound. Dr Adams thought I was having a heart attack. Amy was sent into watch TV. I told Dr Adams what had happened, not just tonight, but in all my dreams. I also told him about Dan's dreams. Dr Adams mouth actually dropped open. Dr Adams sits down and says, "In all these dreams you saw yourself with a gunshot wound, and in Dan's dreams he has a gun, Danielle sees someone plunge a knife into Amy, but no one was ever able to see who actually hurts Amy, until tonight, when you saw yourself stab her". Dr Adams keeps talking stating that in the courthouse, I was Amy in the shower. And now I see myself in Amy's bedroom. Dr Adams then thought out loud, "I think when you touch Amy your not you when you see what you are seeing. Maybe you are the person that harms Amy, and you're seeing that through someone else's eyes". I sat down and said, "I didn't see myself stab her, I fell, and when I got up Amy was bleeding." Before we could finish discussing this Danielle was at the door. Dr Adams asked me not to discuss this with anyone, He appeared to be scared.

9:45 pm

I needed a drink so I went around to the bar and Johnny Downs was there, he called me over and says, "I clicked onto that SEE MORE icon on the Sogods website". I thought, fuck me, I just wanted to do anything except talk about this shit anymore, but I had to ask, "What did you see?" He said, "It was an announcement urging his followers to pray on February 11th at 2:11 am". I said, "February 11th that is Dan's sentencing day". John said, "That's my wife's birthday, I am not allowed to forget 2-11." I can't believe I didn't notice that Dan's sentencing was on 2-11. After several more beers, and quite a few shots later, I had to head home.

12-10-97 / 1:33 am

I was going to bed drunk and I could not wait to sleep, I wanted to dream, I had beer muscles and I was going to control the shit out of any dream that entered my head.

I couldn't get my key in the door, and I fell asleep on the front porch. I sat down to find the correct key and just fell sound asleep. I woke up in the morning when the paperboy threw the morning paper at me. I was still drunk and I felt like shit, not from just the alcohol but I wanted to dream and I didn't. After digging my keys from the cracks in the boards of the porch I went in and turned on the computer, it lit up and went right to the Sogod website. There was nothing new on the site. No new entries. The SEE MORE icon was still blinking in the corner. I had to click on it. It was a letter addressed to me, it read:

Don't stop you are close, 211 approaches, we will all pray.

Each time see who is not there, reflections tell the truth.

And she wont be re-united.

Take your time, you will save her, or die.

Hope to see you in my hell.

I thought, how the hell did Johnny mistake this for, we will pray on February 11th. I was starting to think John was trying to keep me away from this site. I scrolled down and read more, what followed was a rambling mess. It appeared to be written in red crayon, or maybe even blood. It was written exactly like this:

Summer is coming, soon all the kids will be

Home. I will go on to better things

Everyone will want to join with me.

I think all will see I am the only god.

Snow will cover the streets.

Not everyone will feel the cold.

Only the best will last thru this cold weather.

There is a way to join, and you will feel no pain.

Watch your back around your friends.

Half the people you meet want to kill you.

Animals will want to eat you.

Take away your fear, and help us.

Yesterday was the first day.

October was the start.

Using dreams is only one way.

Thursdays are the devils days.

Heart attacks are not what they appear to be.

I know you will want to die.

Not knowing when is the problem.

Knowing how to read this is the key. Don't look up.

I hit print. The screen went back to the front page. I clicked on the SEE MORE icon again. It opened to show a message asking all followers to pray on February 11th. This is what Johnny saw. I tried to get back to what I was looking at to no avail. The printer came to life. Before I could see what was printing, there was a knock on the door. Danielle was standing there when I opened it. "Can you do me a big favor?" she asked. "Can you watch Amy this morning, I have to get to work and her teacher is running late?" Danielle had hired another home schoolteacher that doubles as a baby sitter for Amy, she is like a teacher slash friend for Amy. Her name is Joy, she is a pretty little thing, about 25 years old and hot as hell. "Sure" I said, "I'd do anything to spend time with Joy". Danielle turned to leave, then turned and placed a playful punch on my arm. I said "Amy, I meant to say spend time with Amy".

I was sitting in Danielle's living room watching TV, I could not figure out how to work Danielles remote. I was stuck on PBS watching Rugrats. It was almost 10:00 am, where the hell was Joy? Another question, where was Amy? I went up to her bedroom but she wasn't there. I looked into her mother's room, not there either. I called out for her, no answer. I went past the bathroom and heard splashing in the tub. Found her, I didn't look in, who else would be taking a bath in Danielles bathroom. I went to go back down stairs when I heard someone else's voice coming from the bathroom, it sounded like a mans voice. Maybe it's not Amy in there. I gently knocked and poked my head around the door and looked in. Amy looked like a kid that was just caught with her hand in the cookie jar. She was sitting in a tub full of bubbles. I went in and looked around the room. There was no one else in there. Amy just sat quietly and smiled as she watched me. "You okay pumpkin" I asked. She shook her head yes. "Is there someone else in here?" Amy waited several seconds, and then whispered, "Yes". I asked, "Who, where?" Amy pointed into the bubbles. I could not see anything in the tub but bubbles and Amy's head. I rolled up my sleeve and put my hand into the water, the water was ice cold. There was no one in the tub but Amy. "Why are you in your mothers bathroom anyway?" Amy just smiled and blew bubbles into the air. "Get out and get dressed, I'll make us some breakfast". Amy reached out for me as the doorbell rang. I said hurry up kiddo, Joy is here. I went down and answered the door. No one was there, as I slowly closed the door someone put his or her hand on my shoulder and scared the shit out of me, I think I even pee'd a little. It was Joy, "I let myself in, didn't mean to scare you, you must be Joe" She said as she reached to shake my hand. "I'm Joy nice to meet you." She said as I shook her hand. I was stunned at how youthful and breathtaking she was close up and said, "The joy is all mine." She laughed and said rolling her eyes, "That's the first time I heard that one". Amy came down the steps in a bathing suit, "What are you wearing?" I asked. She pointed to the hot tub in the yard as she headed for the back door. "Oh yea, I could go for a soak, Join us" Joy said as she took off her sweat suit and started to walk towards the back door in what I could only describe as the most beautiful thong underwear I have ever seen. I declined the offer, and went back home to sleep.

I just got up to my bedroom and I was about to collapse into my bed when I heard giggling coming from the back yard. I looked out and saw Amy and Joy in the hot tub. They were sitting on the edge with there feet in the water. They were talking, but I could not hear what they were saying. Joy suddenly stood up, she reached up and took her top off and laid it across the side of the tub. Amy then stood up and walked thru the water towards her. Amy appeared to be in some sort of trance. I wanted to yell for Amy to get out of the way, that her head was blocking my view. Amy then wrapped her arms around Joys shoulders and laid her head against her breasts. Joy then grabbed a hold of Amy bathing suit and started to take it off. As she started to roll the top down over Amy's shoulders, Joy looked up at me and smiled. I turned and tried to hide, but lost my balance and fell. I woke up in bed. It was 2:11 pm. Was I dreaming, was Joy and Amy in the hot tub? I got up and looked out the window at the hot tub. The cover was on and the gate around the tub was shut. It was overcast and it appeared that it was going to snow at any second. As I went to turn from the window I saw Joy's bra hanging out from under the hot tub cover. The phone rang, it was Danielle, and she was asking if I wanted to come over for dinner tonight.

5:30 pm

I arrived at Danielles for dinner. Amy answered the door and let me in. As I took my coat off and threw it over a chair, a folded sheet of paper fell from the pocket. Amy picked it up and handed it to me. I unfolded it and saw that it was what I printed off the computer, I thought I did that in a dream. Danielle came into the living room and sat next to me and asked me what was wrong? I asked her if I watched Amy today. She slapped me on my shoulder and said, "Joy was here all day". You didn't ask me to sit with her this morning until Joy got here? I asked. "No" she said. "Joy arrived early, and I was able to stop and enjoy breakfast before work this morning." She then asked again if I was all right. I said, "I don't know, the dreams are back." Fear came across her face. She then told me what I had told her a hundred times, that dreams are not real, unless you make them real. I then asked her if the hot tub was up and running. She told me the tub was empty, that she drained it last summer when the heater broke. I got up and told her I needed some air and I went outside and walked around to the hot tub. I could not open the cover it was locked. I pulled the garment out that was hanging from the tub stuck under the cover. It was a black bra, the same bra I saw Joy wearing in my dream. I tried to pry the cover up, I could see a little, there was no water in it, just a foul odor. I turned around to go back in and Amy was standing behind me, again I think I pee'd a little. "You scared me," I said. She took my hand and walked me to the edge of the yard. There were trees and then a little embankment that went down to a creek. She didn't say a word, she just pointed to a pile of rocks about halfway down the path. We then walked over to the rocks and I bent down and started lifting the rocks up. Danielle came out on her back porch and started calling me. I turned to get Amy, but Amy wasn't there. I looked up at Danielle and saw that Amy was standing next to her on the deck, they were at least 200 yards away. I dropped the rocks I was holding and waited until they both went in before walking back up to the house. I never noticed that the rocks I dropped were now covered with flies.

7:35 pm

I sat thru dinner without speaking a word. Danielle seemed upset. She excused Amy from the table and asked me what I was doing down by the creek. I told her Amy took me down. "When was Amy out back with you?" she almost screamed at me. "Tonight" I said, "When I was out back". I pulled the bra from my pocket and told her where I found it, and how I knew it was there. Danielle grabbed it from my hand blushing, she said in a low whisper, "That's mine". She then stated that Amy was with her in the kitchen the entire time I was out clearing my head. I put my head in my hands as I sat at the table. Danielle got up and hugged me from behind. I held her arms as she held me. "I can't tell the difference anymore between reality or dreams," Maybe I should see Dr Adams I thought.

12-11-97 / 2:11 am

I'm sitting in Danielle's bedroom. I get up and walk down the hallway to Amys private bathroom. It's a mess, there are towels on the floor, toothpaste left open on the sink. The little trashcan by the toilet is knocked over. Someone is in the shower. The water isn't running, but someone is standing behind the shower curtain. I reach out and pull the curtain back. There is no one there. I put the seat down on the toilet and sit with my head down. I hear water running and look up. I look directly into the shower and Amy is now standing there with her back to me, she is showering, I call to her, as she turns the bathroom door opens and there is a flash. I jump up to see who it was. Nobody, I go out into the hallway and see Amy being pulled into her bedroom. I turn around and look back into the shower. Again it was empty. I then noticed that there is a small mirror on the wall, its reflection covered by steam. This was the shower where the photograph was taken. I walked down to Amy's bedroom and she is lying on the bed wrapped in a towel. When I walk in she clutches her towel to keep it shut. I sit down next to her on the bed and reach out to touch her leg, I tell her it's all right that I would never hurt her. She smiles and says, "I want my dad." I tell her that I will go and get him. I then hear someone whisper for Amy to remove the towel. Amy clutches the towel tighter. I look around the room, but there is no one else here. I then turn back around and realize that I am reaching to grab the towel from Amy's grasp. I don't want to do this but I can't stop. Amy is now crying, she says, " I'm going to tell my dad". I then pull out a knife and plunge it at her chest. I wake up before the knife makes contact. My sheets are soaked with sweat. Its 2:11 am.

7:15 am

I am knocking on Dr Adams door, but part of me wants him not to be in. A young boy, his son opens the door and he brings me into the kitchen where Dr Adams is placing freshly cooked breakfast items on the table with the help of his daughter. "I'm sorry." I said, "I didn't know you were about to have breakfast". Dr Adams seeing that I look like I haven't had a minute of sleep, told his kids to eat, and placed a napkin over his plate which looked like a piece of black cloth. He then led me into his study. "You look like hell," he tells me. "Funny, because I feel like shit"

I said as I sat in a big soft chair, Doctor Adams stood in front of me, he appeared to be nervous and it seemed like he was rushing me, I told him about the dreams, and how sometimes I cant tell if I'm asleep or awake. He opens his desk drawer and grabs a red rubber wristband. He tells me to wear this all the time. "How will this help me?" I ask. He says when you are awake and you have the band on, If you think your dreaming just pull on it and let it snap back onto your wrist, if it is painful you are awake, but if your dreaming the shock of the snap will wake you up. Doctor Adams held out the band so that I had to stand to take it from him, when I did I noticed he was wearing a wristband, and his wrist was covered in welts, he started to escort me towards the front door. On my way out I noticed that the two children that were in the kitchen with him were not in any of the numerous photos he had displayed through out his home.

8:45 am

I was told as soon as I arrived at my office that Dan was being transferred from upstate to Northeastern Mental Hospital. The report said that he was having suicidal thoughts. I called and spoke with his Doctor, he told me that Dan had made claims that he had killed his sisters daughter. The Doctor went on to say as far as he knew, Dan didn't have a sister. As far as anyone knew he just showed up in town about 13 years ago. He worked odd jobs, was living at fleabag hotels and then one day he put a trailer on the outskirts of town. He lived there with a dirty little girl, Judy I think her name was. Then one-night years ago he was in a bar fight with one of our nurses. "Danielle?" I asked. The doctor seemed surprised and asked, "Yes, do you know her?" I told him "Dan is her ex-husband." There was long silence, He then said, "No, I don't think Danielle has ever been married". I then asked, "Dan is Amy's father?" He said, "Might be, Danielle don't speak much about her personnel life inside of here, but that would explain why she refused to press any charges on him that night. Dan did beat her pretty badly", he was then called away from the phone. He did not put me on hold and I could hear a female voice telling him Dan was in cardiac arrest. The phone then went dead and I reached down and snapped the band on my wrist. Just pain, not dreaming.

3:30 pm

I didn't hear anymore from the Hospital, and Danielle was not returning my calls, so I decided to go and see what was up. I was granted entrance to the ward but was denied any visit with Dan. A Doctor came up the hallway and asked me why I was here to visit with Dan. By this mans voice I could tell it was the same Doctor I was speaking to on the phone. I told him I was a friend. The Doctor told me that Dan had left his visitor card blank, and hospital policy states that patients must list anyone they want to visit. I was going to show my prison ID but Danielle came around the corner and had me buzzed in. She took me to a small conference room. She told me that Dan had almost died, that his ventilation hose got kinked under a wheel on his bed. She said his heart stopped beating for a long time and that the heart monitor never alerted staff, he should be dead. "Why is he here?" I asked. The prison Doctor had him sent down to be evaluated. He can't sleep, and when he is sedated he wakes up screaming," she then said, "There was a note in his file that stated he was observed killing and eating flies." Before I could question that, Danielle said, "He thinks he killed Amy". I then told Danielle that the doctor told me he has made claims of killing his sister daughter. "His sisters kid?" Danielle asked puzzled. "There was no mention of a sisters kid in his report, he never mentioned any sister to me". She then told me that she was only able to read some of his report, that Dan first complained of dreams and the dreams keep intensifying, and now every time he falls asleep he kills Amy. Danielle said she could not read the rest and that she is not allowed to treat him, or should she be reading his chart since he is Amy's dad. She then said. "But I do know he tried to hang himself before being sent down." Just to be sure I asked, "So there is no sister?" Danielle shrugged her shoulders and said, "Maybe Judy is his sister". I held Danielle's arm as she tried to exit the room and said, "Danielle I need to see him, it is very important." She asked if I was still having dreams, I lied and told her no. Danielle looked up and down the hallway, she then told me it would be impossible to get into his room, too much security. Danielle was then paged, to where I didn't care. She told me to stay put and that she would be right back to walk me out. I walked out into the hallway. A huge security guard asked me where I was going as soon as I stepped out of the conference room. "Smoke" I said. He then smiled and pointed down the hall. I walked down towards Dans room. Dan appeared to be knocked out, he was sleeping and handcuffed to the bed. As I slowly walked up to his door Dan called me. The guard was now talking to a nurse and forgot all about me. I ducked into Dans room. He wasn't awake, I'm not sure if he was even alive. There was no sense in talking to a man in a coma and as I went to leave I reached out and touched Dan's arm. The touch put me inside of Dan's head. I was in Danielles house and I was running up the stairs to Amys bedroom, I kicked open the door and saw someone sitting next to Amy, this person was struggling with Amy trying to pull off her bath towel, as this person turned to look at me I was unable to see their face as it was blocked by the flash from the gun I had just shot. The person falls face first onto the ground by the bed. I look at Amy and she is bleeding, there is a knife stuck in her chest. I then look down at the person on the floor, everything turns to black and white, everything except for the red band around his left wrist. I didn't see the person face, but I knew it was me lying on the floor. I am then shook out of it by the security guard, "You trying to get me fired" he says. As he walks me out of the room, Dan turns his head and says, "You see Joe, every night, every fucking night, I get there a second too late". I look up at the guard, he keeps walking like he didn't see or hear anything.

7:15 pm

I stop by the police station to see Johnny Downs, He was just about to start his shift. I asked him if he knew anything about Dan and Danielles fight. He smiles and says he forgot all about that night. "It was a crazy night several years ago in early February," he said. "My shift was ending when I got the call. I get there and several patrons of the bar are holding Dan and Danielle is kicking and punching him. She stopped as soon as I hit my bubble lights. Dan was let go by the crowd and he fell to the ground. Danielle turned and her whole face was swollen and bleeding." I asked him if there was a police report. "No, neither of them wanted to press any charges and it was at the end of my shift and I really didn't want any paperwork to hold me up". I asked him if he ever found out what happened. He told me one witness stated they were arguing over a kid. She was heard yelling I gave you and your whore the trailer. You can have another kid with her. I didn't know who she was talking about because Judy looked like she was two months past her due date.

Johnny said Danielle took Amy away from Dan because she found out Judy's baby was his. Danielle wanted to keep Amy away from Dan and Judy because of the drug use. Then Dan found out that Danielle cleaned out all of the bank accounts leaving him with only the keys to the trailer. Another witness stated Dan walked in the bar and walked straight up to Danielle and slammed her head into the wall yelling this is never going to happen, and that he will do whatever it takes to protect her. Then neither were arrested or charged. Right after Danielle and Amy were discharged from the hospital they got their life together. Her parents gave her the house that they are in now, and Dan slipped into drugs and booze. I thanked John for the information. I didn't tell him I found it hard to believe that they could have such a violent fight in public and all that came from it was Danielle spending a couple days in the hospital. John called it a "Slip and Fall", and said all the witnesses refused to give any useful statements and it appeared the whole town forgot about it, including John. Turned out Amy was still considered a newborn and stayed with Danielle in the hospital until she was released.

11:30 pm

I got home and my computer was on. I went to shut it down when I noticed written on the screen blinking was: Read it, Read it up, Read it Down. It was signed Sogod.

I hit print and the screen went black. The computer just shut down. I reached into my coat pocket and took out the folded piece of paper. I read it, I read it forwards and backwards. I checked out the words, up from the bottom, and down from the top. No matter how I read it, it meant nothing to me. I could not stop reading it. This was one of those puzzles inside a puzzle that I thought would keep me up all night, I was not going to sleep until I solved it. Only problem was, would I even know when I solved it. I sat for hours. I made photocopies of the printout, I highlighted words, letters. Still nothing. Then at 2:11 am I saw it. It was like the letters on the page were showing me themselves. The first letter of each line were the only letters in upper class. The last line of the riddle says: Knowing how to read this is the key. Don't look up. Reading the capitol letters down said: SHE IS NOT WHAT YOU THINK. Puzzle solved, but who is she, Danielle or Amy, maybe its Judy. The more I find out the more confused I get.

12-13-97 / 8:00 am

I walked out the door to go to work, Danielle was in her driveway with Amy and Joy. Her car wouldn't start. "Need a hand," I yelled over. Danielle looked up from under the hood and said, "I need a ride".

As we drove towards the Hospital, I asked Danielle about the fight with Dan. She appeared shocked that I even knew about that. "It was nothing," she said. "He was drunk, I was drunker and things got out of hand." I told her I was told both Dan and she were beaten pretty badly. "A lot of blood but not much in the injury part". I then asked her if Dan was trying to get Amy back when this happened?" Danielle suddenly became annoyed, stating "Me and Dan were talking about getting married and then right before Amy was born I found out about his crack whore baby he was about to have with Judy. After Amy was born I took her away, emptied all of our savings, well my savings, that bastard spent all of his money on

107

that whore and drugs. Dan would not have been a fit father, so I left him. He found out and went off. Maybe I should have just left town. Maybe I should have left him some money, but after he spent it, he still would have come back and it still would have happened". I said he got the trailer. She looked at me and said, "The only thing I left him were the keys to that trailer, I couldn't just leave him homeless." So the fight in the bar was after you left him, I asked. "Yes, the next day", she said annoyed that I asked, "He contacted me from a homeless shelter that he moved to with that bitch. If I knew he was still together with her I would have let him rot in that shelter, but I had to tell him where the keys to the trailer were. That stupid motherfucker was going to live in the shelter, the dumb fuck didn't even know I left him the trailer. When we talked, he never once mentioned Amy, he didn't want to see her, or talk to her. It was like he forgot all about her. The next night he came in the bar, it was the first time I heard him say her name". Did he file for custody I asked? "Not then, he just wanted me to give him money, but several years later he cleaned up, and he was still with the super bitch, but I agreed with the custody agreement he had served me." She then snapped. "That's it, don't bring it up anymore, he is gone and Amy is starting to forget all about him, and I just don't need to be reminded of this shit anymore". She got out of the car in front of the hospital and slammed the door. She took a few steps, then turned around swung the door open and said "Thanks for fucking up my day". She then slammed the door again and stormed into the Hospital. I sat and wondered what happened to Judy's baby.

10:00 am

Out of the blue Officer Downs called me and asked how everything was going. I didn't want to tell him anything about my dreams or the Sogod website on the computer so I lied. He then asked me if I had contacted anyone about what I saw in the Photo of Amy in the bathroom. I told him no and questioned why. He said Dan's lawyers were trying to get him a new trial based on that photograph. "Holy shit" I yelled. "Danielle is going to hit the roof. Do you think he'll get a new trial?" He told me it looks like it, and if he is granted a new trial, then he will also get a lower bail. "That don't matter" I said, "The guy don't have a can to piss in, who would put up his bail". Stranger things have happened John said. "You don't have to tell me about strange things". Before he hung up, I asked him if he could get me any information on Danielle and Dans custody paperwork. He told me he would see what he could do. "That's all I ask," I said. As I hung up the phone the alarms went off inside the AD/SEG Unit.

10:25 am

When I arrived on the Unit, several officers are trying to subdue an inmate in the middle of the dayroom. It was Ronald Mason, he was in AD/SEG for biting the ear off his cellmate because he wouldn't give him a cookie. He was huge, he was 6-4 and 300 pounds of muscle. There were five pretty good size officers trying to hold him down without much luck. When I walked in Mason looked up at me from the floor and just stopped struggling. His body froze. The officers were still unable to move his arms or legs to secure them, it was like he was made out of granite. He looked right at me. I have spoken with Mason many times before, so I knew it wasn't his voice when he spoke, it was Johnson. He said as I started to snap my wristband, "The rocks, go back to the rocks" He then went limp. He was shackled put on a gurney and taken down to the hospital where he claimed to have no knowledge of the incident or even what he said. I sent officers to search his cell, I was called over as the officers were refusing to go in the cell. Inside his cell, the floor was covered in shit, there was writing on the walls, it appeared Mason had used his own shit as ink. Written in shit on the wall was "Below the rocks the truth will be found". It was written over and over. The smell was awful, and the cell was infested with flies. When I turned to leave, written above the doorframe was: "You wont see it, but she will see you, save her". I was snapping my band again. Pain, only pain. Then I was notified that Inmate Mason had died in medical.

5:30 pm

When I got home from work I went over to Danielles, but there was no answer at the door. Danielles car wasn't in the driveway. There was a note from the towing company taped on the door. I knocked again thinking Amy and Joy should be home. Still no answer. I walked around back and no one was in the yard. I walked down to the embankment where Amy showed me the pile of rocks. The snow on the ground made it a little harder this time to walk. I slid down past the tree line. I searched for the rocks by kicking at the snow. I could not find it. After about ten minutes of searching it was getting pretty cold. I didn't have any gloves on, so I decided to go back, I was thinking maybe there are no rocks, maybe it was just another dream. But I slipped again and fell onto the pile of rocks. I brushed the snow away and started to remove the rocks one by one. They were little rocks and appeared to have been put there by a child. Under the rocks I found a small stuffed bunny, some little trinkets, and an envelope stuck inside a plastic bag. Inside the envelope were some photographs. All had Amy in them. There was one of Amy and Dan. Written on the back it said Mommy and Daddy will always love you. Amy looked to be about 5 years old and she was holding the stuffed bunny that was in the hole. There was another photo of Amy sitting on a horse. On the back was written, taken on a happier day, Love, But I couldn't read the name, it had been scribbled over. There also was a key that had rusted over, and Amy's birth certificate. It stated that Amy was born on 12-28-1997, but it appeared to have been altered, the font size of the print seemed just a little larger then all the other print. Her Parents were listed as Daniel, and Danielle Williamson. I sat there in the snow looking at all this stuff. I could not make any type of connection from it. The key I found, I was hoping opened the hot tub. The writings on the wall kept going through my head. Below the rocks the truth will be found. What did I find? I found out Amys birth date. That her parents were Dan and Danielle. I already knew that. And written above the cell door. "I wont see it, but she will see you." That one was correct, because I didn't see shit. But who will see me. I then looked up and saw Danielle in the kitchen window looking down towards me. I didn't think she could see me. I was pretty far down behind the trees. But how long was she there. I watched and waited for her to leave. The cold was biting all over my body. She finally left and turned the light off. I then realized that it was dark out. I looked at my watch and it was almost 8 o'clock at night. I then walked the tree line onto my property and entered my house thru the back door.

12-14-97 / 2:11 am

I wasn't dreaming because I didn't go to bed yet. I kept looking at the stuff I took out of that hole. I tried everything I could think of to see who signed the one photo but to no avail. I went up to the bedroom and sat on my bed, I was half afraid to sleep. I heard some noises coming from the yard and I looked out and saw someone walking in Danielles yard towards the creek. I grabbed my coat and headed down. I went out my backdoor and walked up the way I had come home earlier. I expected Danielle to be down there looking for the rocks. It wasn't Danielle, it was Judy. I watched as she found the rocks and the hole. She sat down in the snow and started to cry. I came up behind her, she didn't notice, or she just didn't care that someone was there. I put my hand on her shoulder and asked her what was wrong. She didn't look up. She sobbed, I was told to come here. That I would see who it was that was causing me such pain. "Someone is causing you pain?" I asked. She pointed to the hole and said, "She must of gotten here first". I bent down and lifted her to her feet and asked, "Who told you to come here?" She said, "Dan, he said I would find what I needed here". I told her "Dan is locked up at the Hospital, when did he call you? He doesn't have any phone privileges." She stared at me for a long time and said under her breath. "He told me in a dream". I held her up as we went back to my house. We started to walk the tree line back when we heard someone coming. It was Danielle, she was walking towards the trees holding a flashlight. We were able to get to the fence before she cold see us. I watched as Danielle stood over the hole shining the light in it. It appeared to be the first time she ever saw it.

4:00 am

I woke up to the sounds of someone going thru the drawers downstairs. I got up and looked in the spare bedroom that Judy fell asleep in but she wasn't in there. The room looked like it had been tossed. I went downstairs and found Judy opening drawers, cabinets, she was throwing everything over her shoulder. I knew what she was looking for, but I asked her anyway. Judy jumped, as I must of scared her. She said she had a dream that I had taken the stuff out of the hole and hid it in here. I grabbed her around the waist and led her to a chair. As we sat down I told her it was only a dream and that I didn't know about that hole until I followed her out there. She appeared confused, she then said, "Since I started having these dreams they all in some way became reality." You had dreams that came true I asked. She told me that Dan started having them first, she said Dan just started obsessing over getting Amy out of Danielles house. She then said "That", and then she stopped and said, "I can't say." I gently squeezed her hand, "Cant say what?" I asked. "Dan told me someone was touching her, hurting her." a long pause, "killing her." Did he say who was doing this to her. Judy looked up and said, "At first it was a doctor, but now, now it is you". I then snapped the band on my wrist, still not a dream. "They are just dreams" I said. "That dream hasn't come true, I haven't harmed Amy in any way what so ever, and I never will." It appeared that Judy wanted to believe me. "That was his dream," she said. "My dreams started back up when Dan went to jail". She then explained that Dan would visit her every night in her dreams. Dan told her to go and get Amy the day after he was sent to jail. But when she tried to get her Danielle flat out refused. "Amy is her daughter," I said. Judy became upset, "She should have been with Dan and I. Dan did not have these dreams before she took her away". I then asked, "What other dreams did you have that came true?" Judy told me that Dan instructed her to let people know to look at the photos again. Judy then told me that she could tell the shower photo wasn't taken at the trailer. I asked how she could tell. She said, "We don't have a shower".

10:00 am

I was sitting in the living room thinking if I should have shown Judy the stuff I took out of the hole. This stuff is supposed to show me the truth, but let Judy know who is hurting her. I don't even know what that means, maybe if I showed her the stuff, she could give me an explanation of it. There was a knock at the door, it was Danielle. She came in and asked if I heard any noises out back last night. "No" I said, "I slept like baby, didn't even have a single dream." She looked at me funny then sat down. I noticed that she had an identical red wristband on. She told me when she got home from work she noticed footprints in the snow. She said she could have sworn she saw someone down by the creek. "I didn't see anything," I said again. She then said she heard voices again late last night and when she walked down she found a hole dug up, she said it was fresh because there was no snow in it. "Kids" I told her, "They probably hid something in it and came back last night to get it." She looked at me like she knew I was lying "Kind of out of the way to hide something" she said. "Kids will be kids," I said. I then changed the subject and asked, "When is Amys birthday" Danielle said happily, "She came into my life right after Christmas on December 28th, I will be having a party for her. It's a surprise, so don't tell her." I then heard something fall over upstairs. Danielle also heard it and looked up at the ceiling. "Is there someone up there?" she asked. "Hope not" I then said. "I did leave a window open to air out the middle room, I spilled some paint and the smell was giving me headaches. Something probably just blew over. If there is nothing else I should go check", knowing Judy was still up there I had to get Danielle out of the house. Danielle said she had to do some sort of errand and got up to leave. She approached me and gave me a kiss on the cheek. This surprised me, since we haven't really been on good terms. She then said, "Lets start over, come over tonight, Amy is going to a Christmas show with Joy." She then shut the door just as Judy started to come down the steps. "I thought you left," I said. She then held out the stuffed bunny that was in the hole. "Where did you get this?" She demanded. "It is one of Amys toys, she must of left it here", I told her. "I know" she said, "I gave it to her the day she was born." I asked her. "Are you sure? They make a lot of stuffed bunnies". She clutched the rabbit to her chest "Yes I am sure, I wrote on the tag, Love always". She then walked out the door and down the street. I was going to call her back and ask her about her baby, but she was all ready up the street. Again I snapped my wristband.

6:10 pm

Dinner with Danielle was surprisingly romantic. She had made a beautiful meal. The entire house was candle lit. After eating she led me to the bedroom. We undressed and fell into bed. But something was wrong, something felt out of place. It was a terrific night but there was just something that was not right. Danielle appeared to be very unprepared in the act of lovemaking. Fumbling around, it was like she was waiting for me to tell her what to do. She seemed embarrassed when I touched her. It was like being a 16 year old again. She noticed that something was bothering me. I told her she was acting like a kid having sex for the first time. "Don't you like that?" She whispered into my ear. "Isn't it every mans dream to have sex with a young girl?" So she is role-playing I thought. So I started to act like a horny teenager, but this seemed to anger her. She snapped "Don't act like you don't know what your doing" she yelled. "I can't keep teaching you the same things over and over." I started snapping my wristband. Not dreaming. What happened next can only be described as rape. She raped me. I felt ashamed as I slowly fell asleep in bed next to her. I woke up to find my hands and feet tied to the bedpost. I called out for Danielle but there was no answer. Several moments later I heard someone walking towards the bedroom. I was shocked and embarrassed when Dan came to the doorway. He looked at me and said "If you liked Danielle as a child last night then you're going to love this." Dan then stepped away from the door and Amy was standing behind him. Amy then walked into the room and up to the bed and ran her hand over my chest. She then reached down to remove the sheet that was covering me. Dan held her arm, "Not yet" he said. Dan then told Amy to get into bed with me. Amy stood by the bed staring into

space like she was in a trance or drugged. I tried to snap
my wristband but my hands were tied. Amy then crawled
into the bed with me. "Don't be scared" Dan said. I didn't
know if he was talking to Amy or me. "This is what you
want, this is what you both want". Amy was now lying
next to me on top of the sheet. I looked at her, I looked
directly into her eyes. Amy smiled as I softly whispered to
her, "It's okay, lets do this". Dan smiled and sat down in
the corner of the bedroom to watch. Amy was now on top
of me with her head lying against mine. Dan was getting
impatient and yelled for Amy to take her robe off. I gently
turned Amy's head with my chin and whispered to her
as Dan strained to hear what I was saying. "Bite my neck
baby girl, bite it as hard as you can." Amy lifted her head
and opened her mouth wide, Dan jumped up and tried
to stop her. He tried to pull her away, but it was to late.
I heard a gunshot as Amy bit down waking me from my
dream. It was 2:11 am.

12-15-97 / 6:45 am

As I was getting dressed for work, Judy called. She told me Dan came to her again in her dreams last night. "What did he say?" I asked. She told me that Dan told me that he is late every time he tries to save Amy in his dreams. So he sent Judy in her dream to Amy's bedroom last night. I asked Judy what she saw. She told me when she looked into the room Amy was in bed with someone and she was ripping the flesh from their neck with her teeth. Judy then said there was another person in the room, this person was running towards the bed. When I asked who that was she stated she was unable to see anyone's face other then Amy's. Judy then told me she thought that the person that was running towards the bed was going to hurt Amy so she shot them. Judy said she woke up when she pulled the trigger. I then told her that I was looking out my bedroom window at Amy saying goodbye to her mother right now, and that Amy is fine. Judy then asked if Dan was able to have visits yet. I knew he wasn't allowed visitors but I told her to call the hospital. Judy said Danielle would never let that happen. She then asked if I would visit him. I told her I would try and asked her about her baby. The phone went silent, and I thought she hung up. I was just about to hang up when I heard Judy whisper. I lost him.

8:15 am

Dan was being discharged from the hospital back to the prison, but because of the new trial motion he was being sent to my prison and he is to be housed in the AD/SEG unit. When he came in I met him in the reception area. Dan seemed distant, he didn't want to talk to me. Once he was up on the unit I went over to see him, but he still didn't want anything to do with me. I got up and I told him about Judy, about her dreams and how she says he is visiting her in them. I asked him if he was having the same dreams. Dan just sat silently. I then told him I could arrange for Judy to visit, but he would have to talk to me. Still nothing, I turned to leave and Dan spoke. He asked, "Why Joe, why do you hurt her?" I turned back towards him and asked, "You talking about Amy? Tell me about your last dream". He said he got out of the Hospital and ran to Danielles house. Dan said Johnson was standing outside when he ran up and Johnson handed him a gun. Dan tried to throw it away but it would not leave his hand. He then runs up to Amy's bedroom and kicks open the door. He fires the gun before he even saw who was is in there. The bullet hit Amy in the back and she fell off the bed. Her mouth was full of blood. Dan then told me when he looked up, I was lying on the bed with a gaping hole in my neck, and Danielle was in the corner laughing. He put the gun up to his head and he started to pull the trigger, but he woke up before the shot. I looked at Dan as he was wreck, and he looked like a frightened child that wanted someone to tell him everything was going to be okay. I could not say anything, I put my hand on his shoulder. Dan softly said, "Why wont they let me die?"

11:00 am

I left work early and I wasn't feeling all that great. I was thinking it might be the lack of sleep. I pulled into a coffee shop drive-thru to get a cup of coffee. As I sat waiting for the line of cars in front of me to move I noticed Joy's car in the Funland parking lot. She probably took Amy there. As I pulled up a little further I could see Joy through the window as she was sitting by the ball pit watching the kids play. I did not see Amy anywhere. As I pulled up a little more I then saw Amy in the ball pit. She looked like she was having a grand old time. Joy looked out and saw me, she smiled and waved, and as she waved she knocked over her soda. The soda spilled on her shirt and lap and she appeared embarrassed as she got up to get napkins.

Amy was now out of the ball pit and looking at me thru the window. I raised my hand to wave when suddenly someone's arm reached from behind her, I could not see whose arm it was but I could see a dragon tattoo that ran from the wrist to the elbow. Suddenly Amy was pulled back away from the window. I looked over at Joy, she was still trying to wipe the spilled drink off her pants. I jumped out of the car and ran to the front door, shoving the doors open and almost knocking over several children as I ran to the ball pit area. Joy seeing me rushing in turned to see what Amy was doing. We both got to the ball pit at the same time. Amy was lying in the pit with her eyes closed. I jumped in the ball pit as security was right on my tail. Two security guys grabbed me as I grabbed Amy. Amy just looked up and smiled as she reached out for me. Then another hand reached out from the pit. It was a little boy about 10 years old. I was able to see he had a removable dragon tattoo on his arm just as security pushed me face first onto a table. Joy was confused, asking me what my problem was. The cars behind me in the coffee line were honking their horns. I told everyone what I thought I saw. Joy seemed to understand, Security wasn't so forgiving. They wanted to notify the police. After about a half hour of talking they didn't, they escorted me out of the building telling me to never come back. Joy had moved my car over to the Funland parking lot. She and Amy were sitting on the hood when I came out. "Sorry" was all I could say to them. Joy slid off the hood and kissed me on the cheek and said, "That was very noble of you Joe, you must love Amy very much, and I bet there is not a thing you would not do for her". I just rubbed the top of Amy's head and asked if they needed a ride home. "No" Joy said, "My friend is coming to pick us up." Just then an old white VW van pulled up, the driver looked to be pushing 50 and he could have been Joys father. He had long black hair and a ton of piercing. He reminded me of a heavy metal rocker. Joy ran over and planted an open mouth kiss on him. He was not her father. Joy introduced me, she said to call him "H". He stuck his hand out the window to shake mine, he was wearing more bracelets than a man should ever wear. As I shook his hand Amy was sort of hiding behind me. "And who is this" he says as he reached out to rub Amys head. His bracelet collection slid down his arm. He had a dragon tattoo that went from his wrist to his elbow. Amy grabbed onto my leg, she did not want to go with them. I told Joy that Amy could come with me, that I felt like eating some ice cream, I then asked, "Anyone else want some ice cream?" Amy smiled and raised her hand. Joy didn't even answer, she just jumped into the van and they drove off.

12:45 pm

As we returned from eating ice cream I saw Joy standing on Danielle's front lawn. She was in her underwear and picking up articles of clothing that Danielle was throwing at her from the front door. Tattoo boys van was nowhere to be found. I thought I heard Danielle yell, "You'll get us all locked up". Amy and I got out of the car and Amy ran up to her mother. Danielle grabbed her hand and took her in and slammed the front door shut. I walked up to Joy and handed her shirt to her. "Thanks" she said. "That bitch is crazy". I asked her what happened? Joy told me she had thrown her shirt and pants into the washing machine to wash out the soda that she had spilled on them. She was sitting on the sofa watching TV drinking her energy drink, some sort of drink she mixes herself, she said it was her own creation she makes from fruits and vegetables that she brings to Danielle's every morning. She then said she must have fallen asleep and was dreaming, it was an exotic dream with her friend Henry. I had to ask, "The dude with the tattoos in the van, the guy you introduced as H, his name is Henry?" Joy said "Yes, why?" "He just doesn't look like a Henry". I said. "That why he likes to be called H" she fumed, then she continued to tell me that when she woke up, that crazy bitch Danielle was standing over her. I asked, "What was Danielle doing standing over you?" Joy finished buttoning up her pants as she told me Danielle was just freaking out, the way a person caught doing something wrong does when they get caught, like a hand in the cookie jar, the next thing she knew she was out on the lawn and Danielle was throwing her clothes at her". Joy puts her shirt on and sits down on the lawn, "You all right" I asked her. "Headache" She says as she rubs her temples. "Danielle just freaked out on me, she didn't even ask what I was doing or where Amy was, I have never seen her like this, she has always been nothing but nice to me. All I was doing was taking a nap, okay I was not fully dressed but its not like I was doing anything wrong. She just turned into one sick twisted BITCH," she yelled out before she got up off the lawn. Danielle came out after Joy left and sat on the porch. As I walked up, Danielle asks me what happened. "Shouldn't I be asking you that question?" I said. Danielle asked me how I ended up with Amy. I told her we went for ice cream but I didn't tell her about the Funland incident. Danielle says, "Maybe I overreacted, but I come home early and I can't find my daughter, Joy is half naked on my sofa. I saw you talking to Joy, what did she say?" she asked. "Nothing, just called you a few choice names." Danielle picked up Joys energy bottle, "Well fuck her, what would have happened if you and Amy had come back before me." I just smiled and said, "I would have sent Amy to bed and" Danielle then reached over and hugged me before I could say anything that would have gotten me into trouble. I could only smile. Danielle then said, "Well Joy is fired. I will have to find another home schoolteacher after the holidays to help with Amy.

10:00 pm

I was sitting on my back porch wrapped in a blanket. I just needed a little air. It wasn't that cold out, it was actually quite nice. I could not understand Danielles' reaction to what happened with Joy. I was still trying to figure out that crazy message I deciphered from the Sogod Website. Who is not what I think. My head started to hurt so I swallowed a couple of aspirins and fell asleep. I was shook awake by Amy. She appeared upset, she grabbed my hand and pulled me towards her house. When we walked in thru the backdoor I saw Danielle by the sink. The door slammed shut behind us and Danielle jumped, she looked over her shoulder but she wasn't looking at us, she was looking thru us at Joy who was in the living room. I watched as Joy sat on the sofa tying her sneaks. When I turned back around I was now alone in the kitchen with Danielle. Amy was no longer in here with us. I walked over to Danielle whose back was to me. I saw her pouring some sort of powder or crushed pills into Joy's energy drink bottle. I asked her what she was doing but she didn't answer me. I was going to snap my wristband, but didn't. I wanted to see what happens, there must be a reason Amy brought me here. Joy came into the kitchen and she stated she was going to take Amy to Funland for the day. Danielle pushed the energy drink bottle out of sight behind the paper towel holder. She tried to talk Joy out of this idea but Joy insisted. Danielle could not say no when Amy came skipping into the kitchen. They all walked out of the kitchen and as they got to the front door Amy turned around and said to me, "Watch". I walked into the living room. No one was in there. I looked around the quiet, still room, the front door suddenly opened and Joy and Henry came in. Joy went down to the laundry room and took her pants and shirt off to put them in the washer. She yelled up for Henry to get her energy drink. At first he could not find it, he then spotted it behind the paper towels. When he handed it to Joy, she was aggravated that he took so long to get it to her. "Stop hiding it" he hissed as he tossed it to her. She took a drink and stated it was warm, Henry only seemed interested in taking the rest of Joys clothes off. He told her if she wanted to keep it cold then she should not leave it out on the counter. After another drink she pushed him away and asked him if he had put something in it. Henry got angry and said, "Don't need to drug you, you horny bitch." She pushed him off of her, adjusted her bra and sent him packing. He left in a huff storming out without shutting the door, "You waiting on the old neighbor man to get back with Amy so you can have a three-way?" he yelled as he kicked the paper off the porch. I turned around and Joy was passed out on the sofa. Danielle was standing over her. Danielle reached down and pushed up her bra exposing Joy's breasts. Danielle then reached inside her own blouse and caressed herself. She then took a photo of Joy, Danielle then proceeded to take several more photos of Joy in different stages of undress. Danielle then licked her finger and slid it from joys breasts to her crotch. Danielle then adjusted joys clothing. Just as Danielle stood up Joy opened her eyes and the fireworks began. Danielle screamed at Joy, telling her that her friend is going to get them all caught. Joy yelled back that she is able to see whomever she wants to and that she doesn't belong to anyone. "Not when your with Amy", Danielle yelled as she pushed Joy out the front door. Danielle then yelled, "You'll get us all arrested" before she slammed the front door shut. I turned around and Amy was sitting on the sofa. Standing behind her was Dan and Judy. Amy smiled and said, "My daddy is coming to get me". Dan looks at me as he pulls out his gun and holds it to Amys' head. I snap my wristband and wake up on my back porch.

I rubbed the sleep from my eyes as Amy came out of her backdoor. As she threw a bag of trash in the can she saw me and waved, she then ran over to me, she put her hands on my knees and pushed herself up to my face and gives me a little kid kiss on the lips. "Good morning" I say, "Is your mother getting ready for work?" Amy jumps up and sits on my lap and says "Yes" I reach for my wristband but I can't still be dreaming. I gave her a little hug and held it for a few moments. She appeared to be embarrassed, almost ashamed, she laid her head on my chest. I told her it was all right. Amy then raised her head to look at me as her hand went under the blanket I was wrapped in. She started to rub my chest. The blanket started to fall off me and I realized that I was naked. I grabbed Amy by her arms and tried to push her off me. She jumped off me and stood in front of me as I tried to cover myself with my blanket. Standing in the yard watching us are Sogod and

Dan. Johnson then slowly pulled out a gun and handed it to Dan. He takes it and points it at me, he pulls the trigger and I see the bullet coming towards me. Right before it hits me, Amy stands up and the bullet comes thru her head. I wake up. Its 2:11 am.

12-16-97/ 5:45 am

I look out my bedroom window and see Danielle and Amy walking from their house. I grab the key I found in the hole off my dresser and I head out to the hot tub. The key is rusted but with a little effort I was able to get it into the lock. At first it wouldn't turn, then with one last try the key turned and the lock sprung open. I lifted the cover, as about a thousand flies flew out and circled the tub. There was a horrible smell inside the tub, it contained a few inches of the most disgusting water I have ever seen. Sitting on one of the tub seats was a blanket. I reached down and grabbed it. The blanket was a boys maternity blanket and when I picked it up off the seat it was covered in maggots. It was wrapped around a strong box. I tried to open it but it was locked. I was startled when Danielle pulled back into the driveway. I threw the blanket back in the tub and put the box under my coat and waited for Danielle to go in. I walked down past the front of the house. Danielle's car was in the driveway with the engine still running. I looked in and saw Amy in the back seat, she appeared to be asleep. I went to walk around and Judy got out of the passenger side. "Judy, hi" I said. She told me that Danielle was letting her watch Amy today. "Great" I said back as I tried to shove the box further into my coat, Danielle came back out the front door, "Morning" I waved as she asked, "What's up?" I told her I saw her car running and just wanted to check to make sure everything was all right. "Your so sweet" she said and gave me a hug. She then whispered in my ear, "Since Joy is gone I had to ask Judy to watch Amy". I looked at my watch realizing that I was late for work, "Have to get going myself" I said and headed to my own car. I almost dropped the box when Danielle hugged me.

6:15 am

Driving to work, I could not get the dreams out of my head. Why do I keep getting into situations with Amy? Why did I dream of Danielle taking photos of Joy? Why did I find all that shit in that hole? I zoned out and was struck by a car as I went thru a red light. I am hurt pretty bad and I cant free myself from the car, I slowly passed out.

7:10 am

I wake up at Northeastern Hospital in the Emergency Room. There is a nurse sitting at the nurse's station right outside my room. I try to speak but can't, there is a tube down my throat. Danielle comes rushing in. She sits by my bed and holds my hand and sits quietly in the dark. I am looking right at her. Another nurse comes in and writes something on my chart, she checks all the machines that I am hooked up to. She then puts her hand gently on Danielle's shoulder as Danielle quietly starts to sobs. Officer Downs walks in and Danielle gets up and hugs him, they hug the way friends hug when someone is about to die. I lay there on the bed, I'm screaming in my head "look at me, look at me, I'm awake". They both just sit quietly. Johnny then leans over and asks Danielle if she told me something. "No" she says back never turning to look at him. "Do you think he knows?" he asks. Danielle doesn't answer. "Tell him now" he says, "It will make you feel better to say it out loud" Johnny gets up touches my hand and leaves the room. When he touched my hand I saw him at this very hospital, he looked much younger. Danielle came walking down the hallway with her face all bandaged and she was holding a baby. Amy I was guessing. She looks at Johnny and asked, "Is it done?" Johnny shakes his head yes. Danielle went to walk past but John grabs her arm and whispers in her ear. "So are we". I then opened my eyes and I was back in my hospital room, but Danielle wasn't there anymore. The room was dark and empty. I then heard voices in the hallway. A mans voice was saying that I would be taken off life support tomorrow morning. Danielle came back in and sat with me. Through tears she whispers, talking so low that I have to strain to hear her " I'm sorry Joe, this whole nightmare will become clear with just a little bit of information, please don't judge me or think any less of me. I can't stop your dreams, no one can. The dreams are in your head to help her, to help us. I just hope without you Amy will still be able to someday tell her story, this whole situation is ....I am suddenly aware that I am still in my car and the sounds from the Jaws of Life crushing the car door is deafening. Officer Downs is pulling me from the wreckage. I am placed into an ambulance. I grab John by his arm, No flash of sight, and I ask if he knew Danielle before the bar fight. "Yes" he says, "I knew her, but I didn't know who she was". I could tell he was lying.

10:00 am

Once at the hospital, the staff and myself were amazed that I had survived the accident, I didn't only survive but I only had a few cuts and scrapes. They wanted to hold me overnight for observation. I didn't complain, but I did however refuse any type of sedative or medication that would hinder my dreams. Danielle came in to visit, she brought some flowers and sat them on the bed tray. Amy sat in the corner of the room, she appeared to be refusing to look at me. "What is wrong with her?" I asked Danielle. "She thinks you tried to leave her today." I called her over to the bed. "Amy girl" I said. "I am not going anywhere,

I had an accident. I will be here for you for a long time"
Amy smiled and said "I need you to stay close to me". I
held her hand, no flash, I didn't enter any of her thoughts
or memories. Maybe I was dreaming and I went to snap
my wristband but it wasn't there. Danielle asked me what
I was looking for, when I told her, she told me they cut
it off when I was brought into the ER. When Danielle
went out into the hallway to talk to a nurse, Amy reached
into her pocket and pulled out a wristband. She handed
it to me and I put it on, Amy snapped it, just pain, not
a dream.

12-17-97/ 2:11 am

My dreaming started as soon as I fell asleep, I was able to get up and walk around the Hospital hallways. There was no one else in the Hospital, the room and hallways were dark. I looked up and saw a light coming from under a door at the end of the hallway. I walked down towards the room. I slowly pushed the door open and walked in. I saw Judy laying on a gurney. She was wearing a hospital gown that was soaked in blood and she was clutching the stuffed bunny that I had found in the hole. She took out a pen and wrote on the tag. She then handed the bunny to Dan and said, "Give this to our child." Dan crying said. "He didn't make it." Judy sits up in the bed, she grabs Dan and demands, "Then get me another one". I turn to leave the room, "Come back" someone says behind me. When I turned back around, Its Amy and I was in her bedroom, she is much younger, about 5 or 6. She was sitting on her bed and she was clutching the rabbit. Dan walks in from the shadows and grabs the rabbit from her hands and rips the head off. The stuffed toy starts to bleed. This is from a dirty little whore, and if you accept things from dirty whores, than you too will become a dirty whore. A man then walks out from the shadows and he hands Dan some money. Amy covers her face with her hands as she lies on the bed. When Dan pulls her hands from her face, Amy now appears to be older, about 19 or 20 years old. Dan pulls the cover from Amy and she is naked. She has burses on her back, arms and legs. The man starts to take his pants off. Dan walks up to me and says, "This is her future, the future they want to give her". I wake up its 2:11 am.

10:00 am

I sign myself out of the Hospital, I have a little pain, only minor details after what I been thru. I caught a taxi home and sat in the dark with the shades all pulled shut. Thinking about my dreams and reality, or at least what I thought was reality. I knew Danielle and Dan were Amys' parents, Judy been acting like she should be, is it because she lost her child? What did Officer Downs, and Danielle do in the Hospital? What was Dan and Danielle's fight really about? Why did Johnson (Sogod) start all this shit? Was Amy being molested, am I molesting her in her dreams, did Dan take those photos? There are so many questions. Why do I keep dreaming that I am the one that is hurting Amy?

There was a sudden banging on the front door. I could tell it was urgent by the loudness of the banging. I opened the door and it was Dr Adams. He pushed past me and stood in the living room. He had his hands on his waist and his head was down, he was out of breath, gasping for air. I snapped the band on my wrist, just pain. He looked up and said, "Joe I don't where to start, I did some research and I found out Judy had a baby born a couple weeks after Amy was born, it was a boy, and it was stillborn. Dan was listed as the father. I told him that I already knew that. He then looked at me and asked, "How?" Before I could answer, he said "never mind, this is where it gets weird. I could not locate any record of Amys' birth. She has a birth certificate and is on record with the state, but the Hospital has no record of Amy being born that night. The only other birth recorded that night was a baby girl that died, she was given the name Judy Lynn. Now even weirder. Judy Lynn's birth was recorded in the hospital log but then nothing. No record with the state, I can't even track down any parents." I then asked him if the records could have been destroyed in the fire. "There would still be something", he said as he sat and held his sides. There was another knock on the door. It was Dan, he was released on bail and given a new trial. "What are you doing here?" I asked, "Isn't part of your parole that you stay away from Danielle and Amy?" Dan looked scared, "Arrest Me," he snapped back as he pushed past me into the living room. When he saw Dr Adams he went off. He lunged right at him knocking him to the ground throwing punches. I had to pull him off of the Doctor. "What the fuck is he doing here?" Dan yelled. "Dr Adams is Amy's Doctor," I told him. "Not anymore" Dan yelled as he tried to break free from my grip. "Calm down", I yelled as I held Dan up against a wall. All my recent injuries were starting to throb. "He is the mother fucker that tried to set me up, he is probably the one that put those other pictures in my trailer." Dan continued to yell at Dr Adams saying that the doctor is who he sees hurting Amy. I had to tell Dan that his dreams were messing with his head, I told him how I was having dreams where I was the one who was hurting Amy. Dan looked up and said "I have had dreams too where you hurt Amy". Dan's anger seemed to turn towards me now. I told Dan that Danielle was having dreams where he was hurting Amy. Dr Adams now sitting and wiping blood from his mouth asked Dan if he knew of Judy having a baby. Dan calmed right down. He appeared shocked at the question. "She lost her baby on the same night Amy was born". "Tell us about that night", I asked. Dan told us that Danielle went into labor early on December 28th, her due date was not until 2-11, Dan had not seen Judy for several months and he didn't even know she was pregnant. He was not allowed to be in the delivery room with Danielle. He was told there were complications. He seen Judy in one of the other rooms and she told him she had fallen. He noticed that Judy had blood all over her clothing that were lying on the floor. A Police Officer then came in and escorted him from the Hospital and told him he had to stay out. That he was bothering the other patients. Dan said he walked around to the front entrance and was able to get back into the maternity ward. Danielle was hysterical, she wouldn't let anyone near her. There was a baby, Amy was lying on the table next to her and a nurse and doctor were examining or cleaning her. The same cop then runs in and pulls the curtain shut. Danielle yells became quieter. Both the Doctor, and Nurse came out from behind the curtain and walk right past Dan, he could see Danielle and the cop hugging. He looked down towards Judy and she was now screaming. Dan ran down and Judy told him her baby had died. He said he was in shock. Dan said to Judy "I thought you fell", Judy said she did, She said she landed on her stomach. Dan asked her if the baby was his. Judy said no. Do you remember seeing any other women having babies that night? we asked. "There may have been another, That fucking cop took me out back and he stated everything was okay, and that Danielle and her new daughter were doing fine." Dan said he asked the cop why he couldn't tell him this inside, why was he so involved and why was he hugging Danielle? The cop just told Dan to go home and come back in a couple of hours. This cop told Dan that Danielle didn't list him as the father and that was why he couldn't be in there. I said, "But you are listed as the father, I saw Amys' birth certificate". Dan then told us, he went home and got drunk, high and fell into a stupor. He didn't make it back to the hospital for several days. When he did Danielle told him he was the father and that Amy was his daughter. "I held Amy that day and didn't ever want to put her down, even when the nurses came in to check on her." Dan said. "Danielle was like a changed woman, she was nicer to me and she didn't even ask where I've been for the past two days. It was like at first she didn't want me there, now she don't want me to leave". Dan stated he noticed a stuffed bunny on the bed that Danielle told him the woman next door sent over for Amy. It was her first toy. We all then heard a car pulling up out front. It was Danielle coming home from work, it was 3 o'clock already. Dan jumped up and ran out my back door. Dr Adams stood up and said he too had to go, "Something is just not right with Dan's story" he said. I walked him to the door and said, "That's because he is lying" As Dr Adams left, I whispered to myself, "And so are you." Just as I shut my door the phone rang. It was Danielle, she was upset and I had to go over, but before I did I snapped my wristband, still just pain.

3:30 pm

I walked over to Danielle's and Joy was just leaving. Danielle met me at the front door and I asked her what Joy was doing here? "She came to get her two weeks pay". Danielle said as she hugged me and started to cry. I asked her, "What was wrong?" She said, "Dan is out of jail". I acted surprised and asked, "Who paid his bail?" She said "I don't know, and all I did to get rid of him". I told her there is a restraining order and he is not allowed anywhere near her or Amy. She didn't seem to care about Dan coming around and said she had to pick up Amy and asked if I would be here when she got back. "Yes, I will wait, I'll order us a pizza" I said as she left. As soon as she drove away I went looking for her camera, I found it, but it had no memory card. I looked for it in the computer, but it wasn't there either, then I saw her laptop and there it was. I opened it up. Not only were there photos of Joy, but the shower photo and other nude photos of Amy were also on the card. Danielle then came in and caught me just as other photos stared to open, she told Amy to go upstairs. She walked over and slowly shut the laptop, I was able to see the other photo just for a second, but it appeared to be photos of Doctor Adams kids, they looked younger, and they may have been naked. Danielle put her hand on mine and said, "Let me explain". Danielle started off by saying her dreams became so real and that she had to do something so she set up Dan, she said her dreams told her to, and they showed her what would happen if she didn't. She said after she saw the photo that Dan took of Amys back, she came up with the idea of planting other photos that everyone would think Dan took. She even said since both Doctor Adams and myself knew Dan had taken that first photo, who would believe he didn't take the others. I asked how could she live with herself if Dan was sentence to a long prison term, she said she didn't care, and if he wasn't in jail, he would only wind up dead. This way both Amy and Dan are safe. I asked, "Safe from what? If you took those photos then Dan wasn't hurting her. But Danielle really believed Dan was going to cause Amy to be hurt. She told me she was having dreams almost every night and in everyone Dan was touching Amy, and in every dream Dan would kill her because Amy said she was going to tell. I asked Danielle if the dreams stopped after he was arrested. She said "No, only now she is older in my dreams and she is a prostitute, but at least she is alive." I then asked if anyone else was in the dreams, she said, "Joy was in my dreams and that's the real reason I fired her and took those photos, she was getting to attached to Amy" I then asked her what Joy was doing in her dreams. She said, "Joy just watches, she does nothing, I just don't want to talk about it." I got the feeling she was hiding something, or maybe making the entire dream thing up. I then told her about my dream, the one I had in the hospital where Amy was older. Danielle appeared shocked, she was shocked even more when I told her Dan was there. Danielle then sat silently as I got us a drink, when I returned I asked her if she called the police and told them to look at the photos again. Danielle looked up surprised." I didn't call the police." I asked, "Then who did?" I didn't tell her Judy was the one who sent the letter, Judy told me she didn't sign it. I then asked Danielle if I was in any of her dreams. Danielle said, "At first you were her knight in shinning armor, and that I would rush in and save Amy". I took Danielle's hand and asked, "At first?" Danielle looked away and said, "Now you are the one that takes her away from me". I got Danielle a drink and asked her to tell me about the night Amy was born. She appeared confused and said, "Amy was born on 12-28-97, I had a very difficult delivery, Amy didn't want to come out. The hospital kept her over six weeks." Was Dan there? I asked. "No, and I was so angry that I wanted to kill him. He showed up like 3 days after Amy was born blabbering about not being the father and I had to reassure him that he was the father. Then I found out that Judy was right next door giving birth and I would have bet my life that Dan was the father of that bastard." I acted dumfounded and asked "Judy has a kid?" Danielle smiled and said, "No it died during child birth, I guess god didn't want that slut to have a child". I then smiled at Danielle and asked, "What was the first gift Amy received? Danielle seemed bewildered at all these questions, she didn't answer, and she said that I was bouncing all kinds of questions at her that had no reason. As she walked me to the door I told her I was just trying to keep the conversation going. Danielle held my hand as she kissed my cheek and asked me if I would be able to watch Amy for the next few days. She said since I was out of work and she still needed to find another sitter. "Sure, no problem" I said. I started to walk down the walkway. Danielle yelled at me, "A Rabbit". I turned and asked "What?" Danielle said the first gift Amy received was a little stuffed rabbit that Dan brought for her."

12-18-97 / 2:11 am

I found myself in Amys bedroom again, I was looking at what I expected to be Amy laying under the sheets on her bed. I walked over and slowly pulled the sheet from the bed. It wasn't Amy lying there, it was Judy and she was in labor. She was in pain and bleeding. Dan walks up to us. Looks at me and reaches inside of Judy and rips the baby from her and tosses it into a trashcan. Judy starts screaming, her screams were deafening and I had to hold my ears. Dan then yells at her "This was not part of the plan". He grabs the rabbit from Judys grip and says, "This is for my real child". I wake up and its 2:11 am. I then slowly shut my eyes and drift back to sleep.

7:00 am

I wake up still freaked out about the dream, but at least I wasn't hurting Amy. I turn on the TV. The porno channel is on and its not scrambled like always, maybe it is a free preview. I flip to the morning news and head into the shower. When I get out of the shower I hear the sounds of the porno channel coming from my bedroom. I snap my wristband but my wrist is wet and it slips off and falls to the floor. I bend down to get it and slam my head into the sink and my head starts to bleed. I take my towel and hold it up to stop the bleeding and walk into my bedroom naked to turn the TV off. I reach for the on off switch and notice that Joy is in the porno, she was really giving it to another female. I feel myself getting excited. The camera shot widens and Joy is with Danielle. Now I'm going out of my mind. I then go to look into the mirror on the wall to check out the cut on my head. There is a black cloth covering my mirror. I grabbed the cloth and pulled it away but it is stuck. I try to hold up the cloth and I turn to see my head but I catch the reflection of Amy sitting on my bed watching the TV. I turn and cover myself with the towel. "Amy what are you doing in here?" She points to the TV. I turn it off. Amy kneels on the foot of the bed and she is now the same height as me. As she reaches for me, I go to push her away. But she just wipes away the blood that was about to run into my eye. I then go to wipe her hand off on the towel I have wrapped around me. Amy pulls her hand away and reaches in and starts licking the blood from my head. She wraps her legs around my back. I tried to push her off and we both fall onto the bed. I hear Joy coming towards the bedroom asking what's taking so long. She says she has to take Danielle to work. She comes into the bedroom and starts yelling. Amy jumps from the bed and turns the TV back on. Only now the porno was showing Amy in my bedroom lying naked on her belly and I was standing over her slowly pulling the sheet from her body. Joy then swung a table lamp at me, but I woke up before she connected to the phone ringing. My heart was pounding, I was out of breath. I grabbed the phone it was Danielle, "Where are you?" she yelled into the phone, "I have to be in work at 8:30" I looked at the clock it was 8:15. "I'll be right there," I said.

8:30 am

I waved as Danielle pulled out of the driveway on her way to work. I then went back into her house. I wanted to spend some time alone with Amy, I wanted to ask her a whole lot of questions. I went up to her bedroom, before I entered I snapped my wristband to make sure this was not another dream. I knocked on the door as I slowly pushed it open. Amy was just waking up, she sat up on her bed and started to rub the sleep from her eyes, "Morning" I said. Amy smiled and held out her arms to give me a hug. I sat on the bed and went to brush her hair from her eyes. Amy grabbed my hand and held it against her face and I noticed that she felt warm, almost hot. I asked if she was okay, she said yes. I then moved my hand down from her cheek to her chin and lifted her head so we were eye to eye. I then asked her if anyone was hurting her. She shook her head no. I then asked her why she pointed to Dr Adams on Halloween when I asked her the same question, she shrugged her shoulders. Is he hurting you? Again she shook her head no. I then asked if her mother or father were hurting her, I asked if her father was bringing any other people into the house to hurt or touch her, I asked if Joy ever touched her? Amy got up off the bed and yelled "NO" and tried to run from the room. I grabbed her by her arm and swung her back towards me, she slipped and fell onto the floor. I bent down to help her up, she reached up and hugged me as I lifted her up from the floor. As I carried her downstairs to the kitchen Amy kept a smile on her face the entire time. I made her some breakfast and watched her as she ate. She didn't appeared to be a child in distress, she appeared to be happy, content. Maybe my dreams were just that, dreams. Maybe I let Johnson get into my head, somehow he was head fucking me, or it could be stress. But how do you explain everyone else's dreams. If they were actually having dreams. Amy finished her breakfast and was putting her plate in the dishwasher. I knelt down to help her and she turned her head and gave me a little kiss on the cheek. I patted her head as she then ran in to turn on the TV. This was not the action of an abused child. I then snapped my wristband, still not dreaming.

10:00 am

I received a call from Officer Downs, he told me that he could not get any information on Dan and Danielle's custody dispute. I told him to forget it, I told him I thought all my problems might be in my head. Downs stated "Good, about time you moved on." Amy and me then walked down to Dr Adams, Amy had an early morning appointment. Dr Adams asked if I wanted to join in but I declined and waited in the living room, I again looked around at all his photographs he had displayed, I still could not find any with his children. After about an hour Amy came running out of the office, she grabbed my hand and attempted to pull me towards the front door. Dr Adams came out and asked if he could speak with me. Amy became violent pulling on my arm and yelling she wanted to leave. I looked up at Dr Adams, I could tell something was wrong. I reached down and took Amy's arm and asked her to sit down, she yelled "NO". And continued to try and leave the office. "Can I call you?" I asked the Doctor. "ASAP" he said. Amy calmed down as soon as the door shut behind us. She did however keep looking behind her as we walked up the street. I held her hand, she was squeezing my hand tight, so tight that I had to pull away. I knelt down in front of her, I was face to face with her and I looked into her eyes, she was terrified. She rushed into me hugging me tight. I could feel her tears on my cheek. "Everything's okay" I said. "I wish you would just tell me what's wrong".

1:00 pm

I tried to call Dr Adams as soon as we got home but Amy became highly upset whenever I picked up the phone. She followed me wherever I went in the house. Amy finally fell asleep in front of the TV and I went into the kitchen and called Dr Adams on my cell phone. Dr Adams seemed upset that I waited so long to call, I tried to explain that I didn't want to upset Amy, the Doctor didn't want to hear it. I asked, "What's so important?" Dr Adams said, "During my session with Amy, she was hypnotized, she acted out like she was being chased. She fell, she put her hands down covering herself clutching her clothing and she started to cry, just as I went to wake her up she shouted, Joe stop it, please stop it". Dr Adams then said that I was the only Joe that Amy knows. There was an uncomfortable silence. Dr Adams then asked if I was in any way hurting Amy. "No" I said. "Amy could have been asking me to stop someone else from hurting her". I then told him about the questions I asked Amy this morning, leaving his name out and that Amy said no one was hurting her. I told him Amy appeared to be a normal 11-year-old child all morning, all morning up until his fucking session. Dr Adams then asked, "When you questioned her, did you ask her if you were hurting her?" I hung up and Amy was standing behind me, she then sat down on the kitchen floor and wet herself. I bent down to pick her up, her skin was on fire, she was burning up. I carried her up to the bathroom. I filled the tub with cold water and told her to get in the tub and that I would call her mother. After getting off the phone with Danielle I went back to the bathroom. Amy was sitting on the edge of the toilet. She appeared to be out of it, the way an adult would be after a night of heavy drinking. I then took Amy's shoes and socks off and told her to take the rest of her clothes off and get in the tub, telling her that she would feel better, but she just sat and stared. I lifter her shirt off and I had to help her stand up as I reached for her pants. Amy started to urinate again. I then left her pants on and picked her up and placed her in the tub of cold water. I used a rag to wet her head, letting the water run down her chest and back. She slowly started to come around. I poured the cold water down her back. Amy then looked up at me and smiled, she no longer felt hot and she reached for the cup I was using to pour the water on her and she started to do it herself. I got up and left the bathroom. Danielle was coming up the steps as I went into the hallway. "Is she okay?" Danielle asked as she rushed into the bathroom. I went downstairs and started to clean up the urine in the kitchen. Danielle came in several minutes later and hugged me, "You're a good friend," she whispered in my ear. "Can you now go up and clean up the urine in the bathroom?" I stood up, "You are kidding me?" I asked. She laughed and said, "Yea, I cleaned it up". Danielle then asked me why I left her pants on". I told her, "I felt embarrassed for her, what 11 year old wants anyone seeing them naked, plus they were soaked with urine". I then told her about what Dr Adams told me. Danielle became upset, she then told me that recently every time Amy sees him he has a big resolution and accuses her or Dan, and now me of being the problem with her. I then told her that Amy was very upset and angry today after her session with him. Amy made it clear as day that she was not going to let the doctor treat Amy anymore and she did not want me to talk to the doctor either. Danielle became highly upset, calling Dr Adams a fake and a witch doctor. I had to tell her to calm down. Danielle gathered herself and said, "Ever since Dan was locked up, Amy's mood swings have been getting more violent and more common." We both then went upstairs to check on Amy, she was sleeping on the floor at the foot of her bed. I picked her up and laid her down on the bed as Danielle covered her up with a blanket. I then bent down and gave her a kiss on the forehead, her skin was cool as a cucumber. Amy opened her eyes and smiled at me, she then reached up and pulled me closer and she gave me a little kiss by my lips, she then slid out her tongue and tried to lick at my mouth. I pulled away. Danielle was by the door and didn't appear to have noticed what had just happened. I then snapped my wristband, please be a dream, Just pain. Danielle asked me why I keep snapping that if it hurts so much. "Habit" I said. Danielle walked down the hall, I turned around and looked at Amy as she tried to sleep. I bent down by her side and quietly asked "Amy, Did I ever hurt you?" She looked up at me, her smile left her face. She then rolled away from me. She didn't answer.

12-27-97/ 6:00 am

It's been over a week since I sat for Amy, and I haven't had a single dream. But I know they will be back. In a weird way I need them to come back. This morning I woke up actually feeling great, no aches or discomfort, I felt sort of on top of the world. I do still have to see the county doctor and get cleared to return back to work. After Amy got sick on me Danielle took personnel time off to watch her. The last time I seen Amy was Christmas morning when I gave her a Clair doll, she was so excited that she said "Thank you" at least a hundred times. I haven't seen or heard from Dan or Judy since he stopped by the day he was paroled. His court date keeps getting postponed. I tried to call one night but there was no answer. Some times I think with the way Danielle handles her anger issues, she may have had him killed, she did set him up with those photos and what is to stop her from killing him, I hope she don't dream about killing him.

Danielle also stopped Dr Adams from seeing Amy. I did see Dr Adams Christmas eve. He told me he was still investigating the hospital and the night Amy was born. He seemed to be obsessed with it. That was the last time we talked. He told me that there was no record of Dan and Danielle ever getting married or any custody hearings between them. I told him that I didn't think they ever got married. The Doctor then told me that he has knowledge of what is going on, but before he would tell me, he wanted to make sure he would be safe, that he needed proof to keep himself alive. When I asked him what he meant, safe from whom? He told me something odd. He told me to stay away from Amy, and when he walked away I heard him say, "No one can save them."

I put on my coat and headed out the door and I saw Danielle standing in her driveway, she was smoking a cigarette and as I got closer I noticed that she had dark circles under her eyes, a drastic change from Christmas night when she was full of such cheer. "What's up?" I asked. She turned and said, "Amy's 12th birthday is tomorrow". I told her I was looking forward to it. "I'm not," She snapped back. "I worry about her". I asked if she was having dreams again, she said no, but I could tell she was lying. "By the way, you look like shit," I said as I turned to walk back home. She turned and flicked her cigarette at me and said "Thanks". She then turned and walked towards her front door. "When did you start smoking?" I asked as I stepped on the butt she just flipped at me. She just kept walking, lifting her right hand only to flip me off. I was worried about her, more so about Amy. But I had to see the city doctor, I have to get back to work and forget about all these people before I go insane.

10:45 am

After a two-hour exam the Doctors would not let me return to work. I was told I was still suffering from the blow to my head. The doctor told me that I appeared to be having trouble with my memory and I may have a concussion and more tests were set up for after the holidays, he then asked me if I was seeing things that were not there, or hearing voices. I laughed and told him no. If I had told the truth I would have been there for hours.

I was headed home when I thought I'd stop by and see if Officer Downs was in the district. He wasn't, but a big bald muscle bound cop behind the counter asked if he could help me. I told him I was waiting on a few things from Officer Downs. This guy would not let shit go and he insisted on knowing what it was that I was looking for. I didn't want to get John in trouble. So I told this guy he was getting me some information on some cases I needed for court and I showed him my prison ID. This guy says hold up I'll get it. He came back with an envelope marked "Prison" he flips it to me and says, "There was no name on it, it has been here for several days, is this what your looking for?" I opened it and saw it was copies from the courts. I took it, if it was not mine I'd give it back later. I sat in my car and opened the first package. It was a report on custody requests filed over the past ten years. There was no mention of Dan or Danielle ever filing for custody of Amy. In the other package was a DVD. I put it back and drove home.

1:35 pm

I slipped the DVD into the machine and it started right up. It was surveillance of the bail desk at the courthouse. The surveillance showed nothing of interest. I was about to shut it off when I noticed the time on the digital clock behind the bail counter, it was 2:10 in the morning. The clock then changed to 2:11 am as a man in a hooded sweatshirt walked up to the desk to pay Dan's bail. I could not see his face, it was like he was hiding on purposes. But when the bail was paid, this man took his receipt and pushed his hood off his head, he then turned and looked directly into the camera. I had to pause the DVD. I could not believe my eyes, the video was grainy, but it was Johnson. For the first time in over a week I snapped my wristband, just pain.

6:55 pm

I was sitting in the bar having a few beers and feeling a little edgy. John walks in with a couple of his cop buddies and I waved him over. "What's up?" he asks, he appeared agitated. "I just wanted to thank you for the information you left at the station." He looked confused, "What information?" I told him a big bald muscle head dude gave me a package marked Prisons. He then told me that they don't leave packages at the desk or do they have anyone with that description working the desk, and if I was given a package, he didn't leave it. He then asked me what was in it. "Nothing important" I said. John got all interested all of a sudden and almost demanded to know what was in the package. I lied to him and told him it listed a fake name of the person who bailed out Dan, and some hospital paperwork. "What kind of paperwork?" he again demanded. "Calm down" I said, "It was nothing useful, just the diary from the day Amy was born". Information we already knew about I told him, I then asked him, " Why are you so interested all of a sudden?" John said, "I thought you were past all this private eye shit, so why are you still poking your nose around?" John got up to leave, "I wasn't poking, I went looking for you and I'm handed a package by someone who you say doesn't even work there and now your all bent out of shape. What crawled up your ass?" He put out his hand to shake and said "I just don't want some rookie cop using my name when he gives out shit at the front desk." I told him I understood. John let go of my hand and said, "It's been a rough day, we just pulled a body out of the river." I thought back to Danielle killing Dan, "Was it Dan?" I asked. "Why would you ask that?" John questioned. "Just a feeling" I tell him. John tells me it was an older man and they have no ID yet.

Amy 12th Birthday
12-28-97/ 4:00 pm

I'm wrapping Amy's birthday gift, it's a little kid's make-up kit that Amy pointed to when she was looking through a Christmas wish book when I hear a car pulling up out front. I looked out and saw that it was Dan and Judy. They both got out and started walking towards Danielle's front door. I watched as Danielle opened the door, I was expecting a big fight but Danielle gave Dan a big hug, and then invited them in. Now I'm in a hurry, I have to see what that was all about. When I walked into Danielle's living room Amy was sitting on Dans lap, she was ripping into wrapped gifts. When she saw me she jumped down and ran over to me giving me a big what did you get me hug. I handed my gift to her and walked over to Danielle who was pounding down a drink. "Don't ask," she says as I walked up. "Dan is her father and it is her birthday," She said as she poured herself another drink. "Nuff said" I say and walk into the kitchen to get myself a drink. It's a pretty big turn out for a small gathering. Danielle walks in and starts complaining about the mess people are leaving around the house. "Nice turn out, I thought it was just going to be a couple of people," Danielle tells me that it just got out of hand. I noticed that Dr Adams was not here, I go over to the kitchen table where Joy is sitting with another woman. I put my hand on her shoulder and say "Hi". Joy gets up and gives me a big hug. I look over Joys shoulder as she continued to hug me and see that Danielle is giving me the evil eye. I separate from the hug and excuse myself and walk back over to Danielle and say, "Some guest list, I can almost understand why Dan and Judy are here, but I never would have expected to see Joy, please don't tell me Dr Adams is hiding in here somewhere?" Danielle chokes on her drink. She wipes her chin and tells me that Dr Adams was found dead in the river yesterday. I was shocked, I asked her who was taking care of his kids. Danielle now looked shocked, "What Kids?" she asked. I told her I seen him having breakfast with a boy and a girl, the girl was older, she could have been over 18 years old, the boy was about Amy's age. Suddenly I hear Dan yelling and I look into the living room and I see him throwing my gift across the room. He looks over at me and gets up and tries to charge at me. Other guests grab him. Danielle is asking him what his problem is. Dan points at me and yells,

"That fucker is giving Amy make up" He then attempted to break free from the other guests as he yelled, "You want her to be pretty when you fuck her?" Danielle gives Dan a look, like she wants him to shut up and then walks me back into the kitchen. I say to Danielle almost apologetic, "Amy wanted the make up kit". Danielle says, "Fuck him, I knew I shouldn't have let him come here". I then tell Danielle that I am just going to leave, "Tell Dan when he calms down he can come over and talk if he wants" I then left thru the back door.

8:23 pm

There is a knock at my back door. I jumped up expecting it to be Dan, but it was Judy. She comes in and apologizes for Dan's outburst. "It's okay," I said as we sat down. I then asked Judy, "What happened, did Danielle have a change of heart?" Judy tells me that Danielle just called out of the blue late last night. Dan spoke with her for hours. Judy said she fell asleep, and then this morning Dan told her they were invited to Amy's birthday party. Judy then gets up and walks to the side window and stares out at Danielle's house. "Something wrong?" I ask. Judy says, "I just get the feeling they may be getting back together, Dan doesn't tell me things and he disappears all the time, when he returns he wont tell me where he went." I ask Judy if Dan and Danielle were ever married. Judy tells me that Dan talked about it a long time ago, but she didn't think they were ever married. I told Judy that on Amy's birth certificate they are listed as the parents and that Danielle shares Dan's last name. Judy then became quiet and continued to just stare out the window. As I approached her she turned around and said, "You cant believe a word he says, the man lies and he will tell you what ever you want to here as long as it benefits him". I put my hand on her shoulder and asked her if Dan was coming over. Judy looks likes she is about to cry. "No" she says, "He asked me to leave so he could discuss something with Danielle, and now I look over and the only light on is coming from an upstairs bedroom." I look out and see that the light is coming from Amy's bedroom. Judy then picks up her purse and starts to rummage thru it. "Looking for something?" I ask. She says she can't find her cell phone and walks out the front door.

12-29-97/ 2:11 am

I got up from a dreamless sleep and looked at the clock as it blinked 2:11 am. I snap my wristband, just pain I am not dreaming. I get up and look out my bedroom window and Dan's car is still parked out in front of Danielle's house. There are no lights on. I then see a light from a cigarette out back. Danielle and Dan are standing by the hot tub. I quietly sneaked downstairs and out back. I can't see them, which means they cant see me, but I can hear Danielle telling Dan that everything will be okay and that no one will ever find out. Dan's voice had a lot of concern when he told Danielle that if Judy finds out or he refuses, it could get ugly. I could not help but wonder who he was, and what it is that they are worried he will refuse, and what don't they want Judy to find, that they having an affair, because Judy already thinks they are having one. I then hear Danielle say, "He already took care of two motherfuckers who were causing problems and the same will happen to anyone else that attempts to leave." I thought leave what? I then hear Dan ask, "What about Officer Downs? He can become a loose cannon". Danielle says, "I have more then enough shit on that motherfucker that if he ever opens his mouth I'll ruin his career, and marriage, plus he will never try to leave, he loves what he is doing too much". Then there was an awkward silence. I started to think they might have gone back inside when I heard Dan say, "Can you really trust Joe?" Danielle answers, "He is our only hope, he doesn't have a clue that he is being shown the way, but he has been asking a lot of questions lately, if he shows any signs that he cant handle it, he will be dealt with". Were they talking about me, what is it that I am being shown? Then I heard Dan say, "I just can't understand why you would tell Amy? Just promise me that you wont let her get hurt." I saw the cigarette get flipped into the yard. "It is really not up to me who gets hurt?" I then heard Dan say, "I just worry about Amy". Danielle was now whispering, her voice was low, but I heard her say, "She has been prepared and knows what to expect, she knows what she has to do, and now because of my dreams I know she will be safe in the end." Dan then says, "Your fucking dreams, this all revolves around your fucking dreams." Danielle became defensive, "I have to believe in them, they are what keeps me sane." Danielle then asked Dan, "When was the last time you had a dream?" Dan then flipped his cigarette onto the lawn and said, "Not since I had a dream that you set me up." Danielle's voice raised a little when she said, "I had father bail you out." I heard her backdoor opening as Danielle asked, "Do you even know who bailed you out?" I didn't hear Dan answer, just the sound of the door shutting. I snapped my band. Not a dream, Can Johnson be Danielle's father?

8:00 am

I was jarred from another dreamless sleep by the phone ringing. Officer Downs was on the other end telling me that the accident investigation team had finished with my car and they packaged everything up that was in it. I had forgotten all about that box and I was going to ask John about it, but didn't know if I could trust John now. John then told me that I could pick my stuff up at the police evidence room. I then mentioned to him that I saw Danielle and Dan together last night. There was a long pause, he then said "Good for them," He then added, "That is if you are no longer seeing her". I told him I didn't know what we had, I feel like she is using me for some unknown reason, I guess we are just neighbors for now.

11:45 am

I heard a commotion in the back yard and saw that Danielle was out there running around like a chicken with it's head cut off. I stuck my head out the window and asked, "What's up neighbor?" Danielle seemed to tense up, she then turned dropped the maternity blanket I left in the hot tub on the ground and ran over to the fence. She tells me that someone stole some stuff from her yard. I asked her what was missing. She yelled "What does it matter what is missing, its the point that someone stole shit that don't belong to them." I looked over her shoulder and noticed that the hot tub cover was open and Amy was poking at the water with a stick, she was leaning in over the edge, and she slipped and almost fell in. She hit the side of the tub with a thud. Danielle turned around and started to yell at her. Amy appeared to be injured but Danielle was too upset to care. She yelled at Amy, telling her to go in the house and that she was only in the way. I was shocked at how she was treating Amy, "Calm down" I said with a weary smile, "Call the police." Danielle then looked me right in the eye and said, "It was probably the fucking police that stole my shit." She then turned and walked towards her backdoor. Amy looked up from the back steps and saw her coming, so she got up and ran into the house. "FUCK" Danielle yelled as walked in the house after her.

2:30 pm

Dan pulled up to a screeching stop in front of Danielle's house. He jumped out and ran right in. I could hear yelling coming from the house. They soon came out into the back yard. I looked out and saw Danielle showing Dan the hot tub. Dan just stared into the tub as Danielle was talking to him, even after she stopped talking Dan just stared into the tub for a long time, Dan then turned and said in a low whisper to Danielle, "Without that you no longer have any leverage on any of them," he then banged both hands on the side of the tub and stormed back inside. Danielle looked up to see if I was watching before she followed Dan inside.

My phone rang, it was Officer Downs and he told me he had picked up the stuff from my car last night. He forgot that he had it and he told me it was in his trunk. He said he was on his way to Times Square for New Years Eve. "No rush". I said "Get it here when you can". As I hung up the phone I noticed that Dan was now standing on Danielle's front lawn, he was glaring at my house. He started to walk over when he saw me in the window. It was an angry walk and I prepared myself for a confrontation. I met him at the front door, he grabbed my arm and said in a low voice, "We have to talk." He looked scared, I told him to call me. He said "No, now", and walked me back inside. He went right into my kitchen and grabbed two beers. When he came back in he threw me one. He then said, "Something is wrong" He was sitting on the coffee table and he appeared to be nervous, he was sweating thru his clothing despite the fact it was cold out. "What's wrong?" I asked as I sat down across from him. Dan told me that Danielle has been buddy buddy with Judy all of a sudden. He went on to say that he started noticing that Judy had money and she would not tell him where she got it, and when he asked her, Judy gave vague answers. Dan said he thought she was back on drugs, or fucking for money. He raised his voice a little as he said, "The bitch doesn't work." He then told me the other day he found an envelope in Judy pocketbook filled with twenties, and again Judy would not explain where the money came from. Dan's voice raised again as he told me it was at least a thousand dollars. Dan then lit a cigarette and told me that they got into a huge argument and Judy locked herself in the bedroom. He could hear her on her cell phone but he couldn't hear what she was saying or whom she was talking to. Then later that night when Judy fell asleep. Dan said he hit the call back button and Danielle answered. Dan said they started talking but he didn't mention Judy or the money. Then out of nowhere Danielle invited both of them to Amy's party. "Why wouldn't you ask about the money?" I questioned. Dan said, "I did last night after everyone else had left the party." I asked him what Danielle said. Dan said, "Nothing, she denied it." Dan told me he lied and told Danielle he heard Judy talking to her last night about the money. Dan said Danielle denied ever talking to Judy. He told me he pulled out Judy's cell phone and hit the re-call button again to prove Judy called her last night. Dan told Danielle he did this last night after Judy got off the phone and that's when she answered the phone. Dan said he was waiting for Danielle's phone to ring but it didn't. Dan said he could hear the ringing in Judy's phone but Danielle's phone didn't ring. Dan said that Danielle reached out and took the phone from his hand and closed it. Danielle told him that she was at her fathers last night when they spoke on the phone and that she was wondering how he got her fathers number, that she figured he got it off the bail papers. Dan said he was confused and asked Danielle why would Judy have her fathers number? He asked Danielle if her father could be giving Judy money. He said Danielle laughed and told him that her father died several weeks ago. Dan then put his head in his hands and said. "That impossible, you said he bailed me out". I reached over and snuffed out the cigarette that Dan seemed to have forgotten about, and it was ready to fall from the ashtray. I then asked, "Danielle's father bailed you out?" Dan pulled another cigarette out and lit it. Dan looked up at me and said, "That's what the police told me". I asked if Danielle knew that. He said Danielle laughed at him when he mentioned it to her and said someone was just fucking with him. I almost blurted out that I overheard Danielle telling him he was bailed out by her father, but I caught myself and then asked Dan if he knew Danielle's father. Dan said, "Not really, I met him when I was younger, but I never got to know him." I looked at Dan as he started to sweat thru his clothes onto my chair and asked if the old man he saw in the shadows when he dreamed was Danielle's father. Dan grabbed another cigarette and almost lit it before he realized he still had one burning in the ashtray. I got up and said, "The old man they almost accused you of murdering." Dan still appeared to not know who I was talking about. I then got up and put the tape in that showed the man that paid his bail and told him to watch. Dan said he really didn't want to see another porno. I thought this guy was way past stoned and I just told him to watch as he sat there shaking. I copied the phone number from Judy's phone as Dan tried to focus on the TV. Dan then turned white as he pointed to the TV and said, "That is the man in my dreams."

1-5-98 / 6:00 pm

Danielle had taken Amy away to visit family the day after I spoke with Dan. I hadn't seen or heard from anyone since they left. The night I spoke with Dan confused me more than a little. Dan and Judy's stories were similar only to the point that they both appeared to be trying to make the other look bad or guilty, and don't get me started on Dan's memories of Johnson. I haven't had any dreams since I last spoke with them but I could not get all this information out of my head. One of them was lying, maybe both. It was like I was in the middle of a real life puzzle, and I was going to solve it or die. I started a journal of all the information, dreams, and every one else's dreams. I entered them into the computer in a file marked "Dream Child." I would read thru all of it and would add stuff when it came to me. I also kept hard copies that I hid in the drop ceiling. Lately I hadn't entered anything.

I went to get a beer when John came to my door and handed me the stuff from my car, "Happy New Year" he said as he handed me a milk crate full of useless shit. "This crate has my entire trunk smelling like a diaper full of Mexican food." You're in a good mood I said as I searched the crate for the black strong box. "Hell yea, the misses and me got away for a while. We cleared out some cobwebs, I cleaned out my pipes, several times". He then asked if there was anything of value in the crate. I told him that I couldn't remember what I had in the car so probably not. He then took the strong box out from inside his coat and asked "How about this?" For some reason, I told him that I was led to that box in a dream. John's mood then turned black all of a sudden. "Where did you find it?" he asked. Knowing he had some sort of past with Danielle I said, "It was in the woods behind the prison". He then suddenly became happy again, and shouted, "Lets break this bitch open." Easier said then done, no matter what we tried we could not get that box open. It appeared to have two separate keyholes. I was sort of relieved that we couldn't get it open, I really didn't want it to flip open in front of John and have whatever evidence Danielle has on him to be in the box. John kept calling it the box from hell. Exhausted, I threw it in the closet and said I'll get a locksmith to come out. Johnny looking out the window then asked me when was the last time that I had spoken with Danielle. "About a week ago" I said. "She is out of town visiting with family". Johnny then asked

"Her father?" I slowly shut my closet door and thought to myself, John knows Danielle's father was dead. I went to grab a couple of beers and said "I don't know, the last time I saw Danielle she was talking with Dan about money." I then said, "You do know she is the one that set him up with those photos?" Johnny seemed surprised, not at the statement, but that I knew it. Johnny then sat down in front of me and said "Joe, Listen, You have to stay away from her, if you can afford it, move. Just forget about her. She is nothing but trouble." I then tried to ask a question but John stopped me. "Just listen, I am in more trouble than any one person should have to be in and all because of her and her fucked up father. She can hurt me, her people can hurt me, and they will hurt my family. I don't want you getting locked into the same shit I am in." Again I tried to say something, but John cut me off again. "Just leave it alone, just be a good neighbor, don't get involved and stop digging, you will live longer, a lot longer. Your best move is to take an extended vacation". John finished his beer and got up. "It will all be over when you return." Before I could question anything he was telling me, John turned and left.

1-6-98 / 2:11 am

I woke up and saw a light on over at Danielle's. There was no car in her driveway. I got up and grabbed a flashlight and snuck over and went to get the key from the hide-a-key rock she had on the lawn, but the fake rock was empty. I walked up to the door and saw that the key was in the door, I slowly turned the door handle and put the key in my pocket. As I slowly walked in I thought whoever got the key from the rock may still be inside. I then slowly shut the door and quietly walked in. I stood in the middle of the living room masking the light from my flashlight with my hand and listened, there was no sound, just a dead silence. It was so quiet that the hair on my neck was standing up. I was too terrified to move. My heart was pounding in my ears, I then heard flies as they flew around the room. Suddenly there was a scream from upstairs. I ran up and saw light coming from under Amy's bedroom door. I kicked the door open

173

but the room was empty and dark. I looked around with the flashlight. Standing in the corner with her back to me was Amy. I pointed the light on her. The light traveled from her feet to her head. She was completely wet. She slowly turned around and she held her hand up to block the light from her eyes. She slowly walked over to her bed. Lying face down in her bed was a naked man. Blood was running from under him, flowing across the sheets and dripping onto the floor. Amy reached down and rolled the man over, it was Dr Adams. It looked like he had drowned, his skin was gray from being in the water for a long time. His neck and chest had deep cuts on them. Amy now walked around the bed and was approaching me, she reached out and took a hold of my hand. I looked down at her as she smiled and said, "He was about to tell, wasn't he?" Amy then sat down on the floor in the puddle of blood and started to cry. I bent down and asked her what was wrong? She tells me through the tears "You will do this to me if I tell". I lifted her chin to look at her, "I would never do that to anyone, what are you going to tell?" Amy got up and walked back into the corner of the room and without turning around said "It can also happen to you, he knows what you are doing." I looked down at my chest and watched as large cuts started to appear. The blood from the cuts started to float in the water I was now under. I snapped my wristband and woke up. I am a little excited, and a lot terrified that the dreams are back.

10:00 am

I went out to clear my head so I thought I go for a good run. I ran through the neighborhood. It was cold out and I didn't see many people on the streets. I stopped in at the coffee shop to get a cup of decaf and a donut, just what I needed after running. I sat in a booth and saw Judy come in. I was going to call her down but she sat down in a booth with another man. After several minutes she got up and went to leave, but the man whose back was to me reached out and grabbed her arm. Judy looked terrified, this man then handed her an envelope and let go of her arm. Judy opened the envelope, and I was able to see it contained money, a lot of money. Judy then put the envelope in her jacket pocket and almost ran from the shop. I got up and walked to the counter to pay my bill, as the cashier was making change I turned and saw that the man Judy was sitting with was Officer Downs. He got up and threw some money on the table and walked out. I waited a few minutes before I left. When I walked out it was starting to rain, I was doing a fast walk home when Officer Downs pulled up and asked if I needed a ride. On the way back to my house I asked John what it was he gave Judy in the coffee shop. John was surprised at the question. He stated that I didn't need to know, he then changed his words and said without looking at me that I didn't want to know. I asked him what kind of trouble he was in? He said nothing he couldn't handle, nothing that would not soon be over. As we pulled up in front of my house the rain was turning to snow. John still would not look at me, he just stared straight ahead. When I opened the door, John spoke. He said "Joe we are friends, but if you keep digging into what you know nothing about just because you are having dreams, or your stupid compulsion for solving problems, you will get hurt." I then asked him if he knew who stabbed Dr Adams. Johnny then looked at me for the first time since I got in his car, he said, "Dr Adams wasn't stabbed, he drowned. All evidence shows he slipped on the dock and fell into the cold water." I got out of the car and started to walk up to my front door, John rolled down his window and yelled out asking me who told me Dr Adams was stabbed. "No one" I said. John then asked if I saw it in one of my dreams. I don't know why I just didn't lie but I told him about the dream, probably because John was good at reading peoples lies also. I did however leave Amy out of it. I then asked if Danielle was in anyway related to Robert Johnson, John asked "Who?" I then said Sogod. John looked away and asked if I saw that in a dream too. John then said before he pulled away "See, your dreams are not real, I think its your concussion playing with your head."

2:00 pm

After returning from the coffee shop I sat and went thru all the information I had complied in the computer. I added Judy receiving the money from Johnny and our conversation. I then remembered getting Danielle's dad's phone number. I called the number but there was no answer, nor did a machine to leave a message on. I must have called 10 times. I laid down and fell asleep in the living room in front of the TV.

I woke up to a story on the news about Dr Adams death. The newscaster was saying what Johnny had told me, that it was an accident. They also reported that Doctor Adams was survived by a brother that lived in North Dakota, they didn't mention any children. I clicked off the TV and I could hear water running upstairs. I went up to the bathroom and opened the door. The room was full of steam from the hot water that was running in the shower. The shower curtain was pulled open and there was no one in there. I reached in and shut the water off. I turned around and Amy was standing behind me. Her hair was dripping wet and she was wrapped in one of my oversized towels. She scared me so much that I slipped and fell into the shower. Amy reached out and tried to help me up. I got up and sat down on the side of the tub. I reached out and felt Amy's face. She reached up and placed her hand over mine as she shut her eyes and smiled. I knew I was dreaming and I was about to snap my wristband, but I didn't have it on. As Amy stood in front of me dripping wet, I got up and asked her what she wanted. Amy looked into my eyes and said "I just want to make you happy." I told her I was happy and that I could not be happier. Amy then asked me if we could go home.

I told her that I was home and asked if she wanted me to take her home. Amy shook her head yes and asked if I would walk her home. Amy then gently guided me to sit back down on the edge of the tub. She then reached out and held my hand as she sat down on my lap, Amy then started to kiss my hand and then she tried to put one of my fingers in her mouth. I pulled my hand away as Amy leaned in and licked just under my ear and whispered, "I won't fight you no more". I tried to push her off my lap. Amy held on and said, "I want you to show me, I just want to learn". I watched Amy's face as tears swelled up in her eyes as she said, "Just promise me you will take me home." I was then able to stand Amy up, and I held her face as I wiped the tears off her cheek, I told her I didn't want to do anything to her but help her. A look of relief came across her face as she then walked into me and laid her head on my shoulder. When I reached to brush her hair from her face Amy turned her head and tried to kiss me on the mouth, I tried to pull away but she held on. I felt her trying to force her tongue into my mouth. I then stood up and Amy fell from my lap, her towel almost fell off of her. I reached down to cover her with the towel, she violently pushed me away from her and rolled over on all fours. Her gentle tears were now uncontrolled sobs. I heard her say, "You always promise, you always promise." She was actually starting to scare me, I would not have been surprised if her head spun around. I stood up and looked into the bathroom mirror. It was covered in sweat from the hot water. But I was sure it was not me that I was looking at. I reached out to wipe away the mist but my phone jarred me awake. I let the machine pick it up. It was a mans voice, he left a message. "Hi, I don't know who this is, but someone from this number has been calling my line." I picked up the phone, but it was just a dial tone. I called the number back and again no answer. I listened to the message a couple times. I thought I heard that voice before, it sounded a lot like Johnson. But it couldn't be.

5:30 pm

Danielle and Amy came over for a visit. When I opened the door Danielle told me that Amy wanted to come over and see me. I gave Amy a pat on the head as she walked in. Danielle and me went into the kitchen and I made us a couple of drinks. We sat at the kitchen table and talked. I asked if she knew if Johnny Downs knew Judy. Danielle appeared to be telling the truth when she said "I don't know if they know each other, but I think they know who each other is". She then asked me why I would ask her that. I told her about what I saw at the coffee shop and how weird Johnny got when I questioned him. Danielle appeared to be indifferent on the subject. As we drank I started to make Danielle's drinks a little stronger, and as she became more and more drunk she started to open up. She told me that Dr Adams became obsessed with Amy and she said he was even snooping around the hospital, asking for all types of records. "What was he looking for?" I asked. She said she didn't know, but she found out he was asking for shit when one of her friends in Hospital Records called and told her. I asked if she confronted him. She told me that he died before she could ask him anything. She then said she thought that John might also have something to do with it. When I asked why? Danielle said he did a lot of illegal shit in the past, shit that could get him arrested if anyone found out. She then told me that Doctor Adams might have come across something from John's past and confronted him with it. I was stunned, "What information could Dr. Adams find on John snooping around the hospital?" Danielle said as she poured herself another drink, "He was suspected of stealing drugs from the hospital several years ago, that was probably what he was doing with Judy, buying or selling her drugs." Danielle then looked out the kitchen window towards her hot tub and whispered, "I had evidence." I then asked about Dan. Danielle said that his new trial has been postponed again, the lawyers are looking into additional evidence. I then asked if he knew that she had set him up with the photos. Danielle seemed to sober up a little when I asked that question. She told me that at some point she may have to tell him, but she wanted to wait until his trial was over. I then asked her what if he is sentenced to a long prison term? I even told her, if what she did ever gets out, that she could be arrested. I then asked if Johnny Downs was involved with this.

Danielle got up from the table and laughed. She then said, "This is nothing, this is so small compared to what that motherfucker has done, stealing drugs will be the least of his worries". She was way past drunk as she was slurring all her words, plus she was lying to protect either John or the doctor. Danielle then collapsed on the recliner. I looked at the clock it was almost one in the morning. Amy was asleep on the floor in front of the TV. I picked her up and carried her up to the spare bedroom and I laid her down on the bed and gently removed her shoes and socks. Amy reached up half asleep and gave me a little kiss on the lips. I waited to see if she tried to force her tongue on me. She didn't, she just rolled over and fell right to sleep. I then went back downstairs and grabbed the strong box from the closet. "This must contain whatever she has on Johnny." Danielle started to move around on the recliner, I put the box back and went to bed.

1-7-98 / 2:11 am

woke up to find Amy in my bed on top of the covers. I snapped my wristband, but I was awake. I reached over and brushed the hair from her face and gave her a little kiss on the cheek. I then went to throw the covers over her. That is when I noticed she had taken her pants off, she was now wearing only a pair of panties and a T-shirt that that had rose up. I just stood there and stared at her exposed flesh. I was frozen, I didn't want to touch her, and at the same time I did. What bothered me is that I was awake. I finally realized what I was doing and threw the cover over her and went downstairs to see how Danielle was doing. She wasn't where I had left her. I looked in the kitchen and noticed that a new bottle of booze was open and half empty. All my doors were locked, so she had to be in here somewhere. I then heard someone walking around upstairs. I didn't know if it was Danielle or if Amy woke up. I walked up to the spare bedroom but it was empty, I looked into my

182

bedroom and I saw Danielle sliding from under the covers, she was wearing only her panties. Amy appeared to still be asleep. Danielle saw me in the doorway and appeared to get upset and yelled, asking me what I was doing in her bedroom. I told her this was my house and that she got drunk and fell asleep downstairs. Danielle then tried to pull the covers off the bed to cover herself, but Amy was tangled in them. Danielle was in a highly agitated state and she demanded to know why Amy was in my bed. I told her that she had slept in the other room overnight but must of crawled into my bed in the middle of the night. Danielle, now almost screaming pulled the covers off of Amy and asked, "Why is she naked?" Danielle's screaming woke up Amy who was trying to cover herself with the blanket Danielle just pulled from her. I told Danielle that Amy was dressed just minutes ago when I woke up and found her lying on my bed. "BULLSHIT" Danielle yelled as she stood up and tried to walk towards me. She was still drunk and she stumbled and started to fall. I caught her and tried to sit her back down on the bed. But before I could Danielle threw up down my back. She pulled away and ran into the bathroom and slammed the door shut. I stood by the bathroom door and I could hear her throwing up for several minutes, when the sounds stopped I walked over to Amy who was now lying on my bed under the covers, she was watching me, following me. It was like she was waiting for me to say or do something. I found her panties and shirt on the floor and I bent down to pick them up and noticed that

Amy was now in such a position on the bed that it appeared her hands and legs were again tied to the bedposts. I sat down on the bed as her mother started puking again, I was just hoping she was aiming at the toilet. I laid Amy's clothes next to her and again I brushed the hair from her face. She appeared cold and distant, like she wasn't even in the room, in her mind she was somewhere else. I told her to get dressed. She grabbed her clothing and sat at the head of the bed in a ball clutching them. I found her mother past out on the floor of the bathroom. She didn't throw up in the toilet as I had hoped, but good for me most of the vomit was in the tub. I quietly shut the door shaking my head. Amy was still on the bed now dressed holding her knees in tight to her chest, but again it was like she was not there. I sat on the bed and pulled the blanket up to cover her. Amy then looked at me, smiled and said, "Done". I didn't know what to say, I told her it was okay and that she should go back to sleep. Amy reached out and hugged me, she hugged me tight burying her head in my chest. I'm not sure if Amy or Danielle said it, but I heard someone whisper, "Help me". I held onto Amy until she fell back to sleep. I then went to the spare bedroom. I snapped my wristband, Dam it I was wide-awake.

9:35 am

Danielle came in the room and woke me up, She looked like shit and she said she was sorry. She told me she cleaned up the bathroom and then asked if she did anything stupid last night. "You don't remember?" I asked her. Danielle shook her head no and at that point she looked like Amy. I told her that she flipped out a little when she thought I was in her bedroom and then got even hotter when she found Amy asleep in my bed. I didn't tell her that she somehow became naked. I also told her how she vomited on me in the middle of her rant. Danielle just held her head, "I am so embarrassed" was all she said. As Danielle stood up she still felt dizzy, "I guess I'm still a little drunk," she said. I started to feel bad for making her drinks so strong. I told her to lie down and that I would make Amy some breakfast. Danielle refused and stated she had to go home, she said she just wanted to lie in her own bed. She did however ask if I could watch Amy until she got her head together. I walked Danielle to her front door, and when she could not get the key in the door, I took the key and then led her to her bedroom. She sat down on the bed, then fell back into what I was hoping wasn't an alcohol-induced coma, but when she started to snore I left.

I went back over to my house and Amy was still asleep in my bed. I shook her awake and told her to get ready for some breakfast. When Amy came down to the kitchen she appeared to be cold, I told her to get a sweater out of the closet. She smiled twirled around and skipped towards the closet. I was making some bacon and eggs and did not realize that Amy was gone for some time. When I went into the living room I saw Amy sitting on the floor by the open closet door. As I approached her she turned her head and looked up at me, she was trying to open the black box I found in her hot tub. She tried to lift it towards me, "I can't open it," she said. I reached down and said, "You cant lift it either" as I took it from her. She then got up and skipped into the kitchen. I looked at the box in my hands, it was still locked. I walked into the kitchen and Amy was already eating. I sat the box down in-between us on the table. Amy never looked at it. After she finished her breakfast and went to get up from the table I pushed the box towards her and asked her to open it. Amy shrugged her shoulders and said, "I need the keys". I asked her where the keys were. Amy pointed towards her house as she wiped her mouth on the sleeve of my sweater that I wanted to wear today. Amy then ran into the living room just as my phone rang. I picked it up and was asked if I was the man that kept calling, "Calling who" I asked. "Me" the voice said on the other line. It was then that I noticed on my caller ID that it was the number I took from Judy's phone. I then said I need to know who I'm talking to, to know if I called you. The voice said "Mr. Johnson, who is this?" It didn't sound like Sogod, I then said, "I don't know any Johnson." I then heard another voice on the line that sounded familiar ask, "Who you talking to old man?" The line then went dead.

2:00 pm

When Danielle came over for Amy, I in jest told Danielle that she still looked like shit. Danielle laughed and said, "You would too if you drank as much as I did". I then asked her, "What made you open another bottle after we went to bed?" She just smiled and asked "Any more questions, Colombo?" In my best Peter Faulk impression I asked, "Mame, What's your maiden name, I know you go by Williamson, but rumor has it you never married Dan." Danielle at first thought my impression was funny, but then became confused at the question. Danielle stated that I didn't need to know everything and I should stop asking so many questions. She appeared to be getting very angry, and she was stuttering. She held my arm and told me to just be there for her. Danielle appeared to be afraid. She did smile when Amy walked up on us. Danielle then told me that Johnny Downs was able to list her last name as Williamson on the Hospital paperwork, and he forged a marriage license, she said she really thought she and Dan would stay together. "I'm not proud of it, but I have been a Williamson ever since". She then told me her parents disowned her when they found out she was an unwed pregnant woman. She told me she was better off without them. " But you still stay in touch with them, didn't you visit them over the New Year?" I asked. "We visited my uncle, he is the only one that never judged me," She said as she handed Amy her hat and gloves. I then told her to tell me her last name wasn't Johnson. Danielle's face froze,

"No" she said, "Johnson is not my birth name". She did not appear to be lying.

10:00 pm

I was getting really tired, I didn't get that much sleep last night and I just wanted to go to bed, but as shit happens John came over for a visit, and he brought in a six-pack. I told him I was tired and I didn't want to drink, but then thought one might help me sleep better. John told me he knew he has been freaking me out a lot lately and that he was about to try and make some things clear. He told me he was going to let everyone know what was going on. He was certain that he would go to jail, but he had to clear his concise. I asked him if this was about changing Danielle's last name on Amy's birth certificate and creating a forged marriage license, or stealing drugs. John guzzled a beer and said, "That's the tip of the tip of the iceberg." John drank the other five beers before I could finish my one. I asked about the death of Dr Adams. He grabbed the bottle of beer from my hand and said, "I had nothing to do with that." I told him I wasn't accusing him of anything, that I just wanted to know what was up with the investigation. He said, "There was ice on the deck, he must have leaned on the railing and it broke, he slipped and fell into the icy water. It turns out he couldn't swim, who knew?" As he got up to leave I went to shake his hand. He slapped it away and gave me a hug. As he pulled away I noticed he was fighting back tears as he said, "If anything happens before I can tell my story, check behind my prison graduation photo." John then walked out to his car. From my porch I could see that Danielle was watching him from her bedroom window. She watched him until he was out of sight.

I started to clean up the empties when there was another knock at my door. This time it was Danielle. She was blunt, she wanted to know what John was doing here. She did not believe me when I told her we were friends from the Prison and he came over to shoot the shit. She insisted to know what we talked about. When my answers did not satisfy her. She got up and said, "Watch that motherfucker, he is up to something." She then walked to the front door and opened it, but before she walked out she turned and said, "I know he stole that shit from my yard, and I know he killed Dr. Adams, Accident my ass."

1-8-98 / 2:11 am

Even tho I was dead tired I could not fall asleep. I was tossing and turning ever since I laid down. I could not stop thinking about what John said and I could not understand why Danielle would not tell me her maiden name. I got up to get a drink and noticed that it was 2:11 am. I thought to myself that I should be dreaming. I walked down to the kitchen and before I turned on the light I heard talking outside. I looked out the window and saw Danielle on her cell phone. She was yelling at someone on the phone. I heard her say, "You know what we did. We will all go to jail." There was a long silence as she listened, then she suddenly yelled, "Judy will never say a word, she got her money, she is gone, and for Dan, that asshole doesn't even have a clue as to what is about to happen to him. Another long pause, then Danielle said very calmly into the phone, "You were there from the beginning, you had to know it would not go away when we got older, you had no complaints for the last 12 years, and now that the shit almost hit the fan you tell me you want out, then leave, I am not the one you have to worry about." There was another pause, Danielle sat down and held her head as she listened. Then she said, "Yes, I was there too, but not by choice, and Amy is now in the same situation." She listened again and then said, "I did it, but you covered it up, you found away to make it go away, just like you always do, you made people believe it was an accident." Danielle waited again, then she held the phone away from her ear and yelled at it, "You are an expert at making events look like accidents, don't make them make you the next accident." After another pause Danielle calmly said, "Jut trust me, let it be, I cant tell you how I know, but I have the knowledge, don't be worried about the stolen shit, I know it will all be alright in the end." After listening again for several more seconds Danielle put her head in her hands again and almost yelled into the phone when she said, "Yes motherfucker, my dreams have shown me that it will all be alright. Tell me what you dream about." She listened again and then said, "That's not gonna happen," before slamming her phone shut. She sat on her back porch, looked up to the sky and said to herself, "If you don't have it, then you are a stupid motherfucker, someone out there has more evidence on all of you then you could ever imagine." I knew from her conversation she wasn't talking to Dan or Judy. It could have been John, or maybe the mysterious

Mr. Johnson. Something was not right. I called one of my friends at the prison and asked if he could get me an address from a phone number. I told him to call the phone company and use the prison as a reason for needing this information. I told him to say an inmate may be sending contraband from there. He told me he didn't want to get in any trouble. I told him to use my name, he then told me he would see what he could do. I gave him Mr. Johnson number. I then sat in the living room and slowly fell asleep.

5:10 am

I had another dream, I was tying Amy to her bed, she was in the position she was in my bed last night with her arms stretched up to the headboard and held in place by rope, her legs were spread and tied to the footboard. As I finished tying the last knot Amy looked up at me and she asked me if it was going to hurt. I rubbed the back of my hand across her cheek and told her to go to her special place. Amy turned her head away from me. I sat on the bed and stared at the floor. After several minutes I stood at the foot of the bed and I reached down and slowly started to pull the sheet from Amy's body, her head was still turned away from me and she was humming. There was a box of sex toys on the floor. I looked back up at Amy, this was a child lying on that bed and all I wanted to do was untie her, I wanted to run, but I did neither. I just stood there with the sex toy that I didn't remember picking up in my hand. I walked around the bed and sat next to Amy. I was wasting time, I was waiting for Dan to come bursting in the room and stop me, but Dan never came, no one came. I got up on the bed with Amy and I could see a tear track on her face. I bent down and put my face close to hers and whispered as I snapped my wristband, "Everything is going to be all right, I will make sure of that". When the band hit my wrist I woke up and I was soaked in sweat. What is happening to me? Why do I have these dreams about Amy? When Amy asked me if it was going to hurt, did that mean it hasn't happened yet? I stood up and looked out at Danielle's house. It was still dark out and there wasn't a single light on. A light snow was falling. Everything looked just so peaceful. My ringing phone broke the quiet. When I answered it, I got the address for Mr. Johnson. I wrote it down and placed it on the table next to my keys. I don't know why, but first thing in the morning I'll take a drive by. I then fell into my bed and I was asleep before my head hit the pillow.

2:50 pm

I slept for over eight hours and I had to force myself to get out of bed. My head felt like I was drinking all night. I sat up on the edge of the bed and thought how I just wasted all that time sleeping and I didn't even have one single dream. I turned on the TV to see that the light snow I saw last night had turned into a Nor-Easter. Almost 40 inches of snow had fallen overnight and everything was closed, schools, Malls, and of course every road. I jumped up and I could not even see my car as it was completely covered in white. I could not see where the pavement ended and the street began. There was so much that I had to do. I needed to get that box open, and I wanted to go by Johnson's house just to make sure it wasn't Sogod, but worst of all, I was out of booze. I called John at the police station, maybe he could get a plow to go up the street. I was told he didn't make it in. I called his house but his machine picked up. "FUCK" I screamed as I slammed the phone down. I sat in front of the TV and watched the special newscast of the blizzard of the decade. Almost everything that was reported went against me. It was reported that all side streets would not get plowed for several days and the main roads were open to emergency traffic only, and rolling blackouts were happening all over the place. I found the half empty bottle Danielle left in the kitchen and drank it down.

6:26 pm

I wanted something else to be on TV besides this storm shit, it was really starting to depress me. My eyes were getting heavy as I sat there staring at the TV. I was jarred from my seat by banging on the back door. I got up and the empty bottle fell from my lap and broke on the floor. Standing at the back door was Danielle and Amy. Danielle was all bundled up but Amy was wearing only a sweater and hat. Amy ran in as soon as I opened the door. Danielle asked if Amy could stay with me, she said she had to go in to the hospital. I looked past her at all the snow and said, "How the hell are you going to get to the hospital?" Danielle turned and started to walk up to the front and said, "Snowmobiles". I looked up and saw two snowmobiles out front, both had flashing lights and big red crosses on their hoods. Danielle struggled to get up to them, but as soon as she reached them she was gone. I walked back into the house and Amy was flipping thru the channels, and every time she flipped she mumbled under her breath "Shit", click "Shit". I reached down and took the remote from her hand and told her that there was nothing on and turned the TV off. Amy was still in her sweater and hat so I asked her if she was cold. She shook her head no and removed her hat and kicked off her shoes. She then stood up to remove her sweater and as she pulled it over her head she stumbled and stepped on the broken glass from the wine bottle. She fell to the floor and screamed. I pulled my shirt off and wrapped it around her bleeding foot. I picked her up and carried her up to the bathroom and sat her down on the edge of the tub and started to remove my shirt from her foot. There was not a lot of blood and I told Amy not to look and turned on the water. The warm water washed away the blood to show a piece of glass that was protruding from the bottom of her foot right behind the big toe. I gently removed her sock and then without warning Amy, I pulled out the piece of glass. Amy didn't even notice what had happened. What she did notice was the blood that was now pouring from the wound. I wrapped her sock around her foot and took off my wristband and used it to hold her sock tight against the wound. I told her to stay where she was and I ran to get some gauze. I ran downstairs and picked up my cell to call Danielle but I had no reception. I found some medical tape, iodine and gauze in the kitchen. I went back upstairs and as soon as I got to the bathroom door the lights went out. Amy screamed again and tried to stand. I was able to grab her and sit her back down. It was pitch black in the bathroom. I could not see my hand in front of my face. I lifted Amy by putting my arms under hers and sat her down on the toilet. I told her to lift her leg. I felt her foot and the sock was completely wet with blood or water, maybe both. I again told her to sit tight, that I was going to get a flashlight. Amy reached out and grabbed me, "NO" she screamed as she held on to me. Before I could make a decision the lights came back on. I was kneeling on the floor and Amy was hugging me tight. I looked over her shoulder and saw that her pants were floating in the tub water that was now running over the edge. I gently pushed her away and saw that she had for some reason removed her pants and was wearing what looked like a pair of adult thong underwear, her shirt was long and came down to just above her knees. I asked her as I leaned over to turn the water off why she took off her pants? She said, "They were getting wet" I then asked, "If you didn't want them to get wet then why did you leave them in the tub?" Amy laughed and leaned into me and started to kiss my chest. I pushed her back and demanded that she stop her nonsense. Amy then straddled my leg and started to try and grind on my knee, again I pulled her from me and sat her down on the side of the tub. Amy then leaned back and fell into the tub causing more water to spill out onto the floor. This had to be a dream and I went to snap my wristband but it was still wrapped around Amy's foot. I then got up as Amy stood up in the tub and started to remove her top. I wanted to look away but couldn't. I was then brought out of my dream by a banging on the back door.

8:35 pm

I looked around the room and I was back downstairs sitting in my chair. The newscast was still being shown on the TV and the empty bottle was still on my lap. The banging on the back door continued. I got up and placed the bottle on the table and answered the door. It was Danielle and Amy. Both were dressed in the same clothing of my dream. Before Danielle could say anything I looked over her shoulder and saw the snowmobiles. "You have to get to work?" I asked. Danielle said thanks and started her walk towards the snowmobiles. Amy was sitting on the couch flipping thru the channels only this time she was silent. I looked at the bottle on the table and told her to take her hat and sweater off, "stay awhile" I said. She smiled and did exactly as she did in my dream, she kicked her shoes off and threw her hat on the floor and stood up to take her sweater off. As she started to stumble I reached out to catch her but she fell sideways knocking the bottle off the table and breaking it on the floor. I was able to hold her up and away from the broken glass, but as I caught her my hand cupped over her breast area. She reached up and pushed my hand away and stepped onto the broken glass cutting her foot. This time I took her into the kitchen where the medical supplies were. Amy looked a little surprised when I pulled the flashlight out from under the cabinet. I told her to sit on the table. Amy refused and she would not take her eyes off the flashlight. She appeared to be terrified by it. I picked it up and turned it on and off and said, "It's a flashlight, it can't hurt you." I put it back down on the table and attempted to help her up, but she pushed me away. "Amy" I said, "Stop acting like a five year old. I have to get the glass out of your foot". Amy remained defiant. I then took the flashlight and put it up on the counter across from us. Amy then sat up on the table, but I noticed she kept an eye on the flashlight. I removed her sock and as Amy continued to watch the light I pulled the glass from her foot. I then wrapped it with gauze. But before I put the tape on it, I snapped my wristband, but I wasn't dreaming. I then grabbed the medical tape and the lights went out. There was some light coming in thru the kitchen windows, but not enough that I could see what I was doing. I reached for the flashlight and as soon as I turned it on Amy freaked out, she started yelling "To Big, To Big". As I shined the light on her she was laying down on the table in a ball, clutching her legs up to her chest. I held the light under my arm and lifted her leg. I secured the gauze with the tape, I then shut the light off. Amy sat up and hugged me. She was shaking. I lifted her chin and told her I was sorry and that I didn't mean to touch her the way I did when she fell. She then took my hand and kissed the palm and said, "That's okay". The lights came back on and Amy got down from the table and said, "I'm tired" as she went up the stairs. I yelled up for her to sleep in the guest room. I didn't get a reply.

10:45 pm

When Amy fell asleep I took her house keys and made my way over to her back door, it wasn't that difficult I used the same path in the snow they used to come over. I let myself in and started to search the house for any key that I may be able to open that black box with. I searched every drawer, counter, bowl and hook in the house. Nothing, no key. It must be on Danielle's key ring. The last room I searched was the spare bedroom. This is a room that I have never been in, the door was always shut. This room was empty except for a four-post bed, dresser and a nightstand next to the bed. I searched both the dresser and nightstand, both were empty. The closet only had wire hangers on the polls with nothing on the shelves but dust. As I went to leave the room I saw flies coming from under the bed. I bent down and saw a storage box. When I opened it, I could not believe what was in it. It contained a black rubber mask, a ball gag, and several different size vibrators with grease and jellies. There were several packs of condoms and ropes with restraints. Everything in the box appeared to be brand new. Most of the contents still in its original packages. I always thought Danielle was a prude, but she is actually a freak. Then I thought maybe Amy saw her mother using this stuff and she thought I was going to use the flashlight on her in the same way and that's why she said it was too big.

1-9-98 / 12:30am

I returned to my house and saw the message light on the phone blinking. Shit it was Danielle that called, and the time stamp was 11:00 pm. I was just going to call her back when the phone rang, it scared the shit out of me. Caller ID said Danielle. I let it ring a couple of times and then right before the machine picked up I answered it. I acted like I was asleep. Danielle said, "Did I wake you?" Don't worry I told her, I than asked, "What's up?" She said she was just checking in, she then asked if everything was okay? She said she called earlier and my machine picked up. I told her about Amy's foot and that the power went out and that my phone wont ring when the powers out. Danielle then told me she might be stuck at the hospital for at least another 24 hours. I told not to worry that I got plenty of food, and if I run out, I'll eat Amy. Danielle laughed and said you would need a lot of seasoning with her. I hung up and went to check on Amy, She wasn't in the guest room or the spare room. She was spread out on my bed, her little body had actually covered 90 percent of the bed space. It looked like there was more than just her under the covers. I noticed she had left the bathroom light on and I went over to shut it off. Amy then still asleep rolled from under the covers onto her stomach. She was sleeping topless and she was wearing the thong underwear. I kept thinking does Danielle know about this? Amy is only 12 years old, her body is just starting to develop and she should not be wearing a thong. As I stood there going over all that in my head I didn't take my eyes off of her. Amy is just a kid but the way the light was hitting her she was beautiful. I wanted to go over and touch her perfect skin. I then came to my senses and flipped the light off and went to the guest room. Before I lay down I snapped the wristband, not a dream.

1:45 am

I woke up and looked at the clock, it wasn't 2:11 am, that number, that time, I see it all the time, every time I wake up in the middle of the night I expect it to be 2:11 am. I snapped my wristband just to be sure I was awake. I could not fall back to sleep. I just could not get that image of Amy lying in my bed out of my head. I even started to fantasize about going back into my room and lying down next to her and reaching out and touching her. I didn't want these thoughts in my head but they would not leave. I slowly drifted back to sleep. I woke up to the sounds of the plow trucks going down the street. I jumped up and smelled something cooking. At first I thought Danielle came back early, but when I entered the kitchen Amy was standing behind the table putting a plate of scrambled eggs down. She had my Bar-B-Q apron on that said, "Kiss the Cook". Amy looked up at me and smiled. I said, "Morning" I then told Amy that her mother called last night and said she would not be able to get back until tomorrow. Amy just shrugged her shoulders and turned to get plates from the cabinet. Amy was still only wearing a pair of thong underwear under the apron and I laughed a little. Amy turned and looked at me, I could tell she wanted to know what I thought was so funny. I asked her if she knew what she was wearing. She turned and looked down her back and turned a bright red. I told her it was okay and then asked if her mother knew she was wearing that type of underwear. She shook her head yes and tried to pull the apron completely around her as she sat down, she said, "My mom gave them to me". I was shocked that Danielle would give her such an item. Amy's cooking was quite good, she did however burn the toast but I told her that is just how I like it. All through breakfast Amy appeared shy about getting up, probably because of what she was wearing. I went into the closet and got her a sweatshirt and handed it to her. Amy put the sweatshirt on over the apron and then took the apron off. The sweatshirt almost came down to her ankles. She put the dishes in the sink and said, "I'm going to take a shower." As Amy went upstairs I went down into the basement and changed into my running shorts and started to run on the treadmill. After about an hour I got off the treadmill and took my shirt off and wiped the sweat from my body. When I turned the treadmill off I could still hear the water running upstairs. I headed up to the guest bathroom but it was empty. Amy was in my bathroom. I knocked on the door, there was no answer. I pushed the door open and I could see the outline of Amy's body behind the glass shower doors. I lightly knocked. Amy pushed the door open enough to stick her head out, her fingers were all pruned up. "What is taking so long?" I asked. She pointed to the empty towel rack. I said "Sorry" and went to get a clean towel from the other bathroom. I gave Amy the towel and she wrapped herself up and left the bathroom. I yelled, "I hope you left me some hot water". I got in the shower and was washing my hair and soap went into my eyes, and as I went to rinse my face I felt a hand reaching around me. I reached out and felt someone standing in the shower behind me. I pushed their hand away from me and washed the soap from my eyes. Amy was standing in the shower. I tried to cover myself with the washcloth, "Amy" I said, "What are you doing in here?" She just stood there staring down at me. I stepped out of the shower grabbed a towel and slipped on the wet floor, I tried to grab the sink to stop myself from falling. I saw a reflection in the bathroom mirror as I fell past it.

I didn't know whose reflection I saw, I only knew it wasn't me. I woke up before I hit the floor. I was so startled that I fell from my bed crashing onto the floor. My clock fell from the nightstand with me. It flashed 2:11 am.

4:00 pm

The whole day was a waste as Amy and myself just sat around watching TV and eating junk food. I almost jumped every time Amy moved. I couldn't tell the difference anymore between reality and dreams. I was afraid to touch Amy, or have her touch me.

About 4:00 pm as I was sitting on the loveseat with my feet up on a stool Amy came in from the kitchen. She was wearing one of my sweatshirts and I was afraid to ask or look to see what she had on under it. She had a bowl of chips and sat down next to me and snuggled in real close, she then put her legs up over mine. I looked down at her as she looked back and smiled as she held the bowl of chips up to me. I knew I was awake because I had already snapped my wristband so many times my wrist was about to bleed. When Amy finished the chips she put the bowl down lifted my arm and laid her head on my chest. I started to fall asleep but fought to stay awake. Soon Amy was sound asleep on my lap, a gentle snore breaking the silence every so often. I gently put my hand down on her hip. Then very slowly started to pull her sweatshirt up. Amy except for the occasional snore quietly slept. Finally the bottom of the sweatshirt was up by her waist. I was sort of relived when I saw she had on everyday cotton panties, no thong. I gently put the shirt back down. I could not clear my head, did she ever have a thong on when I wasn't dreaming. I just didn't know. I then fell asleep.

5:25 pm

When I woke up Amy was now laying with her feet over me. I lifted them up and went to the window and the streets were still only plowed in my dreams. I called over the neighbor kids that were shoveling out walkways. They agreed to do my walk for fifty bucks. I stood by the window and watched them work and just as they were finishing up the plows came barreling down the street. As I handed one of the kids the money, Amy came up behind me to the door. The kid I was handing the money to saw Amy and said, "Hey dude, been out playing in the snow yet." Amy's eyes lit up, as she shook her head no. The kid with the money took off her hat to wipe the sweat from her forehead, and that is when I realized this kid was a girl. I looked at Amy and could tell she wanted to go out in the snow. Before I could say anything. The girl with my money introduced herself to me, she said, "I'm Susie, I live two houses down across the street, why don't you let Amy come out and help us dig out your car." Amy looked up at me and ran to get dressed before I finished saying yes. Susie stood there waiting, I asked, "How much is this going to cost me?" She put her hat back on and said, "It's on me dude." As we stood there waiting for Amy to come back down I noticed that Susie appeared to be older but she acted so much like a child. Amy then came down wearing what she came over in. I had to find her some gloves and I gave her a small coat that I had in the closet that I didn't even know I had. I stood by the window and watched as the two other kids left, they weren't going to dig out a car for nothing. I watched as the two girls shoveled, dug, and kicked at the snow. One strange thing I did notice was that it appeared that Amy and Susie didn't talk to each other at all.

8:15 pm

Amy and Susie came stumbling in the front door, Susie was kicking the snow from her boots as she said, "Dude you will need a bulldozer to get that car out." I asked them if they wanted some hot chocolate, again they were both past me running into the kitchen before I finished my sentence. Susie asked where she could take off her coat and boots that were dripping onto the floor. I told them both to take their wet things and hang them in the pantry. Amy came out again wearing what appeared to be just my sweatshirt. Susie came out later wearing jeans that appeared to be wet from the knees down and a T-shirt that had "Wasted Youth" written across the front in glitter. I offered to give her a sweatshirt, but she declined. Susie was older than Amy, she had to be 18 or 19 years old, but again I could not understand why she acted like she was ten. They took their hot chocolate and went down to the basement. Occasionally I could hear them laughing. I sat in the kitchen eating some pie. Susie appeared at the kitchen door shivering. I told her to sit down and I went and got her a sweatshirt and a blanket. When I returned to the kitchen she was on a cell phone, I didn't know or ask who she was talking to, when I entered the room she hung up and stated she had to leave by 10 O'clock. Susie grabbed the blanket, shirt and ran back down to the Basement. She had forgot to take her phone. I went down to give her phone back to her, if I would have checked the last call, I would have seen Mr. Johnson's number. I could hear both girls giggling. I pushed the door open and saw both girls wrapped up under the blanket. They were watching TV. I told Susie to be ready to go by 9:45 pm and tossed the phone back to her. She yelled, "Thanks Dude" as I went back up and finished my pie.

9:40 pm

I grabbed Susie's coat and stuff from the pantry and went down to tell Susie to get ready. As I approached there was no sound, no giggling, no TV. I looked inside and saw Amy and Susie hugging and kissing on the floor. They both then rolled over and Susie was naked and she was starting to reach for Amy's pants. I turned back and snapped my wristband. I snapped it so hard that my wrist started to bleed. I then yelled "Susie, its time." and walked back in. Amy was now sitting on the sofa, the TV was on and Susie was sitting on the floor covered by the blanket. I tossed her coat to her. She looked at me and said "Thanks dude". Amy got up and went upstairs. I put my hand out to help Susie get up. She looked up at me and said, "I got it dude" and started putting her coat on as she sat under the blanket. I looked at my watch and said, "Lets go" as I pulled the blanket from her. She was fully dressed. I just stared at her clothing, it can't be, there was no way she could have gotten dressed that fast. I think I am dreaming while I am wide-awake.

1-10-98 / 2:11 am

I was sitting in the living room watching some soft porn that for some reason again wasn't scrambled. I was just about to go to bed when I noticed Amy was behind the couch watching the TV. I grabbed her and pulled her over the back of the couch and started to tickle her. I told her, "You are not allowed to watch this stuff". I was more embarrassed that Amy caught me watching it, then that she was watching it. When I stopped tickling her, she sat up put one hand over her mouth and pointed to the TV, it was two girls kissing, I looked back at Amy, as she would not take her eyes off the screen. I leaned in and whispered in her ear, "Did you ever do that?" Without taking her eyes off the screen she shook her head yes. I was a little surprised, I asked if she did it tonight with Susie. She turned and said "Noooo". I then asked, "Who did you do it with." She didn't answer and just stared at the TV. I then grabbed the remote and shut off the TV. Amy turned and started slapping me. I had to grab her arms as she continued to try and hit me. I pushed her down on the floor and was lying on top of her. She continued to struggle. I yelled at her, "Don't make me call your mother" only then did she stop. She then got up and stormed off to bed. I got up and sat on the sofa. I knew this wasn't a dream because my face was still stinging from her slap. I didn't even have to look at the time.

6:10 am

I heard snowmobiles coming down the street and I looked out the bedroom window. I could see them speeding down towards me. As they got closer I could tell they weren't the hospital snowmobiles as they just rode past. I then looked over at Danielle's and saw her walking towards my front door. I opened the window and told her I'd be right down. I went in the bedroom to wake up Amy. I shook her awake and as she rolled over I half expected her to start slapping me again, but she slowly opened her eyes, smiled and said, "Morning" as she rubbed the sleep from her eyes. I let her know her mother was here. She threw the covers off and jumped off the bed and bent down to grab her pants off the floor. I wasn't sure if I was dreaming or awake. Amy was wearing an oversized T-shirt, and when she bent over to pick up her pants I saw she had on the thong underwear again. I went down to let Danielle in and tell her Amy was getting dressed. Amy then came bouncing down the steps. Danielle had brought over Amy's winter coat and had laid it on the floor, as Amy bent down to pick it up the back of the thong underwear came up above her jeans. I watched as Danielle stuffed it back down into Amy's jeans. Amy stood up and put her coat on. Danielle came over gave me a hug and thanked me for watching Amy. I grabbed her arm as she turned to leave. "Danielle" I said, "I have to ask why you would let her wear thong underwear?" Danielle turned red and said, "The night they called me into the hospital I didn't do the wash and I had to give her my t-shirt and a pair of my underwear, my ride was waiting and I didn't know they were thong until she put them on." She then said "Its better then no underwear at all". I laughed and said, "Not by much". Before they left, I asked Danielle, "Do you know a girl about 18 named Susie" Danielle had a look on her face like she was thinking, and then said "Yea she lives next door to me, a tomboy, a future lesbian, I think she is older, maybe 20, Why do you ask?" I told her that Amy and Susie watched TV in the basement last night for about an hour. Danielle quickly turned around, "I don't want them to be alone, I don't trust her," she snapped at me. Amy had walked out and was now over on her porch banging on the door. Danielle looked over at her, and then coldly said, "It don't matter, Susie won't be around much longer."

8:30 pm

I spent the entire day digging out my car and when I finally finished I was too tired to do or attempt to go anywhere else. When I got back inside I saw that there was a message on my machine. I didn't recognize the number so I left it blinking and fell onto my sofa. I wished I had a beer but I was way too exhausted to go to the store to get any. I fell into a dreamless sleep. I woke up sweating because I never took my coat off. I went up and turned on the shower. I then went into my bedroom and emptied my pockets and noticed that I still had Amy's house keys from the night I snuck into her house. I looked over at Danielle's and all the lights were out. I'll give them back tomorrow. I took off the rest of my clothes and walked naked to the bathroom. I stepped into the shower and the hot water felt like heaven, I leaned my head back under the stream and closed my eyes. When I opened them I could not see because the water was still rolling off my face but I could have sworn someone was in the shower with me. I quickly wiped my face. But I was alone. I reached down to snap my wristband but I had taken it off when I emptied my pockets. I figured I was over tired and turned and leant against the wall, letting the water flow down my back. I then felt a small body hugging me from behind, I felt the searching hands reaching around trying to grab me. I quickly stood up and turned around, but again I was alone in the shower. I jumped out and wrapped myself in a towel and almost ran to my bedroom. My wristband wasn't on my dresser. I started to look behind the dresser and on the floor. Then I heard, "Is this what you are looking for dude?" I turned around and Susie was lying on my bed, she appeared to be naked covered only by the sheets and she was swinging my wristband on her finger. I walked over to the bed and demanded that she give me the wristband. She slowly pushed the sheet down exposing her breasts and laid the band on her stomach. "Take it," she said. I looked at her and asked her what it was she was doing in my house. She put her finger thru the wristband into her belly button and said, "I saw the way you were looking at me the other night". I told her to get up and get dressed and to leave the wristband on the dresser. I then turned to leave the room and Amy was standing in the doorway. Amy was wearing a very adult nightgown, she walked past me like I wasn't even there. Amy approached Susie on the bed and lifted up the sheet and started to crawl up towards Susie. I yelled for both of them to get out of my house and pulled the sheet from them. Amy was slowly starting to pull down the same thong underwear she had on earlier from Susie's hips. I reached in and grabbed my wristband and quickly put it on and snapped it. I didn't wake up, but both Amy and Susie disappeared from my bed. I bent down and felt the bed where both were just laying, the bed was warm to the touch. I sat with my head in my hands as I was actually starting to believe I was going crazy.

1-11-98 / 9:35 am

I went over to Danielle's to return Amys house keys but there was no answer. Danielle's car appeared to have been dug out and was gone. I had the address in my pocket for Mr. Johnson house and decided to take a ride over. I had to chip the ice away from the car's door just to get in. The car started right up, but being a rental the rear window defroster was broke. I floored the engine and pulled up a little and then got stuck on an icy patch, I tried to reverse but the wheels just spun. I did this for several minutes and got nowhere. I was just about to give up when someone tapped on the passenger side window. I had to lean over to roll the window down. It was Susie and her friends. Susie asked if I needed a push. I told them to be careful. The four of them were able to push me out into the street. Once out there I called Susie over and she leaned her whole upper body in thru the open passenger side window and I handed her a twenty. She took it, folded it up, and then looked around to see if her friends were watching as she stuffed it down her shirt, pulling her shirt down to expose most of her breasts. I said thanks for the push and attempted to wave. Susie grabbed my wrist with her left hand, she took off her right hand glove by pulling it off with her teeth. She then sucked on her index finger and then wiped it on the palm of my hand that she was still holding. I pulled my hand back. Susie then threw me a kiss and pushed herself out of the window and ran to catch up with her friends that were halfway down the street.

11:10 am

On the way to Johnson's address I realized I was about to drive past the Hospital. So I decided to go in and give Danielle her keys back. I walked up to the front desk and asked to see Danielle. I was told that she wasn't in, the receptionist then stated she hasn't been in all year and that she was taking a leave of absence. I got back in the car and was wondering where she went for the two nights when she left Amy with me, and then I started to doubt myself, and thought maybe Amy never even stayed with me. Maybe they never came back from their family visit over the New Year. Then I looked at Amy's keys on the seat and realized they had to have come back. I finally pulled up to the address I got from Mr. Johnson phone number. Danielle's car was parked in the driveway and so was John's. I wasn't ready to just walk up and knock on the door. So I decided to park up the street and wait. Then just my luck it started to snow.

1:15 pm

The snow was getting heavy and I was just about to leave when someone came out the front door. He was all bundled up and I couldn't see his face, but I knew it wasn't either Johnny or Danielle. This person walked up the street coming towards me but he stopped when the white VW van Joys boyfriend drove pulled up next to him. They talked for several minutes until a car pulled up behind them. They didn't move until the car started to honk its horn. The passenger side van door opened and Susie jumped out and stood with the unknown man. The van then pulled away and Susie flipped the bird to the car that was behind it as it drove past. The two stood in the snow talking and then the man got in a car and Susie walked towards the house. I decided to follow the car. I followed him several blocks to a strip mall, he parked and went into an adult bookstore. I waited for about 20 minutes and when he didn't come out, I walked up to the store. A man came out but it wasn't the man I had been following. I entered the store and the only person inside was the man I followed. He was behind the counter. He didn't even look up as I walked in. I guessed he was an underpaid, disgruntled employee that had to come to work in the snow. I tried to see his face when he decided to glance up at me, I smiled and felt my entire body go numb, as I could have sworn it was Sogod. As I got closer I could see it wasn't, but this guy could be Sogod's twin brother. I started looking at a rack of DVD's but kept my eye on the guy behind the counter. After several minutes he looked over at me and asked if I needed help. I quickly replied "Just looking." He then said, "You must be pretty horny to come out in this shit". After several more minutes he said "Hurry up, I'm about to close up." I then started to walk towards the door, I was shocked at how much this guy looked like Sogod. I noticed he was looking at me like he knew me, he got up and came from behind the counter and quickly walked towards me, he stood there a few feet away looking me up and down, I felt like he thought I was going to shoplift. "I think I know you," he said. I told him, "I don't think so, I never been in here before". When I turned to leave, he stood in front of me not allowing me to pass, he looked me up and down again, "Yea" he said as a evil smile came across his face, "I know you, why don't you tell me what you're looking for." Then he looked around the shop and said "I have everything." I told him I was sure he had me mixed up with someone else and that I didn't know what I was looking for. He then said, "Everyone has a fantasy, you into fat chicks? Orientals?" He then paused before he said, "You I bet are into some jailbait". My expression must have changed because this guy says, "Oh, I just knew you would want some young stuff." He then walked over and picked up a DVD from behind the counter, the DVD was titled "My first time". The girl on the cover looked to be about 16 or 17 years old. He then put it in a bag and said, "Its on the house, I just know you will be coming back." We both then walked out. He locked up the store as I drove away. I wanted to go back to the house but I was afraid he would recognize my car. So I drove home only stopping on the way to stock up on some beer

6:00 pm

Driving was terrible, as I pulled up I noticed Danielle's car was in front of her house. I came in and threw the DVD on the coffee table. I now had 4 messages blinking on my machine. They were all from the same number that I didn't recognize. I hit the button to listen them, they were all from Dan. First message he said he was away and needed to talk. I thought to myself, I haven't heard or thought about Dan for a while. The second message Dan sounded a little nervous, he said that he really needed to talk to me. The third one Dan accused me of ducking him and he even yelled if I was there to pick up the fucking phone. The last one was a little nerve wracking. Dan said, "If your not going to pick up the fucking phone, then I'll just have to come and see you myself". Then a pause, then it sounded like he tried to slam the phone down but missed. I then heard Judy tell him to leave it alone before the phone went dead. I deleted the messages and went to bed.

1-12-98 / 2:11 am

I was in a dreamless sleep when there was a banging on the front door. Before I could get up to answer it Danielle came busting through. She came to me in a panic and told me not to believe anything that Dan is going to tell me. I took her arm and led her to a chair. She sat down and told me that Dan was trying to make it look like she was going crazy. At that moment I think I would have to side with Dan. I got her a glass of water and waited for her to calm down. When she asked for another drink, I asked her what it was that Dan was doing. As Danielle took the drink she said he was going to try and take Amy away from her. Danielle couldn't, or didn't want to answer when I asked her how she knew or why Dan was going to take Amy away or why he would tell me about it. Danielle then started to cry as she looked at the floor and would not make eye contact. Danielle told me that Dan had done something terrible in the past and he now wants to make it right and that he now believes the only way to do that is to tell this crazy story he thinks is true. She then said that Dan is afraid and wants to take Amy away to make sure she is safe, She then told me if that was to happen it would only make things worse. I was trying to get a read on Danielle, she appeared to be telling the truth, I then asked her, "Make what worse?" Danielle then started lying as she said, "Her life, Dans life." Danielle then started what I believed to be fake tears. As I sat down next to her and held her, I quietly asked, "What terrible thing did Dan do?" She whispered, "Dan is about to get himself in a lot of trouble, other people involved know what he did and they will do anything to stop him from telling the truth. When I asked her what the truth was, she gulped the rest of her drink and sat the glass on the table, she then looked up at me as she pushed herself up from the chair and said, "The truth can never be told". She then wiped the tears from her face and hugged me. As we hugged she whispered in my ear. "I have to do what I have to do, and even if Dan don't believe, I still believe in you". Danielle then let me go and looked in my eyes and said, "I just know you will be there for us, I just hope no one else knows." Danielle then walked out. I looked at my watch, it was 2:11 am. I snapped my wristband. I wasn't dreaming, but I wished I were.

10:36 am

I got up and made myself some breakfast. I took my plate into the living room and sat down at the coffee table and flipped on the TV. The screen was all snow, the cable was out. I then grabbed the DVD I got from the adult bookstore and put it in. The name of the DVD was titled "My first time". The screen came alive with a woman dressed like a little kid and she had to be pushing fifty. I skipped thru all the scenes and all the women on the DVD were older then me. I took the disk out and put it back into the case, "Young stuff my hairy white ass" I said to the empty room. Just as I threw the DVD on the table someone was knocking on my door. I looked thru the peephole to see it was Dan. I let him in and asked, "Where the fuck have you been?" Dan sat down and told me he had to get Amy away from Danielle and if he didn't she would end up hurt or dead. I didn't know if he meant Danielle or Amy would be hurt. Dan told me that he had an agreement with Danielle and now Danielle wants to break that agreement and other people, dangerous people will hurt Amy. I told him to slow down and then asked what it was I could do. Dan then jumped up and ran to the window, he peaked from behind the curtain and saw Danielle and John coming towards the front door. Dan turned and said we would have to talk later. Dan then tried to leave thru the backdoor but I grabbed his arm and asked him how I could get in touch with him. He pulled his arm free and said, "I will call you, just answer the fucking phone." Just as the backdoor closed Danielle and John came in the front door. John was in his police uniform. I went to the sink and started to wash dishes as they entered the kitchen, I looked up over my shoulder and asked them what was up? John walked to the backdoor and looked out, he slowly shut it and asked if I was alone. I told him "Not now, you two guys are here". I looked over at Danielle and she appeared to be covering up black eyes with her makeup, I pointed to my face and asked, "What's up with this?" Danielle turned away as John asked if I had seen Dan. I told him no, that I haven't seen him in a while and that last night was the first time I even thought about him. John then asked me why I was thinking about Dan Last night, but Danielle interrupted before I could answer and asked if I was sure Dan wasn't here. I told them that I was sure and asked again what was up. Danielle went to my phone and was checking the messages. As I went to stop her, John told me they found Judy dead last night, that her body was half buried in a ditch just outside of town. I asked if they thought Dan did it. John answered, "Not only her, but I think he may have killed Dr Adams and Robert Johnson. John kept looking around the room, he went to the closet and searched in there. I went over and pulled him out and asked if he thought Dan was hiding in my closet. John smiled then went to leave when he saw the DVD on the table and asked, almost demanded that I tell him where I got it. Embarrassed I told him it was taken from an inmate when he came into the prison, and I was supposed to destroy it. John then held it up to Danielle, and made a face before he flipped the DVD back onto the sofa and told Danielle he would call her later. Danielle looked like a scared little child as she just stood by the phone. When I asked her if she was all right. She looked straight at me and said, "I don't think Dan killed anybody". I told her I didn't believe it either. Danielle stood silent for a few more moments, she then said, "I have proof he didn't". She then tried to leave. I stopped her and pulled her back in. Again she started to cry and refused to sit down. She wandered around the living room. I asked her to tell me what the evidence was that she had that would prove Dan didn't kill Johnson the Doctor or Judy. She didn't answer my questions stating she just wanted to leave. I then reached for and snapped my wristband, again I wasn't dreaming. Danielle then said as she ran out the door, "The way John and Dan are acting, they will be next."

John was driving the streets after leaving my house, he was looking for Dan, he then reached inside his police jacket and pulled out the black strong box he stole from my closet and set it on the seat next to him. He then looked up to the sky and said, "Fuck with me now."

11:45 am

Both Danielle and John seemed to be interested in the DVD so I put it back in. The DVD just starts playing. I fast-forwarded it thru all the scenes to the end. I sat thru the credits. The DVD just starts over again. I didn't see anything that would help me figure out what the fuck was going on or why they were so interested in this DVD. I went to hit stop on the remote then decided to hit menu search instead. The screen went black. I sat there for what seemed like five minutes staring at a blank black screen. Just as I was about to turn it off the screen lit up with a menu directory. There were scenes, deleted scenes and extras. I hit extras. I watched as an older man about fifty years old sat on a sofa with his back to the camera. The camera angle swings and what looked like a young girl walks up on him, her back is now to the camera. The man tells her to get from in front of the TV, it was a very poorly made DVD. The girl who was dressed in a catholic schoolgirl uniform reaches behind her and unzips her uniform and lets it drop to the floor, and she gets on her knees in front of the old man. The camera angle switches again and the scene is now being shot from over the mans shoulder. I can now see the top of a girl's head. The girls face was not shown, just the top of her head. When the scene was over and the man yelled at the girl to get out. This is the first time I was able to see the girls face. I couldn't believe my eyes. It was Susie. She stood up and I could see that this DVD was made several years ago. Susie appeared to be about 14 or 15 years old. I then hit skip and the next scene and the following 3 after that were all the same. They all had Susie in different sexual position with other men and one with another very young female child.

1-15-98 / 12:00 pm

I spent the last few days trying to figure out if Susie being in a child porno had anything to do with Danielle and John. Maybe they made it. Then I thought that Dan wants to take Amy away to keep Danielle and John from using her in porno. Amy has been acting strange lately, almost like she wants to be in a porno. I could not help but think that John was behind it and Dan was trying to stop him, or was Danielle trying to put Amy in the porno despite Dan. Then what is John's part in all of this? I had been trying for the past few days to contact Danielle or John with no answers. Dan hadn't called back either. The good news was I hadn't had a bad dream in several days. I then decided to go back to the adult bookstore.

5:30 pm

When I entered the bookstore the man behind the counter saw me and came right over to me. "Did you like what I gave you my friend?" he asked as he put his arm around me. I told him that if that was the first time for the women in that DVD then they all waited a long time. I didn't tell him about finding the extra shit. This guy then tightens his grip around my shoulder and starts to escort me to a back room. He softly says, "I hope you are not the law". I put my hand out, "Joe, not the law". He looks me straight in the eyes as we stood there what appeared to be minutes, but was only seconds. He grabs my hand and says, "Bill, Bill Johnson". The hair on my arms and neck stood up. This had to be Robert Johnson brother, if not his twin. We entered the back room, and as we entered I saw two people leaving out the back door, Bill yelled goodbye to them. I wasn't sure, but I think it was John and Susie. But just as I strained to see. Bill grabs me and pushes me face first up against the wall, "What the fuck are you doing?" I yelled. Bill told me he had to be sure as he frisked me up and down, he then spun me around and lifted my shirt looking for wires. I grabbed my shirt and pulled it down. I shoved Bill away from me. He reached for a gun that was on his hip. I put my hands out, "That wont be necessary". I then said, "You must have some really sick illegal shit in here." He slowly took his hand from the gun and told me to sit. I sat at a table that had a portable DVD player set up. He reached over and pushed play. The screen lit up. It appeared to be a schoolroom. There were 4 young kids, three girls and a boy sitting at desks, one girl appeared to be older then all the other kids and she looked like the girl I saw at Dr. Adams, but she looked younger. As the camera showed the other kids, the boy was not the kid that I saw at Dr Adams. I thought to myself thank god because he would have been about five, this was an older DVD. The other girls all appeared to be no older then 13 years old. The teacher looks up from her desk and says, "I have to go but I'll be back in a few minutes" she then gets up and leaves the classroom. As soon as the door shuts behind her the three girls started to attack the boy in ways I haven't even thought of. The boy appeared to be scared to death. It was one of the most disturbing things I have ever witnessed, but I had to sit there and act like it was the greatest thing I had ever seen. Bill was sitting across from me, his gun now lying on the table in front of him. He was watching me watch the DVD. Bill finally leans over and thankfully shuts the DVD off. He says, "If you want to see more it will cost you five hundred dollars, usually they run between one or two thousand, but first time customers get it at a bonus price. Cash, no check, no credit cards". I tell him I don't carry that amount of cash. Bill gets up takes the DVD from the machine and puts it in a case, he looks back at me, "This one is two hours long and there are many more" I just sat there, I was about to pull my pockets out to show him I had no money. Bill then walks over and opens the back door to let me leave, as I walk up to the door he grabs my arm, "You will come back, I already know you will?" I shook my head yes and told him I would, and then I started to walk towards the parking lot. "Don't be embarrassed to check out the extras on the DVD you got, it has some of my earliest work on it." Bill yells. "You would not believe who buys these tapes".

8:15 pm

As I drove out of the strip mall parking lot I thought about going to the police, but I decided to drive by Bill Johnson's house first. When I pulled up to the corner I saw John and Susie walking towards the house, John appeared to be pulling Susie by her arm. When they got to the door Susie pulled away and ran into the house. John then turned to look around, it appeared like he was looking to see if anyone was watching. John then turned and walked up the street. I turned and drove home the long way, I didn't want John to see me, but first I stopped at the bar, I really needed to put on a load.

1-16-98 / 2:11 am

woke up in Danielle's back yard, my clothes were all wet from the snow on the grass. I get up on my knees and brush myself off. I'm really hanging from the shots I did at the bar. I look up and see Amy sitting on her back porch. She see's me looking up at her and smiles, she asks me if I'm drunk. I then ask her why she would ask me that? Amy laughs and says, "Because the yard is not a bed". I go to snap my wristband but it is not on my wrist. I look on the ground for it. When I turn around Amy is standing right in front of me. She unwraps the blanket she has on and placed it over my shoulders. She reaches out and takes my hand and leads me into her house through the backdoor. When I ask her where her mother is, Amy points upstairs. I drop the blanket on the floor. Amy runs over and picks it up and takes it upstairs. I washed my face and hands in the sink and sat down at the kitchen table. I was so tired that I started to fall back asleep. I then caught myself right before I fell into a deep sleep and got up and splashed some more water on my face. Amy still hasn't come back downstairs. I walked to the bottom of the steps and looked up. There wasn't a sound. I slowly made my way up the steps. When I got close to the top I saw Amy sitting outside of Danielle's bedroom door on the floor. I asked her what she was doing. Amy put her index finger up to her lips and put her head up against the door. I bent down and could hear Danielle moaning in the bedroom. Amy looked up at me and asked in a whisper if her mother was okay. I bent down to stand her up. "She is fine," I said. Amy then pushed the door open. Danielle was lying on the bed pleasuring herself with a vibrator. I reached for the door to close it before Danielle could see us standing there. As I reached for the handle Danielle looked over and asked me to come in. I turned to take Amy away but she wasn't there. Danielle then said, "Don't be shy, please join us". When I turned back around Danielle was sitting naked on the edge of the bed and Amy was standing next to her. I walked in and said, "This is not right, you should let Amy go to bed". Danielle looked over at me and said, "Amy is in bed" as she slowly laid Amy down on the bed. Amy made no sound, nor did she protest what was happening. I walked over and sat down on the edge of the bed next to Danielle and took the vibrator out of her hand. I then told Amy to go to her room. I then turned to see where Danielle went. I was then hit in the face with a punch and knocked out.

I woke up in my own bed, the sun was shinning thru the frost covered windows. I checked my wrist and the wristband was there, just another dream. I then went to lay my head down and felt pain from a bump and burse on my temple.

1:00 pm

I decided to go and confront John on what was going on. I wasn't going to leave until he gave me some answers. I pulled into Johns driveway and saw his wife Lisa coming out carrying luggage. Before I could open my mouth Lisa yelled, "He's not here, hasn't been home in days." She threw her bags into her car and started to pull away. She then stopped and rolled down her window and said, "And if you see him, tell that bastard I left and took the kids." I looked into the back seat as she backed out, Johns two girls looked like the two other girls that were on the DVD that Johnson had shown me, only they too were now older.

8:15 pm

I drove around town looking all over for John. I called his cell and left several messages. I was just about to give up when I spotted his car parked on an isolated road down by the river. I parked across and walked down to where his car was. I didn't see John anywhere and started to think he jumped in the river and killed himself. As I got closer to his car I could see he was sitting in the drivers seat. His head was back against the headrest and he wasn't moving. "Please god" I said to myself, "Don't let me find him with a bullet hole in his head". When I walked up to the driver side window I saw that he wasn't dead, he was in the middle of a blowjob. Both John and his date noticed me at the same time. John became embarrassed as he said he could explain. I didn't think he needed to explain anything to me, and then I saw that his date was Susie. John tried to get out of the car but Susie tried to go back and finish her job. John had to push her off of him. I started to walk back up to my car. John got out and chased me down. He grabbed me from behind and asked me to let him explain himself. I told him I was just at his house this morning and that Lisa left with the kids. He said, "Its for the best". I was standing there looking at a broken man. When I turned to leave John said, "I can't get out." I turned back and asked, "Get out of what?" John told me he is in too deep and the only way out is jail, or death. John smiled as he told me he was sort of relieved that Lisa took the kids, "At least now the kids will be safe, and now that they don't have anything against me to hold on to them". I asked "Safe from what? From who? Hold on to them how?" Before John could answer Susie walked up on us, she appeared to be high or drunk. "Dudes, I'm up for a threesome," she slurred. John looked at me, and then turned back to Susie and told her he didn't think I was into it. "Fag" Susie said as she turned away and walked back down to John's car, stopping only to lift her skirt to squat and pee in the middle of the walkway. John just stared into space. I reached out and took his arm, "What the fuck is wrong with that kid?" I asked as John stared into space, "Let me help you". John pulled away and said, "Jesus himself couldn't help me". He then started to walk back down to his car. John stopped for a second to say, "I am glad Lisa left, my girls are too old, it is me they need". Susie was now sitting on the hood of John's car, when I looked over at her she smiled and flipped me the finger.

1-18-98 / 2:00 pm

I lay in bed staring at the clock, I watched every minute change from 1:30 to 2:00. I thought if I waited until after 2:11 to go to sleep that maybe I wouldn't dream. Anyway every time I closed my eyes I saw Susie's head bobbing up and down on John's lap. I leaned over and lit a cigarette, a habit I just picked up since leaving John and Susie at the river. I was afraid to turn the TV on. I kept thinking there would be a news story about Susie's dead body being found floating down the river, or of Johnny killing himself. I got up to snuff the cigarette out and I looked over at Danielle's house. The light in Amy's bedroom was on and her shades were up, I could see her posters on the wall above her beds headboard. Just as I was about to turn away Danielle got up from the bed and stood in front of the window, she was topless and sweating. She walked to the window and slowly closed the shades. I quickly turned and looked at the clock as it flipped to 2:11 am. I snapped my wristband, but I knew I wasn't dreaming.

9:45 am

I pulled into the parking lot of the adult bookstore. The store don't open until 11:00 am. What the fuck can I do for an hour and fifteen minutes? I walked over to a fast food place to get some breakfast. The kid behind the counter was one of the kids that was with Susie the night she shoveled my sidewalk. I ordered my food and sat down. After about 15 minutes I saw Susie walk in with the girl I saw at Dr Adams house, it appeared that she was wearing a wig. Susie walked behind the counter and up to the kid, she grabbed a sandwich from under the hot lamps, she then tried to grab the kid's package as he told her to get out from behind the counter. He appeared to get very embarrassed when she turned around and open mouth kissed the girl I thought was Doctor Adams daughter. The manager then came from his office and chased them from the store. The manager then called the kid back into his office. He came out several minutes later and left the store. I got up and ran over to him in the parking lot. He looked a little shocked when I asked him to stop. He turned and hollered, "For the last fucking time, NO motherfucker, I am not interested". Calm down I said. I just want to ask you about that girl. "The bitch that just got me fired, that cunt has got me fired from every job I have ever had," he yelled as he continued to walk away. I said, "Yea, that bitchcunt, Susie." He then stopped walking and asked me how I knew her name, before I could answer, he said, "Never mind, you're about the age she goes for." I said "No, that is not it, she cant stand me either". This kid then turns around in a hostel manor and says, "You think she don't like me motherfucker, well your wrong, she loves me, but only because she has to, I'm her brother." I then said, "Dude, I don't know your name, but I just want to help her". The kid then says, "She don't need help, that bitch needs an intervention, or probably an exorcism." He then pulled his bike out from the bike rack. He turned back and looked at me. "Mister, she has more money then you, me and my parents, she supports them, us. If I was to get her help, I'd probably end up on a milk carton".

11:10 am

I walked into the Adult bookstore. Bill winks and gestures towards the back room. When I went in it was empty. I looked around and all the boxes of tapes and DVD's were gone except for a few large crates in the corner. Bill suddenly enters. "Where are all the movies?" I asked him. Bill points to the crates and says, "They are packed up, and ready for shipment next week". He then grabs a DVD from inside his desk drawer and says, "Don't worry my friend, I saved you one." He then asked if I had the money. I gave him five hundred dollars in tens and twenties. He didn't give me the DVD until he counted the money. He then flipped the disk to me. As I was leaving his mood turned dark. "Joe" he said, "All my disks are being shipped to countries all over the world and you my friend are the first person in this country outside of my circle of friends to ever view one of my movies". I turned and asked "Your movies, do you make them?" Bill then said proudly, "The girls in these movies are mine, sick bastards all over the world buy my movies, it like the law enforcement over seas don't care". I shook my head, "Nice" was all I could think of saying. Bill then put him arm around me and walked me out the back door. I then asked him, "So you are not afraid that you might get caught?" Bill laughed and said, "I have so many connections, and nobody on this planet is smart enough to trace them back to me." I was a little confused and asked, "Why trust me Bill, why would you let me buy one of your movies?" I asked as we walked out. Bill turned me towards him and said, "I have made millions and millions of dollars selling these movies, but I haven't made a new one in several years. The girls are now all to old, the sick bastards only want young stuff." I thought that was why his storeroom was empty. Bill then said, "Now Joe I am about to leave this country to spend my money, and you ask me why I trust you with one of them?" I just stared at Bill waiting for him to stop talking so I could leave. Bill grabs my shoulder and says, "Ever since I made the last film I wanted to make one more film for quite some time now, but everyone involved thinks

I should just quit and disappear, and that is what I was going to do before you walked into my store." I looked at him like he was nuts. He patted me on the back and said, "Joe, I have a higher connection that lets me known to make this film, he lets me know I can trust you, and I now know I can because you have earned my trust in my dreams". I tried not to look scared shitless as he said, "My prior doubts about making this last movie have all but vanished, because you have shown me that this one last movie should be made." I shook his hand and asked, "I told you this in a dream?" Bill looked up towards the sky and said, "I have seen you save me." Bill then shut and locked the door.

1:50 pm

When I pulled in thru the gates I saw that John's car was in my driveway. John was sitting in the driver side seat. I was a little afraid to walk up, I didn't want to see any one else in the car with him. But this time he was alone. He got out and said, "Its about time, for someone who's not working you are never fucking home". I told him I had a few errands to do. We went inside and sat in the living room. John started the conversation by saying, "Joe I have to tell you about Susie." John asked me to be quiet and to not ask any questions or he would get up and leave. He went on to say, A long time ago when he was a child he went with his father who was a very corrupt cop to an adult bookstore run by two brothers, his father told them a story about a mother that lived at a homeless shelter that was under investigation for trying to sell her kids, a boy and a girl. John's dad suggested they take the kids and make porno, the deal was, they make the movies, and John's dad would not extort money from the bookstore anymore. The brothers were already making child pornography, but they became partners with John's dad and they came up with another plan. John's father and his partner went to the homeless shelter to check it out. They tipped the mother off about the investigation. Then after the investigation died the Johnson's made her an offer to buy the girl who was about 7 years old. They had her home schooled by people they knew in the porno business, they had the kid think that sex was a natural thing to do, which wasn't hard, because her mother had already sold her for sex. They cleaned them up and when the kid started to develop they use her in films, the kid was sheltered and kept away from other kids, it was less likely she would run to the cops. The girl still lived with her brother and mother who they kept stoned, and after they made the film, John was sure they were going to kill the family, but they made a small fortune selling the tape. John said he was not that knowledgeable of the way they sold them, but shortly after that first film the Johnson brothers got a silent partner that took over the selling of the tapes, then soon after that they were all rich. They purchased land and built in home film studios. Later they tried to get the girls brother to join but he refused. So John's father made him have sex with the girls. I looked at John as he sat in the chair across from me with his head down and asked "You had to be in your late twenties, and your father forced you into this?" John lifted his head, "I started at age 15, they shot a test film as they trained the girl, I didn't mind doing it, afterwards my dad would be so proud of me." I could not believe John has been doing this since he was a kid. John then stood up and he put his hands on my shoulders and told me that he was not proud of what he has done and that is why he is glad his wife took the kids away. I asked him why he didn't just leave with them before? John said he thought about it, then he told me when his father found god and tried to leave, he was found dead in an alley outside of town, his fingers were all cut off and shoved down his throat. John then got up and put his jacket back on. I stood up and asked, "Did they ever find out who killed your father." John zippered his jacket and said, "He was the first of many unsolved deaths in this town." I got up and asked how Susie became involved in all of this. John looked back at me and said, "The girl I just told you about, was Susie." I stopped John from leaving and asked if his kids were even his. John turned to walk out, he didn't speak, nor did he look at me, he just asked that I don't say anything, he told me he was in the process of trying to make things right, he then dropped his head and walked out the door.

9:00 pm

Danielle stopped over to see how I was doing. It wasn't long before I turned the conversation to John and his past. Danielle seemed shocked. I asked her if she thought this is what Dan has been trying to do with Amy. Danielle got angry and stated she had to go and pick Amy up. I asked her if she wanted company. Danielle didn't answer, she just stormed out of the house slamming the door. Danielle was pissed, but I got the feeling she was not pissed at me.

1-19-98 / 2:11 am

I thought it would be fitting to watch the DVD at 2:11 in the morning. The DVD was not the same one that I had viewed in Bills back room. This one showed a girl no older then 13 tied down on a four-post bed. She was assaulted over and over again. After the attack was over the camera zoomed in on the little girls face. I hit pause. She was smiling, she appeared to be looking at someone out of the camera's view, and she looked proud. I turned the DVD off and there was a breaking news story on. The report was on the shooting death of two people, one of whom was a city cop. When they put up a photograph it was Johnny Downs, he was found shot in the head behind the wheel of his police cruiser, the reporter also stated that a younger female was shot in the passenger seat and they were waiting to notify her family before releasing her name. I just knew it was Susie. The reporter looked at the camera as he said the bodies were discovered in a police cruiser that was parked down by the river. The reporter said the events leading up to the execution style killing were sketchy, but early reports say both were also shot in the groin area.

6:35 pm

Since Johnny was dead I decided to call in a tip to the police hotline telling them about the child pornography that was being made and sent out of the Adult bookstore. I called from a pay phone in the prisons parking lot under a surveillance camera that I knew did not work. I figured with the store shut down, all might be well. I didn't know if the police would go directly to the store and raid it, or set up some sort of sting operation, so I decided after I called that I would stay away from the store for a while.

1-21-98 / 12:00 pm

Danielle and Amy haven't been home the past couple of days. I found myself getting up and checking their driveway every time I heard a car drive by. I was in the kitchen making lunch when the story of the raid on the adult bookstore was broadcast on the news. I saw Bill blocking his face as he was led from the store in cuffs to a police car. The newscast also showed cops putting boxes from the store into a police van. What caught my eye was Danielle's car parked in the lot next to one of the police vans. This was a live broadcast so I jumped in my car and headed down to the strip mall.

3:30 pm

When I arrived at the bookstore several police cars were still there. Danielle's car wasn't. I saw Jimmy Northan, a Police Officer I knew from Johnny. When

245

he saw me he came over and asked me what I was doing here. I told him I was driving by and I was just being nosey. He told me to leave because they were ordered to video record everyone that comes to the store and take down their license plate numbers. I told him that I had nothing to hide, and I told him how sorry I was to here about John. Jimmy seemed distant about John. Jimmy then told me that John may have been involved with the store. I acted shocked and asked how could he be involved with this place? I then asked if it was a crime to sell porno? Jimmy then started to walk me back to my car. He said, "This place may have been selling child pornography." Jimmy then leaned in towards me and whispered, "Keep this between us, besides the young woman in his car, we also found some DVD's and tapes in his car." I asked what kind of DVD's. Jimmy said, "Children, some as young as ten years old". I asked if they were traced back to this store, and if that was why they were searching it as I got in my car. Jimmy leaned in the window and told me the FBI was pissed, that they were investigating the owners and this raid may have compromised it. Jimmy also told me that the tapes found in Johns car were in the process of being reviewed when the tip came in, so the Police Commander jumped on it and set up the raid before notifying the FBI. I then put my car in gear as Jimmy slapped me on my shoulder and said, "But so far I don't think there was anything illegal in the store."

11:00 pm

I flipped on the 11 o'clock news to see if there was any more information on the bookstore. It was still the lead story. The police were saying that it turned out there was nothing in the store that would make them think anything illegal was going on. Bill Johnson was interviewed, he was angry, as he was let out of the police station he screamed that this was nothing but a witch-hunt. Henry, Joy's friend was walking with Johnson carrying a briefcase and dressed in a thousand dollar suit. I almost chocked on my beer when they said he was Johnson's lawyer. As they were shown leaving, again I saw Danielle's car parked behind Johnson as they walked away from the camera and headed towards the parking lot. I was just about to turn the TV off when an update on Johnny killing was shown. Nothing new was added except they showed a photograph of the young girl that was killed. It was Susie.

1-22-98 / 2:11 am

found myself in Danielle's house. I was standing in the shower of Amy's bathroom. I could here people talking in the bedroom. I peaked out from behind the shower curtain and saw Amy sitting on the closed toilet seat, Joy was kneeling in front of her and she was cupping both of Amy's hands on her lap. She was telling Amy this is what she has been getting ready for and promising Amy that it will be fun and it wont hurt. Amy then smiled back at Joy as she stood up, both of them then left the bathroom. I walked up to the door and peaked out into the bedroom. I saw Susie sitting on the edge of the bed in a silk robe. Joy walked Amy up to Susie and she took Amy's hand and placed it on Susie's hip. Joy then reached around and untied Susie's robe. As I tried to lean out and see if there was anyone else in the room the bathroom door creaked open. Joy suddenly turned and came towards the bathroom. I was trapped, I had nowhere to go. When

Joy came into the bathroom I was just about to snap my wristband. She saw me and her face went from fear to comfort. Joy smiled at me and said, "What are you doing hiding in here, come on out and watch, this is what you have prepared her for." Joy then took my hand and started to walk me into the bedroom. I reached for my wristband and pulled it. Right before I let it snap against my wrist I saw Danielle's reflection in the bathroom mirror that was slightly open and showing the bedroom. I would have been able to see more but a black cloth half covered it and the wristband snapped onto my wrist and I woke up on my living room floor.

As I pulled myself up I saw all the empty beer bottles and felt the pain of another hangover. I looked over at Danielle's, there was no sign of life in the house. I sat back down on the sofa and found a bottle with some beer left in it, I then fell back to sleep.

9:35 am

I woke up when I rolled off the sofa, I got up and picked up all the beer bottles. As I threw the bottles into the recycle bin I saw Danielle's car in the driveway. I wanted to go over but what reason did I have. Just then Amy came out the back door and waved to me. I walked over and asked her how she was doing. Amy told me she was hungry. I asked her where her mother was. Amy said they got home late and her mother was still sleeping. I told her to go in and leave a note for her mother and to come over for some breakfast. I was grilling some pancakes when Amy came in. She wanted to help so I let her flip the cakes. She seemed happy. We sat down to eat. Amy sat right next to me. She was so close I had to push her chair away a little. I sat and watched her eat, the butter and syrup started dripping down her chin. I grabbed a napkin and went to wipe it away, but Amy pulled away and said, "That's not how you do it." I looked at her and said, "No, show me" Amy got up and dipped her finger in the syrup on my plate, she then wiped it on my chin. She then took my face in her hands and licked the syrup off my chin. I grabbed a napkin and said "Gross" as I wiped my chin. Amy laughed and said, "No its not, get mine". As she pointed to her chin. I looked at her and wondered if this was just a childish game, or was there something else involved. I then thought to myself, she is a 12-year-old girl and I hoped she was just playing a game. I grabbed her face and pulled it close to mine and I licked the syrup off her chin. Amy was laughing so hard she said she was going to wet herself. I then grabbed her face again and went to give her a raspberry on her cheek, but when I pulled her face towards me she turned and gave me an open mouthed kiss, sliding her tongue into my mouth. I gently pulled away, I didn't want her think I was mad or upset. Amy just sat back down and continued to eat her pancakes like nothing happened. I looked up and saw Danielle coming across the yard. I got up to let her in.

Danielle came in and smelled the pancakes, "Hope you guys left some for me." Danielle sat down at the table across from us. Amy hopped off her seat and put some cakes on a plate for her. I got up and started to wash out the pan. Danielle showed Amy that she got some syrup on her face and Amy quickly sucked the syrup off of Danielle's face. Both laughed and when Danielle turned and saw that I had a horrified look on my face, she said, "Its not that bad, your looking at us like we're freaks" I forced a smile, "Its early" I said.

1:43 pm

Danielle and I sat in the living room small talking when I changed the subject to John's death. Danielle acted shocked, I had to tell her he was killed several days ago, I was surprised she didn't here about it. Danielle told me they were out of town and asked how it happened. As I told her I mentioned they also found illegal porno with children in his car. I could have sworn I seen a little smile come across her face. I also told her about how the police raided the adult bookstore in the strip mall, Danielle then said she heard about that. I thought to myself, she knew about the raid, but was clueless to John's murder. And when I mentioned that Little Susie was also found shot to death inside of John's car, Amy gasped and dropped her video game. Danielle then started to cry what I perceived as forced tears. Amy picked up her video game and came over and sat on Danielle's lap and gave her a hug as both were now crying over Susie. Danielle then got up and said she had to leave. I walked her to the door and said, "I didn't know you guys were that close." Danielle then took my hand and said she just wanted to be alone. I told her Amy could stay with me until she was up for company. Danielle grabbed Amy by her wrist and said, "No, she wont be a bother".

1-23-98 / 2:11 am

I had just finished a workout and I was sitting on my exercise machine watching TV when Amy came down the basement. She said her mother had been drinking and had fallen asleep in bed. I told her she could stay here for a while and then we would go and check on her mother. Amy asked me what I was sitting on. I told her it was my work out machine. She asked how it worked. I took my shirt that was draped over my shoulders and tossed it on the floor and started to pull on the bars showing her how they lift the weights. "Cool" she said, and then she asked if she could try it. I got up and adjusted the weights, and said, "Give it a try Arnold". Amy looked at me funny and asked, "Who's Arnold?" I flagged her as she took her coat off and threw it on the floor, I bent down and picked up her coat and my shirt and placed them on the table. I then turned around and Amy was sitting on the machine, she had taken her top off, she was wearing a pink wife beater t-shirt that said, "OLD ENOUGH" across the front. Amy was pulling on the bars. She asked if she was doing it right. I said, "Yes, but why did you take your shirt off?" She replied, "That's how you did it." I bent down and picked up her shirt. Amy was really going to town on the machine, She was starting to sweat thru her t-shirt. I told her to stop before she hurts herself. She appeared to get upset and she let go of the bar letting the weights crash against the machine. Amy then stood up and sort of stomped towards me. She snatched her shirt from my hands and walked over into the corner and turned her back to me before she lifted her t-shirt off and wiped the sweat from her face and chest. She then looked over her shoulder to see if I was watching her. I told her to put her shirt on and to stop playing games that we had to go check on her mother. Amy then said in a defiant tone, "No, not until you kiss me again". I turned and saw that Amy had sat down on the sofa in a defiant way with her arms crossed across her chest. I said "Kiss you again, when did I kiss you before?" Amy said, "In the kitchen" I then reached down for her and said, "Lets go, its not going to happen". Amy then stood up and said as she pulled her shirt back on, "Why, are you gay?" I turned and looked at her. "Because my mom says the only men that will refuse to kiss me are gay". I then sat down on the sofa and I put my head in my hands, "I'm not gay Amy, and your mother is wrong, there will be a lot of men, I mean boys that wont want to kiss you, and they will not all be gay". I then looked up at Amy and she had tears in her eyes. I looked over her shoulder at the clock on the wall, it was 2:11 am. Now I knew I was dreaming. I looked back at Amy as tears were now rolling down her cheeks. I then reached up and wiped the tears away with my finger. Amy grabbed my hand and put my finger in her mouth as she got up and sat down on my lap. I pulled my finger from Amy's mouth and turned her face towards mine, "We have to go check on your mother." Amy then leaned in and kissed me. It was a closed mouth gentle kiss. During the kiss I looked over her shoulder and saw that it was still 2:11 am. I then realized that Amy was slowly moving her hand down my chest, I felt myself starting to get excited. I reached for my wrist and snapped my wristband. I didn't wake up, I was horrified, I wasn't dreaming. I pushed Amy off me. She fell to the floor and looked up at me like a scorn puppy. "Come on we have to check on your mother". I went into the bathroom, I was embarrassed, and I looked at myself in the mirror and saw that I was crying.

1:10 am

I took Amy home and as I was tucking her into bed when Danielle came to the bedroom door in a flowing nightgown, she stood in the doorway and said that I would make a great father. I turned and could see how the light behind her was making the nightgown she was wearing almost invisible. I didn't say a word, I just though how beautiful she looked. She then walked over and sat on Amy's bed and leaned down and gave Amy a kiss on the forehead. We both went to leave when Amy reached for me, I bent close to her and Amy reached up and gently bit the side of my cheek. "Goodnight" I said as I left the room. Danielle took my hand and walked me to the front door. Should I tell her what has been happening? I decided not to. Not yet.

7:00 am

I got a call from John's wife Lisa and she asked if I would be able to be a pallbearer for John. I told her that it was short notice since the funeral was is in 6 hours, She told me that she had found a letter this morning from John with some requests in the case of his death and one was that I be a pallbearer. I then agreed, but before I could hang up Lisa also said, "John has also asked that I give you several of his things from when he worked with you at the prison". That's was when I remembered John telling me to check his prison photo if anything happened to him, I also remembered that un-openable black box sitting in the back of my hall closet.

1:00 pm

During the service for John I noticed that Danielle, Joy, Bill Johnson, and Joys friend Henry were all seated in the back row. They were all kind of disrespectful during the service making noise, even laughing at one point. After John was laid to rest I saw Lisa approach them and give each one a hug, it wasn't long before she was smiling and laughing with them. As I went to leave Lisa asked me when I could stop by and pick up the things John wanted me to have. I wanted to get them now, but told her to call me whenever she felt up to it. She squeezed my hand and turned to walk back to the others then she stopped and said, "The sooner the better, I want everything about him out of my house as soon as possible".

6:30 pm

After stopping for a few beers after the funeral I decided to stop by Johns. Lisa met me at the door and walked me into John's office. His office was a shrine to his days spent with the prison and the police force. Lisa flipped on the lights and said, "Take what ever you want, I am only going to burn the rest". Lisa was in the house alone, she went back upstairs and sat in a big chair and just stared out the front window with a large drink in her hand. I just didn't want to grab his prison graduation photo and leave so I grabbed a box and filled it with stuff that I didn't want. When I left I waved goodbye and told Lisa if she needed anything to call. Lisa didn't even turn to see what I was taking, she just waved from in front of the chair and said, "I don't ever want to see or hear from anyone that ever knew that bastard". This comment struck me as odd, seeing the way she carried on after the funeral with the ones that are most likely responsible for his death.

8:55 pm

I dumped all the shit I took in my garbage can and grabbed the photo and turned it over, there was nothing there. I ripped off the backing, still nothing. I started to think I might have the wrong photo. I then noticed that the backing appeared to be thicker than it should be, it was two pieces glued together and when I ripped them a part a disk fell out.

10:00 pm

I put the disk in the DVD. The TV lit up with an empty chair, John then came from behind the camera and sat down. He looked into the camera and said:

"Who ever is watching this, I am truly sorry. I just need someone to know what I have been living with for many, many years. It all started when my father talked the Johnson brothers into getting involved with child pornography. It ballooned from there. I know when I got older I did it for my own greedy self, but I didn't want money, I wanted the kids. I know what I did was wrong and I probably deserve what ever it is that has happened to me for you to be watching this, but my children don't deserve to go thru what I have gone thru. I love my wife and my children very much, which is what makes me even sicker. When my wife and children started to get dragged into what I done, I had to push them away, and that is why I am dead. I was able to destroy the evidence that would have shown that my father and me were the sole guilty people, by doing this, I thought my children could get out. Now I'm not trying to make excuses but the children that we used were never harmed, then my own daughters started to get dragged into this." Then John went silent and would not even look at the camera. He then got up and left from in front of the camera. When he came back he had an envelope in his hands, he was crying as he held the envelope up to the camera. He wiped his face, regained his composure and continued:

"In this envelope are the names of the people that if I was killed are the ones that not only killed me but were involved in every unsolved murder in this town. These are dangerous people, keep them away from my children. This is enough evidence of events that will put those people away for a long, long time. I could not release this before my death because the evidence inside also shows what I did, how I was able to forge and manipulate hospital records." John then took the envelope and taped it between a photograph of himself with his two children. The DVD then shut off. I jumped up. I remember seeing that photo on the wall in his living room above the fireplace. I ran out and got in my car and as I was pulling out Danielle came running up and flagged me down, I told her I was in a hurry and I'd see her when I got back. Danielle yelled she can't find Amy. I slammed on the breaks causing the disk I just watched to fall onto the floor of the car. Danielle almost ran into my car when I stopped. As I got out of the car I stepped on the dick breaking it into several pieces. I realized that Danielle was in a complete panic. "Where was Amy when you last seen her?" Danielle told me they were watching TV. That she fell asleep on the couch and when she woke up Amy wasn't there, Danielle said she looked all over and she isn't anywhere. Danielle fell to the ground in tears. I lifted her up and walked her back to her house. I tried to calm her down, Amy may have fallen asleep and didn't hear you calling. Danielle sat down inside and I searched the entire house, there was no sign of Amy anywhere. When I came back in from searching the yard. Danielle was standing on the back porch. "Did you see her?" Danielle asked as I walked up. I shook my head no and hugged her. I told Danielle that we have to call the police. Danielle pulled away. "No, not yet, they might have her" Danielle then walked into her kitchen. She took the phone and sat down at the kitchen table. I watched her as she sat and stared at the phone, it was like she was willing it to ring. I gently took the phone from her hand, Danielle looked up at me. "Who might have her?" I asked. Just then Amy came running in thru the front door, Danielle jumped up as Amy ran straight up to her bedroom and slammed the door shut. Joy came in behind her. Danielle grabbed Joy and demanded to know what she was doing with Amy. Joy started to say something, and then she saw me and quickly pulled from Danielle's grip and stated that Amy came to her front door crying. Amy at first would not tell her what was wrong, and became violent when she suggested that she be brought back here. Joy then told us as she was driving Amy around town, Amy said she was upset that Susie had died. Danielle then put her hands up to her face and gasped. Danielle then slowly turned and went upstairs to see Amy. Joy then went to leave, but turned and looked at me, "I left several messages". I looked over at Danielle's phone and saw the message light was blinking. Then thought how could we have missed that.

11:50 pm

Amy finally calmed down and she fell asleep in Danielle's arms. Danielle asked if I would take her to bed. I reached down and lifted Amy from Danielle and laid her down in her own bed. As I turned to leave Danielle was standing in the doorway of Amy's bedroom, she looked like a train wreck. I told her that Amy would be okay. It's just a shock for a young kid to hear that one of her friends had died. Danielle looked down at the floor and said she should have told her. "Don't blame yourself," I said as I leaned down to give Amy a little kiss to her cheek. Amy looked up at me and whispered. "Are they going to kill me next?" I looked up and Danielle was gone. I told Amy, "As long as I am around, no one is going to hurt you." Amy's smile came back across her face. She rolled over and shut her eyes.

1-24-98 / 1:00 am

It was now too late to go back to Johns and see if I could get that photo. Lisa was pretty pissed when I was there earlier and I'm sure it wont be a problem getting it tomorrow, after all, John is in it, Lisa is not going to want it. I sat with Danielle on her couch and held her until she fell asleep. I couldn't help but think there is something going on with her. I got up and watched her sleep. I wanted to shake her awake and demand she tell me what the fuck is going on. But I just quietly left, putting a cover over her before I did. On the way out I saw a little key hanging from a hook above the door. I grabbed it just in case it opens that little black box.

As Danielle slept she was dreaming, she was standing looking out a window at a beautiful sunset, the sun was slowly disappearing into the ocean. She then saw Amy running, laughing and playing with a dog on the beach. As she watched her she thought how happy she looked.

Danielle then heard someone calling Amy. Danielle watched as Amy looked up and ran to a man and hugged him as the dog ran circles around their feet. Danielle strained to see who the man was. Suddenly Amy turned towards her and the man held her hand as they walked towards the window, the man was me. Danielle pulled away from the window revealing the prison bars that covered it.

2:11 am

I woke up in a field, the sun was shinning and there was a warm gentle breeze. I sat up and looked around. I was in the largest flat field that I have ever seen. There was nothing but flat land as far as the eye could see. I then heard a fly buzzing around my ear and when I went to swat at it I felt a hand on my shoulder and turned to see Amy standing behind me. I stood up as Amy took my hand and we started walking. Neither of us said a word. We walked for quite some time. Then I saw something on the horizon and as we got closer I could see they were tombstones, there were six of them. As we reached the stones I read the names, Robert Johnson, Dr Steven Adams, Johnny Downs, Susie Henderson, and Judy Johnson. The sixth stone was blank. I turned to ask Amy why she had brought me here but she was gone. I reached out and touched Johnson's stone. I was suddenly in Northeastern Hospital. I walked into Johnson's room. I had no control over what was happening. I walked over to a table and crushed up several pills and then mixed the crushed pills with saline and sucked it up into a needle. I walked over to Johnson as he lay sleeping in his bed. I inserted the needle into his IV line. Johnson suddenly opened his eyes and said as he grabbed my arm. " You think I can't stop you if I am dead?" I continued to push the rest of the solution into his IV. Johnson screamed, "Your own eyes will show him the way". He was very angry as I pushed his hand away and started to walk from the room. When I got to the door I turned around and said, "You never wanted to stop shit old man, if you wanted to, you would have." As I walked thru the door I was back in the field. I walked over to Dr Adams stone and gently touched it. I then found myself standing on the docks by the river. I hear someone behind me ask, "Why so paranoid all of a sudden? You knew she would tell someone eventually." I turned to see Dr Adams walking up. He than says, "Just be thankful it was me, and not a cop." I extend my hand to shake his as he asked, "You have my money?" When our hands touched I pull him in and stabbed him in the chest. The look on his face was of disbelief as I pull the knife out and slid it across his neck. The Doctor then falls back and breaks the railing falling into the water. I throw the knife in and watch it sink. I turn around and I am back in the field. I look around to see if Amy is watching, but I am again, alone. I then reach for Johnny's stone. I am now standing in the shadows of the trees down by the river watching

Johnny's car parked a few feet away. The passenger side door opens and Susie gets out, she is topless and I can see Johnny reaching for her, Susie slaps his hand away and yells, "I have to pee", as she runs down to the water. I look in my hands as I am putting a silencer onto a gun. As I approach the car Johnny see's me coming and rolls the window down. "What the fuck are you doing here? You can't prove a fucking thing now." Was the last thing he said before I pulled the gun from under my coat and shot him point blank in the head. I then reached in and pressed the gun up against his exposed penis and without hesitation I fired again. When I turned around I was once again back in the field. As I raised my hands I saw the blood on them that had just splattered when I shot John. I rubbed them together to try and stop them from shaking. I then reached out and touched Susie's stone. I was standing on the walkway between Susie and John's car as Susie came walking back up. When she saw me she folded her arms across her chest to cover her exposed breasts. She looked scared as she walked towards me, "Dude, I'm doing what you asked, Johnny really believes you wont hurt him." Then as she approached me she said in a low whisper, "He hasn't told me where the shit is." She then brushed her shoulder against me as she walked past heading towards the car. As she reached for the car door I grabbed her by her hair and swung her around and slammed her back up against the car. She didn't scream, she didn't say a word. I leaned in our noses were touching.

I looked into her eyes, she was terrified. A tear ran down her cheek as she said, "I'm sorry, he makes me do this." I pulled her face into mine and kissed her, she slowly wrapped her arms around my shoulders. Still holding her hair I spun her around again opened the car door and pushed her in. When she saw John she went to scream but was cut off when I put the gun into her open mouth and blew the back of her head off, chunks of her skull to hit the windshield. Again I pushed the gun down into her vagina, but before I pulled the trigger I watched a stream of blood run down her chest and drip off her nipple. I then slammed the door shut and I was back in the field. I then knelt down in front of Judy's stone. Her last name was Johnson, was she related to the Johnson brothers? I leaned forward and was transformed into a speeding car that I was driving, Judy was sitting in the passenger seat, and she was angry and yelling about her son. I suddenly turned up a side street leading out of town. Judy became a little quieter but she demanded to know where her son was. About five miles up the deserted road I pulled over and got out and walked around to Judy who was refusing to get out of the car. I reached inside my coat and pulled out an envelope. It was overstuffed with hundred dollar bills. When Judy saw this she got out of the car, still angry she said, "Why are you giving me more money, I am not leaving without my son?" I then said, "Your son will be here soon, this is a little extra to make sure you say gone". Judy was still keeping her distance from me as she said, "I am going to be a very good mother" I then held the envelope out towards her, "I am not the only one that kept your son from you." Judy then came closer and swung a fist that struck the bridge of my nose, causing it to start bleeding. Judy then backed away from me saying, "I always knew you took my son away from me." I then looked up at Judy as I spit out blood that was starting to fill my mouth, "Why the fuck did you do that?" I asked. Judy then approached me yelling, "WHERE THE FUCK IS MY SON?" I reached out pushed her up against the car. "He is on his way," I calmly said as I held out the envelope to her. She had such anger in her eyes as she stared at me, when she looked down to take the money, just as her hand touched the envelope, I slid the tip of a needle into her arm and injected into her blood stream enough of a deadly mixture of narcotics to kill ten people and said, "You would have been a great mother." Judy tried to run but quickly succumbed to the drugs running thru her system. I got a shovel from my trunk and started to bury her in the ditch she fell into. She moaned in either pain or ecstasy every time the dirt fell from the shovel. I then looked up and saw headlights coming down the road. I blew Judy a kiss and said, "You just couldn't stay away, you had to find your son." Judy was reaching up as a mixture of what looked like blood and puss started to escape from her mouth and nose. I threw the shovel into the weeds and got back in the car and drove away without turning on the headlights. I turned to see if the other car was going to stop, but when I did I was back laying in the grassy field. Amy was sitting next to me, Singing. I pushed her away from me and went to touch the stone that didn't have any name on it, there was only a date 2-11-09, but before I could touch it Amy snapped my wristband waking me. I sat up in my bed in anger and ripped the wristband from my wrist and threw it across the room. "FUCK" I screamed as I looked at the clock, I wasn't surprised that it was 2:11 am

2:30 pm

After the dreams of the killing spree I went down stairs and got a drink and fell asleep in front of the TV. When I woke up it was 2:30 in the afternoon, and the drink I got had spilled down the front of the chair. I got up and showered, grabbed a six-pack from the fridge and headed over to Johns house.

4:14 pm

Lisa answered the door and when she saw me she tried to slam it shut. I pushed it open and walked in behind her. Lisa said, "You don't take directions too well, do you?" I told her I was sorry but I needed to get another photo of John. Lisa kept walking and pointed to the fireplace and said, "Too late, they are all ashes now" I looked up to where I saw the photo last night and there was just a faded outline where the sun discolored the wallpaper. I looked into the fireplace and could see the photo simmering in the ashes. Lisa was now sitting in her chair, she was loaded on booze or pills, I didn't give a shit which. I pulled what remained of the photo from the ashes. Lisa looked over and tried to grab it from my hand. "You can't have that," she screamed. I pulled the photo away as Lisa fell to the floor. I pulled a part of the burnt envelope from behind the photo. I then dropped the burnt photo onto Lisa who was still lying on the floor trying to figure out which way was up. She swatted it away and yelled for me to get the fuck out of her house.

10:00 pm

The only readable part of what I pulled off the photo was the names Danielle, Amy, Judy, Timmy and half of Johnson's name. They all appeared to be on some sort of a list, the paper it was on had a Northeastern Hospital watermark. There were also birth certificates that appeared to be originals, but the names and dates were burnt off of them. I knew all of the people on this list except for Timmy, if I held the paper up to a light it looked like his last name started with "JO". Could this be another Johnson, could this be Judy's son? It was all useless. As I sat at my desks looking at the burnt papers I could feel that there was someone else in the room with me. I reached into my desk drawer and slowly pulled out my prison stun gun. When I swung around in the chair. Dan was sitting in the dark, he said the stun gun wouldn't be necessary as he lit a cigarette. When the match lit up his face was illuminated and I could see his face was swollen and bruised. I turned on the room light and asked him what had happened. Dan got up and walked over to me, he bent down and took the stun gun from my hand, and as he sparked it he said, "This must hurt." He then put the gun back in the drawer and partly closed it. Dan then said, "Joe, forget about it, stop looking around, just let it happen". I told him I was confused, that at first he wanted me to help him find out who was hurting Amy, and now he was telling me to back off, to stop looking, and let it happen. I didn't know what he wanted. Dan sat down across from me, he lifted his head to look at me and said, "I can't beat you, and I know that, I'm a 110 pound drugged up loser. But it is not only me, a lot of people are about to come into a lot of money, and I have seen all the people that have tried to stop it, well ... they are all dead, and Joe I don't want to be dead." I then stood up. Dan pulled a gun from his waistband and quietly told me to sit back down. "Joe, I had a change of heart about it a few weeks ago and Judy and I took the money and left. I was supposed to stay gone, Danielle had promised me that that Amy would safe, but I had to come back and make sure she was safe. I knew if I tried to interfere someone would know and I would end up dead, just like all the rest." Dan then said as he looked at the floor, "I was beaten just for coming back". I then tried to reach into the desk drawer and grab the stun gun. Dan then jumped up and kicked it shut on my hand. As I yelled and held my throbbing fingers Dan knelt down beside me and pushed the barrel of his gun up against my neck. "I am not allowed to hurt you, I don't know why, so just fucking drop this," he said. I looked up and said thru the pain, "Drop it Dan? You are one of the reasons I am still looking, but I still don't have a fucking clue what it is I am looking for." Dan pushed my face away with the gun and I fell to the floor holding my hand. Dan grabbed the burnt bits of paper off the desk, crumbled them up and shoved them in his pocket and said, "Just drop it, it will all be over soon and no one else has to die." He then walked towards the front door, he turned and said, "If you had a clue as to what was happening, you would already be dead." As Dan left all I could think about was that Lisa must have called him and told him that I came and took that shit out of her fireplace. Did she know what was hidden behind it?

1-25-98 / 2:11 am

After Dan left I drank the rest of the beer in the fridge. I past out at the kitchen table with the stun gun in my hand. I started dreaming in a whirlwind of dreams, at one moment I was lying in a field with Amy, then I would be running from Dan and Johnson as they shot at me. Every time I found myself trying to hide, Joy would call me into a safe place, but I'd only be safe for a little while, soon others would be coming to get me. Finally I was hiding in a dark corner as several people came into the room, but they couldn't see me. Amy then walks in and points to me in the corner, as the crowd came rushing forward I was shook awake in the kitchen by Amy, but before I could tell the difference between my dream and what was happening I pressed the stun gun into Amy's chest and stunned her to the floor. I looked up at the clock to see that it was 2:11 in the morning, and then in a fit of anger I threw the stun gun at the wall, smashing the clock and knocking it to the floor. I then bent down to pick up Amy, I carried her into the living room and placed her on the sofa. I knelt down beside her and laid my head on her chest trying to hear her heartbeat, "I'm sorry, I'm sorry, I'm sorry" I kept saying over and over. Amy starts to stroke my hair and I hear her whisper, "Its alright". I look down at her and she is smiling. I lift her shirt and see that there are two red marks between her ribs. She squirmed when I touched one of the marks. I asked her if it hurt? "Only when you touch it." She said as she pulled her shirt back down. I stroked her cheek and told her I would get her some ice. When I came back from the kitchen with the ice Amy was laying on the floor. I took the ice that was wrapped in a towel and placed it under her shirt on the burn marks and then laid a blanket over her. I sat on the sofa and asked her why she was lying on the floor. She didn't answer, she just stared straight up at the ceiling. I then asked her what it was she was doing over here at 2 in the morning. She then slowly turned her head towards me, she smiled and said, "I could not sleep, I had a weird dream where everyone was chasing you, trying to hurt you, so I came over here to see if you were okay", She then lay silently on the floor before she said, "Cause I need you to be safe, I need you to save me". I sat in silence. Amy then sat up, "You wont hurt me, will you Joe?" I patted her on the head, "No, baby, I would never hurt you" I then watched as Amy fell asleep on the floor, it wasn't long after that I fell asleep also.

9:30 am

I woke up to find myself alone in the house. I wasn't really sure if Amy was even here last night at all, then when I walked into the kitchen and saw the broken clock on the floor I knew some of what I did was real. I walked out front and stood on the porch. I looked up and down at the houses. Dr Adams house was up for sale. The family moved out right after the Doctors death. Susie's house has been dark since her death. I then saw Danielle and Amy come out and get in their car. "Good morning", I yelled as I waved. Danielle waved back as she stood looking over the car at me. "Stop over tonight". She said. I told her that I would try. I then looked down at Amy sitting in the passenger side seat. Amy smiled at me and lifted her shirt to show me the two red burn marks on her torso. She then stuck out her tongue and pulled her shirt up over her face, when she pulled it back down she was holding her finger over her mouth telling me to be quiet. Danielle was now getting into the car. I looked at Amy and make the gesture that I was locking my mouth and throwing away the key. Amy pressed her face up against the window as they drove away.

1:00 pm

After returning to my warm house I remembered the key I took from Danielle's the other day. I went to get the box from the closet, but it wasn't there. I pulled everything out of the closet, I then searched the entire living room. I thought this little box may or may not be a key to what is happening. It was no bigger then a portable DVD player, but it must of weighted 15 pounds, it didn't get up and walk away. There was then a knock at my door, I kicked all the shit I took out of the closet back in and forced the door shut. Dan was standing out front. I let him in as he said he came over to see Amy, and asked if I knew where they were. I told him they left earlier this morning. Dan then asked if he could wait for her. He threw his keys on the table and I noticed that there was a similar key on his ring to the one that I took from Danielle. After last night I was a little apprehensive about him being in my house, but after seeing that identical key and remembering Dan and Danielle's argument by the hot tub made me think they knew I had the box, and maybe one of them stole it from my closet. Dan sat on the sofa staring at the TV, Law and Order was on and Dan said out loud to himself, "I could write a great story for this show." Dan then turned and told me that Danielle was selling her house and she and Amy were moving away. I must of appeared shocked because Dan then says, "Cheer up, this will solve all your problems". Dan then got up and placed his hand on my shoulder and said, "Your only problem will be forgetting about her, am I right?" I thought, was he talking about Danielle or Amy as he walked away and went into the kitchen to grab a couple beers. Dan sat and drank at least five beers, but he didn't make me think for a second that he was ever going to leave. The entire time he talked about Danielle and Amy moving away. He would return the conversation back to them moving every time I tried to discuss what happened with the burnt papers he took from me. He would only talk about Amy and Danielle. I tried to get him to tell me where it was they were moving to, but he told me he wasn't allowed to give out that information yet. But I was willing to bet he didn't know or was not told. I then made up a dream, and told him I dreamt that I found a black strong box. Dan almost did a spit take. "Where did you see the box?" he asked as he wiped his chin. I got up and walked into the kitchen, "It was a weird dream, the box was floating in dirty water, and when I picked it up several people started to chase me." Dan then yelled in, "Who was chasing you?" I told him I didn't know, and I started to look for my stun gun. Dan came in and grabbed his sixth beer and asked me what I was looking for. I shrugged my shoulders and said "Nothing". Dan got up in my face, "Your looking for that box, you got that box?" I pushed him away, "No" I said, "I don't have any box, it was just a dream." Dan then grabbed his keys from the table and made sure the key I saw was still on the key ring. Danielle was pulling into her driveway, and Dan said he had to go. When he left I thought by the way he acted, he knew what box I was talking about, but he also had no idea where it was.

9:30 pm

Just as I was about to shut off the lights and go to bed Danielle was at my door, "I thought you were going to stop over," she said as I opened the door. "Sorry, slipped my mind" I told her. Danielle sat down and opened a bottle of wine that she brought in with her. We drank for a while, I then asked her if she was moving. Danielle appeared shocked that I knew this, she then looked at me and asked, "Did Dan tell you?" I answered, "Yes, he did, and he seems happy about it". Danielle then told me she was sorry for not telling me. Danielle told me she hasn't even told Amy yet. I asked Danielle several questions, why was she moving? Where was she moving to? Each time I asked a question she would gently dodge them and would change the subject. But before she left she hugged me on the sofa and gave me a wonderful passionate kiss. Seeing an opportunity I tried to play it further but she shot that down and told me that she thought she and Amy needed a change, a chance to start over. She promised to call me when they got settled, but I knew she was lying.

1-26-09/ 2:11 am

I dreamt about the field again. This time Amy wasn't there as I walked to the tombstones alone. I went to the last one, the one without a name. I reached out and touched it. Nothing happened. I knelt down in front of the stone and ran my fingers over the date, 2-11-09. I jumped when I felt a hand on my shoulder, I turned around and again Amy was standing behind me. She walked into me and hugged me. I slowly shut my eyes as I heard flies buzzing around my head. When I opened my eyes I was back in Danielle's house. I was sitting on the end of the bed in Amy's room. There was no one else in there with me. It was dark and the only light was from the street lamps outside her bedroom window. I then noticed that the bed was the only item in the room, the bed was naked there were no sheets, pillows or covers on it. I got up and walked into the hallway and found Amy's little stuffed rabbit on the floor. I bent down and picked it up. I smelled the bunny, it smelled like Amy. I walked thru the house and all the rooms were empty. There was only dust on the floors. I sat down on the steps and started to feel sad, but I didn't know why. I guess I just needed to know they were safe. Suddenly the front door was kicked open and Dan came running in. He ran right past me like I wasn't there as he took the stairs three at a time. I followed him up to Amy's room. Henry was holding Dan back. Dan was screaming that he changed his mind and he reached into his pockets and started to throw money at them. Henry then punched Dan knocking him to the ground. Bill then came out of the bedroom holding his handgun and said, "I knew this piece of shit would try to fuck this up". After loading the gun he handed it to Henry and told him to shoot if Dan even thinks about getting up. Bill then turned and saw me standing there and he quickly approached me. He reached out and took my arm and started to walk me towards the bedroom. Right before we got to the door Bill stopped, he swung me around and said, "You want to back out too bitch, I still have another bullet", I just stared at him, I didn't know what the fuck he was talking about. Bill then shook me and yelled, "You getting cold feet too motherfucker, I'll kill you myself". I pushed him away and looked at Dan bleeding on the floor. "No I'm good." Dan then yelled, "You are such a little fucking bitch." Henry then kicked him back down to the floor, and as I went to enter the bedroom Dan yelled, "You touch her and I will kill all you mother fuck" was all Dan could say before Henry started to pistol-whip him. When I entered the room Amy came running over and hugged me tight. I looked down at her and brushed the hair from her face. Amy looked up and said, "You said we wouldn't have to do this, you told me you would never hurt me". All I could say back was "I know, I wont". I then knelt down to look her in the face. I held her shoulders and said, "You have to believe me, it will all be over soon, just let me help you" Amy looked surprised, she took a step back and said, "I don't need you to help me". Amy then looked out at Dan and said, "Help my daddy". Amy then dropped her robe and climbed into her bed and pulled a sheet up over her. Lights came on and a camera started to roll. I took a step towards the bed as Bill walked to my side, "Lets do this." I shoved Bill away from the bed. Dan who was able to fight off Henry and take the gun away from him came into the room and fired one shot. The bullet hit me in the side and I fell on top of Amy as everyone else in the room was running from the gunfire. I tried to push myself up off of Amy's body. I then felt Dan holding the gun against my head. Amy got up and ran to him. Dan was crying as he said, "You did this, you promised me everything would be fine in the end" Dan pushed the gun into my neck, "Welcome to the end, die bitch". I saw the gun flash, I tried to pull away and avoid the bullet. I found myself back in the field by the tombstones. I reached for my wristband and snapped it. I didn't notice that there was now a name on the sixth tombstone. It was Danielle.

6:30 pm

I picked up my mail and noticed that there was a letter from Johnny Downs. When I opened it another disk fell out. The letter said:

> Joe, this disk was in the black box I stole from your closet, I know you took it from Danielle's hot tub. There were other things in the box but I had to destroy them. I hope this helps.

I was going to throw the envelope out when I realized there was an old key in it. I was just about to put the disk in when Danielle came over for a visit. I put the disk on the counter near the sink. And sat down with Danielle, after a few drinks I again asked her when she was moving? She told me she wasn't sure of the date, but that it would be quick and would probably happen overnight. "So you are just going to get up and move in the middle of the night without warning?" I asked. Danielle took a drink and said, "I don't think I will even have time to pack". She then told me she wasn't going to tell Amy until the time of the move. I asked if Dan knew where she was moving. Danielle told me that no one knows when or where she will be moving. She then got a little defensive and told me she really didn't want to talk about it anymore and asked me to stop asking, she told me that there were people who would be highly upset if they knew she was even thinking about leaving. Danielle then again promised to call me when she was settled if she was able to. Danielle then got up to open another bottle of wine. "If your able to?" I questioned. I started to think she might be getting ready to go into some sort of protection program. I was just about to ask her, but she picked the Disk up from the sink and asked me what it was. I got up and took it from her hands and told her it was a movie disk. "What movie?" she asked. I don't know why, but I told her it was a porno that I found in the belongings I got from John after he died. Danielle looked at the disk, "Is it so hot you had to cool it off by washing it with your dishes" she slurred with a laugh. I could tell Danielle was getting more toasted with every drink. I took the disk and tossed it on the table. Danielle grabbed the wine and said "Lets watch it." Danielle went into the living room and turned on the TV and dimmed all the lights. As much as I wanted to watch a porno with Danielle I had no idea what was on this disk. Danielle then jumped up and ran back into the kitchen, "I'm going to grab us some chips," she yelled back. I was then able to switch the disk with one of the porno's I got from the adult bookstore. Danielle came back in and grabbed the disk from my hand, "For crying out loud", she said, "You are acting like you never watched a dirty movie with a girl before". Danielle then put the disk in and pushed play. It was the first movie, the one with the forty year olds playing teenagers. I sat on the sofa and Danielle grabbed a throw and snuggled up against me. Before the first scene was over she was snoring on my shoulder. Before I could get up to turn the TV off, I too fell asleep. When I woke up Danielle's head was in my lap, I looked at the TV and saw the extras were about to start. I tried to reach for the remote without waking her up. But as soon as Susie's face came on the screen Danielle sat up and asked, "What the fuck is going on? What was John into?" Danielle then grabbed the remote and watched as Susie preformed on the TV. Danielle didn't say another word. I tried to get the remote from her but she pulled away and said, "Look at her, she is so beautiful, and what is she about fourteen". Danielle just sat and watched as a tear rolled down her cheek. She then said that Susie looked like she was enjoying herself, that she didn't appear to be uncomfortable at all. I grabbed the remote and shut the TV off. Danielle had a look on her face like she was just seeing her newborn child for the first time. "That is wrong on so many levels" I told her. Danielle just sat and stared at the blank TV. She then said, "She didn't look like she was being forced to do any of that". I took the disk out and said that I was going to send it to the police. Danielle then became very upset and told me that Johns name would be dragged thru the mud if I did that. I said "They found DVD's in his car when he was killed, I'm sure they already know." Danielle grabbed the disk and asked, "Were they with children?" I wasn't sure. Danielle then put the disk in her pocket and approached me and started to kiss me on the neck and chest. In-between kisses she would whisper.

"Tell me that seeing Susie's naked body didn't turn you on? Tell me you didn't like the way Susie looked all wet in the shower? Can you honestly tell me you would have turned down Susie if she wanted to fuck you?" Danielle then reached her hand into my pants, feeling that I was excited, she then whispered, "I can tell you liked her". I pulled away to look into her eyes. She came into kiss me on the mouth. I stopped her and asked, "What if that was Amy?" Danielle didn't say a word. She pulled my face to hers and as our lips touched she said, "Amy will do fine". I looked over Danielle's shoulder at the mirror on the wall and a black cloth did not cover it. I might not be dreaming. I then snapped the wristband anyway. I woke up with the credits rolling on the screen. I gently lifted Danielle from my lap and turned the TV off. I then saw out the corner of my eye that Amy was watching the TV behind us. Danielle sat up and stretched. I pulled her close and whispered to her that Amy was sitting behind us and she may have watched the porno. Danielle put her hand on my chest and said, "She'll be all right, I sure she has seen quite a few porno's at Dan's". Again I snapped my wristband. This time I wasn't dreaming. Danielle picked up the empty glasses and took them into the kitchen, I turned to see Amy but she was no longer there.

1-27-98 / 12:50 am

I was about to get into bed when I heard a car pull up out front. I saw a brand new sports car parked in front of Danielle's. I could not see who was in it. Danielle came running out to the car and leaned in the passenger's side window. I slid open my bedroom window, but I was unable to hear what was being discussed. Danielle then banged on the roof of the car and I could tell she was angry, but she was trying to keep her voice down. Danielle then turned and started to walk away from the car. Dan then got out of the drivers side and ran to catch up with her. Dan was all cleaned up, since the first time I met him, his face was clean shaved, and he was wearing what looked like a thousand dollar suit. Dan grabbed her and I could now hear Dan as he told her he was taking the money and leaving for good this time. He said he was going to try and forget all about what they did, and what she was about to do. Dan then got quiet and said that he did not want to end up like Judy.

Danielle hugged him and told him he was doing the right thing. Danielle then pulled away. She looked at Dan for a moment. She then said, "Don't worry about Amy, she will be fine, just go far away, don't ever come back" Dan told her he was not coming back, and that he was even going to change his name. They then embraced again and kissed, when they separated Danielle put her hand up to his face and softly said, "If you do come back again, they will kill you". Dan held her hands and said before he turned and sprinted back to his car, "I hope you know what you are doing," Danielle looked up at my window. I stood back so she wouldn't see me. A gust a wind lifted and dropped my curtains. I felt a chill when I saw how Danielle's expression changed when she saw that my window was open.

2:11 am

I could not sleep so I got up and went down and got the disk from the mail. I put it in the DVD player, the disk played, but it must have been damaged as the sound and picture kept going in and out. I saw John placing some sort of documents on a table in front of him as the camera zoomed in on several of them. I was able to see a date on one "12-28-97" I could see the name Timmy again, only this time his last name was visible and it was Johnson. I wasn't sure, but the more I watched, the items appeared to be what Lisa burned. Then just before the DVD player rejected the disk, John put the key that was in the mail on the table. The key was shinny and new and had a label from Northeastern Hospital attached to it. I then went to add all this information into my computer log but when I flipped my laptop on, the Sogod site was up. There was nothing new on the site, same old shit, I then clicked on the time line icon. I noticed there was an entry that was made two days ago. It said:

> In just a few days, this trip will be over.
> For Amy and Danielle it will just begin
> The best of days will follow for Amy
> Her time on this planet will blossom
> Everything she has learned will empower her
> You will one day see the truth
> Let it be in this life, not death
> Everyone has taken Amy into his or her hearts
> And so have you
> Very soon her beauty may blind you
> Even I can see it now
> Any more time spent looking
> May place
> You with the dreams of the small child
> Watch what is happening
> If she falls someone will be there for her
> Let them live
> Let them love
> Danielle has seen the ending
> I can only hope
> Everyone can see her shine.

I knew this puzzle from before, the first letter of each statement spelled out:

IF THEY LEAVE AMY WILL DIE.

If Sogod had posted this, he would not have used an identical puzzle that I was already able to solve, someone else must have posted this. I called a friend that could track websites, maybe I could get an address as to where this was being sent from. I was told he would get back to me.

9:45 am

I received a call from my buddy telling me the web site has been dormant for several weeks now. That the entry I asked about was placed onto it from an outside source and he was able to trace it to the public library next to the high school around the corner from Bill Johnson's house.

12:15 pm

I went to the Library and was surprised when a security guard at the door stopped me. He asked if I had a card for the library, I told him I just needed to use the computers. He said the computers were for the high school students only during school hours. I flashed him my prison ID and told him the prisons believe some prisoners may be talking to some of the children that use them. He was defiant in his stance at first, but then he told me they only have one that is working and it was going to be in use all day. He waved over a library aid to come over and take me to sign up to use the computer tomorrow. We walked back to the sign up book in the back. The guard appeared to be very interested in who I was. I signed the book for tomorrow and flipped the pages back in the book to see if I could see who used the computer the day and time the message was listed on the Sogod site. The book only went back to the start of today. When the aid saw me looking she asked if she could help me. When I told her what I was looking for she looked over my shoulder at the Security guard who was watching us and told me to wait. I sat down and watched the traffic going by the high school across the street. I then saw Bill Johnson pull up and park across in front of the school, he was on his cell phone when he got out of his car and started to walk across towards the library. I looked up and saw the security guard was also looking out at Johnson, and he too was also on his phone, they both hung up at the same time and the guard then looked over at me. The aid walked past me and placed a book on the shelf with a note sticking out of its pages. I saw Johnson was almost across the street and his gun was under his jacket on his hip. I got up and grabbed the note from the book and went out thru the back entrance. I watched thru the window as Johnson came into the library. The security guard met him and they both walked back to the computer logbook. Johnson looked thru it, he then wrote down my information from the sign up sheet. Bill then stood there with the guard and looked around the library. He shook the guard's hand and left. I then unfolded the note that the aid left in the book. It stated that two computers were working on that day, it listed the names of the person that used each computer during the time that the message was posted on the site. One of the names was Dan Williamson. I walked to my car and was about to get in when the library aid came over and handed me my sign in sheet from the computer log. I asked her why she was giving this to me. She said, "Those men wanted to get your information so I pulled it before they could see it", I told her that I watched one of them copy my information from the book. She told me she filled out a phony name and address slip in the book. She then went to leave but I grabbed her arm and asked her why she was doing this. She looked back and smiled, "Everyone in town knows what they do, and I just know from my dreams that you are the one to stop it."

3:30 pm

I tried to call Dan but only got his voice mail. I saw Danielle and asked if she knew where he was or how I could get in touch with him. Danielle seemed more interested in why I wanted to get in touch with him then giving me any information, but before I left she told me she wasn't sure where he went. As I walked back towards my house I saw Amy in the backyard playing with her dolls. Amy was dressed like a woman in what appeared to be clothing you would see on a college student at a rave, not a 12-year-old child. I went into my kitchen and looked out at Amy in the yard as she played. I then noticed that Amy had taken all of the clothes off her dolls, it looked like a flesh colored plastic orgy. Amy looked up and saw me watching. She put one of the dolls up to her face and licked it. She then waved and smiled. I went to snap my wristband, but thought why? I sat down and called Dan again. This time I got a message that said the subscriber I was trying to reach was no longer available.

7:20 pm

I was returning from getting some dinner when I noticed the adult bookstore had reopened. I went in and saw a young little red haired girl behind the counter. She smiled then looked back at her book when I walked in, I didn't notice the book she was reading was titled, "Controlling Dreams". I browsed and made my way towards the back room. I then realized I was the only one in the store. I looked back up front and the redhead was gone. I looked up at the front door just in time to see her locking the door from the inside. Just as the key clicked in the lock I was grabbed and pulled into the back room. Henry threw me into some boxes and I fell to the floor, as I went to get up I was kicked back to the floor. I rolled over on my back and Bill Johnson was standing over me. He had his gun in his hand, "Who the fuck are you?" he quietly asked. I looked up at him, "You know me, I've been in here before". Bill then stepped on my groin and asked again who I was. I grabbed his foot to try and take some of the pressure off of me. "I don't know what you mean, my name is Joe Pratt". Henry then bent down and grabbed my wallet, "He is Joseph Pratt". Henry then grabbed Bills arm and showed him my license, "Look at the address, I knew I met this motherfucker before," he said to Bill just before he punched me, knocking me out cold.

I woke up secured naked to a chair, I was alone in the room. The little red-haired girl came back and quickly whispered in my ear that everything will be okay as long as I don't panic. I thought I am naked taped to a chair, why would I panic. She then called out, telling them that I was awake. Bill came in and sat behind a table across from me. Henry then walked up behind me and threw my prison ID onto the table. Bill grabbed it and slapped me across my face with his gun. "You're a fucking undercover pig, you are the mother fucker that tried to shut me down". I spit out the blood that was filling my mouth. "I'm not a cop, why would an undercover cop carry his police ID, I work, well I used to work at the prison." Bill looked back at the ID. Henry walked around and was looking over his shoulder, "Could be," he said. I told them to call the prison and ask for me. Bill took my cell phone and dialed the prison, he was told that I was out on a medical disability. He sat across from me at the table. He sat in silence for a while, like he was thinking about his next move. I spit some more blood on the floor and said, "You said yourself, you wont believe who buys this shit". He then told Henry to go back out front and open the store, but before Henry left Bill grabbed his arm and whispered something to him. Henry then looked at me and smiled. Bill pulled the duct tape from my feet and then sat back down putting a silencer on his weapon. Bill looked at me and said, "Joe, my dreams tell me to believe you, the day after you appeared in my dream, you walked into the store out of the blue. I let you in on what it is we had in here. The next thing I know my store is raided and I'm taken off to jail. I had to be placed into protective custody, I was labeled a child rapist and called short eyes by the other inmates. Lucky for me I have informants in the police department." Bill got up and looked out into the store. "All my dreams tell me that I can trust you and let you know that I will make one last movie. I will tell you this, doing this last movie will make millions and millions of dollars in a very short time. Just by supplying sick fucks like you young girls on DVD. My one problem is I only have one more child available to me. The children in the earlier films belong to me, some were sold by their drug addicted mothers, they were taught to think sex is part of growing up, most have been sold for sex by there parents before I got them, I cleaned them up, put them in nice homes and took care of them. I have never forced or hurt any of the children that performed for my cameras. They are all paid well, their families are paid well, and now this last film will cost noting to make, and put a ton of money in the bank." Bill then called for Henry to send in Sugar. Bill then looked back at me, "You now know more than you should, you know more then Henry, and Henry wants me to kill you. I could flip a coin, but I have a better idea." Sugar walks in the room, she is the little red head from the front desk. Bill gets up and walks up behind her. "Sugar here is 17 years old". Bill leads her to stand in front of me. Bill walks over and grabs a camera, and as he starts filming says, "If Sugar likes you, I'll let you live, if not, Henry gets to rip your heart out. And FYI, watch out, she like to bite". Sugar started to do a slow dance in front of me, she then leaned in and licked my ear, she then leaned over to the other ear, but this time she whispered, "I am 21 years old." She then stands back up and continues to dance. Bill yells, "Fuck this shit, do it." Sugar drops to her knees and lifts her shirt off, she starts to press her naked chest into my crotch. My hands are still tapped behind my back and I have no other option but to let this happen. She slowly starts to grind on me. Bill came in closer with the camera, "I can tell you like Sugar, but does Sugar like you?" Sugar then pulled a knife from her boot as she was back up in my face, she whispered again, "Just let it happen" she then reached around me and cut the tape from my wrists. Bill yelled, "Give me a money shot". Sugar stands up and lifts her skirt to reveal she is not wearing any underwear. She straddles me and starts riding me like a trained professional. As she pumped up and down

I looked into her face, she did appear to be older then 17. She kept the same look on her face the whole time she was with me, I felt like I was being judged by her, it did not feel like she was being forced to do this. I then suddenly pushed her off me and threw her over the table. Henry started to rush at me, but Bill stopped him. I was able to stand up just in time to release myself down Sugars back. I then fell to my knees and I tried to locate the knife Sugar used to cut me free. Sugar rolled off the table and bent down and kissed me on the mouth. My first intent was to push her away, the pain was so intense from being hit in the face with Bills gun. But I had to let her do what she wanted so I kissed her back and even held her after it was apparent she wanted to stop. Bill then grabbed her by her hair and pulled her up and away from me. She looked back down at me and said as she wiped my blood from her lips, "Sugar likes." She then slid her knife back into her boot. Bill ejected the disk from the camera and put it in a locked file cabinet. They both then left the room. I got up and found my clothing and pulled myself together. I went to the door and heard Henry telling Bill that just because I busted a nut, he still didn't trust me. When Henry came back into the room I asked him if I could go. Henry said, "If it was up to me you would be dead by now". I then looked up at him and said, "Dude, I pretty sure you are not in charge of shit". Henry ignored me. I then said, "Did they name her Sugar because she tastes that sweet?" Henry continued to just sit and stare at me as I tied my shoes, I then said, "What I would really like to find out is what Joy tastes like?" Henry then pushed over the table and came charging at me. Bill came in and got in the middle. Bill told Henry to lock up the store. Bill then asked me how I knew Joy. I told him Joy babysat for my neighbors kid. Bill said "Amy." I didn't answer, I went to walk around him and leave, but I then turned and asked Bill if he had Amy on DVD. I didn't know if I wanted a yes or no answer. Bill patted me on the back and told me to never come around the store again or the performance that just happened would end up on you-tube, and I would be the new short eyes at the prison. Bill then shoved me from the store and slammed the door shut.

Back inside Henry wanted to know why Bill would not let him kill me. Henry yelled at Bill telling him that I knew too much and that Bill just told me more. Henry was very argumentive with Bill. Bill then having enough shoved Henry into a chair and put the nozzle of his gun in Henrys mouth and very quietly told him, "Shut the fuck up". Henry gently pushed the gun away. Bill sat down across from Henry. Henry looked over at Bill and asked in almost a whisper, "Why?" Bill without looking up said, "He is in my dreams, he is with my brother" Henry sat at the table with a very confused look on his face, but before he could ask Bill to explain, Bill says, "I saw him kill the people that wanted to stop me in my dreams," silence filled the room until Bill said, "When my brother tells me to kill him, I will".

1-28-98/ 2:11 am

I fell into a dream, I know I'm dreaming as I am sitting on a large leather chair with my feet up on an ottoman. There is a glass of wine on the table next to me with a fly walking around on the rim. I look around and there are no windows or doors, just six walls. As I turn my head back around to face forward Sogod, Robert Johnson is sitting in front of me. He welcomes me to his home. "Trace the outline of this room," he says. "Look at the 6 walls", Sogod watched me as I again looked around, "Joe you are in my coffin with me, why did you come here?" I can't answer him, I was unable to talk. Sogod then says, "You have 14 days, I feel it in my heart that you want to give up, I can't let that happen. Amy needs you to not let that happen. I have kept you safe until now, but there are people out there that will try to stop you, but I can and have made the others doubt them" Again I try to talk, scream, I can't. Sogod gets up and walks to the head of the room. He turns and looks towards the sky and his eyes roll back, the white of his eyes fade to black. With his arms stretched out touching both sides of the room he slowly starts to raise off the floor, blood starts to run from his blacken eyes, his ears, his nose, and his mouth. Blood is dripping from his fingers. He is at least thirty yards from where I sit. I reach for my wristband, but before I can snap it. Sogod is in my face and he catches my wristband preventing me from waking myself up. "This is the only way to stop what I have started, Dan is correct, if you let her leave, she will die". He then let the band snap against my wrist.

12:30 pm

I went out to try and find if this key John sent me was going to fit any lockers at Northeastern Hospital. When I went to back out of my driveway I saw Henry sitting in a white corvette across the street. When I pulled out, I drove past his car, he didn't look up. I went to get gas first and brought a bag of candy. I waited several minutes in the Mini Mart before going back to my car. As I walked back I looked around but didn't see Henry or the white corvette. I may becoming just a little too paranoid. When I arrived at the hospital I met Danielle and Amy in the lobby. I had no excuse at all for being there and thought Danielle was going to question me about that. But Danielle appeared more concerned about hiding why she was there. I don't think she knows that I know she quit her job at the hospital. Amy was begging Danielle for some money to get some candy from the machines. I bent down and gave her the bag I brought at the Mini-Mart. When I looked up I saw Henry sitting in the white corvette in the parking lot watching me. Danielle also seen him and excused herself. I didn't ask where she was going nor did I care. I watched Danielle walk thru the lobby and saw that there were several personnel lockers on the wall. The sign said they were for electrical devices such as cell-phones that were not allowed on the hospital floors. I noticed they were out of Henrys site and I tried to fit the key into one of them but the key was way to big to fit. A staff member came over and told me that they were no longer in use and if I had a cell phone to just to turn it off. Just then I turned around and saw Henry walking into the lobby. I quickly ducked behind a counter. Henry walked quickly by, but I could tell he was looking for me. When he disappeared around a corner I quickly left the hospital, but on the way out I took a pair of pliers off of a workers cart and used them to pull two of the stems from the passengers side tires of the white corvette.

3:35 pm

I stopped at the hall of records and I used my prison ID that almost everyone mistook as a police ID to try and get the blueprints of the hospital. But the man working the counter stated I still needed to get written permission or a warrant if I wanted a copy. As I was walking back to my car a kid came running up calling me. He appeared to be familiar but I could not place him. He told me he could get me what I needed. I asked him how much. He said, "Just find out who killed my big sister." Then I realized he was Susie's brother. He told me to meet him at the fast food joint in the strip mall at 10:00 pm tonight. He then turned to go back into the building. I asked him why he thought I was trying to find out who killed Susie. He turned and said, "Because I watch you doing it every night. In my dreams."

9:30 pm

As I drove to the strip mall I kept thinking about Susie's brother and the girl at the library saying that I am in their dreams, it made me wonder if this whole town was watching me thru these cursed dreams. As I pulled around the corner I saw Henrys white corvette in the gas stations parking lot. As I drove by I saw Henry looking over at me. When he saw me looking he flipped me the bird. All I could do was smile. I pulled into the strip mall and saw that the adult bookstore was still open. I quickly drove down to meet with Susie's brother. I parked out back, out of site of the bookstore. It wasn't long until Susie's brother tapped on the window. I opened the door and he got in. He shut the door and said, "Drive". I pulled out onto the road and saw that Bill Johnson was locking up the bookstore and when he turned to look over at us, this kid hid in the passenger seat. I didn't want to look down at him, I didn't want Johnson to know anyone was in the car with me. We drove for about ten minutes in silence. This kid kept looking over his shoulder to see if we were being followed. His paranoia was making me even more paranoid. I asked him if the tube he was carrying was the blueprint. Looking straight ahead he said, "Pull into the train station parking lot. I pulled in under a lamppost, I saw that this kid looked terrified. I said, "Dude chill out, I'm not James Bond, your just going to give me some blueprints." He handed me the tube, "Pete" he said. I shook his hand and told him my name was Joe. He said, "Yea, I know". I took the tube and opened it. The tube contained the correct blueprints. Pete got even more nervous so I put them back in and closed the tube. Pete then looked around one more time. He handed me an envelope with a Post Office box number already addressed on it. "When you find out who killed my sister drop me a letter. I don't need to know how you find out, but I would like to know that whoever did this suffers a little." He then got out of the car and jogged into the train station.

11:55 pm

I pulled up to my house and looked around to see if I saw a white corvette or Henrys VW van, neither were around. There were only two familiar cars parked in the community. Danielle and Amy were pulling into their driveway just as I was getting out of my car. Amy waved and ran into her house. Danielle came over and asked if everything was okay. I said, "Sure, why do you ask?" She said because of me being at the hospital today. I lied to her and told her I had to see someone about getting back to work.

1-29-98 / 12:10 am

When I got in the house I threw the tube on the table and ran to the bathroom, I had to pee so bad I didn't even have time to turn on any lights. When I came out I saw headlights go past my front window. When I peaked out I saw that Henry was back, he was parked across the street just sitting in his car. I then went up to my bedroom and grabbed my handgun, checked to make sure it was loaded and then clipped it on the front of my pants. I then slowly pulled the closet door shut and turned the light on. I unrolled the hospital blueprints. There were two other sets of lockers. There were lockers in both employee restrooms. I had to think of a way of getting into them. I sat back in the closet and fell asleep.

2:11 am

I woke up to someone running around inside my house. I got up and turned the closet light off and peaked out.

I was able to see my bedroom door. The silence was errie. I then saw a light from a flashlight getting closer to the door. Then someone was standing in the doorway shining a light into the room. I could not make out who it was, but I was guessing Henry. After standing there for several moments he bent down and shined the light under the bed, the light was then pointed straight at me. The light was coming thru the crack in the closet door I was peaking out of. I slowly pulled my gun from its holster. Suddenly the light was gone and so was whoever was holding it. I snuck out and went to the door. I leaned around and saw the light quickly coming back at me. I lifted my gun and pointed, my finger was on the trigger. I was just about to shoot. The light fell to the floor and Amy screamed. I flipped on the hall light and saw Amy ducking on the floor. "What are you doing sneaking around in my house?" I yelled. "I almost shot you". Amy was now sitting on the floor covering her head. I sat down with her and pulled her onto my lap and stroked her hair, I told her it was all right, that she just scared me. I then lifted her face and asked in a gentler tone, "Why are you here?" Amy said, "I could not find you, I got scared". We then went to the living room and I looked out the window, Henry was still across the street and he appeared to be sleeping. I turned to tell Amy to come on that I would take her home and stay with her. But Amy wasn't in the room. I then felt her behind me as she was pressing her body up against me, her arms came around me and she was holding me in a tight bear hug. I tried to spin around, but she held on tight. I then asked her to say something, to tell me what's going on. Amy said, "I want you to hold me, I want you to teach me how to be a woman, I know you wont hurt me". Amy then let go of me. I turned around and Amy was sitting on the floor naked, she had pulled her knees up into her chest and she was rocking back and forth. I grabbed a blanket off the back of the sofa and knelt down to cover her. Amy lifted her head and said, "I am no longer scared because my dreams tell me to stay with you". I then snapped my wristband and as soon as the rubber hit my wrist there was a knock at the door. Amy jumped up and ran upstairs leaving her clothing in a pile on the floor. I still wasn't sure if I was awake or dreaming. I opened the door and Dan came in. "Is Amy over here?" he asked in a panic. I told him she was okay, that she was upstairs. I told Dan to sit down. I then grabbed Amy's clothes up off the floor and went up to get her. Halfway up the steps I heard a gunshot come from my bedroom. I ran up and saw Amy laying facedown on my bed, her right hand was still holding my smoking gun. Her face was looking away from me, I walked around the bed to see if she was shot. Dan came running in. "What did you do to my baby?" he yelled. I then looked out the window and saw Henry running towards my front door. I knelt down beside the bed, Amy eyes were closed as I reached out for her. Dan was now hysterical and he lunged at me, scratching the side of my face, telling me not to touch her. Amy opened her eyes as blood started to wet the bed sheets. Henry then came bursting into the bedroom. "You just killed all of us," he yelled as he lifted his gun from his hip and fired. I then woke up slumped in the corner of the closet. I pulled myself up and went into the bathroom. As I splashed water on my face, I noticed the water that fell from my face back into the sink had a pinkish tint to it. I looked into the mirror. I had three scratch marks on my face.

11:45 am

I woke up and really didn't want to get out of bed, I just wanted to sleep until after 2-11. I rolled over and looked at the clock and it was almost noon. I forced myself to get up and start the coffee machine. As I waited for the coffee to perk I looked out my window and I saw Danielle coming out her backdoor. She appeared to be sneaking around the back of her house. Danielle snuck to the side of her house and looked up front where Henry was still sitting in his car. I watched as she stared up at him for several minutes before returning to her back door. I didn't even drink my coffee, I put on my running clothes and grabbed my keys and went out the front door. I stretched on the pavement for a few minutes I wanted to make sure Henry saw me before I started my run up the street. I jogged up to the corner but stopped before turning, I looked back at Henry, and he didn't follow at all. I know he saw me, I made sure of that. Then I started to think Henry wasn't following me at all. Maybe he was watching Danielle and Amy, did he know Danielle was aware of his presence. I then ran up to the coffee shop and had a cup. On my run back Danielle drove past me honking her horn and waving, two cars behind her was Henry, he never took his eyes off of Danielle's car as he drove behind her.

2:25 pm

I noticed Danielle pulling into her driveway, she got out and went inside. Several moments later Henry pulled up across the street and parked, again he didn't get out. I grabbed my keys and headed back up to Northeastern Hospital. Again Henry didn't move. Once in the hospital's lobby I realized I had no idea how I was going to get into the employees restrooms. I just headed directly towards them. I came across a doctor's lab coat and quickly picked it off a hook as I walked by. I came up on the women's room first. There didn't appear to be anyone inside when I peaked in. I saw the lockers up against the wall right across from the door. No one was in the hallway so I quietly entered the room. I locked the door behind me and went to the lockers, the key I had did not fit into any of the lockers that I tried to put it in. I put the key back in my pocket and went to the door. Just as I unlocked it two female employees came in, they both appeared shocked that I was in there, I was a deer caught in the headlights. Suddenly one said, "Doctor, the men's locker room is around the corner". I said "Sorry, I should have known that I was lost when there were no urinals in the bathroom." I then went to the men's room, this was a little easier to get into. I just walked in and put the key into the first locker. It slid right in, but didn't turn, I was able to try several more lockers before employees started to come in, it must have been change of shift. Again I put the key back in my pocket and left the locker room. I sat outside and waited, but I didn't get another chance to go back in. As soon as the last man left the locker room the clean up crew went in. When they came out they locked the door. I got up and left the lab coat sitting on the bench. Just as I stood up Bill Johnson came around the corner with a Hospital employee. When he saw me he asked if everything was okay, I told him that I was fine. I noticed he was looking at the coat on the bench. Above my head was a sign that said X-Rays and had an arrow pointed in the direction that I came from. I told him I just had my hand checked out in x-ray. Bill looked at the coat, then at my hand. He then said he hopes everything turns out okay. The employee was opening the locker room door as I walked away. Bill entered the men's room and handed the man what looked like a fistful of money. Bill told him this was not all of it, and he would get the rest when the job was finished. As the employee walked down the hallway I went back and peaked in. I watched as Bill went to a locker and opened it up, he took out an old VHS tape and a large office envelope. He put the Tape under his jacket, he then opened the envelope and searched thru all the documents that were inside. He then lit them on fire and dropped it all into the toilet just before it burned his hand, he then flushed it down into the sewer. I then hid behind a corner and watched as Bill came out and walked down the hallway towards the lobby. He didn't lock the door and I was able to get back in. I put the key into the locker I watched Bill open. It was the right locker as the door sprung open. It was now empty, as Bill got to it first. I then went into the bathroom hoping I could retrieve something from the toilet, but it was all gone. Just as I was about to leave, the locker room door swung open. I hid inside the bathroom stall as Bill and Henry came in. Bill reached over and locked the door. Just as Henry tried to ask Bill what was going on, Bill grabbed him and slammed him up against the wall. Bill whispered, "What the fuck are you doing here, where is Danielle?" Bill held Henry by his neck choking him. "Don't tell me you lost them again". Henry could hardly speak, "Danielle is at the store with Joy". Bill then let go of Henry and he fell to his knees on the floor. Henry looked up at Bill and said, "What about Dan?" Bill replied as he slowly put a silencer onto the nozzle of his gun, "Dan is already dead, he just doesn't know it yet". Henry then asked Bill what it was he was doing here? Bill then pulled the tape from his jacket and said, "This tape is the only thing that could get me ass fucked everyday in prison". Bill then looked down at Henry and said, "This tape and you" as he pressed his gun into Henrys mouth and shot thru the back of his neck. As Henrys body slumped onto the floor Bill looked up as he wiped Henrys teeth and gums from the silencer, he slipped the gun back into his waistband and went and looked out the locker room door. The same hospital employee that let him in came in with a large laundry hamper. They picked up Henry and put him in the hamper, threw some sheets and towels over him. Bill then watched the door as the blood was cleaned up from the wall and floor. Bill then told the man to wait a few minutes before he took the body out. Bill then reached inside his jacket and handed the man another envelope "We were able to finish sooner then I thought," he said before he left. The man opened the envelope and I could see that it was full of cash. He then smoked a cigarette before he pushed the hamper out the door. I waited several minutes maybe an hour before I came out of the stall. When I exited the Hospital the man that pushed the hamper out held the door for me.

10:00 pm

I watched the early news to see if anything was being reported on Henry. There was nothing. I kept switching channels, maybe a body was found, something. It was like it never happened. The phone rang and scared the shit out of me. I looked at the caller ID. The call was coming from Bill Johnson's adult bookstore. I let the machine pick up.

"Joe, you there, this is Bill. Listen I know I told you to never come to the store, but I have something you will have to have". I sat there staring at the phone, his message was calm, and it was like he was talking to a friend. I went upstairs and got my gun.

11:36 pm

I stood outside the bookstore it was closed so I tapped on the glass. Bill came from the back room and opened the door. I lifted my arms for him to pat search me. He pushed my arms down and told me that wont be necessary. He then locked the door behind us and escorted me to the back room and hit play on the TV he had set up, I was hoping he was not going to show me Amy in a porno. It wasn't, it was the surveillance footage from the Hospital. I asked what this was all about? Bill didn't answer. I watched as I walked into the locker room, followed by Bill and Henry, Bill then fast-forwards to where Bill comes out followed a couple minutes later by the Hospital employee. He jumps to when I come out. Bill hits stop. "You stay in shit don't you?" I turn to see he is now holding his gun on me. Bill then asks me why I was at the Hospital, I told him that I was not sure, that I had a dream that sent me there. Bill then walks to the back of the store and unlocks the door. "Lucky for us Henry is a memory, right now he is fish food". I tried to remain calm but I could not control the sweat that was running down my back as I asked Bill why he was telling me this and what it was he expected me to do. Bill looked directly into my eyes, I was looking into the most uncaring, unsettled eyes I ever seen. Bill was so cold and uncaring, he put his hand on my shoulder and said, "Because in my dreams I am told to keep you alive, keep you close. My dreams tell me I will fail without you. In my dreams you took me to the hospital and you showed me that Henry was a snitch, I knew you were going to be there. Henry was killed because you told me to kill him". As I walked out the door Bill grabbed my arm and whispered into my ear, "I don't know why, but I feel you will help me, you will show me the ones that want to stop me, you will save me". I pulled away, I wanted to tell him he was fucking nuts but he had a bigger gun then me. As I opened the back door I asked, "In your dreams, who is it that tells you to keep me alive, and does he tell you to share any of the money with me?" Bill says as he turns and walks back to the store, "It is My Lord and savior, he is so good, he is so fine, he is Sogod", and just as he shuts the door he says, "No money".

1-30-98 / 2:11 am

I sat staring out my front window, I just didn't know what to do. Henry's body was not found, most likely it never will be. No one knows he is dead, all the other proof I could give is in my head, If I go to the police they most likely they would only care about me having sex with what could be seen as a under age girl. Bill will be clearly heard but not seen saying that Sugar was only 16, and I could barely hear Sugar tell me she was not a minor, I am sure it wasn't picked up on the tape. Plus at no time was I threatened on that tape. Maybe I could get that DVD from the store. Then I thought I should tell Danielle, but what if she is in with Johnson, she would only run and tell him, and why did Bill have Henry following her? Is that why Bill killed him? Who paid Dan to leave, knowing what I know, Dan is probably dead and buried in a shallow grave somewhere. I should just let it go and wait till 2-11 and hope it all just disappears and

313

I don't die. My head was filled with so many questions as I slowly fell asleep, and the bottle of beer in my hand fell and broke on the floor. I got up to clean up the mess. When I returned, Sogod was sitting in my chair staring out the window, looking at Danielle's house. I reached for my wristband, Sogod continued to stare out the window as he said, "That wont be necessary." Without turning around he continued, "If you give up, I will have no other option than to leave Bills dreams, and without me in his head, you will be dead before sunrise." I walked to the front of the chair and said, "I don't know what else to do, the further I get involved, the more trouble I get myself in. I find myself getting more and more confused." Sogod still just looking forward said, "Stop trying to figure out why, It will all come out in the end, 2-11 will be the day that puts this place in hell, you will see, you really have no choice but to save her, or you will die with her". I told him I didn't have a clue to what that meant and asked him to just tell me what it was that I was supposed to do, when I was supposed to do it and who it was I was going to save. I then bent down to pick up the broken glass. Sogod didn't answer me. When I looked up to demand he give me answers, he wasn't there. I then snapped my wristband, but I wasn't dreaming.

Danielle was deep into a dream, she was running around the house looking for Amy. She looked out her back door and saw Amy walking into my house. Danielle ran out and quickly walked over to my front door and walked in. She walked into the living room and approached the back of the sofa, she saw Amy as she was getting up off the sofa pulling her shirt back on. She heard Amy say, "It's a date". Amy then turned around and saw Danielle standing there. Danielle asked, "What date?" Amy then said, "Joe is going to fuck me before he kills me". Danielle woke up, her heart was pounding, she then sat up and wondered why her dreams went from me helping Amy to hurting her.

2:15 pm

I saw Amy sitting on her porch and she appeared to be cold. Against my better judgment I walked over to her. When she saw me she smiled. I asked her if she was okay. She told me that her teacher got a phone call and had to leave. When I asked her what she was doing sitting out in the cold. She stood up and wrapped herself around me. "I'm locked out, I came out to get the mail and the door shut behind me". I told her to come and sit in my house, that her mother would be home soon. Amy ran in and quickly turned on the TV and pulled a game-boy from her pocket and started playing. I went into the kitchen and made some hot chocolate. Amy sipped the drink and she got some cream on her nose. I leaned over and wiped it off with my finger. As I licked the cream from my finger Amy asked, "How many times a week do you have sex?" I told her that was not a very nice question, and that it was none of her business. Amy then said to me in between sips that she is going to do it at least twice a day. I was surprised and asked, "When you get older?" Amy put her cup down and looked over at me and said, "Pretty soon I will be old enough." I told her she was wrong, and that she had many, many years before she should even be thinking about that. Amy then reached over and put her hand on my leg, "Maybe you can show me, I know you will be nice". I pushed her hand away and stood up snapping my wristband. "Amy this behavior must stop and if it don't I will have to tell your mother." Amy's eyes started to swell with tears, "I'm sorry, I thought this is what you wanted" I sat down and hugged her, "In ten years Amy you will be so thankful that we didn't". Amy then looked up and asked, "In ten years if I still want to, can I ask again?" I looked into her eyes, as she appeared to want me to want her, to reassure that I will still be here in ten years, I told her "Sure, we will make it a date". She reached up and kissed me on the cheek and said "It's a date then". Danielle then walked in and freaked out, "What's a date?" Amy jumped up and said, "Me and Joe set a date in ten years". Amy noticing that Danielle was mad then grabbed Danielle's keys and headed out the front door. Danielle stood there, "What just happened in here?" I told her Amy was growing up pretty fast and she wanted a date with me, so I told her to call me in ten years. I expected Danielle to laugh, or at least smile, but Danielle's mood became more defensive, "What kind of date? Don't be putting thoughts into Amy's head, she is still just a kid," she scolded as she turned to walk out. I jumped up, "Amy started this conversation, Amy has been acting like a 25 year old stoned on ecstasy all of a sudden with talk of sex and she is not getting those thoughts from me". Danielle quickly turned around, "How dare you think this is my fault, If anything, she saw sex watching your porno's". I then told Danielle I didn't think it was her fault that Amy was acting this way, but she has to be getting it from somewhere. Danielle appeared to want to tell me something, or scream at me, but she did neither, she just turned and walked towards the door in a huff. As she opened the door I yelled, "Maybe I'll go over to Bill's bookstore and grab another movie". Danielle turned and quickly walked back up on me, she was pretty close to my face. Her face was calm but she had a lot of anger in her eyes, "Stay away from that fucking store" she said as she gently grabbed my collar, "And stay the fuck away from Amy". She then pushed me away from her, "THEN HOW WILL I SAVE HER?" I yelled. Danielle stopped for a few seconds then left without shutting my door.

1-31-98 / 2:11 am

I drank myself into a drunken stupor and fell asleep at the kitchen table. I woke up when Amy came in my back door. She sat down at the table across from me. She appeared to be in a very agitated state. When I asked her what was wrong she told me that her mother went out and left her home alone again. We sat at the table and talked for over an hour, Amy was getting tired and could hardly hold her head up. I told her to go upstairs and lay down. Amy got up walked over to me and took my hand and we went up to the spare bedroom. She kicked off her shoes and crawled into bed. I pulled the sheet up and tucked it under her. I stood there and watched her sleep for several moments. She looked like a little angel. I then bent down brushed the hair from her face and gave her a little kiss on the forehead. When I stood back up, Susie startled me as she was standing at the foot of the bed. Susie looked at me and said, "Dude, go ahead, you know you want to".

I said, "Excuse me." Susie walked over to me and put her arm around my waist and said as she slowly started to pull the sheet from Amy " She is sound asleep, touch her". As Susie continued to pull the sheet I saw that Amy was lying on her side with her back to us, still sleeping. Susie sat on the bed and placed her hand on Amy's hip, Amy didn't move. I grabbed Susie by her arm and stood her up. Susie then stood behind me and wrapped her arms around my waist, "Go ahead dude" She whispered as she gently bit at my ear. "You know this is a dream, no one can get in any trouble", Susie then tried to guide me towards the bed, I could feel her breath on my neck. I looked down at Amy as she rolled over and sat up on the edge of the bed. She reached out and started to unbutton my shirt, I didn't protest, but I wanted to. Amy got up on her knees on the bed and was face to face with me, she slowly leaned in past my head and kissed Susie. I grabbed Amy by her shoulders and gently pushed her down on the bed and told her to go back to sleep. I turned and grabbed Susie and shook her, as I demanded that she tell me who killed her. Susie looked right thru me, she walked around me like I wasn't there and stood by the bed and lifted her dress off over her head before she laid down next to Amy on the bed. I reached for my wristband. Susie saw this and said, "Dude, both of us, it's a dream come true" She then pulled the sheet up to cover them "If you don't show her, someone else will". I let the band snap. I woke up and almost fell out of the kitchen chair.

10:55 pm

I decided to review all the information I had entered into a log on the computer. There may be something I missed, but nothing jumped out at me. Then I saw the name Timmy Johnson. I had logged this name from the paperwork I had found. I decided to go to the Hall of Records in town to see if I could find any info on little Timmy.

12:35 pm

I checked all avenues at the Hall of Records, Birth records, Death records, Hospital reports, even name changes and could not find any mention of a Timmy Johnson in Buffalo. I was about to give up, and then I decided to look in the archives. I found a story that was published in the Buffalo Times in February of 87. It was about the body of a baby boy that was discovered just off the grounds of Northeastern Hospital. The story said the body was discovered when a construction crew that was digging a trench for the Hospitals expansion project found a small coffin. The baby was only several days old. It didn't list a name or cause of death, but did say tests showed he was a twin. Directly under that story was the birth announcements, the first boasted of a baby girl being born to Judy Johnson, the article didn't list the fathers name, nor did it list the baby girls name. It made me think, Dan told me that Judy gave birth to a boy that died. Did Judy actually give birth to Timmy and when he died, someone replaced Timmy with Amy? Then how did Amy end up with Danielle?

6:10 pm

When I got back home there was a note taped to my door from Danielle. It was a computer-generated note. When I opened it, inside it said:

"SORRY"
I was quite the bitch last night
I am a little stressed out
Call me.
Love Danielle.

    I folded it back up and threw it on the table. I looked over and didn't see Danielle's car in the driveway. But before I let the curtain fall shut I thought I saw Amy run past the kitchen window, I quickly pulled the curtain back up, but didn't see any more movement in the house. When I sat down in the living room I sat on Amy's gameboy that she must of left here last night. I then decided this gave me a reason to go over. When I knocked on the front door I could hear people jumping and fumbling around. I knocked again and Amy yelled, "Just a minute" As I waited I leaned over to look in the window. I was able to catch what looked like someone running up the steps. Amy then opened the door in her pajamas. She appeared to be out of breath. I asked her if she was all right. Amy smiled, "Just exercising, Danielle is not home". I looked at her and asked, "Danielle's not home?" Amy said as she rolled her eyes, "Sorry, My Mom is not home". She then stared up at me smiling. I pulled out her game-boy and said, "You left this at my house last night." Amy thanked me as she took the game-boy from my hand. Amy still seemed very uneasy as she kept looking over her shoulder. I leaned in to give her a hug and whispered in her ear, "Are you sure you are okay". Before she could answer Joy pulled the door open the rest of the way and rubbed the top of Amy's head. Joy then grabbed me and gave me a big hug, "It's been a while," she said. As she hugged me I could see what looked like sleeping bags laid out on the floor in the living room and the coffee table was pushed up against the wall. Joy then released me and asked, "What's up?" Amy showed her the game-boy and said almost apologetic, "Joe brought my game over". Joy then said, "Cool, lets go play it". Amy then ran back inside. Joy, holding my wrist tight asked, "Is there anything else?" I took a step back, "No, nothing else, I'm good". Joy sucked her finger and said as she closed the door, "I bet you are, I just bet you are".

8:00 pm

I received a call from Joy, she said that Amy was requesting that I come over and join them in game night. I told her that I was tired and I was going to go to bed early. Joy then put Amy on the phone and Amy complained that it wasn't any fun playing games with just two people. I told Amy when her mother returned she would play. Amy said her mother would not be home until tomorrow and insisted that I come over. I told her I would think about it, all I heard as I hung up the phone was, "please, please, please, please." I looked over at Danielle's, and then decided to go and join them. Amy opened the door and quickly pulled me into the house. "Take your shoes off, we're going to play twister." Joy came in from the kitchen with beers, "No twister yet" she said as she handed me a beer. We sat around the kitchen table and played board games. Amy was fighting to keep her eyes open, when Joy noticed she said, "I guess this is why they are called BOARD games". She then told Amy to go to bed, Amy protested and wined she wanted to play twister. Joy told her that they would play tomorrow as she patted Amy's butt on her way upstairs. I grabbed my coat as Joy came back downstairs, she walked over and put her hands on my shoulders and pushed my coat off. She was extremely close, she then said as she looked into my eyes, "We can still play twister" She then kissed me. I then reached for my wristband as Joy pulled the game from under the sofa with her foot. "Lets make it interesting" she said to me with an evil smile creeping across her face. "How's that?" I asked. She then looked up the bedroom stairs and pulled her top off as she said, "Lets play naked twister". I grabbed her and pulled her in for another kiss. After the embrace,

"I asked who's going to spin. She then reached down took my hand and started to lead me towards the stairs. "You'll spin, I promise you, you will spin," she said as she lead me to the spare bedroom.

1-1-98 / 2:11 am

I woke up next to Joy in Danielle's spare bedroom and reached for my pants on the floor. Joy woke up and pulled me back into the bed. "That was wonderful," she said as she stroked my chest. "Its late, I have to get home." Joy appeared to be insulted, and I tried to explain that the last thing I needed was for Danielle to catch us together in her house. Joy then asked if I was dating Danielle. "No, its just, well, I would not want to come home and find anyone fucking in my spare bedroom". Joy then reached down and grabbed me by the short hairs and said, "What we did was not FUCKING, we made love". I gently removed her hand from me and kissed her palm, "Sorry, but I didn't mean us" Joy then rolled over on top of me, her hair falling on my face. "How old are you?" she asked. "30" I lied, I am actually 38. She leaned in and kissed me, "I just turned 22, so you're old enough to be my father". I held her face, "I could be your older brother, but not your father, who gives birth at 8?" Joy just made a face like she was doing the math and then questioned, "I know you will have sex with a 22 year old, me, what's your cut off age, youngest and oldest?" she then leaned on her elbows on my chest and waited for me to answer. I looked up at her and said, "I never thought about it, as long as I am attracted to a woman, age really don't matter". Joy now started to slowly grind her hips on mine says, "So if you saw an attractive ten year old, you'd do her". I told her there is no such thing as an attractive ten year old. Joy was now sliding down onto me, we were about to make love again, Joy started out slow and gentle, she then became violent, bucking back and forth bringing me to completion. She then collapsed on top of me, both of us sweating, and exhausted, Joy then took a playful bite at my ear and asked in a whisper, "How old did they tell you Sugar was?" Joy then rolled off of me as I asked, "Who is Sugar?" Joy turns her head and strokes my face, "You're joking, how can you forget your first underage blowjob". I stared up at the ceiling wondering if Sugar was really underage, or that Joy doesn't know. Joy then turned my face to look at her as she said, "Since Susie is no longer working, Sugar is the last of the best underage pros around, I taught her myself, want to see" Joy then tried to go down on me. I grabbed her and pulled her up. She complained that I was hurting her arms. "Sugar was a mistake", I told her, "I wasn't given a choice". Joy pulled away, "Why you getting so bent out of shape, I did 50 year old guys when I was 16, I don't judge, I was hoping that someday the three of us could play naked twister together. I just lay there silent, ashamed, embarrassed and a little confused. Joy got up, "You're starting to bring me down," she said as she walked into the bathroom. I rolled over on my side just looking out the bedroom window, I was too tired to get dressed, let alone get up. I then started to think that Sugar may have been underage, then why did she tell me she was 20, then I thought that Joy might run back to Bill and tell him that I wasn't into Sugar and that could make Bill not be so trusting. I was just about to fall asleep when I heard Joy come back in the room. I didn't even turn to look at her. She got back into bed and spooned me from behind, "Sorry she whispered, I won't bring Sugar up ever again," She said as she reached over and gently hugged me. Half asleep, I was too tired to protest, but I did say, "Sugar really wasn't a mistake, it is just that I was embarrassed". Joy didn't respond she just occasionally kissed the back of my neck and tried to reach down and grab me. When she couldn't reach she adjusted herself and was about to grab hold when I realized that Joy was as tall if not taller then me, she should not have a problem reaching over me. Just as she was about to grab hold, I slowly opened my eyes and saw Joy standing at the side of the bed, I then rolled over and came face to face with Amy who was still reaching for me. I quickly reached down and snapped my wristband. I woke up in the same bedroom just as Joy came back in from the bathroom,

"What's wrong with you now, you still mad about the Sugar comment?" I didn't answer, Joy then told me to leave. I slowly got up and watched as Joy got back in bed, turned her back to me and pulled the sheet up to cover herself. I then bent down and kissed the back of her head and told her that naked twister threesome with Sugar might not be that bad of an idea.

1:30 am

When I got back to my house I realized that I had left my wallet over at Danielle's, I would not be able to explain to Danielle how I left it in her spare bedroom and so I went back over to get it. The front door wasn't locked and I slowly walked up to the spare bedroom. As I approached I could hear Joy on the phone. I stood outside the door and listened, "I don't think he is the one for her", I could hear whomever she was talking to yelling on the other end, but I could not understand what was being said. Joy then said, "I just don't think he would do it". Then silence, I peaked in and saw Joy was still on the phone and she had a confused look on her face, like she didn't understand what she was being told. Several times she tried to say something, but was cut off and she just listened. Joy then said, "Okay, okay, I will see what I can do, but you do realize your whole plan is coming from your fucking dreams, what if he runs to the cops" Again I could hear hollering coming from the phone. I peaked in again and saw that Joy was holding the phone away from her ear. When the yelling stopped Joy put the phone back up to her face and said, "He told me that he wasn't dating Danielle, he left about an hour ago". Silence again as Joy listened. Then before she hung up she said, "Just because he agreed in your dream doesn't mean he will in real life." She then said, "What time will you get here tomorrow?" She then hung up. I leaned up against the wall. I didn't know, but I was guessing that she was talking to Bill about me. I was sort of relived that she didn't mention my comments about Sugar to whomever she was talking to. I walked back to the top of the steps and called for Joy. She came and stood in the bedroom doorway, "Joe, what are you doing back here?" she asked. I told her my wallet must of fell out of my pants. Joy turned the bedroom light on and my wallet was lying on the floor by the bed. She bent down and picked it up, "Did you leave this here so you would have a reason to come back?" she asked as she handed it to me. I knew she was just told to try and get me to do something and I wanted to stay to find out what that was. I looked back at her and asked, "Did you want me to come back?" Joy opened her robe and let it drop to the floor. I snapped my wristband. I wasn't dreaming, but I was in a dream.

7:15 am

I woke up again in Danielle's house. Joy was not in the bed. My clothes were folded and sitting on a chair with my wallet on top. I was upset that I didn't have a chance last night to find out what Joy wanted me to do. I was just about to throw the sheet off of me when Amy came in and crawled up on the bed next to me. She propped herself up on the pillows and asked if I liked Joy. I told her we were friends. Amy smiled and asked me if she was my friend. I leaned over and kissed her nose, "Yes we are, we are like best friends". Amy then said, "If we are best friends, then I don't want you to have sex with Joy again". Before I could say anything Joy came in the room and got in the bed on the other side of me. Joy looked over at Amy and told her not to be so jealous and that she would soon have her turn. Surprised, I turned and looked at Joy, She said, "Yea, I heard about your date in ten years". Joy then reached in under the sheet and did a reach around and grabbed me. Amy also pulled in and hugged me. I whispered to Joy that I was naked and very uncomfortable. Joy let go of me, calling me a prude as she got up letting the sheet fall, almost exposing my naked body to Amy. Amy stuck her tongue out at Joy as she left the room. After Joy shut the bedroom door Amy turned to me and said, "You are my best friend too," and gave me a hug. Amy then started to gently kiss my neck. I gently pushed her away and told her that I had to get dressed. Amy got up and went into the bathroom. As I stood up to put my pants on I saw Amy's reflection in the mirror as she was standing in the bathroom door watching me as I got dressed. I pulled on my pants and sat down on the bed. I snapped my wristband. I wasn't dreaming.

8:30 pm

I decided to just stay in, stay away from Danielle, Amy, Joy, and the world. Then I received a call from a person that stated he was a Special Agent with the Witness Protection Agency. He told me he needed to speak with me, but not on the phone, he asked if I could meet him. He gave me the location and told me to be there in an hour. I went on the Internet and looked up the address he gave me. It was an isolated stretch of road just outside of town. I was beginning to think this was some sort of set up. All I could think was that Joy said something to Bill and he was going to have me killed.

Then I started to think maybe they were trying to find out if Danielle and Amy told me anything about leaving. Then again it could be legit. I swallowed several aspirins, grabbed my gun and headed out the door.

10:15 pm

As I pulled up to the address I saw it was an old abandoned gas station. I pulled in and drove around back and noticed a black SUV with tinted windows, it flashed its lights. I felt my hip to make sure my gun was still there as I pulled up next to it. A big man in a dark suit got out and walked up to my window. "Joe?" he asked. With my hand on my gun I shook my head yes. He reached down and opened my door. I slowly got out as he gestured that I get in the back of the SUV. I looked around and saw two other people hiding in the brush behind the gas station. "Who are they?" I asked. He put his hand on my shoulder to guide me towards the SUV, "They are hear to keep us safe". When the SUV door opened, I saw two men I never seen before sitting in the back. I was then frisked and the big guy took my gun and put it in his waistband. The big guy stayed outside and stood by the SUV after shutting the door. I sat in the back seat across from the other two men. When I looked over at them they flipped open their ID wallets and showed me that they were WPA agents. "What's up?" I asked. One agent, Henderson, told me that the Miami DEA had completed a drug sweep of one of the biggest drug gangs in South Florida. One of the people picked up was a Randy Wilson. I shook my head and told them that I had no idea who Randy Wilson was. They slid a photo over to me, when I looked at it, I saw a photo of Dan. I said, "This is Dan, Dan Williamson." Henderson took the photo back and his partner said that this might be why he was not on any gang lists. Henderson than said that he was not seen in any of the video of the drug gangs under surveillance either. I watched them as they whispered to each other, I was wondering why they didn't fingerprint him. Henderson then slid the photo into an envelope and told me that Dan had told them a story about child pornography in an attempt to get a lighter sentence. I then asked why the Witness Protection Agency was involved. Then other man, Agent Witcher reached into a bag and pulled out some photos, "Whoever this guy is, he is a smart man, but a dumb criminal," he said. The first photo were mug shots of Bill and Robert Johnson. "He told us these two have been generating child pornography for years out of a small adult book store not far from here, and that they own every house in a secluded gated street, they used to use those house as sets for their films. He then said that all who live in that community are involved. I pointed to Robert Johnson and thought that they should know this, but I said it to them anyway, "This guy is dead". I was then shown a photo of myself coming from the bookstore. I was asked to explain what it was I was doing in the store. "I brought a DVD, millions are sold every day, that is not a crime is it?" Officer Henderson then leaned over and put his hand on my leg, "Dan or Randy has told us, if anyone could prove his story it would be you". I could now see Officer Henderson's gun under his suit jacket. It was not a government issued gun and the serial number on the bottom of the handle was scratched off. I looked out the window and saw the other three men standing together smoking cigarettes. I could tell these guys were not professionals, I knew they were not who they said they were. "I looked back at the two sitting across from me, "I really don't have a clue as to what it is Dan is talking about. I have been in that store several times and not once have I come across any child sex tapes. I do know Dan and I believe he would do and say anything to save his own ass". Henderson then asked, "Why would he pick this store, these people?" I told them he must have seen the coverage of the police raid on the store and he is playing you guys off that, blowing smoke up your ass. They asked me more questions that seemed either irrelevant to the subject or questions that if they were who they said they were, they would have already known the answers. Henderson finally gave me his card and told me to call if I wanted to talk. I sat in my car and watched them as they drove away. I don't know who they were, but I was sure they weren't Witness Protection, DEA or FBI. I know if Dan were arrested, even under another name, these people would have known, they would see his upcoming trial on possession of child pornography. Dan would have told them about his dreams like he did in the county jail, he would have told them about Danielle and Amy. These guys didn't mention either of them in there questioning. I believe these guys were working for Bill and they were trying to see if I would talk. I looked at the card as I flipped open my phone and called my friend Officer Franks at the prison. "I need another location on a number." I told him the number as I sat in my car and asked that this be kept between us. He told me he would call me back on a secure line.

1-1-98 / 12:30 am

When I got home I realized I never got my gun back. I thought I'd call the number on the card in the morning and ask for it. I grabbed a beer and sat in the dark. Maybe John was right, maybe I should just move.

2:11 am

I woke up to Amy knocking on my back door. I asked her what was wrong when I let her in. Amy told me she was playing hide and seek with Joy. I looked at the clock and told her it was two in the morning. Joy poked her head out of Danielle's back door. Amy quickly ducked down from the window. I said out loud to myself, "I don't have time for this shit", and when Joy looked over I waved and pointed down. Joy got upset and went back inside slamming the door shut behind her. Then it dawned on me, Joy must of thought I was pointing at my crotch. I

bent down and grabbed Amy's hand and stood her up. I
opened the door and told her that she had to go home.
Before Amy could leave we saw Joy pull out of the driveway
and speed up the road. We just both looked at each other.
Amy said, "Where the hell does she think I am hiding?" I
smiled at her and asked her if her mother was home. Amy
just laughed and said, "We are home". I turned around
and we were in Danielle's house. Amy ran into the living
room as I looked to make sure I had my wristband on.
When I walked into the living room Amy was setting up
the Twister game in the middle of the floor. Joy and Susie
were sitting up on the back of the sofa. I looked around
the room and every mirror was covered with a black cloth.
Joy got up and handed me the spinner and said, "You got
winner." Joy then ran to the Twister mat. Both Joy and
Susie were wearing only robes, I watched as they untied
their robes, letting them fall open. Bill walked up behind
me, "They are waiting for the first spin," he said softly as
he held a video camera on the girls. I just stood there, I
could not move, I refused to play, I looked at Amy as she
sat on the floor, she appeared to be waiting for me to spin.
Joy yelled at Bill as she pulled her robe shut and started to
tie it, "See I told you this would not work". Bill reached
over my shoulder and spun the spinner, "Susie, left hand
red" he said as he put his camera on a tripod. Susie then
slowly bent down to touch a red circle with her right
hand. I smiled at Amy as she looked up at me from the
side of the game. "That's the wrong hand dumb ass," Bill

said to Susie. I then slowly reached for my wristband. Bill put his hand over the band and said, "I know you want to play, and you know you want to play". Tears started to well up in my eyes. Bill spun again, "Joy, right foot blue". I looked over at Joy as she dropped her robe, I wanted to run, but I couldn't. I tried to snap my wristband, but I couldn't. Then I thought, what if this is also Bill's dream, what if Bill is seeing this. Joy got fed up with the time between spins and got up and told Amy to take her place, Joy walked over to me started to gently kiss my face and neck as Amy jumped up eager to play. Bill grabbed Amy as she started to remove her shirt and told her that she was just here to watch. Amy's smile left her face and she sat back down with a thud. Joy then led me to the game as Bill took the spinner and kept spinning. Susie was bent over on the mat, her ass pointing up. Bill yelled, "Joe, right foot green." As Joy pushed me down and I fell onto Susie. Joy sat down next to Amy and whispered something in her ear. Amy's face became darker and said, "I have been waiting for this to happen, but with me". I was jerked awake by the phone. I let it ring. I could not stop shaking.

8:55 am

I woke up feeling very uneasy and depressed. I felt vulnerable, alone. I made coffee then sat at the kitchen table and stared at the cup until it was too cold to drink.

The ringing phone brought me into a little reality. I let the machine pick up. It was Officer Franks from the prison, he started to leave a message but I quickly picked up. Officer Franks told me the number I gave him was traced back to a cell phone. I told him that didn't help me. Franks then said, "Cheer up, the cell phone was purchased by a William Johnson, he then gave me Johnson's address. It was not the house that I had seen him in around the corner from the bookstore, it was in a different part of town. Franks then asked if that was enough. I just hung up, I didn't answer him. I picked the card up off the table, "Fuck me". This has to be the same Bill Johnson.

12:15 am

I drove out to the address Officer Franks gave me. It was over a hundred miles outside of town. As I approached the address the houses got bigger and bigger. 6289 was the address. I was in awe as I sat outside a gated mansion. The address label above the secured gate was 6289. I could see several landscapers riding mowers over the vast lawn, one of the mowers engines kept stuttering. Then a man walking his dog asked if I was looking to buy. I pointed to the house and asked, "This house is up for sale?" The man told me it went on the market several days ago. I asked if it was his. He laughed, "God no", he said. "That belongs to Bill and Danielle Johnson". I was in shock and asked, "Did Bill marry a young girl?" Again he laughed, "No,

Danielle is his daughter". His dog then started to pull, he waved and said, "If you got an extra 3 million laying around, snap it up".

2:40 pm

As I drove back home, even tho I suspected it, I could not believe Bill was Danielle's father. I opened my cell phone and called the number on the card. It rang several times before a woman picked up, "How may I direct your call". I asked for Agent Henderson and I was put on hold. Several moments later Agent Henderson came on the line. I told him that he still had my weapon. He seemed honestly disappointed that I didn't call with information. He then told me that my weapon was being checked against any unsolved crimes and that it would be returned as soon as it clears. I knew I would never see that gun again. Before he hung up I heard the stuttering lawnmower in the background. The same one I heard while parked outside of 6289.

10:50 pm

I sat in front of my computer, I had so many theories going thru my head, all of them came back to Amy being set up, prepared, taught, whatever they wanted to call it to be some type of sex slave or porno kid. Was Amy about to become the next Susie or Sugar? Did Dan know? Was he paid to leave? Does Danielle know? Is that why she is leaving town, to keep them from using Amy? As much as I didn't want to do it, I had to find Danielle and find out what was going on. Only problem was Danielle hasn't been home in days, I know she wasn't relocated anywhere because Amy is still at the house with Joy. Then I thought maybe Johnson got rid of Danielle.

1-1-98 / 2:11 am

I dreamt about Sogod again. We were both back in his coffin. He told me to see whose seeing what I'm seeing. I really got to tell this guy that just when I think I am about to figure this shit out he plays these riddles that fuck me up more. I asked him to be clearer and to just tell me what to do. Johnson then screamed, "SAVE HER". I felt the spit from his scream hit my face. "Save who?" I asked. Sogod now calm puts his hand on my shoulder. "Joe, stop trying to figure out what or why, just save her". As he said that a look of terror came across his face, he then tensed up and told me not to let them leave. I walked towards him, "I can't stop them from leaving. " Sogod held out his hands and said, "They can't leave, he wont let them." As I was now becoming more confused, Sogod slowly shut his eyes and held his hands up towards the ceiling. The room started to shake and cracks started to appear on the ceiling letting sunlight shine thru. I looked at Johnson as he fell

to his knees, the roof was being ripped off. Then just as
the ceiling gave way and came crashing down, Johnson
let out a scream, as his body transformed from the inside
out into thousands, maybe millions of flies, the flies took
the shape of Johnson as he stood back up, then they flew
apart and left thru the hole in the ceiling. I didn't snap
my wristband, I knew I had to be dreaming. I just laid
down on the floor and fell asleep.

As I was dreaming about Sogod again, Dan was
having his own nightmare. Dan was standing in my yard,
he was confused as to why he was there. Suddenly Amy
yelled from the car for him to hurry up. Dan turned and
saw Amy sitting in the back seat of his car, Dan got in
the car and they drove away. Dan drove as Amy slept in
the back seat, Amy woke up when he pulled into a water
park. Dan had a strange feeling about himself. He could
sense that Amy was distant from him, almost like she
didn't even know who he was. As Amy ran into the wave
pool, Dan then had to hide behind a game booth when
he saw Danielle, and Joy walking around the park. Dan
hid in the shadows as he watched the two of them stop
just feet from him, Danielle asked, "Where the fuck are
they?" Both stood looking around before Joy asked, "This
is where he told you to meet him". Suddenly Amy came
running over and gave Danielle a big wet hug. "Did you
see your father?" Danielle asked as the hug parted. Amy
shook her head no. Danielle then became nervous and
said as she wrapped a towel around Amy's shoulders, "We

have to find your father". Bill then walked up on them and said, "Why, are you three going somewhere?" Amy wiping the water from her hair looked up at Bill and said, "I am going to live with my Dad". Danielle turned white as Bill grabbed her by her arms and pulled her in close. He whispered softly to her, "I told you what would happen if you tried to leave". Danielle was almost hysterical, "That's not what she meant to say," Danielle cried, "She was mistaken, she is going to live with her father after." Bill without letting his grip go from Danielle's arms, told two other men to go and find Dan. Bill then pulled Danielle in for a kiss as Joy plunged a knife into Danielle's side. Her eyes opened wide as the pain reached her brain, just as she went to scream Bill kissed her again and pulled the knife up her side and across her chest. Danielle fell silent to the ground as Amy ran to her. Bill then grabbed Amy by her hair and pulled her head back. As Amy looked up at him, Bill started to slide the knife across Amy's neck. Dan then woke up in a panic, slowly realizing it was a dream he called Danielle.

3:30 am

I woke up on the floor next to my bed. I snapped my wristband to make sure I wasn't going to pull myself up and find naked teenagers in my bed. I went downstairs to get a beer. I had a message on the phone. I pressed play as I opened the fridge door. "Joe, its Danielle we need to talk, I need you to get Amy out of the house. I'll call you tomorrow and let you know where and when we can meet. Please bring Amy with you". She sounded scared, but at the same time it sounded like she was reading from a script. I looked at my machine and the address tag listed the call as unknown. Nothing I could do until she calls me back. So I guzzled my beer, put my index finger in my mouth and simulated blowing my brains out before I laid back down on the sofa and turned on the TV. I watched the news, the big story was how the Yankees are buying every free agent on the market. Then a story came on about a graveyard that was vandalized overnight. Headstones were turned over, and graffiti was painted and several graves were dug up. They showed workers and police swatting at flies at one of the graves, I knew this graveyard, Sogod was buried there. Was that what happened in my dream? Did someone dig him up last night? I was too tired to check it out and I soon fell back to sleep.

7:30 am

I woke up when Danielle called back. She sounded a lot calmer. I asked if everything was okay. She reassured me that she was fine. She then told me that she had called Joy and told her that I was going to take Amy out today. Danielle then told me to bring Amy to the indoor water park up the turnpike. I'll meet you there at noon by the front entrance. Danielle then hung up. Just then Amy and Joy came in thru the back door. Amy was carrying a backpack and a towel. Joy looked at me in my pajamas and asked if this is what I was wearing. I told them to have a seat and I went upstairs and changed. I grabbed my bathing suit and grabbed a towel, I then wished I still had my gun. As Amy pulled me towards the door I Asked Joy if she wanted to join us. Amy almost crushed my fingers as she squeezed my hand, I pulled away as Amy gave me a dirty look. Joy declined the invitation saying this was her first day off in a long time and that she was going to enjoy it. She gave Amy a kiss on the cheek and then slid her tongue into my mouth as she grabbed my ass. This also seemed to anger Amy who pulled me harder towards my car.

On the ride to the water park Amy fell asleep in the backseat. When I pulled into get gas I reached over and opened her backpack. She had a bathing suit, some toiletries, and then I noticed a mini tape recorder and a bag of pills. Amy woke up just as I flipped the pack shut. I then realized I still had the tape recorder in my hand so I quickly shoved it into my pocket as Amy wiped her eyes. Amy then jumped out of the car and said she needed to use the bathroom. I then opened the bag of pills but I could not ID any of them. Amy was coming back so I threw them back in her bag. As we drove up the turnpike I asked Amy what she had in her backpack. She said, "My bathing suit and stuff". I asked "What kind of stuff?"

She opened the pack and started going thru it, "Some cream for my hands, toothpaste", she then grabbed the pills and held them up, "I don't know what these are," she said as she shook the bag, "Maybe aspirin." I took them and sat them on the dash. Amy then said she wanted to change into her bathing suit. I told her to wait, that we were almost there. Amy then climbed into the back of the car. I watched her in the mirror as she just stared out the back window. I picked the bag of pills up and tried again to see if I ever seen any before, none of them had any markings on them. I felt Amy moving around in the back and I looked in the mirror but I could not see what she was doing. I adjusted the mirror and saw that Amy was changing into her bathing suit. She seemed to be having trouble tying her bikini top. She then caught me looking at her in the mirror and giggled. I flipped the mirror back up and said, "I thought I told you to wait". She said sorry as she continued to giggle. I waited several moments and then I told her to get back up front with me. Amy then climbed up clutching her top to her chest, she turned her back towards me and asked me to tie it, and when I told her to wait until we hit a red-light, she kept saying, "Tie it, tie it, tie it." I had to pull over and tie her top. Then once we pulled back on to the road, she started with the, "Are we three yet" brain cell killer until she finally fell asleep. We had to travel about twenty more miles once we got off the turnpike. Danielle had told me to take a shortcut that would save us some time. The shortcut was a winding road that was a little scary, it went up a mountain and in several spots the guardrails were old rotted wood, there were also stretches of road where there were no guardrails at all.

11:20 am

We were standing in the lobby of the park. Danielle wasn't anywhere around. I really wasn't looking for her, I was looking for other people that may be watching Amy and I. Danielle snuck up behind me and handed me tickets to the park. She put her arm around me as we walked in, we looked like every other couple in the park. Amy ran ahead and yelled that she was going in the wave pool. Danielle took me to the hot tubs that were set back by the wave pool. There were several other people in the tub as we sat down. A horn sounded alerting the swimmers that the waves were about to begin. All the kids in the hot tubs jumped out and ran to the wave pool. As the waves started, the remaining adults got out to watch their kids. Danielle and I sat in the tub alone. She slid over next to me. "Amy wont be leaving with me," she said. I asked her if she meant when she relocates, or leaves the park. She smiled and said, "I will probably leave with Dan, we just can't take her with us, at least not now". Danielle then told me that at first, she was hoping that to let Amy leave with Dan. I didn't say anything, I just sat and watched the crowd. Danielle reached over and turned my face to look at her, "When I leave, they will come looking for me, they will think I have Amy." I was still confused. Danielle then said, "If I take Amy and they find me they find Amy, if she is not with me, they don't." I asked who they were. She told me that the less I know the safer I would be. Two kids walked up and were about to get in the tub. Danielle grabbed me and started to kiss me open mouth as she rubbed her hands on my back and chest. One of the kids said "Gross, get a room" as they left. Danielle stopped. She looked at me and said she didn't want to leave without saying goodbye. She then went to get out, I grabbed her arm and asked, "You said you were going to let Amy leave with Dan, so is she?" Danielle stood in the tub and told me that Dan was supposed to meet her here and that he was going to take Amy away with him. I then asked her, "Where was he going to take her?" Danielle sat back down and changed the subject as she asked me if I knew Bill. "We go way back". I said, "He got me laid and then threatened to kill me". Danielle got scared and appeared to be looking thru the crowd. "Are you looking for Dan?" I asked, "Dose he still think Amy is leaving with him?" Danielle continued to search the crowd. She then looked at me and said, "Dan will understand, I can't find Amy." I pointed to Amy and told Danielle that she has been sitting on a beach chair in front of the wave pool. Danielle looked back at me with fear in her eyes, "Bill will do anything to keep Amy here, I should not have asked you to bring her here, this may be a mistake," I asked her what was a mistake. Danielle said she should have come here alone to tell Dan, she then said that she had to go back, and that she has to take Amy back and do what he wants. I asked her what it was that Bill wants? "He would not hurt his own granddaughter?" Danielle put her hands over her face. "What would make you think Bill is Amy's grandfather?" I pulled Danielle's hands from her face as I said, "I did only think she was, now I know." Danielle was getting more and more paranoid and told me, "People who have known less have been killed". I held Danielle's hand, "Bill told me I am in his dreams, that I am the man that helps him but he wont tell me what it is that I help him with or how I help him." Danielle interrupted me, "That is his brother Robert, Sogod, he is controlling Bill thru his dreams, I think they dug his body up last night." I then took both of Danielle's hands and kissed her fingers, "If taking Amy away will keep her safe from Bill then let her and Dan leave now". Danielle started to cry, "If I do that Bill will kill all of us". She then got out and stood outside the tub. She looked back and said, "I don't know what to do. I want to believe that you will save her, but I feel you may also cause her harm." I held her wrist and said, "Stop believing what you see while you sleep, you said it yourself that Robert is controlling all of this, and if they dug him up and destroyed his remains, maybe that will stop the dreams." She pulled away and said, "Bill would never destroy his brothers remains, he took them to preserve them, to keep the dreams going." I stood up and told her how silly she sounded. I thought she was going to hit me. "He has been controlling what happens all my life", she said, "I have to believe what I have seen, and what Dan told me he saw last night, only means that Bill knows we are here." She then walked towards the bathrooms. I then sat back down and watched to see if anyone followed her, but no one followed, it appeared to be an ordinary crowd at a water park. I really didn't know what she meant by believing what she and Dan saw, but I was guessing she has seen the outcome if Amy stays or leaves, and she can't decide if staying or leaving was better. I looked over at Amy as she was now sitting on the edge of the beach chair and several older boys were gathered around her. They all appeared to be ignoring the older hotter girls that they were with to talk to Amy. Amy was smiling and chatting away, several times the boys seemed to be surprised at whatever Amy was saying, as they jumped back and laughed. The three older girls that were sitting there got up and walked towards the hot tubs and they were not happy. Two of them came and sat on the side of the tub letting their feet get wet. The third stood outside the tub, and she was pissed, pacing back and forth. One of the girls said to her, "Fuck him". The girl outside the tub almost screamed, "What is she like ten years old?" Then one said, "They are only paying attention to her because she told them that she wants to learn about oral sex, she is probably a bigger tease then you". Now all three of the girls were in the tub and they were so angry that I don't think they even noticed I was still in the tub. Then suddenly one jumped up and said, "Look at that slut, I'm going to kick her ass". I looked over and saw that Amy was kissing, full making out with one of the boys as the other two laughed and watched, when they saw the girls looking they tried to warn their friend. I reached over and touched the girl on her arm that wanted to get out. She pulled away and yelled, "Don't touch me pervert" I held my hands up and said, "You shouldn't be mad at her, he is the one that is cheating". She looked down at me and said, "You know what old man, you are right". She then stood up and screamed, "FUCK YOU BRAD" as she got out of the tub and walked away. The other girls soon followed. I watched as two of the boys got up and started to run after them saying they were just playing. The third boy slowly walked past the tub slightly turning his head to say, "Bill sent me to see if you came here" as he walked past me. I got out of the tub and snapped my wristband, I was drying off when Amy came running up. I noticed what looked like a hickie on her neck. I said, "Amy I don't know what has gotten into you but you are going to get yourself into trouble". Amy looked up at me like she didn't know what I was talking about. I looked over her shoulder and saw that Danielle and Dan were standing in-between two game counters talking. Dan appeared to be angry. I handed Amy some money and told her to go get us some sodas. I then went over to try and hear what Dan and Danielle were talking about. I went to one of the games and started playing. I could hear Danielle telling Dan that

she should not have had Amy brought here. Dan pulled
her in close and said thru clenched teeth "This wasn't part
of the deal." Dan kept saying that he came here because
she begged him to. He appeared to be trying to convince
Danielle to stay with some plan they had, and let Amy
leave with him. Dan even said that two many people have
died and what ever Danielle was doing would get more
people killed. As I put more money down on the game I
was thinking Danielle was telling Dan that she had
changed her mind and she was taking Amy back with her.
Dan then walked out from in-between the games, Danielle
came out and grabbed his arm and said, "Just go back to
where you were, I know everything will be okay, Amy will
be safe, and we will join you shortly. I have seen what will
happen if I let her leave with you, and you saw the same
last night". Dan pulled free from her grip and glared at
her. "They are dreams Danielle, just that, fucking dreams."
But before Dan disappeared into the crowd he said, "You
know this is so fucking wrong, I will do what I have to
do to protect her from him." Dan then lowered his head
and whispered, "And I thought you would do the same
for her." Danielle stood their just feet away from me as she
pulled out her cell phone. I heard her say, "Call off the
dogs, Dan is going to be leaving alone, I'll be bringing
Amy back with me", she then looked up to the sky as she
hung up the phone and said, "I'm sorry, I'm so sorry".
Bells suddenly went off as the man behind the counter
came over, "We got a winner". Amy came running up

dropping my soda. Danielle turned around and saw us standing there, I had won, I looked at the wheel and it had stopped on the name "AMY", I looked down and my dollar was on "AMY". The man was pointing to the prizes behind him. They were very large stuffed toys. Amy yelled she wanted the huge black and red dog. It was bigger then her. She had trouble carrying it so I had to take it to the car. I had to shove the toy into the passenger seat before shutting the door. I looked up as I shut the door and saw Dan drive by, then seconds behind him was Agent Henderson, or the man that claimed to be Agent Henderson following him out of the parking lot. I got an uneasy feeling in my gut. I then pulled on the car door handle to make sure it was locked and started to walk back to the park. I saw an old red pick up truck parked to the right of the entrance that had a direct sight line to my car, there was man sitting behind the wheel reading the newspaper. It was not hard to miss that the paper he was reading was upside down. I was starting to think that Danielle may have had Dan set up and she was now setting me up. To calm myself, I thought they were just making sure that Danielle leaves with Amy. Then I thought, if Sogod can control dreams, maybe he has shown Danielle that Dan is the one that hurt Amy, but then what did Dan dream? I met Danielle and Amy back in the park and we spent the rest of the day together. I kept my eye on Danielle and the only time she was away from me was when she stood in the food line as Amy and

I searched for an empty table to sit at, Danielle said that she needed some food before she had to drive back. As we left the park Danielle told me that she was sorry that she had to take Amy back home and she promised me that Amy would be safe. I walked them to their car, Amy gave me a hug and a kiss on the cheek, and as I patted her head she told me to make sure her big stuffed dog wears a seatbelt. I then asked Danielle where it was that she was taking Amy. Danielle didn't answer as she embraced me with a long kiss. It felt like the kiss of death, sort of like a French kiss from your sister. It would have lasted longer if Amy didn't pull us apart. Danielle turned and told Amy to get in the car. Danielle then hugged me again and whispered in my ear, "I know you will be safe also". I waved as they drove away. I then put Danielle's cell phone that I took out of her pocket during the hug in my pocket and thought to myself, I will be safe also, I looked back as they drove away, who else dose she think will be safe? I walked past the red pick up truck in route back to my car. The truck was empty and I started to feel a little less paranoid. I sat in my car as I pulled up the last number Danielle called. It was the number that was on Agents Henderson's card. I suddenly went miles past paranoid.

3:30 pm

Dan pulled out of the water park parking lot unaware that he was being followed. He was still unaware when he pulled into a truck stop and went into the bathroom. As he stood by the urinal Henderson came in behind him. Dan nodded to Henderson as he stood at the urinal next to him. Dan finished and went to the sink to wash his hands. Henderson came up behind him and put his hand over his mouth and pushed a hunting knife thru the back of Dan's neck. Henderson then spun Dan around and plunged the knife into Dan's stomach pulling it up to his chest slicing thru several ribs. Henderson then sat Dan's body on the toilet in a stall, washed up, and then calmly walked out.

9:45 pm

As I drove down the mountain I was starting to get very tired, then I felt dizzy. The last thing I remembered was trying to keep my car on the road. What I didn't know was that Henderson had Danielle put the pills that were in Amy's backpack into my drink at the water park. I was already knocked out when my car slammed into the mountainside and then slid across the road and crashed thru the old wooden guardrail and plummeted down the mountainside. The red pick up truck from the parking lot pulled up and stopped so he could watch as my car exploded on impact when it landed several hundred feet below. The man in the truck smiled, flicked his cigarette out the window and made a call. Bill Johnson answered the phone, "He's toast" the man said, "I could see him in the drivers seat as the car went thru the guardrail". He then said before hanging up, "Danielle is going to be pissed, you promised her that he would not be hurt." He then hung up and drove off. The cigarette he flipped was blown across the road, stopping just feet from my face.

What the man in the truck didn't see was that I was thrown from the car when it hit the side of the mountain. I was laying unconscious just several feet from him in a ditch. My car fell empty down the mountainside, the black and red dog was driving.

1-1-98 / 2:11 am

I found myself sitting on a park bench with Dan, "How you doing?" I asked. Dan lifted his head to show me the hole that was left from the hunting knife. I almost jumped off the bench. Dan smiled as he pointed to his neck and said as blood poured from his mouth, "This is the one that killed me". Dan then lifted his shirt to show me his insides hanging out and said, "I can't figure out why he gutted me". I got up and asked him why he was just sitting here. "I'm dead man, actually I am still sitting on a toilet at the truck stop". I tried not to, but I laughed. Dan quickly turned his head and looked over at me. Blood from his neck wound spraying across the bench, "What is so funny? You're lying in a ditch dying." I stopped laughing and lifted my shirt to check for injuries. Now Dan started laughing, "They had Danielle drug you before you left the park. She was promised that you wouldn't be hurt, that is a promise Bill has broken a thousand times. Bill's people

357

watched you crash, they all think you are dead". Dan then stood up as he was staring to disappear and said, "When I told Danielle about my dream, the dream where I saw what would happen to her and Amy if they left, it must of spooked her, Danielle believes you will save Amy, but she is in one way responsible for your death". I refused to believe that I was about to die. Dan continued, "Before I told Danielle about my dreams, she had begged me to take Amy away". I looked at Dan, he was now just a ghost floating in front of me, and I then asked him "Danielle refused to let you take Amy away because of what you saw in your dream?" Dan whispered as he disappeared, "No, because she has seen you save her". I reached down and snapped my wristband. I felt the most pain I ever felt in my life as I woke up on the side of the road.

6:00 am

It had started raining and I decided to try and start walking. I saw that several items were also thrown from my car including the little tape recorder and a pack of cigarettes. I put the recorder in my pocket and almost cried when I saw the cigarette pack was empty. I got about two miles down the road when a car came speeding around the corner and almost hit me. To avoid the car I fell backwards into the brush. The car stopped and a young couple got out and ran over to me, they kept asking if I was alright. I got up and just started walking away from them. I didn't want to get anyone else involved. I heard the man yelling at the woman to go and get me, that they cant just let me leave. I then felt myself passing out, the ground rose in front of me. The last thing I remembered was falling backwards. I hope one of them caught me.

9:15 am

I woke up to the sound of a train horn and dripping water. It appeared that I was in a small cabin located somewhere on the mountainside. It was a small dark windowless room. The rain was dripping thru the tin roof into buckets around the cot I was laying on. All my cuts had bandages and wraps. I sat up on the cot and the young woman from the car was standing in the corner doing something. "Where am I?" I asked. She turned around and smiled as she handed me a glass of water. As I drank it down she told me not to worry, that I was safe. She took the glass from me and told me her name was Karen. I then tried to get up but pain shot thru my ankle and back. She put her hand on my shoulder and told me to lie back down. "Karen, why did you bring me here?" She said her husband Norm did not have insurance and he would lose his license if this were to be reported. I could tell she was lying and tried to tell her that they didn't hit me, that I had fallen earlier. I then started to feel woozy again. Karen said it was the medicine she put in my drink, and that I should just sleep. I think I fell asleep before my head hit the pillow.

2:11 pm

I woke up in Danielle's house, I was in her spare bedroom. Bill came in and told me to hurry up. I stood up and noticed that I had no pain. He then rushed in and grabbed my arm. "We don't have time for this shit", he yelled as he pulled me into Danielle's bedroom. The room was completely different, the walls were painted black and all the lights were red. Bill stood behind me and pulled my robe off and shoved me towards Amy who was lying on the bed clutching the sheet. Amy reached out and tried to pull me onto the bed with her. I pushed her away and looked around the room. There were cameras in every corner. All the people except Bill had their faces covered and again I noticed that all the mirrors were covered by black cloth. I looked down at Amy as she was now sitting on the bed smiling at me. She looked up and asked if I was okay. I didn't respond as I kept searching the room for Sogod. When I looked back, Amy was now back lying under the sheets. She reached out and grabbed my hand pulling me down on the bed. I know I am dreaming and I attempt to get up and talk to Bill, but suddenly I am under the sheets with Amy and I could feel many hands searching my body. I then looked at Amy and my hands were around her neck, I was chocking her. I wanted to stop but I couldn't. Amy was fighting with me, she was scratching at my chest and face, and she looked up and said, "You promised." Suddenly she went limp and stopped fighting, she became motionless. I turned to look at Bill. He stood out of the cameras view. He lifted his hand and fired his gun at me. I woke up as the bullet hit. I sat up on the cot. Fresh blood was running down my chest and face. Karen came running in and asked if I had scratched myself. She went to get some bandages. I got up and grabbed my shirt and told her I had to go. She tried to grab me as she called for Norm. He came in and surprised me when he knocked me to the floor. Karen then injected me with something that put me out before she pulled the needle out.

11:25 pm

I woke up to a pounding headache and as I went to sit up I realized that my ankle was now chained to the bed. I really couldn't understand why they brought me back here instead of a hospital, now the chains made me think they may be a little unstable. I never did believe their insurance story. I was able to get up and walk about two feet from the bed before the chains started to dig into my skin. I heard Karen and Norm arguing outside the room. There voices were mumbled but got clearer as they neared the door. I heard Norm tell Karen if they were to let me go now, I would run straight to the cops. I heard Norm tell Karen that he was not going back to jail. Karen then told Norm that she was sure I had no idea that they were bank robbers hiding out in the mountains. Norm then yelled back, "Everyone watches the fucking news". Karen was telling him to quiet down. I acted like I was still out when they entered the room. Karen whispered to Norm, "What are we going to do with him?" There was a silence. Then I heard Norm say, "Let him die". Norm walked over to the corner where I first saw Karen and he grabbed a needle and said as he handed it to her, "Fill it with an overdose, he'll die in his sleep". I watched as Karen cooked what appeared to be heroin, she then sucked it up into the needle. She turned and asked Norm, "Are we just going to leave him here?" Norm said "What is one more fucking body." Karen gasped and asked Norm if he was going to kill everybody. I didn't know who everybody was, I haven't seen or heard anyone else. Norm then walked up on Karen and said he would drop my body a couple miles down the road and that the police will think I was a junkie that overdosed. Karen smiled as Norm then left the room saying he was going to get the car ready. Karen walked towards me tapping on the needle. She put the needle in her mouth as she tied a rubber tube around my arm. I opened my eyes and asked her what she was doing? She got startled and the needle dropped from her mouth and rolled under the cot. Norm then came running back in. "Hold up" he said in a panic "The Mountains are crawling with cops." Karen jumped up from looking for the needle and both of them went to the door and slowly went out. They left the door open a little and I could see that I was in some sort of shed in the backyard of what looked like a really nice house. They ran a few feet before returning to slam the door shut. I slowly got up and reached under the bed for the needle. I was about to shoot the drugs out onto the floor but I heard someone coming back towards the shed. I quickly put the needle under my pillow as Norm came bursting in. He was holding a young girl who appeared to be terrified. Her hands were bound behind her back and her mouth was covered with duct tape. He shoved her down on top of me in the bed. When she saw me she started to scream thru the tape. Norm gave her a backhanded slap across her face and told her to shut the fuck up. He then grabbed her face and turned it towards his and told her as long as her grandparents get rid of the cops everything will be okay. I now knew who everybody else was.

Up at the house Karen was holding a knife to the grandmother neck inside a coat closet just inside the front door. Her husband answered the door as two State Troopers stood outside. Karen could hear the cops ask him if they saw this man. Karen peeked out the door and saw the old man talking to three police officers as he looked at a photo. She watched as he shook his head no and handed the photo back. The Officer then handed the old man a card and told him to call if he were to see or hear anything. As the old man shut the door Karen pushed the grandmother from the closet and said, "Nice job". Before Karen was able to put the tape back across his mouth, the man had lied and told her, the picture was of neither of them. Karen then asked who was the person in the picture, the old described a man he saw in his dreams, and he described me. Karen then secured the duct tape back across his mouth. Karen then secured the couple and headed back out to the shed. The old man was smiling; he knew he was not going to die.

As the old man was answering the door Norm was pushing his granddaughter face down on the bed next to me. He was sliding a handgun up and down her body. He caught the barrel of the gun in her torn nightgown and slid it up to expose her ass. "Now tell me this is not a nice ass". When I didn't answer Norm leaned over and slapped me with his gun. "Answer me faggot," he yelled. "Fuck you" was all I could think to say. Norm now holding the gun pointed at my head said as he massaged this terrified girls ass, "Fuck me, did you say fuck me". As he held the gun I could see it was a revolver and I was pretty sure it wasn't even loaded. All the chambers looked empty. He then leaned down and tried to kiss the girl thru the tape. I reached for the needle under my pillow. Karen then came in thru the door just as I was about to pull the needle out and plunge it into Norm's neck. Karen yelled as she pointed at me, "The fucking cops aren't even looking for us. I think they may be looking for him." Norm looked at me and asked, "What the fuck did you do?" Karen then realized what Norm was doing with the granddaughter, and she slapped Norm off of her. Norm yelled he was just playing as he left the shed. Karen then pushed the girl to the floor and yelled for Norm to wait up. I quickly bent down and told her to go and listen at the door. She violently shook her head no. I showed her that I couldn't, that I was chained to the bed. She slowly got up and walked to the door. She listened for about a minute before her face changed and she almost screamed thru the tape and started to cry. I waved her back and held her head against my chest. I whispered in her ear that I was going to take the tape from her mouth, But that she cant scream or cry out, I told her that she must be quiet or they would come back in. She looked up and shook her head yes. I took the tape off and asked her what she had heard. She said Norm told Karen that he was going to kill all of us in the morning and they were going to head towards Canada. I told her I would do everything in my power to stop that from happening. She looked up at me and said, "That is what my grandfather keeps saying". I didn't understand, how does her grandfather even know I am out here? Before I could ask her to explain I heard Karen and Norm coming back. I told her I had to put the tape back on her mouth. She understood as I pressed it back on. She then rolled onto the floor as they came back in. Norm walked in and grabbed her from the floor. I stood up but was unable to budge the bed that was bolted down. As I attempted to get to Norm I didn't see Karen coming up and injecting me with something that caused me to fall out on the floor.

1-1-98 / 2:11 am

As Karen slept she had a dream. She was sitting in a holding cell when a guard came in and escorted her into a courtroom. Norm was on the stand and she smiled at him as she was led past him to her seat. Norm's expression never changed, he did not smile back at her. She sat handcuffed and shackled still wondering what was going on as she listened to the questioning. Norm was asked by a lawyer who was pointing to photographs of the old couple, their granddaughter and me, "Who killed these people". Norm looked over at Karen and slowly pointed at her and said, "That bitch right there". Norm was then asked, "Why did she kill them?" Norm answered, "Because she got off doing it, she said it was better than sex". The next question was why didn't you try and stop her? Norm pointed to a lump on his head, "You see this" he said, "She hit me with a shovel when I tried to stop her". Karen had heard enough and jumped up, "That is not true" she screamed. The judge looked over the bench and told Karen to calm down. The judge was Sogod. Karen sat back down and wept into her hands. When she looked up she was lying on a bed in a room surrounded by mirrors. She was about to be given a lethal injection and die for the killings she did not remember doing. Sogod entered the room and held her hand, he leaned in close to her and said, "Karen, all you did was drive the car in the bank jobs, if you would have told Norm no when he told you to kill those people, you would have lived". Sogod then slowly started to push the poison into her arm. Karen woke up and looked over at Norm as he slept like a baby next to her. She then looked at the older couple tied down on the floor. She then rolled over and went back to sleep, it was 2:11 in the morning.

6:00 am

The sun was just about to come up when Norm shook Karen awake. Karen got up and went into the bathroom. Norm came in as she sat on the toilet. "I'll start loading the car, when your done tape these trash bags over there heads." He said as he pointed to the old couple and their granddaughter lying on the floor. Norm then turned around and told her, "And when you are done with that, go out and kill that mother fucker in the shed". Karen reaching for some toilet paper asked, "Why can't you do that while I bag these guys?" Norm screamed, "Don't get fucking scared now bitch". And threw the plastic bags and duct tape at her. Karen came out and got on her knees and started to put the bags over the old couples heads. She leaned down and whispered, "I wont do it tight, and if you relax you should be able to breath for a while". Just as she slipped the last bag over the granddaughters head Norm stuck his head in and yelled, "Hurry the fuck up, if we get caught it will be all your fault". Karen then came out to the shed and went right to the side of the bed and started looking on the floor. I reached over and grabbed her by her hair and pulled her up, "Looking for this?" I asked as I showed her the needle. I looked out the door and saw Norm running towards the shed. Karen grabbed the needle from my hand but was unable to break free from my grip. Norm stepped on a shovel and the handle came up hitting him so hard in the head that he fell down on all fours. Karen turned and started telling me this wasn't what I thought it was and that she wasn't going to do anything. Norm came stumbling in the door. "WHAT THE FUCK IS GOING ON?" he screamed. Norm came over and pulled Karen from my grip and pushed me back down on the bed and yelled for Karen to stick me. Karen looked confused as Norm yelled, "What the fuck bitch, my head is killing me, stick him" Karen looked at the wound on Norm's head and saw that it was exactly the same as the one she had dreamed about. Karen rushed towards the bed and plunged the needle into Norm's neck. Norm screamed as he tried to grab Karen, but the drug was too strong and he collapsed onto the floor.

6:20 am

As Norm lay dying on the floor Karen slumped down in the corner and shook. I yelled for her, but she seemed to be in some sort of shock. She then screamed and pushed herself back further when Norm suddenly shook and convulsed on the floor, a white and red foam starting to escape from his mouth. She looked at the needle in her hand and then over at me. She slowly got up, holding the needle as she walked over to the cabinet where the drugs were kept. I could not see what she was doing. I kept calling out to her the whole time. She then turned from the cabinet with the gun in her hand and looked over at me again. She looked like her soul was beaten down as she slowly walked over to me, I was about to try and fight her off. Her eyes were swelling up with tears. "I'm so sorry" she said as she knelt down beside the bed just outside of my reach. She then placed the key to the chains on the floor by the bed and slowly walked out. I quickly jumped up and grabbed the key and unlocked the chains, my legs hurt and it was difficult to walk at first. I reached the door and looked out just in time to see Karen pull the trigger of the gun I thought had no bullets in it. It must have had one left. The bullet came out the back of Karen's head, causing her hair to fly up, Karen then fell slowly to the ground with a bullet hole thru her head. I hurried as fast as the pain would allow me up to the back door of the house. I pushed open the door and grabbed a knife out of one of the kitchen drawers. I found the three people up in the master bedroom. I tried to pull the bags from their heads but couldn't. I then cut slits in them and tore them open to let in air. The man and the girl were fine but the old woman wasn't breathing. I knew mouth to mouth from my prison first aid training and was able after several minutes to get the woman coughing. I sat on the floor sweating. I picked up the knife and cut the tape from the old mans hands. Neither of us saying a word to each other. I handed him the knife and got up to leave. He reached out and grabbed my arm and asked, "Who are you?" His grip was weak and fell from my arm as I stood up. "I'm nobody, just forget you ever saw me." I told him as I headed out. I grabbed a coat and gloves from the closet and some cash that was on the counter. I had to get as far away as possible before the couple was able to call the police. If I were to get caught up in this Danielle and Bill would know I was still alive.

10:30 pm

It seemed like I walked for hours, I stunk so bad that flies would die when they would land on me. I grabbed a clean T-Shirt in a gas station Mini-Mart and washed up in the bathroom, I locked myself in and fell asleep. It was a dreamless sleep. An urgent banging on the door by a stranger that needed the bathroom more then me woke me up. I went back into the gas station and grabbed some food. The home invasion was all that was on the TV. The story of the bank robbers found dead in the back yard, and how an unknown man saved the old couple and their granddaughter. That was just how I wanted it to be, unknown. I handed the man behind the counter the money for the food. He looked at me and asked, "If you were the unknown man wouldn't you have waited for the police to arrive?" I told him some people just want to stay in the background. As the clerk handed me my change he said, "That family that was saved, the Brinson's, they have more money then this entire town. I would have waited for a reward". I was miles from home and I didn't have the money to call a cab, and when I saw the amount of money that was in the cash register, I thought for a minute about robbing the store. As I walked past the pumps an old man who had to be in his eighties asked me if I knew how to get to buffalo. I pointed to the well-lit sign behind him that said Buffalo 85 miles. He waved and said thanks. I then thought about knocking him down and stealing his car, but I just started to walk up the road trying to figure out how long it will take me to walk to buffalo. The old man pulled up and asked if I needed a ride. I thought another stupid question but I held my tongue, I did need the ride. As I climbed in he told me his name was Clem. I lied and introduced myself as Dan, Dan Williamson. Clem noticed the fresh injuries to my face and hands and that it took me a few minutes to get into the car. He asked if I was okay. I smiled and said, "Nothing a good nights sleep won't heal". He then asked, "Where you headed?" I told him he could drop me off anywhere in Buffalo. Clem talked about all kinds of nonsense, but his stories helped me fall right to sleep.

1-1-98 / 12:00 am

Clem gently shook me awake from another dreamless sleep. "Where we at?" I asked as I rubbed the sleep from my eyes. "Buffalo bus depot". He said. I had a little trouble getting out and Clem asked again if I was okay. I told him that I was assaulted at the rest stop. He asked if I wanted to call the police, I just shut his door and thanked him for the ride. He then reached out the window and handed me some cash. I didn't want to take it but I didn't know if I was going to need it. He asked again if I wanted to alert the cops, I shook his hand and said, "I actually deserved what I got." I thanked him again and walked into the bus station and caught a bus that dropped me off a couple miles from my house. Of course it was raining when I got off the bus. The cold rain felt good against my skin. When I got home the sun was just starting to rise. I snuck in the back. Danielle's car was not in her driveway so I sat in the dark and waited for Danielle to come home.

After several hours I gave up and slid into a tub of hot water and some medical salts and fell fast asleep.

2:11 pm

I woke up freezing in the water. I stood up and turned on the hot water to thaw me out. I stood in the shower a few minutes and just let the water run down my back. I got out and wrapped a towel around me. I walked out into the hallway and Joy was standing there with a surprised look on her face. "Mother fucker" I said just as I was hit from behind and almost knocked out. Joy yelled, "This will fuck everything up". Bill lifting me by my shoulders yelled back at her, "This is just what we needed, now grab the legs and help me". They carried me to the spare bedroom and tied me down on the bed. Joy and Bill then whispered to each other and then Bill left the room. Joy came over to the side of the bed and started kissing my neck and rubbing my chest. I was semi-conscious but I could feel myself getting excited. Bill then came back in and pushed Joy away from me. Bill was holding Amys hand. When Amy saw me she smiled, dropped the stuffed bunny she was holding and said, "I knew you would come back for me", and she tried to jump up on the bed. Bill grabbed her and told her to get undressed. Amy never took her eyes off of me as she continued to try and get on the bed. Joy was kissing and caressing me, but Bill became upset and smacked Joy away from me. He told her to take

Amy's clothes off. I looked over at Amy, her eyes were still fixed on me and she had a huge smile on her face. As Joy approached her I felt useless, there was nothing I could do. Amy then looked over at Bill and then slowly walked over and sat on the bed. Amy then leaned down and rubbed the back of her left hand on my cheek as she reached over and snapped my wristband. I woke up in the tub. The water had drained out and I was freezing. I grabbed a towel and headed to the spare bedroom, it was empty and the bed was still made. I looked out the bedroom window, there was still no sign of life at Danielle's. When I turned to leave I stepped on Amy's stuffed bunny.

6:00 pm

I turned on the 6 o'clock news. The home invasion story was still the top story. I almost fell out of my chair when the newscaster said they now have a description and a possible name for the man that saved the couple. An artists sketch was shown, and I was a little relieved that it didn't look much like me at all. It appeared that Mr. Brinson might have given a bad description. But then they showed an interview with a man that they said might have given the mystery man a ride. Clem was standing in front of several microphones, "I picked up a young fellow 80 odd miles outside of Buffalo, he was hurt, hurt bad, he looked like he was in a knife fight. He had trouble getting in and out of the car. He told me he was assaulted at the rest stop, told me he deserved it." Clem then said "I dropped him off at the Buffalo bus station, he told me his name was Dan, Dan Williamson". Not seconds after he said Dans name I could hear the phone ringing over at Danielle's. I sat up and smiled as Clem told them everything I wanted him to.

9:38 pm

I kept all the lights off, I didn't want anyone to know I was back. I took some painkillers and a lot of alcohol. Almost all my pain was gone. I heard a car pull up outside. I snuck to the window and peaked out. A black SUV had parked out in front of Danielle's. It just sat there for a while with the engine running. The windows were tinted and I could not see who was in there. Then the passenger side back door opened and Amy jumped out. She still had her backpack from the water park, Joy got out behind her and yelled "I be there in a minute" to Amy as she ran up to the front door, Amy stopped, and turned around and yelled back, "Fuck you, I hate all of you". That wasn't the first time I saw Amy angry or curse, but it was the first time that I think she actually meant it. Joy looked over at my house and then said to whom ever was driving the SUV, "I'll go in the back and look around, I'll let you know if I find anything". Joy then reached her head inside to kiss the driver. Amy who was sitting on her porch yelled, "Come on slut I have to pee". Joy turned and briskly walked up towards Amy, I thought Joy was going to hit her. Amy didn't flinch as Joy stopped and said to her thru clenched teeth, "As soon as we get what we need bitch, I will bust you the fuck up". Amy just sat on the porch with her little middle fingers up as Joy walked past.

11:00 pm

I was sitting in the kitchen watching Danielle's back door waiting for Joy to come over. I did the last thing I wanted to and fell asleep at the kitchen table as I waited. Joy and Amy both came out and headed towards my back door as I slept at the table. As they approached the back door a fly landed on my hand, half asleep my hand spasm and the fly circled my head buzzing my ears. As they reached the deck, the fly flew onto my face and into my mouth waking me up. I didn't know if I was dreaming or not so I reached for my wristband as Joy slid a key into the backdoor. I had just enough time to get up and hide in the pantry. I had no idea what they would be looking for. So earlier I had hid my laptop, and DVD's up in the attic, my log and other paperwork was still hidden in the drop ceiling in the living room. Thinking that they may be looking for the black strong box that John took, I grabbed the broken disk he sent and slightly hid it under a chair by the front door. Joy pushed Amy in the back door as Amy asked what it was they were looking for. Joy kept pushing Amy in as she said "Don't start, you know what we are looking for", Amy snapped back, "I hope it is not your virginity because that's long gone". Joy started looking thru the kitchen drawers. Amy opened the cabinet under the sink and started to throw the stuff out over her shoulders onto the floor. Joy ran over and told her to stop it, that they needed to leave the house the way it was. When Joy turned her back, Amy again gave her the finger. After searching each drawer, Joy stood in the middle of the kitchen and said to herself, "If I had it, where would I put it" Amy now standing just outside the pantry whispered to herself, "Up your whore ass". Joy then walked over grabbed Amy by her arm and asked her where I kept my computer. Amy pointed to the living room. Joy left the kitchen and I could hear her going thru my desk drawers in the other room. Amy stood by the door and yelled that she was getting a drink. Amy then opened the fridge and grabbed a can of soda. She opened it and I watched as she drained half the can into the sink. Amy then grabbed a bottle of vodka but it was empty. I then looked and saw that my extra vodka was right by my feet. I looked up and Amy was opening the pantry door. The biggest smile came across her face. I had to hold my hand over her mouth to keep her from yelling. Amy then slowly pulled my hand away and hugged me. I whispered in her ear, "What is Joy looking for?" Amy shrugged her shoulders, "That black box we could not open" she said as she reached for the vodka. We both jumped as Joy yelled I think I found something. "I looked at Amy and told her not to worry, that there is nothing in here that can help them. Joy then started yelling for Amy. I looked at Amy and told her not to tell Joy that I was here. Amy whispered, "I'll come back" and left the pantry as Joy walked into the kitchen. I again snapped my wristband and almost yelled at the pain it caused. Joy walked up to Amy and asked, "What were you doing in there?" Amy just held up the bottle of vodka and walked out the back door. Joy stood there and took one last look around, I saw the broken disk in her hands. "Usually they don't start drinking until after they get fucked". Joy said to herself as she dialed her cell phone. Then I heard her say into the phone as she walked out the back door, "I found the disk, but it looks like it has seen better days." She then listened before saying, "No box, and no papers." Joy then walked towards the back door as she said, "I can just burn the house down with everything in it if you want me to", before she hung up.

1-1-98 / 2:11 am

I was worried that they would come back, or that Amy would tell Joy she saw me so I went up to the attic and watched Danielle's back door. I must have fallen asleep. Joy slamming Danielle's front door and running out to get into the black SUV woke me up. I then noticed the only room at Danielle's with a light on was Amy's. I quickly went over and up to Amy's room. Amy was asleep in her bed. I gently shook her awake. She smiled and hugged me and I could smell vodka. She whispered that she thought I was dead. I held her away from me and asked her what was going on. Amy told me that she was told that Joy was now her mother. I asked, "Why would Joy be your mother?" Amy said she didn't know, she said she heard Bill telling Joy that she was now her mom. I pulled her close and hugged her and said, "Get your stuff we are leaving" Amy looked up at me and asked, "Where are we going?" I didn't know, I had to think, I then said, "It may just be time to go to the police". I then let her go and she looked back up at me, but it wasn't Amy it was Sogod. He stood up and put his hand on my shoulder. "What would you tell the police that can be proven? All of the proof came to you while you slept, and it will all point to you, watch who you tell it could get you killed." I then noticed that all of Amy's mirrors were covered with black cloth. I looked back and asked Sogod why that was. Sogod looked at me and said, "I been telling you to see whose not there, you don't even know who you are anymore". I turned and looked at the mirrors, then back at Sogod but he was gone. I walked over to one of the mirrors and went to pull the cloth from it, just as it was about to fall I woke up to Amy walking the bedroom hall yelling my name.

5:00 am

I was able to talk with Amy for several hours. At times it was like talking to someone my own age, and then she would appear to be dumber then a bag of hair. At first she would not tell me anything about what was happening. Then I let her get a soda, and I didn't stop her as she poured some out to make room for vodka. She soon opened up and told me that her mom and dad had been teaching her about sex. She told me she was about ten and a half when she was visiting Bill with her mother, and Susie and Joy showed her how to masturbate. She told me that she was locked her in the closet with Susie and forced to watch her mother and Joy have sex with men. Amy then told me when she was about to turn eleven, that Joy started coming around her house all the time, and that Joy would tell her stories about sex and all the ways to have it, and how everybody was doing it. When I asked her why she didn't tell her mother, Amy said that she was told that it was a secrete and that everybody was doing it, but nobody talks about it. Amy then told me that recently Joy and Danielle had started to play games with her, games that started out fun, but then they would all end with everybody getting undressed and that sometimes Joy would do things to her. Amy appeared to get sad and said that only her mom would listen to her when she told them she didn't want to do it. Amy started to get drunker and I was going to take her home and let her sleep it off when she got real quiet and whispered to me that one time she found movies that had kids in them. She then looked around the room to see if anyone else was listening and quietly said, "They were having sex." Amy told me that her grandfather Bill made those movies. Amy then laid down on the floor, she appeared to be talking to herself as she said, "I saw movies with Joy and Susie in them, and they looked beautiful. Amy then looked over at me and smiled as she told me that she is going to be in her grandfather's next movie. When I asked her if she wanted to do this, Amy said, "When we are done with the movie, I am going to live with my mom and dad on an island." I then asked her where her mother was now, her smile left her face as she told me that nobody would tell her. We then talked some more I asked if she knew when she was going to make the movie, but Amy didn't know when. When I asked her who she was going to make the movie with, Amy told me that she was told that I was going to be in it with her. Amy then sat up as I thought she was about to puke. She reached for me as tears started to roll down her cheeks, I pulled her up to a standing position and I had to hold her steady. She then whispered, "I heard my grandfather tell Joy that you were dead." I turned and lifted her head to look at me, "I'm not dead pumpkin, I'm right here." Amy held me tighter. Amy really needed to sober up a little, I took the soda can from her went to the kitchen to pour the remainder out and sat the can in the sink. I looked in at Amy as she sat in the living room, she looked so sad and alone. I got her another, vodka free soda and sat across from her and held her hands as she reached for the soda. I put a small trashcan next to her in case she puked. She seemed to force a smile as she said, "I think my mom went away because she doesn't want me to do this." Amy then told me that ever since her mother left she has been giving Bill and Joy a hard way to go. She said that when she tells Bill that she doesn't want to do it anymore, Bill would get mad and start blaming her mother and father, and that she would get scared and worry that Bill would hurt them if she doesn't do it. Amy then looked up at me and said that if I was to do the movie with her it would be okay, that it is just acting and that we could

leave right after it was done and all live together on the
island. I just smiled and said, "Maybe." I didn't have the
heart to tell her that there was no way that could happen.
Amy looked at me with hope on her face and said, "My
mom told me that it would be okay, my mom told me that
you would save me, and when she finds out that you are
not dead, maybe she will come back, and we all can do
the movie together" Amy's smile returned to her face as
she said "Pretty please" with her folded hands in prayer
in front of her. I had to make Amy promise not to tell
anyone, even her mother that she saw me. Amy didn't
understand why. I had to tell her that they would hurt her
and me if she did, they might even kill us like they killed
Susie. Amy then told me that she has been having dreams
where she makes the movie. When I asked her about those
dreams, she said she makes the movie with me. Amy then
started to cry again, and when I asked her why, she told
me in every dream a man that looks like her grandfather
always stops it and tells her she should not be doing this
and that someone will save her. When I asked her to tell
me about her last dream. Amy told me she was in a bed
getting ready to do what Joy had shown her, but that her
mother came in and told her that they were leaving and
that she didn't have to do anything. I asked her where her
mother took her? Amy said to here, to me. It was getting
late and Amy was starting to ramble and slur her words, I
should not have let Amy drink alcohol. I got up and told
her she should get home before Joy wakes up. Amy told

me that Joy had left and that she would not be back until morning. I looked at the soda can in the sink and thought about getting her another one. I went back into the living room and Amy had fallen asleep on the sofa. Her head was tilted back and her eyes were closed, she looked so peaceful. I caught myself watching her sleep. When I looked back up at her face, her eyes were open and she was smiling at me. I told her to get up, that I was going to walk her home. Amy stood up and slowly walked towards me as I told her that she was going to be all right. Amy laid her head against my chest and reached her arms around me. I then reached down and held her face and whispered into her ear, "That man in your dreams is right, someone will save you". I then led her to the back door and told her that I was going to leave, and that I could not tell her where I was going, but I would be back to check on her. I made her swear not to tell anyone that I was here, but if anyone asks, I told her to call me dad. Then as I stood on the back porch, Amy stepped up a step grabbed my ears and kissed me on the mouth, she held her kiss there several seconds and I could feel her tongue again gently trying to part my lips. I then gently pushed her away by her shoulders and looked her square in the eyes, knowing this is what she has been taught, I told her this is not the behavior of a little kid and that someone, someday will show her the right way. Amy walked halfway to her backdoor turning to see if I was still watching and said, "I am not a little kid anymore", she took several more steps and said, "I never really had a chance to be little". I let my wristband snap, but I knew I wasn't dreaming.

10:00 am

I woke up in the Motel that I had walked to after Amy left. I tried to think of any evidence or proof I had that I could take to the cops. I was sure Amy would not repeat what she told me to the police. Dan, I am almost certain is dead, and Danielle is most likely buried right next to him, or is in this up to her neck. Then I though about Dr Adams death and the others, of Susie, Judy, Robert and Johnny. I knew how they happened, but only by my dreams. If I were to tell that to the police I would be arrested for being insane. Sogod was right, What I saw was never released to the public, only the killer would know what I know, I would be blamed. It was 2-7, 4 days until what ever was going to happen, happens. It appears everyone in town knows what Johnson is doing, but no one has ever come forward, either out of fear or they are being paid not to. Johnson has been able to hide everything he has done over the years so well that he has been able to stay off the police radar. If I was to call in another tip about his store it would only just go ignored, or one of Johnson's informants would get it and they would find my tape with Sugar. The only evidence I have is burnt up papers with half names on them and crazy theories. I would be put in a mental institution for sure.

I lay back on the bed, between the painkillers and booze it wasn't long before I was fast asleep.

2:11 pm

I woke to the sound of a honking car horn. I am sitting in my car across the street from Bill Johnson house that is around the corner from the adult bookstore. Bill and Joy come out and drive away down the street. I then see someone peaking from behind the drapes by the front window. Shortly after Danielle walks out and briskly walks in the other direction. I slowly drive up behind her. She knows that someone is following her and I can tell she is getting nervous. I then pull up to her and she almost jumped out in front of me. I roll the window down, "Need a ride?" Danielle looks up and down the street then quickly gets in. When I asked her where she was going, she just says, "Drive, drive, drive". I don't wait, I just start demanding that she tell me why Amy has been brought up to think sex at her age is normal. Danielle tells me that I don't understand. She tells me that she wanted to take her away but was told that both Amy and herself would be killed if either tried to leave. I told her that was a lie and that Amy was home, alive, and that she is the one who had run away. Danielle then turned and looked at me, she had evil in her eyes, "Amy is alive because I am kept captive in this house". I pull the car over and grab Danielle by her head, "You are not in the house now bitch" I then turned her head to look out the window, only now I am standing in the basement of Bill Johnson's house, not with Danielle, but with Amy. I look around and there is only one way out. I run up the steps and bang on the door. I hear footsteps coming towards the door, "Stop fucking banging", Bill yells, "Or I will fucking strap you to the bed again". Just as he said that I found myself strapped to the bed in the basement. Amy knelt down beside me and asked, "After I have sex in Bill's movie are you going to kill me?" I tried to reach out as Amy stood up and walked towards the steps, she looked up and said, "I will do it". I saw she had tears in her eyes when she looked back at me and said, "I believed you, I believed you when you told me it would be alright, that we would be safe." She then said as she started to walk up the steps, "Do you believe that I love you? Because you have never told me that you love me." Bill then opened the door and let her out. I snapped my wristband and woke up in a pool of sweat. I decided to take a walk over to Bill Johnson's house.

5:15 pm

I was standing behind some trees across the street from Bills house. The black SUV was parked in the driveway. I stood there for what felt like hours wondering what to do. I was just about to give up when Bill came out and drove away, but I didn't know if anyone else was in there.

Then I remembered that I had Bill phone number, but my phone was dead. I then picked up a rock and threw it at the house, the rock smashed thru the front window. The only sounds I heard were the birds flying away. I ran across the street and kicked in the front door. There was nobody else home. I ran to the basement steps and put my ear up against the door. I slowly opened the door and went down. Danielle looked up as I came down the steps. "What the fuck are you doing here? I was told you were dead," she said as I shoved her back against the wall, "You are a good actress, I almost believed that you didn't know I was alive?" She slowly slid down the wall to a sitting position. I pulled her hair so she was looking up at me, "Why did you set me up, who wants me dead?" Danielle just stared, "You know who, Bill, he had a dream where you tried to stop him from making his movie. I am sorry, but he said he wasn't going to kill you, just scare you off." I let go of her hair and Danielle's head bowed down as she looked at the floor. Without looking up she asked how I knew she was here. I told her I didn't come here looking for her, that I came looking for Amy, and that I have been having those fucking dreams ever since I meet her crazy uncle in jail. Danielle still not looking up said, "He is not my uncle, he was my father". I grabbed her face, "Do you ever tell the fucking truth bitch, I thought Bill was your father?" Danielle then told me that Bill and Robert adopted her when she was only several days old. They both raised her as their own. "My two dads, how fucking sweet" I yelled, Danielle still looking at the floor whispered, "They adopted me just so they could use me in sex movies." I crouched down in front of her and said, "So now you sold Amy to them?" Danielle still sitting said, "Amy was always theirs, she was born to make them money." I stood up and walked to the bottom of the steps, "Unfuckingbelievable" I said. "Now get up, we have to go to the police" Danielle started shaking, "No, I cant". I asked, "Why fucking not?" Danielle got up and sat on the edge of a table. "I will be arrested and Amy will be taken away from me, and Bill will slip away, Bill has too many friends in high places in this town, he had Johnny killed, and left evidence that will show that I killed him." I turned back and asked, "Did you kill any of them?" Danielle didn't answer, she looked up at me and said, "You have to trust me, they will kill Amy." I grabbed Danielle and shook her, "How the hell can you allow someone to film your own child having sex, I know you have seen what has been going on. Bill will have both of you killed as soon as he replaces Amy with a younger child" Danielle pulled away, "That is what you think? Half of what you think you know is wrong, Bill doesn't replace the girls he uses them to have more children. He didn't kill me when I was done, anyway this film is his last film. The first of its kind, it's been advertised as a porno with a child and her mother, you would not believe how many orders he has for this". This is not happening, what sick fucks would even want that? I snapped my wristband, but I was awake. I then said, "I think it may be a child porno with a snuff at the end". Danielle had a confused look as she didn't appear to know what a snuff was. "A snuff is when one of the sick fucks at the end, kills the other on tape". Danielle shook her head no, "No no no no" was all she kept saying. Danielle then reached up and grabbed me, "Get out, get out before Bill or Joy get back, they are both crazy, they are beyond paranoid and if they know you were here, they will kill everyone." I told her I wasn't leaving without her, Danielle said, "You don't understand, as long as I am here I can control this, I cant tell you how I know, but I know you will stop all of this from happening, I will call you, just let me know where you are staying." I sat on the steps, I wasn't sure if I should trust her. Danielle walked over to me, "Just tell me your not at your house, they are going to search it for a stolen box, they will see you, they will kill you." I looked at her, I looked into her eyes, and for the first time in a long time she appeared to be telling me the truth. I then told her that I did take that box from her hot tub. Danielle became upset and tried to get up, "If they find that box then they will have everything they need to put this all on John and me." Don't worry, I said, "They wont find it. John stole it from me." Danielle then calmed down and told me that she would call my cell as soon as she knew anything. I then asked how she was going to explain all the damage upstairs? Danielle looked up the steps, "What damage? what happened?" Danielle was starting to talk fast, I told her that I broke the window, and that I had to kick in the front door. Danielle was now starting to have another panic attack. I slapped her because that is what I saw in all the movies, and plus I really wanted to slap her for a long time, her face started to swell up. Danielle looked back at me with tears in her eyes, "Hit me again", she yelled. I just stood there. "Hit me again, Hit me, hit me hit me" she just kept yelling as she started to shove me back against a wall. I then swung up and punched her on the side of her face. Danielle fell to the floor holding her face as blood from her nose started to run down over her lips and stain her shirt. Part of me felt like I should tell her that I was sorry, and the other part wanted to punch her again. Danielle then looked up at me and said, "Just go I can handle this, I believe in my heart that you will do what I have seen you do". As I wrote my cell number down I thought that this was all too hard to believe. Danielle then asked if I was the one on the bus and if I gave Dan's name? I shook my head no and handed her my number and told her that I had to charge my phone, but to call me before anything happens, or I would have no other option but to go to the police. As I got up, she asked me if I thought Dan was still alive, I just walked up the steps. Danielle then told me to lock the basement door, I turned and told her that if she fucks me over, she won't have to worry about Bill killing her. Then as I shut the door I heard her say to herself, "I have to trust what I have seen".

7:35 pm

Bill pulled up to the house and saw the broken window and the pushed in front door, the first thing he thought was that Danielle had left. He called out for her and ran into the basement door before he realized it was locked. He then went slowly down the steps. Danielle jumped out with a pipe in her hands. Bill jumped back as Danielle dropped the pipe and ran to Bill hugging him. Bill noticed that Danielle's face was battered and bloody. She told Bill that she thought he was Dan coming back. Bill held her back and asked her if Dan was here. Danielle told him that about an hour ago she heard a bang upstairs and then heard Dan yelling and cursing, she told Bill that Dan slapped her around and then pushed her into the basement and locked the door. She then hugged Bill telling him she thought Dan had killed him. Bill had a concerned look on his face, but he was buying Danielle's story. He then told Danielle that he knew Dan was still alive from the news story. Bill yelled, "FUCK, Dan is back, we have to find him before we shoot the film." Bill then hugged Danielle and whispered to her, "I will not let your brother ruin this".

8:35 pm

I sat on the bed in the Motel staring at my phone willing it to ring. I was just about to fall asleep when it went off. As soon as I answered, Danielle didn't give me a chance to say anything. She just quickly whispered, "Because of the damage to the house when you busted in, Bill is going to wait to shoot the film, I will keep you informed". She then hung up. I didn't know if she was telling me the truth or trying to keep me away until after the eleventh. I was still not sure if I could trust her, but I was starting to think I could trust my dreams.

What Danielle or I didn't know was that Bill had heard the phone conversation, but he thought Danielle was talking to Dan, and that they are working together to take Amy away. Bill decided to keep the shoot for the 11th, only he wasn't going to tell anyone. Bill too was going to trust his dreams.

2-8-98 / 2:11 am

was out of painkillers and the pain in my leg was keeping me awake. I tossed and turned for several hours. When the clock hit 2:11 in the morning I knew I missed my opportunity to dream. I got up and sat in the only chair in the room by the window. I put my feet up and noticed that I had something stuck to the bottom of my foot. I reached down to pull it off and several gunshots came thru the window. I fell to the floor checking my body to see if I was hit. I heard a car spinning its wheels as it pulled away. I slowly got up and looked out thru the broken glass. There was nobody out there, there were no people coming out of the other rooms to see what had just happened. It was dark and silent. I then looked up towards the highway, cars continued to drive by. I opened the door and went out and looked down at the office, the lights were on and the neon vacancy sign was blinking, but I didn't see any employees. As I stood in the middle of the parking lot, I noticed that the lot was empty, not a single car. Just as I went to turn and head back into my room a car came speeding in. It came right at me. I got prepared to jump out of the way when it slammed on its brakes and stopped just inches in front of me. Joy jumped out and ran over to me, "We have to go back inside". Joy slammed the door shut and tried to move the oversized chair in front of it. I told her not to bother that who ever she was running from could get in where there used to be a window. Joy then sat down on the floor in the corner shaking. I knelt down next to her and asked her what was going on. Joy reached up and cupped my face, "Did you ever do something that was so wrong that if anyone ever found out" I interrupted her by saying, "You talking about trying to kill me?" Joy pulled herself up and kissed me hard. She then said, "No, if I wanted you dead, you would be dead". And then she kissed me again not allowing me to read her face. I pulled away and asked if she was talking about teaching Amy about sex? Joy said as she slipped both her hands under my shirt, "No one is teaching her anything, Amy is a very curious little girl, she asks a lot of questions." Her hands were now undoing my pants. I almost yelled at her, "Then what the fuck are you talking about?" Joy then leaned back against the corner, "I am talking about my past, my future, my whole fucking life. I am pretty sure there isn't one mother fucker out there that would want to change lives with me". I stood up and reached for her. She grabbed my hand and I helped her to stand up. She walked over to the bed and sat down. She looked at me and said, "No one would". I sat down next to her and said, "That's not true." Joy continued to pout, I turned her face towards me, "Susie would, and so would Johnny, or Dr Adams". Joy seemed to smile and said, "Then you would want to kill them, again". Joy then stood up in front of me and lifted off her shirt and said, "Fuck me". I just stood there as Joy stripped down to her underwear and laid down on the bed. "Come on, Fuck me like you used to". I looked back at the shot out window and reached for my wristband, but I didn't snap it. I looked around the room for a mirror but there wasn't one. I walked into the bathroom where there was a mirror on the medicine cabinet, but it had been ripped off. I heard Joy moaning on the bed. I turned and saw that Susie was now with her, they were both under the sheets on the bed. Now I knew I was dreaming and I walked over and stood by the bed watching them. I reached out to touch Joy. Suddenly a hand came from behind me and grabbed my arm. Amy then walked from behind me and sat on the edge of the bed and said, "Show me, show me so we can get out of here". Joy and Susie got up and were now sitting on either side of Amy, they were rubbing Amys legs and shoulders. I fell to my knees in front of Amy. Joy reached out and started to gently rub my cheek and said, "Did you ever wonder what spring rain tastes like?" I rested my hands, one on Joy's thigh and the other one on Susie's. Amy stood up as Joy started to lift Amy's shirt off, my face was resting on her belly. I then looked up and saw that there was a large film crew filming us. Amy's with tears in her eyes looked down at me and whispered, "Do it, and we can leave this place and be together forever". I looked up into Amy's eyes, she was smiling, she seemed like she just wanted to get it over with. I then reached up and touched her face and asked, "Who am I?" Amy's face became confused. I pulled myself up to be face to face with her and screamed, "TELL ME WHO THE FUCK I AM?" Just as Amy went to speak, Susie snapped my wristband and I woke up in the motel bed. The window was still intact, there were several cars in the lot and when I rinsed my face with water in the bathroom sink. I looked up and watched it drip off in the mirror. And yes something was stuck on my foot. I looked at it for a while. Then I decided to leave it there.

2:30 pm

All I could do to keep from going crazy was drink, and it wasn't long before I was almost falling down drunk. I spent all day drinking and peeking out the window. I didn't have a thing to eat. I was still on the news, but I was still known as Dan Williamson. There was a report on my death, but my car was found crushed and burned by the highway patrol. They were reporting that a badly burned man was found under it, and they were assuming that it was me. What actually happened was that the car fell onto a homeless man that was living near the lake. At least Bill will still think that I am dead. I got up and went to take a shower, as soon as I was soaped up I heard a knock on the door. I turned off the water and wiped the soap from my eyes. I stood motionless in the shower. I heard the front door slowly opening, I quietly stepped from the shower and took the back of the toilet tank off. I stood next to the bathroom door with the top above my head ready to strike. I heard someone and it appeared that whoever it was, they were looking thru the room. Just as I tried to peek out of the bathroom, the door was pushed open and the door hit my arm causing the tank top to drop and break on the bathroom floor behind me. The maid screamed, I screamed. The maid held her hands to her chest and sat down on the bed. I ran over asking her if she was okay. She looked at me with frightened eyes and asked, "What the hell are you doing?" I told her, "I just got out of the shower when I heard you in the other room, I thought you were a burglar, I am so sorry". She pointed to the broken top and said that I would have to pay for that. I said "No problem just charge it to the room" as I reached to touch her shoulder and she jumped back on the bed. I put my hands up and told her that I wasn't going to hurt her. She covered her mouth as a giggle came out and pointed at me. I looked down and realized I was still naked and dripping with soap. I grabbed the cover off the bed to cover myself. I had to apologize again. She stood up and brushed her maid outfit off and said that she would come back later to clean the room. I told her when she did come back that I would be dressed. She laughed and asked if she could grab a beer from the cooler. She didn't appear to be old enough to drink, but I reached down and grabbed her two. She opened one and guzzled it. Her eyes were sparkling, she was a pretty girl, her nametag said, "Ruby" and the maid outfit sort of turned me on a little. As I watched her down the beer I thought that I had seen this girl somewhere before. She finished the beer and handed me the other beer back and said as she left the room, "I'll drink this one when I return".

6:00 pm

I was lying on the bed when Ruby came back in, again she just let herself in. She grabbed two beers from the cooler and opened them and sat on the bed and handed me one. "I saved your room for last" she said. I sat up and realized that I had never gotten dressed. The sheet fell down to my waist. Ruby reached out and rubbed my chest, "You told me you would be dressed". I smiled and told her that I must have fallen asleep. Ruby was already done her beer and grabbed another. She opened the beer and put in on the nightstand. She then stood up, standing by the bed she took her hair out of a bun and let it fall over her shoulders. As she shook her hair out, I realized that she was the girl I thought was Doctor Adam's daughter. She then unzipped her maid dress and let it fall to the floor,

"Now we are both naked," she said as she climbed into the bed next to me. She kissed me softly on the mouth as she asked if she could invite a friend over. I looked at her with a puzzled look, hoping it wasn't her boyfriend, but expecting it to be Bill. She grabbed her cell phone and said, "Don't worry it's a girl". I raised my hands and said, "By all means," I then asked, "Do you want me to dial?" Ruby playfully pushed me away and told me to go wash up. I got up and went into the bathroom, I heard Ruby say into the phone as I turned the water on, "Come on over, he is really cute". I washed my smiling face in the sink and when I looked up the mirror was not on the cabinet. I looked over at the toilet and the tank top was still sitting on it unbroken. I looked down to make sure I had my wristband on. I then looked out and saw Ruby putting some sort of pill into my beer. She then laid down and pulled the sheet up over herself. I went back in and laid down next to her as she handed me the beer. I took a sip and put it on the nightstand. "Drink up" she said, "You have a big night ahead of you". I turned over and I was going to intentionally knock the beer over when there was a quiet knock on the door. I sat up with the beer in my hand. Ruby got up off the bed and reached for what I thought was something to cover herself with while she answered the door. Instead she stood up with a gun and told me to drink the beer. I slowly put the bottle to my mouth, "GUZZLE IT" she screamed as she stood just far enough away that I could not grab or slap the gun away.

I drank the beer letting most of it dribble down my face. Ruby watched with the gun at the ready, I suddenly fell back on the bed and was unable to move. Ruby answered the door and Bill came in with Amy, when Amy saw me she ran over and climbed up on the bed and hugged me. Bill set up a camera on a tripod then grabbed Amy and pulled her off the bed. Amy swung at him yelling, "FUCK YOU". Bill laughed then shoved Amy over to Ruby and told her to get her ready. When Amy refused to do what Ruby was telling her, Ruby violently started to rip Amy's clothing off. Bill told Ruby to be careful not to hurt her. Bill then leaned down next to me and he turned my face to look at him, he showed me a handgun, "There is one round in the chamber". He then put the gun under the pillow. He then whispered in my ear as he turned my head away "You fuck her, she shoots you, its over." He then pulled my face close to his and kissed me. He then squeezes me between my legs and said, "If you don't, you both die tonight". Ruby then let go of Amy, she sat down and started to pick up her ripped clothing. Ruby walked back to the bed and looked down at me, her face had a look that made me feel that she was sorry. Bill told Ruby to get me ready. Amy then sat on the side of the bed and watched as Ruby strapped my hands to the headboard. She then turned and started to tie my ankles, I tried to kick or turn but the drug would not let me control my body. Bill yelled at her to forget about my legs. Amy then turned towards me and leaned in and kissed me on my forehead, she didn't look scared and she had the biggest smile on her face. She then quietly whispered, "I will be okay". I started to get some movement back and I was able to turn my head away. Amy then reached her hand over me and laid down next to me. Bill yelled again telling her to take the rest of her clothing off and get under the sheet with me. Amy then leaned in again and winked at me. I could feel her reaching under the pillow. Bill was getting more and more upset that Amy would not do what he was saying. Bill then came towards the bed and reached for Amy as she sat up and shot the gun at Bill missing him. Ruby pulled Amy off the bed and threw her to the ground as Bill came running towards me. I got some more movement back and was able to kick my leg up and stop him from pouncing on me. Bill fell to the floor as Ruby jumped on the bed and held my legs. Bill got up with a knife and plunged it at my chest. Just as the blade was about to pierce my skin I woke up tangled in the sheets swinging and kicking. I sat up and looked around the room in a panic, but I was alone. The broken tank cover was still all over the bathroom floor. I sat on the edge of the bed and looked down and saw that whatever it was that was stuck to my foot was still there.

8:45 pm

Just as I bent down and pulled on my shorts Ruby opened the door, I guessed it was Ruby as I just sat down on the bed with my back to whoever it was as they walked in. It was at that moment that I thought about dying, and I wasn't afraid. Ruby then said as she shut the door, "I thought you were going to be dressed this time". I turned and expected to see Ruby standing there in her maid outfit holding a gun. She wasn't, she was dressed in a pair of black low-rise sweatpants with "SEXY" written on the ass and a gray hoodie that couldn't hold another skull iron-on. Her hair was down and she looked even younger then before. I asked her how old she was as I pulled on my pants. She told me that she liked older men and grabbed a beer. She choked on her beer when I asked her if she owned a gun. "Why would I need a gun?" she asked as she wiped her chin. "No reason, just a question". She then came over and sat on the bed as I tied my shoes. She rubbed my back and said, "You are a weird one Joe, lucky for you, you're cute as hell". I sat up and looked at her, she had such an innocent face, "You never told me how old you are". She got up to get another beer, she was pounding them down, she said, "I am 24", and asked me why as she handed me a beer. The beer was still closed and I didn't open it. Ruby then pulled her hoodie off and sat in the chair across from the bed, her shirt was short and revealed a skull piercing in her bellybutton. "You just look to be no older then 17 or 18". Ruby laughed, "I get carded all the time, even when I buy smokes". I asked if she had a cigarette, she opened her handbag and grabbed a pack. I tried to see if there was a gun in there, but I didn't see one. I was able to see that there was a bag with pills in it. She opened the pack and lit two at one time, she came back over and sat down next to me on the bed and handed me one of the cigarettes. I must have looked awkward smoking it as she asked me, "How long have you been smoking Joe?" I flicked the ash completely missing the ashtray, "About 20 seconds," I said as I got up and walked into the bathroom coughing, the mirror was there and the broken tank top was still all over the floor. I looked at myself in the mirror and thought, she keeps calling me Joe, I registered under Daniel. I peaked back in at Ruby as she was sitting on the bed fluffing her hair with her fingers. I sat down on the edge of the tub. I heard Ruby opening another beer, "Joe we are running out of beer". I got up and walked up to Ruby as she pointed at the cooler and told me that there were only two beers left. "I'll go get us some more". Ruby got up and held my face as she gave me an open mouth kiss, I embraced her and let it happen. Her kiss was nervous, her hands shook and she was sweating. I grabbed my wallet from the nightstand drawer and saw the tape recorder that I took from Amy's backpack was next to the bible. I quietly hit the record button and left the drawer open a little. I then headed out to get more beer. I looked around the parking lot, just the same old cars. As I walked to the store to get more beer I kept trying to remember if I told Ruby my name was Joe, these dreams are making me just a bit paranoid.

9:30 pm

I returned to the room and found Ruby sleeping on the bed, the remainder of the empty beer bottles next to her, I picked them up off the bed, and as I was putting the new beer in the cooler Ruby woke up and asked me what time it was. I looked at my wrist and said "Its two in the morning". Ruby jumped up and started to panic, I grabbed her and told her that I was kidding. I showed her that I didn't even have a watch on my wrist. Her smile returned to her face when I said, "Its just past 9:30". Ruby then got angry, "Don't do that," she said as she headed to the bathroom. I quickly pulled the recorder out of the drawer and hit play. Silence, then some sort of rumbling. Then Ruby's voice, "Where the fuck is it?" Then I heard her dialing a cell phone. Ruby was whispering, "Come on, come on answer the dam phone". Then she said, "Hi its me, I am in that guys room, he went to get beer" Then silence as I guessed she was listening. Then, "When he comes back you want me to put two of the pills in his beer and then call you" Ruby was listening again, "I would like to fuck him first before you kill him". She then said, "I may be in the wrong room, I think this guys name is Joe, that's what I have been calling him". More silence, "I can't check his wallet he took it with him". The last thing she said before the tape ran out was, "I guess you will see who he is when you get your cranky old ass over here". I then put the tape recorder in my pocket and removed the battery from Rubies phone, I ripped the motel phone cord from the wall and took sixty dollars from her bag. I looked at her driver's license and her name was Rudy, and I was right she was only 19 years old. I put her ID back in her bag and grabbed the bag of pills and emptied them on the bed. I then grabbed my bottle of aspirins and refilled her bag. I heard the toilet flush so I scooped the pills up off the bed and grabbed a couple beers and dropped two of the pills in one of them as Ruby came out wearing only her underwear, she propped herself up in the doorway and said, "Joe, you seemed to be a little over dressed". I held out her beer and walked over to her. She took both beers from my hands and sat them down on a table. When she stood back up she grabbed me and kissed me. During the kiss I tried to see which beer had the drug in it. I then told her I had to use the bathroom. I didn't pull the door completely shut. I then turned the water on in the sink and peeked out and watched as Ruby dropped two aspirins into one of the beers, she then laid down on the bed, and it appeared that she was praying. I pulled two more of the pills from my pocket and went over and sat down on the bed next to her. "Do you do this a lot?" I asked. She rolled over and handed me the beer with the aspirins in it, "Only when I'm horny," she said. I held up my beer to make a toast, and I was able to see that it contained all the pills foaming at the bottom, "To horny little girls", as we tapped our beer bottles together I knocked hers from her hand. Ruby jumped up from the bed. I reached in and grabbed another beer and dropped two of her pills in as I opened it. I said "Sorry" as I handed it to her. "I got beer all over me", she said as she wiped her stomach. I then lay her back down on the bed and started to lick the beer off her. Ruby didn't need any prodding as she guzzled her beer. Within minutes she was unable to move. I then poured my beer out onto the floor. As I stood up over her she had a look of terror on her face. I leaned down and kissed her, she was trying to say something but couldn't. I pulled the pillow from under her head and held it above her face. I then pulled the case off and went into the bathroom and picked up the big broken pieces of the toilet tank and placed them in the pillowcase. I came back into the room with the case over my shoulder. I walked up to the bed and slammed it down next to Ruby as the fear on her face grew. Ruby was forcing herself to talk. "Please, don't, hurt, me, Joe". I grabbed a couple of beers and picked up the pillowcase and stood over her. I watched as she tried to move. I reached down and squeezed face as I put my face as close to hers as I could without touching her. All she could say was, "Please, Joe". I then whispered into her ear as a tear fell down her cheek, "I am not the one that is going to hurt you" I then kissed her face, "But you can tell that sick fuck that is on his way, that I will be back, and I will stop his fucking heart". Before I stood up to leave Ruby was able to say, "Thanks, Joe" I then screamed at her, "MY FUCKING NAME IS DAN". I turned to leave when I heard a car pulling up. I looked out the window and saw that Bill and Joy were walking towards the room. I quickly looked around the room but there was no other way out. I got behind the door, as I was going to smash the first one in with the pillowcase full of broken porcelain. I looked out thru the peephole in the door and both were walking back towards their car. I was then able to duck out the door and disappear around the corner.

10:50 pm

"Can you believe this shit?" Joy yelled as she entered the room with Bill. Ruby was able to move a little but was still too drugged to get up. Bill sat on the bed and without even looking at Ruby quietly asked, "Where is he?" Ruby again tried to pull herself up into a sitting position and struggled to say, "He left, he left right before you guys came in, you had to see him". Bill then suddenly turned towards Ruby shoving the barrel of his gun into her mouth and screamed. "WELL WE DIDN'T SEE ANYONE" he then looked up at Joy and asked, "Who was he, what did he look like?" Ruby tried to answer but Bill had the gun to far in her mouth. Bill kept looking at Joy, "I was so fucking happy ten minutes ago". Joy sat on the other side of the bed and started to gently rub Ruby's thighs. Ruby started to choke on the gun. Bill then looked down at Ruby and took the gun out of her mouth and wiped it on Ruby's panties. Bill turned away from Ruby again and said, "All this time and I am no fucking closer, and to put a big fucking cherry on top, this stupid whore doesn't even know who she was about to fuck". Ruby was able to lift her hand and put it on Bills back, "He told me his name was Dan". Bill turned back around to look at Ruby, "What?" Ruby smiled and said, "Before he left the room he yelled at me, he told me his name was Dan". Bill just sat on the bed with his head down. Ruby then said, "He got mad when I called him Joe". Bill got up to walk out of the room. Ruby grabbed his hand and Bill looked back as Ruby said, "He also told me that he would be back". Bill looking over at Joy asked, "Why would he come back?" Ruby said, "To kill you". Bill pulled away and left the room. Joy leaned over Ruby's body and slowly licked Ruby from her belly button up to her neck. Joy then lifted Ruby's head and forced her tongue inside her mouth just as she stuck a knife into Ruby's stomach. Joy continued to kiss Ruby as she pulled the knife up towards Ruby's breasts. Joy kept kissing her until blood started to pour from Ruby's mouth. Joy pulled the knife from Ruby's chest and wiped it on the bed sheets. Joy then wiped the blood from her lips and chin but before turning to leave the room, she spit blood from her mouth back on Ruby's dead body.

2-9-98/ 1:35 am

Danielle woke up just as Bill and Joy were getting back and Danielle could tell Bill was angry when he kept slamming doors. When Bill came in and sat down, Danielle asked what had happened. Bill then threw his beer against the wall and both Joy and Danielle jumped as it smashed and stained the wallpaper. "Your fucking brother is going to fuck this up," he yelled at Danielle. "I should have killed him myself when he came back the first time for more money." Joy put her arm around Bill and said, "It will be all right." Bill pulled away, "This is it", he said, "One more time, one last film, and it was his fucking idea, he is the one that suggested we keep Amy, now that fuck up, coked out jerk fuck wants to ruin it, he wants to stop me, that shit stain wants to kill me". Bill was getting more and more upset with each word, "Calm down" Danielle calmly said. Bill turned towards her, "Your fucking brother, he all of a sudden has feelings for her, I think he wants to fuck her himself". Since Bill would not listen to reason, Danielle got up to leave the room. Bill ran over and shoved her over a chair and stood over her, "Now don't think for a second that I don't know you are still talking with him. Did you call and warn him, did you tell him we were coming?" Danielle yelled back at Bill calling him crazy, "I set him up with the photos and lured him to the park so he could be killed, I did everything you asked, it was you and your stupid inept friends that let him live". Bill just stared down at Danielle on the floor, "Fuck you, I knew you and Amy were going to leave with him at the water park." Danielle trying to get up yelled back, "Then why didn't we." Bill still standing over her looked down and said, "I will kill you and Amy in a heartbeat and don't think I wont, all I promised was a film with a snuff at the end and those sick fucks don't care what the kid looks like, or who it is that's fucking her". Bill then said as he stepped over Danielle, "The money is in the bank, and my flight leaves at noon, I will be in my new beach house on my own island and this fucking country can fuck itself inside out". Bill was still rambling as he walked up to his bedroom. Danielle got up and sat on the chair she was pushed over. She looked over at Joy who had a smug look on her face as she leaned against the doorframe and said, "You do know if Dan shows up Bill will kill all three of you". Danielle rubbing her knee snapped back, "You are such a stupid little bitch, he is going to kill all of us, including you." Joy pulled the knife she had just used to kill Ruby out, and came over to Danielle. "Put the knife away Zorro" Danielle said, "Bill just said, HIS money, HIS flight, HIS FUCKING ISLAND". Danielle laughed as she told Joy that Bill has no intentions of taking her ass anywhere.

2:11 am

Joy woke up to find Bill wasn't in the bed with her, she slowly got out of bed and walked towards the steps. There was light coming from under the bathroom door so Joy leaned her ear up against the door and she could hear giggling. She reached for the doorknob then decided not to open it. Joy then heard whoever was in their getting out of the tub. Joy quickly disappeared into the shadows of the hallway. When the door opened Bill came out with a towel around his waist, Danielle then suddenly came running out naked, "Who only has one towel in their bathroom?" She asked as she tried to pull the towel away from Bill. Joy watched as they went into Danielle's room. Joy slowly walked up to the open door and watched as they made love on the bed. Danielle rolled off of Bill and lit a cigarette, she took a drag and handed it to Bill and said, "Do you believe that stupid little bitch thinks we are taking her with us when we leave". Bill blowing smoke rings, put the butt in an ashtray and said, "Her surprise on film when I kill her will make us millions". Joy thought they were talking about Amy until Danielle sat up and asked, "Are you still getting rid of Amy too?" Joy watched Bill as his facial expression changed and he said, "I will tell Joy she has to be in the flick, you know she wont refuse, she cant wait to taste Amy, and I cant wait to watch Joy die, but I was thinking we should take Amy with us to the island". Danielle had tears in her eyes, "You know Amy is the closest thing I will ever have to a real child". Bill shrugs his shoulders, "A three way with a mother and her pretend daughter, now that's fucking hot". Joy gasps and Bill looks up to see her run from the doorway. Joy runs back to their room and searches the drawer for Bills gun, and just as she finds it Bill knocks it from her hand and swings a punch at her face, just as his fist hits her chin Joy wakes up jumping in bed next to Bill, he doesn't move from his sleeping position but asks if everything is okay? Joy doesn't answer, she gets up and heads to the bathroom, she looks in at Danielle who is sleeping naked in her bed and notices the still burning cigarette in the ashtray. She sits down on the toilet and looks at the wet footprints on the floor mat and the tub is still wet. Joy then notices that there are no towels hanging. Joy then walked back to Danielle's bedroom door and leaned back against the doorframe. Joy watched as Danielle slept. Danielle was in the middle of a dream of her own.

Danielle was standing in her bedroom watching Amy sleep in her bed. Suddenly she realizes that there is someone else in the bed with her. Danielle wants to run to the bed but she cant move. Danielle then senses that someone else is coming into the bedroom so she spins and fires a gun she is holding in her hand. The bullet missed the target. She then attempts to fire again but she is hit in the face and wakes up. Danielle didn't notice that Joy was standing in the doorway watching her, Danielle just rolled over and slowly closed her eyes. Joy didn't notice that Danielle woke up, she then returned to the bedroom just as the phone rang and Bill answered. She stood in the doorway as Bill asked whoever was on the other end, "What the fuck is she doing there? Oh never mind just find her and if she dies, no sweat off my sack." Joy then entered the room as Bill yelled into the phone, "Fuck the cops, if they get in the way, kill them to."

When I left the motel I went to a homeless shelter just around the corner. I was told they were full but I was allowed to stay in the lobby and told that I could sleep in a chair. Sleep was nearly impossible as it was freezing out and every time the door opened the cold wind woke me up. I tried to lie on the chair putting my back to the door, my eyes were heavy and I had thoughts of just going to the police. Then the wind hit my back and I waited for the door to close. When the door didn't shut I turned to see Sugar holding the door open. The lady behind the counter was telling her to leave and that she didn't see anyone tonight. When Sugar saw me she walked over and told me to get up. The lady behind the counter again told Sugar to get out or she would call the cops. Sugar ignored her and pulled on my arm telling me that I should go with her. I slowly got up and walked with her to the front door. The lady behind the counter was yelling for me to stay away from her, I ignored her too, but I did snap my wristband.

Sugar took me out behind the shelter to a van. When I got in, without looking at me, she told me that she was sorry and had to show me something. I sat silently in the passenger seat, at least it was warm. We drove out to Bills mansion, I fell asleep on the way and Sugar woke me as we drove by the gate. I remembered the address 6289. Sugar parked the van and jumped out without saying a word, actually neither one of us spoke since leaving the shelter. Sugar walks me out back and she bent down to look thru a basement window. I knelt down beside her and saw Amy sleeping on a beanbag chair. Sugar looking in the window said, "That used to be me, but now I am to old". I looked around the room and it was nicer then my house, and this was just the basement. My eyes went back to Amy as she slept. Amy then suddenly jerked up, Susie pulled me from the window as a big man came walking into the basement with another child, a boy that appeared to be no older then Amy. When Amy saw him she smiled and walked over to a large sofa and sat down. The boy looked familiar, and when he walked up to Amy, I thought he looked like her, he stopped a few feet from Amy and had to be gently pushed towards her. He stood in front of Amy as she reached out and grabbed his jeans and started to take his belt off. The man smiled and turned and left the room. Amy watched him leave and then grabbed the boy and threw him onto the sofa and ran to the door and tried the handle but it was locked. The boy on the sofa then walked up behind Amy and flipped his belt around her, he was able to strap both her arms down. He then spun her around and they were now face to face with each other. He grabbed Amy by her face and leaned in and whispered something in her ear. Amy got her arms free and shoved him away. I could see Amy yelling at him, but could not hear what she was saying, she then sat down in a corner and started to cry. The boy then sat on the sofa and he too appeared sad. The man opened the door and told the boy to leave and slapped the back of his head as he walked past, he then looked at Amy on the floor and laughed before shutting the door. Sugar touched my arm and I jumped, I forgot she was even there. Sugar then said as she helped me up, "Amy is strong, she knows what they are going to do to her is wrong, she is fighting them". I reached and snapped my wristband again, but I still wasn't dreaming. As we walked back to the front of the house Sugar told me that Bill was planning something big for Amy, and after it was done he was going to leave the country. When I asked if she was going with him Sugar stopped walking. I turned and reached back for her, Sugar looked up with tears in her eyes, "I want to believe that I will be okay, but Bill has had everyone that has any knowledge of this killed". I pulled her in and hugged her.

I whispered in her ear "Run away, hide". Sugar pulled away and said, "I cant, I have nowhere else to go." As we walked back to the van. There was a police car behind it with its lights on. I again thought about just trusting them with what I know, I could tell them to check the house. As I was just about to call out to them Sugar pulled me into some bushes. "What the fuck is wrong now?" I tried to ask as she put her hand over my mouth and pointed behind me. The big guy was walking down towards the cops. "Do you think she got in the house?" One of the cops asked him as he approached. The Big guy looked around the area and said, "None of the alarms were tripped, and turn your fucking lights off, are you two trying to wake up the whole neighborhood". The other cop turned the lights off and came out of the police car, he put his hand on the hood of Sugar's van, "The hood is cold so she may have been here a while, what do you want to do?" I didn't know what was going on, the big guy said no alarms went off, I thought how could that be, we walked straight across the lawn. Just then the little boy came walking down. The big guy gave him what looked like a walkie-talkie and told him to wait in the back of the van, he then told the cops to get out of site and watch the van. The big guy then walked to right to the bushes we were hiding behind and dialed his phone, "Bill, Sugars van is parked outside the house". He then said, "The cops are here to". I could hear Bill yelling into the phone. The big dude then flipped the phone shut and walked back up to the house.

6:15 am

Sugar and I were able to sneak back to the main road. We caught a bus back to the homeless shelter where I was able to hot wire a car and grab the pillowcase full of porcelain that I left by the dumpster. I just drove around town and Sugar fell asleep in a ball on the passenger seat. I pulled into a fast food joint and Sugar woke up when I was ordering. "Get me a coffee, large with extra sugar" she asked. As we drove out I asked her what the lady behind the counter of the homeless shelter meant when she told her that she didn't see anyone today. Sugar sipped her coffee and told me that Bill sent her to the shelter looking for Dan. Sugar then sat there silently gazing out the window as I drove, she then asked, "Joe, what are we going to do?" I pulled onto a dirt road that led up to the creek that was behind my house and parked the car under some trees, I grabbed my pillowcase and flung it over my shoulder and started to walk towards my house. Sugar just sat in the car and then rushed to catch up with me when I started to walk away, "You can't leave me here", she pleaded. I turned and said, "You want to know what I'm going to do? I'm going to kill Bill, I'm going to bash his fucking brains in". Sugar grabbed my arm and said, "He will know your coming". I pulled away, "He thinks I am dead, he wont know what hit him". Sugar laughed, "You don't understand, his brother, his fucking dead brother controls all his moves". I stopped walking and looked up to the sky, as I just wanted a sign. "What the fuck are you talking about?" I asked as Sugar stood in front of me. "His brother has some sort of power, he enters Bills dreams and lets him know what's happening, he will let Bill know that someone is coming for him." I put down the pillowcase and looked at Sugar, "I'm not making this shit up you have to believe me". I knew she wasn't bullshitting me, and I said, "I know, his brother Robert also comes to me in my dreams, he told me to save her". Sugar looked confused, "Save who?" she asked. "Amy, I guess". Sugar looked down, "Its to late to save her, its to late to save any of them, maybe he meant me, maybe he wants you to save me, we should just run away, if we run away Bill will see it in his dream and maybe he will leave us alone". Sugar was almost in tears as she pleaded with me to run away from this. I then asked Sugar why Robert would tell me in my dreams to save Amy and at the same time tell Bill what I was doing? Sugar then asked, "When was the last time Robert was in your dreams?" I sat down on a big rock. Sugar was right, Robert hasn't entered my head in several days. As I sat there thinking a fly landed on my shoulder, Sugar was non-stop with the questioning about what we were going to do, where we were going. She was talking a mile a minute. I figured the sugar was kicking in. I looked up at her as she came in and hugged me and started begging me to leave, I watched as the fly jumped from my shoulder and landed on Sugar's back. Sugar then stood up in front of me, and I rested on her chest as she cradled my head. "I cant walk away, but if you want to leave, you can take the car" I said as I held out a couple dollars that she could take for gas. Sugar took my hand and folded my fingers up over the money. With tears in her eyes she said, "I am not afraid of dying, I have been dead for a long time now".

8:55 am

Sugar and I got into my house thru the back door and Sugar ran to the phone, "I got a dial tone". I was confused, who the fuck were we going to call? I looked over at Danielle's house and it appeared to be abandoned, just like all the other houses in the community. I told Sugar to stay off the phone, I was still paranoid and didn't know if it was bugged, "Just keep an eye out" I told her as I went upstairs to get in the shower. As I leaned into the hot water I kept thinking about all the shit that has happened. I really didn't have any clue as to what I was going to do, when I was going to do it, or where I was going to do it. I only knew that 2-11 was D-Day. I remembered how sweet and innocent Amy was when I moved in and how she has transformed in only a couple of months. I wanted to just go and grab her from Bills and take her away, I don't know why, but I just felt like she was going to be safe. I also didn't trust Sugar, why did she just appear and why did she show me Amy at Bills house. What I didn't know was that she was making a phone call as I showered. All she said into the phone was, "We are at Joe's house now". When I returned back downstairs Sugar was asleep leaning on the window ledge. I lifted her up and walked her to the sofa and laid her down and covered her with a blanket. I then fell asleep in the chair across from her.

11:23 am

I woke up and saw that Sugar was still sleeping on the sofa, I looked at my watch, Dam its almost noon, all this kid does is sleep. I got up and grabbed a beer from the kitchen. When I sat back down Sugar woke up and stretched reaching her hands to the sky. Her belly shirt rose to expose her flesh up to the bottom of her breasts. She saw me looking and lowered her arms but held her shirt up, she rubbed her belly, and said, "Nice and tight." As my eyes went from her stomach to her face I saw a red dot on her forehead just as a bullet splattered her brains all over the back of the sofa. I fell to the floor and crawled to the side of the window. Another shot came thru hitting Sugar in the chest. I peaked out but I didn't see anyone, the street was empty and the sky was dark. I looked back at my watch to see it was 11:25 am, the sun should still be out. Suddenly the front door was kicked open and Bill and the big dude from his house came bursting in. The big dude held a high-powered rifle on me. The red dot from the lazar was shaking on my chest, or it may have been that I was shaking. Bill walked over to Sugar, "Fuck Ron, you shot the wrong one" Bill then threw her dead body face first over my dinning room table and turned with an evil smile on his face and said "I got a fucking excellent idea". Bill then grabbed her jeans and pulled them off. "Get the fuck up hump," he yelled at me as the big dude kept aiming his gun at me. I slowly pulled myself up and looked over at my hall mirror and seen the black cloth covering it. Bill became impatient and hollered, "Get the fuck over here while she is still warm". As I approached, Bill grabbed me and pushed me up between Sugars legs. Bill leaned in and pushed me down onto her back, the second bullet went straight thru and I could feel Sugar's warm blood on my chest. "This is what's going to happen." Bill reached in between my legs and ripped Sugars panties from her body. "You are going to fuck a dead girl on tape, I will combined it with your first performance and call it, before and afterlife". I went to reach out and grab Bill but Ron slammed the butt of his gun into my kidney and I slid off Sugar and fell to my knees. I knew I was dreaming, but the pain was real. Ron then picked me up and again pushed me onto Sugars body, "Have him fuck the hole in her head" Ron yelled as Bill pulled out his hand held camcorder and yelled action. I tried to push myself up but slipped on the blood that had started to cover and drip from the wooden table. "I don't have time for this fucking shit," Bill yelled as Joy came running in yelling, "I hope I didn't miss the show". Bill looked over at her and said, "Shut your dick hole and help this sorry fuck out" Joy came up behind me and pulled down my pants, she then reached around and tried to force me into Sugar. "FUCK HER", Bill yelled. Joy started pushing and pulling on my hips. Bill then yelled at her to get out of the shot and when she ignored him Bill yelled shoot her. I heard the shot and felt Joy fall on my back and slide off. "Last fucking time, FUCK HER", Bill yelled. I knew this was a dream, but I could feel pain, and smell the blood, I felt like I had no other choice. Plus I needed to know what was going to happen. I held onto Sugar leaving bloody handprints on her hips. I could not get excited enough to enter her. I then fell to the floor checking to see if I had my wristband on. Joy's dead body was still twitching next to me, her eyes were open and staring. I looked up at Ron as he handed me a gun. I heard Bill on the phone talking with the police, "I saw a guy shoot at a house and then he ran over and kick the door in". I pointed the gun at Bill and pulled the trigger, click, click, click, no bullets. I then fell backwards onto the floor as Bill and Ron left thru the backdoor. I could hear the police sirens in the distant getting closer. Suddenly Sugar shook me awake. I was still in my chair and the police sirens were real and they were getting closer. I was still half asleep and Sugar was in a panic, "They are coming to get us," she hollered as she tried to pull me up. I pushed her away, "No one even knows we are here". Just as the police drove by Sugar dropped to the floor and covered her head. She slowly looked up as the sirens drove past and faded in the distance. I sat up and wiped my eyes and looked over at

Sugar and saw that she was stretching. I jumped up and pulled her back onto the floor. Sugar was lying on top of me as she looked down, "Who is the crazy one now?" I reached up and brushed her cheek, "Sorry", Sugar sat up on me and asked if I was flirting with her. I didn't really hear what she was saying, I just kept looking for the red dot. Sugar then pulled her shirt off and dropped it over my face and said, "I'm going to take a shower, if you want to you can join me" She got up and jogged up the steps. I looked at my watch, "Hurry up we have to be out of here before nightfall". As I sat up on the floor the rest of Sugars clothing dropped from upstairs. I picked them up along with her shirt and went up. Sugar was in the shower and the steam was filling the hallway. I sat her clothes and a towel on the sink and turned to leave. Sugar reached out and grabbed my wrist. "We will both probably be dead in a couple days if not hours." I watched her face, the water running down her neck and over her breasts. "I just want someone to make love to me, and mean it". I leaned in and gave her a kiss and held her cheek against mine. She whispered in my ear "That was nice". I kissed her again on her forehead and left the bathroom.

1:00 pm

When Sugar came out of the bathroom I was sitting in a chair in the bedroom watching the street from the window. Sugar sat on the edge of the bed wrapped in a towel and asked, "Why do we have to leave before it gets dark?" I didn't take my eyes off the window. "Bill is coming for us". Sugar got up and started to massage my neck and asked me how I could possibly know that. I leaned my shoulders into her hands, "The dreams, I believe the dreams are showing me what's going to happen". Sugar stopped rubbing my neck and walked around and stood in front of me, "Tell me what you dreamed about". I reached out and rubbed her cheek with the back of my hand as water droplets rolled down from her still wet hair. "I dreamt Bill and the big guy from his house, I believe his name is Ron, came with Joy and kicked in my front door". Sugar asked me what happened next as she gently sat on my lap and laid her head on my shoulder, "Nothing, I don't know, you woke me up". I held Sugar against me as she sat on my lap, she continued to rest her head on my shoulder. She didn't need to know she was shot. "What are we going to do?" she whispered. I told her that my dreams would show me what to do, or help by showing me what not to do. She then turned my head to look at her, "Are you sure?" I kissed her gently on her lips, "Yes, I am beyond sure", I said as I lifted her from my lap and told her to get dressed. I then went downstairs to get some food.

3:00 pm

I made a couple of sandwiches as Sugar came down and sat at the table with a thud. I slid one of the sandwiches over and asked her what her problem was. Sugar ate the sandwich in three bites, "I just feel like I will never feel true love from another person". I grabbed a beer and dryly asked, "How's that?" Sugar reached over and took half of my sandwich, "I was put into this situation by Bill and Danielle when I was just a child when my cracked out mother sold me to them, I never had a chance to grow up, and no one ever tried to rescue me. They taught me what they wanted me to believe was right. What they taught me was the joy of sex, I don't think that I have ever felt love. I always wanted to as long as I could remember, was to just have someone love me. I just want to fall in love". I was shocked as Sugar had tears in her eyes and she seemed sincere. "You don't have to have sex to fall in love with someone" I said as I cleaned up the table. "Do you think you would ever be able to fall in love with someone like me?" she asked with a puppy dog look on her face. I said what do you mean by somebody like you? Sugar grabbed the crust off my plate and said, "With my past". I handed her the rest of my sandwich and said, "If you were 10 years older I would be madly head over heels in love with you". Sugar finished the rest of my sandwich and said, "Don't lie to me just to make me feel better". I then said, "I am not lying, that right now at this very moment I do have love for you, you helped me when no one else would". A big smile came across her face. "But I am not in love with you". The smile left her face. She got up and grabbed a beer. I was going to stop her but then thought she may be right, we may be dead in a couple hours, let her drink. Sugar took a drink from the beer and then put it down in front of me and threw my empty bottle away. "So you feel love for me, but you are not in love with me, but if I was in my thirties you would not be able to control yourself am I right?" I held her hands, "Right as rain". Sugar kissed my hand and said, "I have no idea what that means, but I'll take it for now".

Just as I was finishing my beer we both heard footsteps coming towards the back door. I hushed Sugar and motioned for her to get under the table. She ignored me and was right behind me as I peeked out the back window. We saw Danielle walking up towards the back porch. I turned and grabbed Sugar by her ears and pleaded with her to hide in the pantry. She leaned in and gave me a big wet Bugs Bunny kiss before walking slowly into the pantry. I then stood behind the door as Danielle slowly opened it and peaked in. As soon as she stuck her head in far enough, I grabbed her and shoved her up against a wall. "WHAT THE FUCK ARE YOU DOING HERE?" I yelled. Danielle didn't try to fight back, she just went limb as I held her up against the wall. "I came to see you". I let her sit down at the table, "How did you know I was here?" Danielle eyes were flashing all around the room. "Who or what the fuck are you looking for?" Danielle looked at me and asked me if I was alone. "Yes I am alone, what the fuck is going on?" Danielle still looking around, "You have to believe me Joe, don't trust anyone". I slammed my hands down on the table, "WHAT THE FUCK IS GOING ON?" Danielle jumped in her seat, "Are you sure you are alone, Dan is not here?" I reached across the table and grabbed her and was about to pull her across the table and punch the shit out of her. Danielle pulled back and yelled, "DAN IS ALIVE", her voice now lowering, "Bill went to pick him up at the hotel you said you were staying at and I was worried that Bill would see you there, but you weren't there, Dan was". I let Danielle go, "Did Bill see Dan?" I asked already knowing the answer. Danielle said no, but when Bill got to the room, there was a dead maid in the bed. I sat and said," I know, Bill had Joy kill her". Danielle looked up at me and said, "Bill is an expert of having other people kill his problems." Danielle appeared to be on the verge of some sort of breakdown, and I could not care less. I got up and walked over to the window to make sure Danielle was alone. "I was there you know that, I hope Bill don't". Danielle turned around and said, "I didn't tell him anything and neither has Amy." I walked over to Danielle and had to restrain myself from just using her face as a punching bag, "Why would Amy say anything?" Danielle started to look around again, I grabbed her face, "Answer me bitch." Amy told me she saw you at your house. I suddenly felt ill, "How do you know she didn't tell Bill?" Danielle finally looked me in the eyes as she said, "She told Bill that she saw her father at your house, and that he told her he was going to save her." I just stared into space. Danielle then reached for my hand,

"Tell me Joe, did you speak with Amy at your house? Or did she really see Dan?" I looked down at her and told her that Dan was dead, and that I don't know if Amy knows that. Because I used Dan's name Bill is chasing me, only he doesn't know it. I then saw out the corner of my eye that Sugar was peeking from the pantry, "Need a drink?" I asked Danielle as I walked over to the pantry door and pushed Sugar back in. I reached for a bottle of wine and told Sugar that it is better if Danielle don't know she is here. Sugar whispered, "Lets hold her hostage." I pointed at my watch and mouthed "Dark soon". I put the wine back down and came out of the pantry. Danielle seeing that I didn't have any wine asked me what was up. I grabbed her arm and lifted her from the seat, "I don't know if you are playing me or Bill, but I do know that I will not let either of you hurt Amy" Danielle pulled her arm from my grip and slapped me, "How dare you, your accusing me of wanting to harm my own child". I grabbed her wrist, "Then go to the cops". Danielle's fight again left her, "You know I can't do that, they will kill me, then what would happed to my daughter?" I pushed Danielle towards the door, "I am not really sure she is your daughter". Danielle walked off the porch a few steps and stopped, she turned around and with fear on her face said, "It don't matter anymore, no one can stop what is about to happen". She then turned and started to walk away. "But you can stop it, IF YOU WANT TO, YOU CAN STOP IT" I yelled. Danielle kept walking. I then said, "Make sure you tell your sick twisted father Bill that I have a little gift for him, tell him that I will end his life, that I will put a hole in his head and piss in it, I will skull fuck his dead ass". Danielle kept walking, "And if I have to, I will take your life too you stupid cunt". Danielle stopped walking, she hated the word cunt, she slowly turned to look at me, "Joe I need you, and if only for the visions I get that you will save her, I haven't told anyone anything about you. I don't only believe that you will save her, but I have seen you save her" she then bowed her head and whispered, "But I have also seen you kill her". I took a step out on the porch, "I would never hurt her". Danielle looked up and said, "It is what it is Joe, Just let it happen" she then turned and started to walk away. "You say no one can stop it, but at the same time you keep telling me that I will save her." Danielle stopped, she slowly turned around and softly said, "It will happen, it will happen before you save her, but she has been prepared, she is strong." I felt defeated, I asked her to help me understand what it was that was going to happen. Danielle said, "As a child I went thru exactly what Amy is going thru, and I can see in Amy that she is enjoying herself as I did. I never thought it would end up this way, I never wanted Amy to get hurt, I never wanted anyone to get hurt, but if you tell or try to stop it from happening a lot of people will die, including you and Amy. I just need you to make sure she is safe after it happens." Danielle then disappeared into the tree line. I turned to go back in and caught Sugar coming from the pantry with a Bar-B-Q fork. I had to shut the back door before she ran out. "Fuck her" I said, "She is to stupid to realize that she is already dead". I stood in the doorway and made sure Danielle left. The one thing she said that stuck with me as I took the fork from Sugar was that Bill is an expert of having people kill for him. I looked over at Sugar as she stared out the window and I thought, is that why she is here?

4:45 pm

Sugar and I packed some food and supplies and then we snuck out the back and headed back to the car. It would not start so I grabbed the pillowcase from the back seat and swung it over my shoulder. Sugar asked me why I kept that with me. I didn't answer and grabbed her by her hand as we started walking. We walked along the creek to an overpass, climbed up and headed back down the street. I jumped every time a car drove by the gate out front. Sugar asked if I was getting a little paranoid. I knew she was feeling it too because every time a car or a noise was heard she squeezed my hand a little tighter. I led Sugar over to Susie's house, it was empty as the family had moved away and the grass on the front lawn was over grown. Plus it was right next door to Danielle's house. I would be able to see if anything was going on from several windows. Problem was, I didn't know if they were going to shoot the film at Danielle's.

Back at Bills, Bill demanded that Danielle tell him where she went. She told him she went to her house to get a few things and that she noticed that someone was at my house, but when she got there they ran off before she could see who it was. Bill gave Danielle a backhanded slap across her face knocking her down. "You stupid bitch you know it was Dan, who else could it have been?" Danielle looked up and answered "A Squatter". Bill looking down at Danielle, "Really bitch, are squatters a big problem in a gated community?" Bill then stepped over Danielle and called Ron on the phone and told him to come over, Bill told him to bring his big gun and Amy with him, and before he hung up he said that they have some hunting to do. When Bill left the room Joy helped Danielle get up to the bathroom to tend to her bleeding nose and lip. Bill stuck his head in and grabbed Joy's arm and pulled her out. "Listen" he whispered to Joy "Danielle is going to be no good for the movie looking like that". Joy stuttered, "I, I, I can cover it with make-up". Bill grabbed Joy by her face and yelled, "NO, You will take her place" as he shoved her back into the bathroom. Joy shut the door and sat on the edge of the tub, as she remembered hearing Bill say he would kill her during the movie in her dream. Danielle was looking at her in the mirror as she said, "You got what you wanted, you got Amy." Danielle then turned to look at Joy and asked, "Did Bill tell you to kill me?" Joy looked up with tears in her eyes, "No, but he is going to kill all of us". Before Danielle could ask how she knew that, Bill opened the door and told Joy to come down stairs. As Joy got up to leave Amy ran in and hugged Danielle. Joy patted Amy on her head and smiled as she walked out. Joy wanted to tell them to run away but she just walked out. Bill grabbed her and told her to come with him and Ron. Joy appeared distant and slow, Bill shook her, "What the fuck is your problem now?" Joy didn't respond, she didn't even look at him.

As Amy hugged Danielle she asked if everything was going to be okay, she asked if they were still going to leave. Danielle told her in a couple days and kissed her forehead. Amy looked up and saw Danielle's bloody face and she started to cry. "What happened?" Danielle told her that she fell, she then told her to go wait in the bedroom. When Danielle returned to the bedroom, Amy was half asleep on the bed. Danielle sat down next to her and rubbed her back. "Amy, do you like Joe?" Amy answered "Un-hun". Danielle asked, "Do you trust him, do you trust him enough to go away with him?" Amy sat up on the bed and held Danielle as she said, "Joe is going to come and get us." Danielle slowly lifted Amy's head to look her in the eyes, Amy smiled and asked, "You are sure that Joe is still alive?" Danielle started to tear up and brushed Amy's hair from her eyes, "You may have to leave with Joe," Danielle said as she fought to keep her tears in her eyes. Amy not looking up asked, "After we make Bills film?" Danielle stood up and watched as Bill, Ron and Joy drove away "Yes baby, after". Amy then laid back down on the bed. Amy made Danielle pinky swear that she would tell no one about Joe, especially Bill. Amy and Danielle hooked their pinkies and swore. Danielle softly cried as Amy drifted to sleep.

Before getting in the car Bill told Ron that Sugar was with Dan at Joes house, he told him that he caught Danielle going over there, and when he questioned her about it, she lied and he told him the story she had told him. Ron got in the back and asked how he knew Danielle was lying. Bill didn't answer. Ron then asked what it was they were going to do. Bill told him to be patient. Bill then reached over and took hold of Joy's hand. "This is what you wanted sweetheart, you always wanted to be in another film". Joy continued to silently stare straight ahead. Bill gently squeezed her hand and said, "If you don't tell me what's bothering you, I wont be able to fix it". Joy quietly asked, "Are you going to kill me?" Bill laughed, "If I wanted you dead, Ron would be wiping your brains off the windshield right now". Joy then said, "In my dreams you". Bill cut her off, "Fuck your dreams, its all nerves, I dreamt last night that Dan hit me in the face with a toilet". Ron laughed in the back, "That's not going to happen, that little prick could barley lift the seat to pee" Joy smiled. Bill then told her to take a look in the glove compartment. Joy found a brand new large hunting knife that Bill told her to put in her bag.

8:00 pm

Ron put his rifle together in the car, he was placing the silencer on as Bill pulled up to the gatehouse. The security guard waved them in. Bill rolled down his window and asked if he had seen anyone. The guard shook his head no and said, "This place is a ghost town." Bill then handed the guard some money and told him to go home. The guard did not care as to why he was being sent home, he was happy to leave.

They then pulled in and parked across the street from my house. Joy got out and surveyed the street. She tapped on the window and said, "All clear" as she got back in. Ron got out and stood behind a tree and aimed the laser thru my front bow window. Joy was sitting in the passenger side seat rubbing her hands together to get warm, she asked, "What is he waiting for?" Bill then told her to be patient, that as soon as he has a shot he will take it. Joy then turned her conversation back to going away with Bill after they make the movie. Bill told her that it would probably be a good idea if everyone went his or her own way. Joy was shocked. Bill explained that as soon as the DVD hit the streets someone is going to take it to the cops, an honest cop. Joy protested telling him that no one went to the cops about the other films. Bill then told her that this film was going to be the first one released in this country. Joy then became even more on edge and stated that if she was going to be in the film, she too should leave the country. Bill understood and agreed, he told her she should leave, just not with him.

Suddenly both of them saw a flash come from Ron's gun, they got out and looked thru my front window as Ron fired again. All three of them then slowly started to cross the street. Joy forgot her knife and she had turn back to the car to get it as Bill kicked my front door open. Joy grabbed her knife from her bag and quickly jogged to the door, she was hoping she didn't miss any of the fun, as she entered the house Bill was standing in the middle of the room rubbing his head. Ron kept saying that he saw someone move. Joy holding the knife asked what happened? Bill threw his hands up in the air and said, "Ron killed the fucking couch."

8:15 pm

As I sat at Susie's bedroom window, I watched as they pulled up, I watched Joy get out, and for a moment I thought she was going to run from them, but she got back in the car as Ron got out and stood behind a tree and fired into my house. I watched all three of them go over and enter my house after Bill kicked the door in. They were inside for quite a while before they came back out. Bill had my laptop under his arm and they all jumped in the car and drove away. I sat at the window as a big smile came across my face and thought to myself that my dreams are winning.

Sugar was in the family room rummaging thru the drawers and closets, I had no idea what she was looking for, nor did I care. I was a little relieved that she wasn't bugging me about what we were going to do. My relief didn't last long as Sugar came back in with a handful of DVD's. She put one in and pushed play. "This is my first time," she said as if she was proud of it, "It was filmed in this bedroom," she said as she stood in front of the TV. I continued to stare out the window. Sugar threw the case at me and asked, "You gonna watch?" I didn't respond. When the DVD started I tried to block out the sound. Sugar said, "Look at Danielle, I can't believe how young she looks". I turned to see Danielle she appeared to be in her late teens or early twenties. When Sugar saw me watching she smiled and said, "That is me and Susie with her". Susie and Sugar looked to be about 11 or 12 years old. I could tell someone off screen was coaching them as they kept looking back at the camera, someone was telling them what to do. I got up and turned the TV off. Sugar snapped and asked me why I did that. I told her the light could be seen from the street. "Sorry" she said as she sat down on the bed. I then asked "How old were you in that?" Sugar laid back down on the bed and started playing with her hair, "It was the morning of my 12th birthday, actually it was my 14th, but my mother was afraid that if she told Bill my correct age he would not had paid as much, and she would not have been able to get high. So she lied about my age". I sat down on the foot of the bed, "So you are 21 now?" Sugar giggled "Yea, it was my 21st birthday the day at the bookstore, I told you that right before Bill had me". I held up my hand to shut Sugar up. "I think Amy was born on 12-28, so has she been put on film yet?" Sugar kicked off her shoes and was rubbing her feet on my back, "I don't think so, Bill has a rule that he wont use a kid until they are old enough." I looked back at Sugar, "How old, is old enough?" Sugar shrugged her shoulders and said, "Bill is a little superstitious, he likes to do the first one on your 12th birthday." I put my head in my hands, "This don't make sense, Amy turned twelve last month." I then asked Sugar if she was sure of Bills rules. Sugar sat up next to me and told me that Susie was older then her, Sugar told me Susie turned 13 about eight months before her fake 14th. I didn't say anything, Sugar flipped around on the bed and put her head in my lap and looked up at me, "I remember, because Bill let me watch Susie make her first film after her 12th birthday party". I got up off the bed and almost knocked Sugar to the floor, "Was that film made in here also?" Sugar rubbed her head then said, "No, I think it was made up the street." I then looked out the bedroom window and realized that every single home in this community was empty. "Stay here" I said, "I have to get something from my house". Sugar got up with a worried look on her face, "You cant, they might come back". I gave her my cell phone and told her to watch by the window and if any one comes near the house dial my house number and let it ring once, and I'll run out the back. Sugar followed me to the bedroom door, "Wait" she said as she grabbed me and kissed me. I held her close to me, my hands rising under the back of her shirt. "Hurry back" she said, "I don't want to be here alone".

10:15 pm

I ran into my living room and grabbed what I had saved from the box and my notes that I kept in a big overstuffed envelope hidden in the drop ceiling. At almost the same time my phone rang once, as a spotlight came shinning thru my shot out window. I stood still in the corner and could see a police car shinning their spotlight on the house. I also saw Sugar walking down the street towards the police car. When Sugar approached the car I was able to get out the back door and hop the fence into Danielle's yard. Then I saw that one of the Police Officers was making his way to my back yard holding a flashlight with his weapon drawn, it made me wonder what Sugar told them. I heard the Officer say "The back door is open" into his radio. He then leaned up against the house as he was told to wait, that backup was on the way. I didn't know it, but Sugar called the cops and reported a robbery in progress just as I left Susie's house. Danielle's basement door was open and I was able to enter before being seen. When I reached the living room I discovered a lot of filming equipment, lights cameras and a bunch of shit I had no idea what it was. I went up to the bedroom and they were just the way I remembered them. I then smelled what appeared to be fresh paint and looked into the spare bedroom. The walls were painted black and the paint was still tacky. All the windows were also painted over but had giant curtains with upside down crosses on them. There were shackles attached to the walls and the bed. This was definitely where this movie was going to be made. I called my cell phone hoping Sugar would answer, she picked up just before it went to voice mail. She asked me where I was, but I changed the subject and told her to stay away from the police. I then heard a cop in the background telling her to move along. Sugar told me that she was the only person that came out to see what was going on. She also said she heard the cops say that the owner of the house was killed several days ago. I started to tell her that it was a long story when she yelled into the phone, "Tell me later" and hung up. I scratched some paint from the window and peaked out to see that Sugar was running up to someone that was walking down the street. Several cops were taping up my house with that yellow police tape. I then saw Sugar in the shadows talking with the man she ran up to, I didn't think he was from this neighborhood, his face was hidden in the shadows, but he did look a little familiar. They talked for several minutes then embraced in a hug before he walked away back down the street.

What I didn't see was that this man had handed Sugar some pills and instructed her to put them all in my drink tomorrow night, he told her to leave as soon as I fell asleep.

Sugar asked him if the pills would kill me. The man told her that he didn't want me dead, that the pills would only knock me out long enough so they can complete what was promised. After about two hours I was able to exit out the back and make my way back to Susie's house.

2-10-98 / 1:30 am

We watched the police as they finished boarding up my front door and windows. Sugar asked me what was so important that I needed to almost get caught by the cops. I pulled out the envelope and emptied its contents on the bed. I then looked at Sugar and said, "Its my house, I wasn't doing anything wrong". Sugar sat down on the bed next to the pile of papers and said, "Do you know that Bill Johnson's twin brother Robert used to live at your house before he got arrested?" Sugar was looking thru the papers on the bed as I felt a horrible feeling boiling up in my gut. Sugar looked up and asked if I was feeling okay. I got up and walked to the window, I was staring at my house. "Johnson started all of this long before I even moved in there." Sugar walked up behind me and asked me what I was talking about. "They knew I would buy that house, they wanted me to buy that house." Sugar walked back to the bed, she then said as she sat back down, "Bill didn't want anyone to move in, he was pissed when his brother sold it from jail, it was the first time what he called an outsider moved in" I felt like I was going to throw up, I held my head, there wasn't anything I could have done, I would have been pulled into this no matter what. This was Sogod's plan all along. I started looking thru the pile of papers, now more determined then ever to figure this out. I told Sugar that Timmy Johnson died at birth on 12-28-97, the same day Amy was born. Sugar looked at me with what could only be described as the most dumfounded uninterested look on her face. "This is it," I yelled as I grabbed and kissed her. Timmy Johnson was Danielle's baby, but he died at birth. So somehow Danielle's baby was switched with another baby. Danielle's baby was switched with Amy, somehow Dan and Danielle, or Johnny Downs switched those babies, and they switched them on February 11th, 211." Sugar dropped all the papers she was holing back into the pile and said, "I don't think so, the boy we saw in the basement with Amy, they call him TJ, I am 100 % sure that it stands for Timmy Johnson." I refused to believe that, "I am sure Danielle took Amy from that hospital on 2-11". Sugar suddenly became even more disinterested, "So what, in less then a day and a half Amy will be a memory. What would we do with this information, and how will it stop Bill from doing what he is about to do? Unless you know who Amy's real parents were, who would we tell?" My excitement level dropped a little. "Let me have my moment", I said. "I love puzzles and I am on the verge of solving this one". Sugar had gotten up and was looking out the window, "The cops are leaving," she said as she turned around and saw that I was passed out on the bed. Sugar pulled my shoes off and then pulled the covers up over both of us. Soon Sugar was sound asleep next to me. I quietly got up and took Sugars purse downstairs. I found her phone and disabled it before putting it back. I searched her coat pockets and found a piece of paper with a phone number on it. I looked at the number then at Sugars broken phone. I picked up the house phone but the line was dead. I then found my cell phone in the inside pocket of Sugars bag. If I had kept checking I would have found the pills she had just received. I was just about to hit send when I thought what if they have caller ID. I then switched my sim card with Sugars and called. "Sugar what's up, where are you?" I felt my rage about to explode, as it was Danielle on the other end. Danielle then asked, "Sugar, are you okay?" I put the phone close to my mouth and whispered, "I knew you were fucking me", Danielle didn't say anything for a few seconds. I wanted to smash the phone. Danielle then asked me where Sugars was. "Sugars dead," I said before I hung up. I went back upstairs and stood over Sugar as she slept. I wanted to smother her with the pillow, but I got back in bed, Sugar rolled over and spooned me, she reached around and held me in her sleep. It took every ounce of self-control not to strangle her.

1:50 am

Danielle looked at the phone and started to shake. Bill came in the room and asked her who called. Danielle sat down and said, "Someone just called from Sugar's phone and said that Sugar was dead." Bill slapped the phone from Danielle's hand, "What the fuck is going on, why would Sugar want to call you?" Before Danielle could answer, Bill grabbed her and threw her to the floor, he called for Joy to bring him some duct tape. Both of them taped Danielle's feet and hands. Ron came from upstairs to see what was going on. "This bitch has been helping Sugar and Dan all along, letting them know what we are doing, but it just back fired because psycho Dan just killed Sugar, didn't he bitch," Bill said as he bent down and grabbed Danielle's face, "You are why they were staying one step ahead of me." Bill then told Ron to watch her. Bill picked up the phone and left the room with Joy. Danielle looked up at Ron and asked him to help her. Ron bent down and placed a piece of duct tape over her mouth, then he picked her up and as he carried her up to her bedroom he whispered in her ear as he put her down on the bed, "Only your dreams can help you now". Bill dialed Sugars number several times, each time he received a message that the phone was out of service. Joy sat down next to Bill at the table and said, "So what if she was talking to Dan, what can they do? You didn't tell her where or when we were going to do this?" Bill threw the phone against the wall, "I told her we were going to wait." Bill looked past Joy, he then focused back on her face and said, "Call everyone, we are going to do this now."

2:11 am

I woke up and Sugar was wrapped up in the sheets. I still wanted her dead, but something was telling me to wait. Sugar slowly started to wake up and when she realized that I was awake she rolled over and gave me a big kiss, smiled and laid her head on my chest. "What was that for?" I asked. I then heard Amy say, "For saving me". I pulled the sheet back and Amy was lying next to me in bed, she appeared to be bleeding from her ears. I looked around the room and we were all back in my house in my bedroom. The mirror above my dresser was covered by a black cloth, I knew I was dreaming so I turned my attention back to Amy as she was now making out with Sugar as they lay next to me, the blood from Amy's ears was starting to soak into the pillows and mattress. I told Sugar to leave, she got up off the bed and sat in a chair across from the bed. She was naked and covering herself with a big throw pillow. I sat up and asked Amy how I saved her. Amy told me that she refused to go thru with making the movie and Bill told her she could leave. I hugged her, trying to see why her ears were bleeding, and asked her why she came over here, Amy looked around confused, and she then looked over at Sugar. "Say it" Sugar whispered thru clenched teeth. I turned Amy's face back to me "Say what?" I asked. Amy started to cry, her blood was now running down onto her clothing. Sugar came over and was kneeling on the bed, she kept yelling, "SAY IT, SAY IT, SAY IT". I pushed Sugar off the bed, she hit the floor with a thud. "Tell me sweetheart", Amy curled up in a ball on the bed and held her bloody ears. Sugar continued to yell "SAY IT" over and over to Amy from the floor. I grabbed Sugar by her arm and pulled her back up and she fell onto the bed next to us. I put my hands around her neck and told her to shut the fuck up. But she continued to chant, Say it, say it, say it. I looked back at Amy, "Tell me, you know I would never hurt you, I will never let anyone hurt you", Sugar pulled free and rolled right up to Amy as she continued her Say it chant. I raised one of my hands and I was going to punch Sugar's teeth out. Amy suddenly screamed at the top of her lungs, "YOU ARE DEAD". Sugars chanting turned into laughter. I grabbed her arm and threw her back to the floor. I pulled Amy into me and hugged her. "I'm not dead, I'm right here". Amy then whispered slowly in my ear as blood started to run from her mouth, "I killed you".

I woke up to find Sugar getting up off the floor, "What happened to you?" I asked. Sugar stood at the side of the bed with her hands on her hips and said, "You tell me, one moment I am sound asleep and the next thing I know you are throwing me out of bed". I rolled over and said sorry. Sugar stood there staring at me for a few moments before she asked, "Joe, was it another dream?" I shook my head no and told her that she woke me up falling from the bed. Sugar then quietly said, "I had one". I rolled over and looked up at her and saw tears swelling up in her eyes. I reached for her to get back in bed, but she pulled away shaking. "Sugar, tell me what you saw". Sugar told me she was in a field and Amy came up to her and led her to a clearing with tombstones. I was able to grab her arm and sit her on the edge of the bed, "Were their six stones?" I asked. Sugar shook her head yes. I told her that I had that same dream several weeks ago and that Amy also led me to the tombstones, but only five of them had names on them. Sugar turned around to look at me and whispered softly that Danielle's name was on the last stone. I thought to myself this might be happening soon and that Bill has already killed Danielle. I pulled her in and asked her if she had any other dreams that she hasn't told me about. I could hardly understand her, as she said no through her sobs. She lay silently for several minutes at the foot of the bed. She then pushed herself up and stood by the bed. I asked her if she was all right. She told me that when she touched the tombstone with Danielle's name on it in her dream, she was transformed into the room where Amy and Danielle were about to make the movie. Bill was very upset and he was screaming at Danielle to just do it. She said that Danielle was sitting on the bed refusing to move or remove her robe. Bill walked over and started to rip it off her. Bill then pulled a gun out and pressed it into Danielle's face as he yelled that this was going to happen. Amy then sat up and slowly pushed the gun away from her mothers face, and looked over at me in the corner of the room. Bill looked at her for a second and then said, "Okay, as long as someone dies". Bill then clapped his hands and yelled action. Amy still hugging her mother on the bed fired a small gun into Danielle chest. Danielle fell from the bed onto the floor landing on her back. She was still alive but bleeding out. Amy jumped off the bed and started to rub the blood all over her body, wiping some on her face and licking her fingers. Amy then stood up as her mother lay dying on the floor. Amy was covered in her mother's blood. Bill yelled "Fucking beautiful". Bill then walked over to Amy and said "You can now leave with Joe," Amy smiled up at Bill as he very calmly shot her thru her ear. The bullet caused blood and brain matter to come out the other side of Amy's head and splatter on Sugar. Bill then looked at Sugar as she stood there in shock and said, "I don't need you anymore either slut". And fired at her. Sugar fell backwards and landed back in the field next to the sixth tombstone. When Sugar looked up at the tombstone, it now had her name on it. As she went to touch the stone again she woke up to me pushing her out of the bed. I pulled her down on the bed and held her until we both fell back to sleep.

4:15 am

I woke up and found myself alone in the bed. I got up and could hear Sugar downstairs. I went to the top of the steps and I was able to see that she was trying to get her phone to work. I thought that I was too close to let her fuck my shit up and I walked up on her. I expected her to try and hide the phone, but she just turned and said, "My fucking phone wont work" as she held it out to me, I slapped it from her hands. Sugar backed away and fell onto the sofa. "What the fuck is your problem?" she asked with fear in her voice. I pulled out the phone number I found in her coat and crumbled it up and threw it at her. Sugar pulled it open and asked me what I was doing with Danielle's number. I told her that I had found it in her coat, I told her she was playing me and I accused her of calling Danielle when we were at my house, why else would she come looking for me there? Sugar attempted to get up, "Listen you don't understand" she said before I pushed her back down. I then demanded, "Make me understand, you have one chance to make me underfuckingstand". Sugar told me to sit. I stood as she told me that Bill had decided to make another movie, and he had been getting more and more paranoid and that he became super paranoid when Dan broke into his house and slapped Danielle around. Sugar told me that Bill saw it happen before it happened in a dream, but in his dream Bill saw me breaking in and taking Danielle and Amy away. Bill became so paranoid and untrusting as he got closer to making this movie. Everything he did was a result of his dreams. Sugar then told me that Bill believed Danielle wasn't only hiding Dan but she was also hiding me as well. If anyone tried to convince Bill that I was dead he would not listen and distant himself from them. Then one night someone called Bill and told him that a Dan Williams had registered at some hotel. Bill thought that it may be Dan and he sent one of his girls, Ruby over to check it out. Sugar told me when Ruby called and reported to Bill that she was at the room, but the guys name wasn't Dan it was Joe, Bill freaked out. Sugar said he was yelling I told you Joe was still alive and that motherfucker is hiding with Dan. Before he called for Joy to go over to the hotel with him, he sent Ron out to kill the people that were supposed to kill Dan and me. Sugar said that Danielle tried to tell Bill that Dan probably told Ruby a fake name. Bill told Sugar to stay with Danielle. When they returned Bill was way past angry, he was yelling that Ruby didn't know who the fuck she was with. Sugar said she asked Bill where Ruby was. Bill told her that she died due to lack of knowledge. Sugar then grabbed my hand and said, "Ruby was my friend and Bill killed her for trying to help him." I pulled away, "That still doesn't answer why you would call and let Danielle know where we were. Sugar looked at me and said that Danielle was into her dreams almost as much as Bill was, that she was so many times going to leave with Amy after Bill told her that Amy was going to be his next girl. Sugar then told me that Danielle asked her to find me and make sure that I stayed and saved Amy, Sugar told me that Danielle begged her to do this. I looked at Sugar and I found myself actually starting to believe her. Sugar then said, "It was Danielle that sent me to the shelter, she told me that you would be sleeping in the lobby". I sat down and held Sugar. Sugar then said that Bill called the homeless shelter just before she was able to sneak out and he gave Dan's description to one of his friends that worked there, and that is why the girl said we don't have nothing for you. Sugar then told me when she was driving me to Bills, that she was going to turn me over to him that night, and that was why she was taking me there. When I was watching Amy in the basement window, Sugar said that she was just about to call and let Bill know where we were, but she received a call from her father. Her father told her to keep me alive and away from Bill, and when she told her father about Danielle, he told her that when she talks to Danielle, she was to only let her know that we were safe but not to let her know where we were or what we were going to do. Sugar said that when Danielle called her when we were back at my house when I was in the shower. Sugar said she lied and told Danielle that she lost me and she didn't know where I went. I worked in a prison for ten years and I could tell when an inmate was spinning me with lies, Sugar wasn't. I asked, "Why would your father want to keep me alive?" Sugar said she didn't know and showed me the pills that he gave her, "He told me to put these in your drink tonight". I took the pills from her. I was really starting to get sick of these pills. "He said they would not kill you, that they would cause like a temporary coma that would last several hours.

Enough time so the film could be made and everyone would disappear before you woke up." I put the pills in my pocket and asked, "How's your father involved in this?" But before she answered I asked, "I thought your parents sold you?" Sugar then told me that he isn't really her father. He is the land developer that built this community for the Johnson's and Bill has all the kids call him father. I got up and walked to the window, "So it's tonight?" Sugar walked up and hugged me from behind and said, "You have to take me with you now, if you bust in and disrupt the filming and I don't do what I was told, I know they will kill both of us". I turned around and kissed her on her forehead, "The money behind this wants me alive, and believe me if they do kill me, I'll make sure you are no where near them, and that you remain safe". I then took Sugar and escorted her back upstairs and told her that she will not leave my sight, I held her as we sat down on the bed, and I held her until she stopped shaking. I got up and went to watch the street out the window, Sugar whispered to herself, "Danielle was only trying to help".

8:30 am

Sugar woke up and rolled over on the bed and looked at me as I sat and stared out the window. "I'm so bored." She then wined, "I'm hungry". I looked over at her, "Are you bored, or hungry?" I got up and grabbed the backpack I filled at my house and tossed it to her. I sat down on the bed as she ripped into a box of cookies and asked, "Did you figure out what we are going to do yet?" I took a cookie and said, "You will have to make a phone call later tonight". Sugar stopped eating and asked, "To who?" I looked into her eyes, she appeared eager to help, or just wanted information to pass on. "You will call your so called father and tell him that you gave me the drug, Then you will tell him you are scared and you want to leave". Sugar said he wouldn't believe her. "You will have one chance to make him believe". Sugar looked up from her cookies and said, "He won't believe me because that is not me, I have never backed down or away from anything, and I am never scared".

1:00 pm

After several hours of card games and endless useless conversation, Sugar said that she saw some wine in the kitchen when she was snooping. I was blown away that she did not bring that up earlier in her mind numbing conversations. We got up and went to the kitchen, as she reached under the sink and pulled out two big bottles of wine I grabbed two glasses from the higher cabinets and knocked over a bag of flour that spilled out onto Sugars head and down her back. Sugar stood up and was covered in the white powder. She looked like a dog sending a cloud of white dust into the air as she shook herself. I really tried not to laugh. She shoved the wine into my arms and stormed up to take a shower. I put the wine on the table and sat by the steps to make sure she wasn't going to try and sneak out. I then noticed all of the DVD's Sugar had upstairs were now on the coffee table. They were all labeled by date only. All of them were made between 1980 and 1990, none of the dates jumped out at me. In the middle of the stack was one without a date listed. I put it in and hit play. It started just like the others I have seen with a young girl about to disrobe. As I went to hit stop it switched to a woman that I think was Susie's mother. She appeared to be setting up a hidden camera. She turned and looked toward the front door and quickly sat dawn, making sure she was in frame. A much younger Bill then walked in with a little girl that looked like Susie, Bill looked around the room, and he appeared to be nervous. Susie could not have been more then 8 years old. The woman gave her some crayons and a book and she sat on the floor and started to color. Bill sat across from this woman. The woman was nervous and she kept looking at the camera. Bill asked her if anything was wrong. The woman shook her head no then asked Bill what was going to happen to the kids that are getting too old. Joy who had to be 15 or 16 walked in and was introduced to the woman as the nanny that had been taking care of teaching the little girls. Joy nodded her head and sat down with Susie and started to color with her. Bill got up and threw an envelope on the woman's lap. She again looked over at the camera and said she feels like a whore. Bill then went to walk out but turned back to the woman and said, "The kids will one day take your place, so don't worry about the kids, worry about what is going to happen to you." I sat and watched Susie as she was on the floor coloring, she was a beautiful happy little girl, Joy sat next to her as she looked up at the woman and said, "I use to be this kid" and reached her hand up under the back of Susie's shirt. A tear slid slowly down the woman's face as she got up and sat down with Joy and Susie. Joy then leaned over and kissed the woman on her neck and whispered, "One day I will be you and this house will be mine." I thought this is how it starts, I then realized I had tears in my eyes also. The DVD then switched back. I got up and pushed stop, the clock on the DVD was 2:30 pm. I could still hear the water running in the shower. I then ran up and looked in the bedroom, there was an ass shape outline of flour on the bed sheet, but I didn't see Sugars clothes anywhere. I ran and pulled the shower curtain back. Sugar screamed and covered herself, "You scared the piss out of me" she said, I then saw her clothes in a pile by the sink and said, "Sorry". Sugar holding herself then said, "No Joe, lucky for me I am in the shower, I actually pissed when you snatched the curtain back". I sat down on the toilet and asked, "How long have you been in there?" She then told me that she did think about sneaking out the bedroom window, but didn't. I ask her what changed her mind. She softly said, "My dreams, I believe Bill wants to kill me". Sugar bent down and turned the water off and wrapped herself in a towel and sat on the edge of the tub, she reached out and cupped both my hands, "You have to trust me, and I have to trust you, we are all we have." She leaned in and kissed my cheek, she then quickly pulled back, "What the fuck dude you stink". I lifted my arms and smelled, "I don't think it me, I think it's the clothes", Sugar then started to pull my shirt off and said that she would throw our clothes in the wash. I agreed and told her to gather her things up, I turned the water back on and got in the shower as Sugar headed towards the laundry room. I again stood in the stream of hot water, she was right, I had to trust her, and she was all I had right now. Suddenly the water turned ice cold as the washer started to fill up. I got out and wrapped a towel around me. When I came out of the bathroom Sugar was just going into the bedroom. I went in and found her towel on the floor and she was bundled under the covers. I sat down and said to her, "I do have to trust you, and I believe you are right about thinking Bill wants you dead". I then lifted the covers to get in bed with her. I pulled the covers up and stared at the ceiling as Sugar fell asleep next to me.

3:30 pm

I got up from a dreamless nap and pulled the covers up to reveal Sugar as she continued to snore next to me. I grabbed our clothing from the wash and dressed in the laundry room. I don't know why, but I folded Sugars

clothes before placing them on a chair next to the bed. I
went down and heard a motor running out front, I peeked
out and saw two men unloading boxes into Danielle's
house. There were no markings on any of the boxes, and
then I saw one carry in tripods and lights. This film was
about to happen. I looked at the wine on the table and
thought about how hungry I was and if I had a glass of
wine it would knock me on my ass. The food I brought
over was completely gone. I searched the kitchen but the
only food in there was spoiled. I then watched as the two
guys shut the truck doors and drove away. I then left
Sugar a note and snuck out to the store and brought some
sandwiches and cigarettes. When I returned back Sugar
was still up in the bedroom, at least I hoped she was as
I quietly walked up the steps. When I opened the door
Sugar was just pulling on her pants. "I got us some food",
I said as I turned to walk back downstairs. Sugar turned
around and had a look of terror on her face. "What's
wrong now?" I asked. She sat on the bed and said she had
another dream. Sugar stared down at her hands in her
lap. I told her to tell me what she saw. She said that her
dream started when she woke up and I came in the room,
and said I got some food. I took her hands and asked her
to tell me how it ends? Sugar looked up and said, "I kill
you". I had shivers, "Why do you kill me?" Sugar got up
and took a pair of scissors off the dresser and threw them
in a small trashcan. "I stab you with them in your sleep
after we make love." That didn't answer why, but the

how was now answered. Sugar hugged me, "Please don't fall asleep". I whispered back," I wasn't planning on it", and thought to myself, now I have a reason not to. Sugar smiled as she wiped away a tear and asked, "Where is the food?" I told her downstairs and followed her as she left the room. I then turned around and grabbed the scissors from the trash and tossed them out the window.

6:20 pm

It was starting to get dark and Sugar and I were opening the second bottle of wine, "Lets play truth or dare," she said as she sat down next to me on the sofa. "Okay" I said, "But no weird shit". She pulled her legs up into an Indian sitting position on the sofa and said, "I'll go first, and I will take truth". I took a sip of wine and said, "Did you ever steal from anyone? And if so, what was the best thing you ever took?" Sugar made a weird sound and said, "This is easy, I stole from everyone I ever met, but the best thing I ever stole had to be this red corvette that I drove around for about an hour before I parked it and called the owner and told him where it was". I didn't know what to think, "I asked why was that the best thing you ever stole?" Sugar answered, "No one got hurt, nothing got broke and everyone was happy in the end. The car was returned missing only gas". I looked at her, "Are you drunk?" She flagged me. "Your turn, Truth or dare?" I didn't know what she would dare me, so I said truth.

Sugar look straight at me. "That day in the bookstore, did you enjoy it?" I forced a smile and answered, "I can honestly say, NO, no I didn't, hell to the no". Sugar appeared to get upset and wanted me to explain, "How could anyone enjoy anything with the possibility of death when it's over". Sugar shook her head "Okay, okay, then did you ever fantasize about me after that day?" I had to think, I didn't want to hurt her feelings so I said "Yes", but I don't think I was lying. Sugar smiled, and said, "Dare". I said "I have another truth for you", Sugar sat up and said "Okay Joe, truth me". I then asked, "What is the worst thing you ever had stolen from you?" Sugars good mood suddenly turned dark, "That's also easy for me, It was my childhood, my heart, my soul, theses are things that were taken from me at a young age and even if the fucker that took them wanted to give them back, IT'S FUCKING IMPOSSABLE". Sugar was yelling by the end and I had to grab her and hold her, she was starting to tear up. I told her I was sorry and said "I'll take dare". Sugar got up filled her glass with more wine and handed it to me, she then started drinking straight from the bottle. She walked around in front of the sofa before saying, "I dare you to kill Bill". I looked at her and asked, "Right now?" She said "I don't care when you do it, I just want him dead", Sugar was starting to get loud again, "I want you to HURT HIM, I want that FUCK to feel the pain THAT I FELT, I want him to feel the pain that I felt when a large man raped me as a child, I want him to feel the embarrassment of having objects shoved in you as grown men laughed, I want him to die slowly, I WANT HIM DEAD". Sugars head fell into her hands as she started to cry. I couldn't do anything but hold her head in my lap. She calmed down after several minutes of sobbing. She then looked up at me and said, "I should have just dared you to fuck me". I just continued to hold her. I thought to myself, Kill Bill I can do that, I don't think I could fuck this kid.

7:00 pm

I got up and sat by the window, I was waiting for any sign of Bill or Danielle. I had no idea what I was going to do when they got here. Sugar was doing what she has been doing 75 percent of the time since she got here, she was sleeping on the sofa. I was now drinking the wine straight from the bottle. Sugar got up and walked up behind me. I didn't know she was there until she started rubbing my shoulders. "I will watch why don't you get some rest". I was pretty tired, drunk and tired. I got up and told her to get me as soon as anyone shows up. I went up to lie in bed. It wasn't long before I was sound asleep.

11:25 pm

I found myself in an empty room, I turned to look for a door but there was none, just four tall walls. I then heard a child laugh behind me and when I turned around I saw

Amy sitting on the floor. I reached out for her. Danielle then walked past me and helped Amy stand up. I turned to see if there was anyone else in the room but it was empty. When I turned back around, Amy was now laying on a huge bed with both Danielle and Bill. Danielle then reached out and started to take Amy's sundress off, Amy reached out for me. I reached out towards Amy but Danielle slapped my hand away. Bill suddenly spun me around and pointed a gun at me, "You were never going to stop this", he said as he pressed the barrel of the gun against my head. I shut my eyes as I heard a shot and jumped in fear, I expected to wake from a dream, but I didn't. I then felt Bill dropped his hands, his gun falling to the floor. I opened my eyes and looked at Bill and saw blood now starting to stain the front of his shirt. I then watched as Bill fell in slow motion face first onto the floor reveling Sugar standing behind him with a gun in her hand.

Sugar then shook me awake, "There is a car parked across the street". I got up and looked out the window. I could see the light from a cigarette flare in the drivers seat. I could not see who it was that was in the car. I asked Sugar if she knew who it was, she didn't look at me, she just shook her head no. After several minutes a man got out and walked to the trunk of his car, he grabbed something and started to walk toward us, he was walking towards the front door holding something in his hands. Sugar looked over at me and asked if she should go see what he wants. I thought to myself that she cannot be that stupid. The man stopped when he reached the front lawn. He looked up and down the street and then pushed a for sale sign into the lawn. He then got back in his car and left. Sugar stood up, "Oh my god my heart is pounding". I put my arm around her, "Calm down, you are going to have to make that call now." I handed her my phone. Sugar took the phone and said, "He won't answer it because he isn't going to know the number". I told her that I had put her sim card in it and that he will know it is her. I handed Sugar a note with things I needed her to say. As she dialed I told her to try and say only what is on the note. "Hi father it's me" she said, "I gave Joe the drug, he appears to be sleeping." I could hear her father yelling on the other end, Sugar then told him that she thought I might be on to her, and that was why she gave me the drug so early. She was then supposed to ask him to come and pick her up, but she didn't. I pointed to the note. Sugar crumpled it up and threw it on the floor. I then pulled the phone away from her ear so I could also hear what he was saying. I heard him say, "Don't worry about it, where is Joe now?" Sugar told him I was in the master bedroom and then she said she thought she should just leave now. He then told her to stay with me, and if I start to come around, she should mix more of the drug in water and pour it in my mouth. Sugar then started to cry, she told him that she was scared, not scared to be in the house, but scared that Bill and Joy might come looking for her. Her father was then silent. Sugar cried into the phone, "Please help me." He then told her not to worry about Bill or Joy, He then said, "I'll call Bill and tell him you two came here thinking I would protect you, I will tell Bill that I killed both of you, He will then stop looking." Sugar than asked, "What about his dreams?" There was an awkward silence until he almost yelled into the phone, "JUST DO WHAT THE FUCK I AM TELLING YOU TO DO, and what ever you do, don't leave that house until I come to get you". Sugar then closed the phone and handed it back to me. "Bill is going to see this in his dream and kill all of us, including father". I put the phone in my pocket and told Sugar that the next time Bill goes to sleep, he wont be waking up, I then asked her, "Do you know how to shoot a gun?"

TWO-ELEVEN
2-11-98 / 12:25 am

I went into the bathroom to splash some water on my face, I was still tired and needed to stay awake. When I returned to the bedroom Sugar was lighting the last of several candles lit around the bed. When I saw this she said, "Don't worry the shades are all closed." She walked over and hugged me. "This may be our last night together, why don't you go down and grab the wine." When I grabbed the wine I mixed one glass with the drug. When I returned to the bedroom Sugar was under the bed sheets. I handed her the glass with the drug and started to take off my clothing. Neither of us said a word to each other. She took a sip and put it on the nightstand. I lay down next to her and started to gently kiss her. Sugar was childlike as she blushed when she moved my hand to cover her breast. I held up my wine glass and said "Cheers". Sugar clinked her glass against mine and guzzled it. She then held me close to her as she whispered in my ear, "How long before the drug works?" I felt a tear fall from her cheek. I held her until she was no longer able to move. When I let go she slumped onto her back. I leaned in and gently kissed her as I pulled the cover up over her. I then sat up on the bed and felt woozy, she must have had some of the drug on her lips. When I tried to stand everything went black and I fell unconscious onto the bed.

2:11 am

I woke up and tried to feel Sugars neck to make sure she still had a pulse but my hands and legs were duct taped. The door opened and Bill came in and cut the tape from my ankles and pulled me from the bed. He shoved me down the hallway and into another bedroom. Amy was sitting on the bed and jumped up as I came in. Bill stopped Amy as she tried to run to me. Joy took Amy back to the bed and attempted to take off her robe. Amy protested and Bill swung me around and slapped me down to the floor. Amy yelled for Bill to stop. Bill then pulled his gun out and yelled, "THEN DO IT". Amy took her robe off leaving her with just a pair of panties on, she then laid on her back on the bed as she slowly put her hands thru ropes that were tied to the headboard. Joy then helped Bill pick me up and they both ripped my clothing off down to my boxers. Bill then pushed me down face first onto Amy's stomach. "Do it bitch, take her panties off". I reached for Amy's hips. "DO IT" Bill yelled, "Or I'll kill both of you". I looked away as I slowly pulled on the panties. I saw a mirror leaning against the wall covered by a black cloth. I suddenly felt calm as I knew I was dreaming. I then felt a fly land on my hand, I watched as it walked up the back of my hand and sat on my wristband, the fly seemed to look at me before flying off. I watched its flight as it flew over and landed on Sogod who was standing in front of me. Sogod walked over and pulled the cloth from the mirror. I saw Amy's reflection in the glass as she slipped one of her hands free from the ropes and she reached under the pillow. I then looked and saw that it was Danielle that was slowly pulling down Amy's panties. I then looked down at myself and saw that I was seeing thru Danielle's eyes, I was Danielle in my dreams, I watched thru Danielle's eyes as Amy tried to show her she wasn't afraid to do this, I saw as Danielle fought with Bill and was forced to do this. I witnessed thru Danielle's eyes as she killed people. Sogod then sat down beside me on the bed and said, "You now know what I meant by seeing who is not there". I reached for him and he took my hand and said, "You were not Danielle all the time, some dreams were all you". I wanted to ask him more but suddenly the bedroom door was forced open. Bill stood off to the side as he held up his weapon and shot. I watched as the bullet went thru the neck of someone that was standing in the shadow of the doorway. That person fell onto the bedroom floor dropping a pillowcase causing its contents to crash onto the floor. I then felt an extreme pain in my neck and everything turned black.

I felt someone slapping me. As I slowly opened my eyes. Sogod was sitting on the bed. Amy was halfway off the bed and blood was running from a wound to her neck. I was lying over Amy's legs unable to move. Joy was slumped in the corner, her face appeared to be shot thru and parts of it were sliding down the wall behind her. I looked over and saw that Sugar was standing in the shadows of the doorway holding the hand of the man she calls father. I looked back at Sogod as he said "Its up to you Joe, its time to take your dreams back, its time to save her". Sogod then started to turn into what looked like flies, as his skin and eyes started to change, I woke up staring at Sugar as she lay next to me staring straight up at the ceiling, tracks from her tears could be seen on the sides of her face, she was still unable to move. I jumped up and grabbed the pillowcase and ran out of the house.

2:15 am

As I got to Danielle's door I looked at my watch, the crystal was broke and it stopped at 2:11am. I pushed the door open and silently made my way to the bedroom steps. I looked up and saw Bill pulling Danielle from her bedroom. I picked up her phone and dialed 911 and left it off the hook. As I walked towards the spare bedroom

I could hear Bill yelling at Danielle to do it. When I hit the doorway I saw Amy reaching under her pillow as her mother was about to take her panties off. It was happening exactly the way my dream went. Bill saw my shadow and grabbed his gun and quickly turned and fired. I ducked his shot, I could hear the bullet as it flew by my head and shattered thru the temple of one of his cameramen. I was then able to stand up and swing the pillowcase up hitting Bill in the face crushing his nose, causing him to drop his gun as he fell to the ground, at the same exact time as Bill hit the floor, Amy pulled my stun gun from under her pillow and shoved it against Danielle's neck and squeezed the trigger and held it there until Danielle passed out on top of her. Ron who was the other cameraman lunged at me. I swung the pillowcase full of broken toilet tank top at his legs knocking him to the ground. Joy stood in the corner, she appeared to scared to move. As Ron attempted to get back up I slammed the bag back down over his head knocking him out. I looked up and saw Bill trying to get to his feet. I kicked the side of his face like it was a football causing blood and teeth to spray from his head and splatter on the bed sheets. I reached for Amy who was trying to push Danielle's body off of her. Joy pulled out her knife and charged from the corner at Amy as she lay on the bed trapped underneath Danielle's weight. I was able to grab Joy but she stuck the knife into my side and I crumpled to the floor pulling Joy down with me. Joy pushed me to the side and stood up as I tried to hold her down, she put her foot on my chest and pulled the knife from my side. Bill was also able to get up and he now stood over me with blood dripping from his wounds and stepped on my hand as I reached for his gun that was still on the floor. Bill bent down dripping blood and picked up his gun as Joy turned towards the bed with the knife. Just as she went to plunge it into a screaming Amy, Bill lifted his weapon and said, "I don't need you anymore slut" and he shot Joy in the face. It was a point blank shot and the force of the bullet hitting her face forced her body to slam back against the wall. Joy's face and the back of her head stuck to the wall behind her leaving a red streak on the wallpaper as she slowly slid down. Amy was pleading with Bill to stop. Bill still standing on my hand said, "It is to late to stop now." He then pointed his gun at my head. He leaned down and I could feel the hot barrel burning my scalp. "My brother was wrong," he said to me, "You failed". I then heard a shot and felt Bills body fall over me. I pushed him off and sat up leaning against the bed. I looked up and saw Sugar standing in the doorway holding a smoking gun, Sugar was shaking as her father slowly took the gun from her hand. Sugar then looked over at Joy's body and softly said, "I was seeing what Joy was doing in my dreams." With one hand holding my bleeding side, I held up the other and asked that they let Amy live. Sugar smiled at me as her father slowly put his gun back under his jacket and said, "We are now even". I looked up at Amy who was reaching out to me. I could hear the police cars getting closer. I looked back at the doorway but Sugar and her father were gone. I heard Amy sobbing and the police running up the steps as I passed out.

2-11-98 / 7:30 pm

I woke up in the Hospital and there were two Police Officers standing guard outside my door. I called out to them but they ignored me. I reached for my wristband as the Doctor walked in. He lifted the sheet to look at my side. If you stay off your feet for a few days it should heal nicely. I asked him what was happening, if I was I under arrest. He wrote in my chart and said, "I don't know, but there is a FBI Agent out there waiting to talk to you if you feel up to it". Agent Brown came in right after the Doctor left and pulled up a chair, he was polite and asked how I was feeling, "Okay" I said, and I then asked him if I was under arrest. He patted my arm and said, "Not yet, Amy has been very informative". I forgot all about Amy and I tried to sit up, "How is Amy, is she okay, where is she?" Agent Brown assured me that she was fine. He then flipped thru some notes and asked, "So tell me how you came upon all of this?" If I told him the truth he would have me committed. I told him as I was coming back home and I noticed that my house was boarded up and police tape was wrapped around the entire perimeter. I saw a light on at my neighbors and when I knocked on the door it opened a little. When I stuck my head in I heard Amy screaming upstairs so I ran up. He stopped me and asked if I was the one that called 911, "I dialed it, but then I heard Amy scream again so I dropped the phone and ran up". He then asked where the sack of broken porcelain came from that I hit them with. "I told them it was there, that I must of just picked it up and started swinging it. He then sat silently as he wrote in his notebook. I asked him if any of them were still alive. He didn't answer, he just looked up from his notes and said, "Funny, Bill was seen coming from a motel near here. When we searched the room the only items missing were a pillowcase and the toilet tank cover, but they did replaced that with a dead girl". I just lay in the bed waiting for the next question wondering why they were watching Bill, and why they didn't arrest him after finding Ruby dead in the hotel room. Agent Brown then said, "The dead girl could not be identified." I still remained quiet. "We also lifted a lot of prints, any possibility that any of them are yours?" I then ask him if I was going to need a lawyer. He dodged the question and said, "Anyway, your telling me you lived next door and you never seen or heard anything like this come from your neighbors?" I acted like I was thinking, and then said, "Nope, never". He got up and started to walk out of the room when he turned around and asked, "How did your rental car fall off a mountain side and blow up just south of the turnpike?" I was caught by surprise and I could not answer. He then said "I'll just write down it was stolen". He turned to leave again but before he did he told me that if there was anything else to call him, then as he left his card on the table he whispered, "That is if you remember who shot Bill". He dismissed the Officers at the door as he walked out. He stuck his head back in and told me that I wasn't being held, but not to leave town. He then turned out the light and whispered "Sweet dreams".

8:00 pm

The Doctor came back in and told me that I would have to stay a couple more days in the Hospital and let my wound heal. I could not do that, I had to find Amy, so I signed myself out. Agent Brown was in the lobby when I got off the elevator. He appeared to be waiting for me, like he knew I was going to leave. I asked him where Amy was. Agent Brown told me that her Uncle picked her up at the police station the night of the incident. I asked for the Uncle's address. He told me that he could not give me that information. He did however tell me that her uncle was a well-respected man and that Amy was now safe. He then offered me a ride home that I accepted. On the ride home he told me off the record that Bill

Johnson had been under investigations for over fifteen years. I was told the investigation was compromised when someone called in a tip about his bookstore. As we sat at a red light he looked over at me and asked if I knew who it was that made that call. I had a feeling that he already knew the answer. He then said that the tipster's tip went thru one of Bills informants with the police and that Bill was able to get rid of or destroy any evidence before the store was raided. After that the FBI wasn't only watching Bill, but the Police Department too. I asked him why they were watching Bill in the first place. He didn't answer at first, he looked at me like I was joking, with a look that said I already know that answer. He then told me that Bill was suspected of producing child pornography. I didn't respond. Agent Brown then looked at me and asked, "What no more questions?" I sat silently, I had a million questions running thru my head. Not questions about what happened, questions as to how he knew I knew. He then said, "During our investigation no one would talk to us, we even sent in people undercover with no luck. Then several days ago we got lucky, someone in the police department, an officer that may have been involved wanted to talk, this officer told us he would explain everything to us, his name was Johnny Downs, but before we could question him he was killed." We then pulled around the corner leading up to my house Agent Brown said, "Didn't you know Officer Downs?" I looked down at the floor as I told him he was my friend. As we pulled up to my house Agent Brown said "Over fifteen years watching this guy and it all came to an end in one night because you happen to stumble into it". I looked up at Agent Brown, "If Bill was under surveillance you must of known what was going on, why didn't you stop him earlier". Agent Brown then told me that Bill was only suspected of making the movies, after we started this investigation, the movies suddenly stopped. It seemed from that point that Bill was always one step ahead of us, it was like he had informants everywhere, but the FBI could not locate any of them, or any of his films. He said they tapped his phones, intercepted his mail. He then paused before saying, "It was like he was being informed by ghosts". I then asked him if it was now over. Agent Brown told me that Bill was just the middleman, an underling and the big guy with the money was still out there. As I went to shut the car door, Agent Brown asked, "You didn't see anyone else in that house that night?" I told him no. I was hoping that my nightmare was at least over.

2-13-98 / 2:11 am

I woke up from a dreamless sleep by the phone ringing, and when I answered it I could hardly hear Amy on the other end. She was crying and whispering into the phone for me to come and get her. I asked her where she was. She said she didn't know, she said that she was tired and had to sleep. I yelled into the phone telling her to tell me where she was, who was there with her and what the room looked like. She could only say again that she was too tired and had to sleep. I then heard the phone hit the floor but it stayed on. I held it tight to my ear and I could hear water dripping, and then I heard a train horn. I knew where she was. I just had no way of getting there. Then I remembered Danielle's car in her driveway.

4:40 am

I pulled up out front of the house that just days ago I was being held prisoner in. I parked down behind some trees and snuck up to the front window. I peeked inside but no one was in there. I was about to go around back when I noticed a photo of the man Sugar called father sitting above the fire place, was this the same man that I had pulled a bag from over his head. I got around back and I could see the shed. There was light coming from under the door. Just as I was about to run down to the shed when the back door opened. I bent down behind some bushes. It was Sugar and an older woman. They both walked from the patio down into the shed. I stood up and felt the barrel of a gun being pushed into my back. When I turned around to see who it was I was slammed across the face and knocked out.

8:30 am

I woke up on the floor of the shed and I was handcuffed behind my back and had duct tape across my mouth. Amy's one hand was also cuffed to the side of the cot that she was sleeping on. I was able to sit up and pull my arms around front. A trick I learned from watching the inmates do it in the holding cells. I pulled the tape from my mouth and shook Amy but she didn't wake up. There was a glass of juice on the crate next to her, I smelled it, as it was probably drugged. I pushed on the door but it was locked from the outside. I was able to push it open enough to peak out. There was now a moving truck parked on the side of the house that was being loaded up with electronic equipment and DVD recorders. Sugar approached the back of the truck and went to put a box in, The man Sugar called father looked in the box and then threw it across the lawn, Sugar turned to look at him just as he slapped her to the ground. I then looked around for cuff keys or anything that I could use as a weapon. I then heard voices getting closer and peaked back out and saw Sugars father walking towards the shed with a woman, I saw Sugar kneeling on the lawn picking up the stuff that fell from the thrown box as the moving men laughed at her. I just sat on the foot of the bed and waited as they unlocked the door and walked in. He had a gun on his hip and he grabbed a metal chair and slid it over to me. "Take a seat," he said. I stood up and watched as the woman checked on Amy. I asked her if Amy was okay before I turned the chair around and sat down backwards leaning my cuffed hands on the back of the chair. He then unlocked a drawer and pulled out a needle and filled it with something and set it on the table next to Amy. He then sat down across from me and said, "She feels no pain." When he lifted his baseball cap to wipe his forehead I recognized him. He was the old man that I had saved in this very house, he was Mr. Brinson and the woman checking on Amy was his wife, but Sugar was not his granddaughter. Mr. Brinson then said, "It was over Joe, you were out, why cant you just leave shit alone?" I looked at him, as he actually seemed disappointed that I was here, I said, "Just let Amy go, why hurt a child?" Mr. Brinson let out a little

laugh as he stood up and looked at his watch, "Let me tell
you a story Joe. Many years ago my drugged out 13-year-
old daughter sold my granddaughter to the Johnson's, the
bitch sold my little Danielle for two hundred dollars and
some crack, the baby was only eight months old. They had
been producing porno and they came up with this idea to
raise her to be in kiddy porno, they taught her shit as soon
as she could sit up. Do you know how I found out?" I
didn't answer, I kept watching Amy and Mrs. Brinson. "I
saw her on TV in a dream that I had every night, the
dreams started about ten years after she went missing. I
then tracked the Johnson's down thru the clues I saw
when I was asleep. It took me over 15 years to find her.
Danielle was celebrating her 16 birthday when I found
her. I wanted to kill the Johnson's, but for a lack of better
judgment I didn't. They had little girls that they had
raised to do these movies, and the kids appeared to enjoy
what they were doing. Danielle also appeared to be happy,
she still doesn't know I am her grandfather. The Johnson's
were making money hand over fist but they were not
careful with it, the FBI was ready to bust up their little
ring. I saw the potential for making a ton of money, so I
joined them. With my connections from the war, and my
real estate business I became the brains, I began selling
the videos overseas, only I knew who the buyers were, I
had to trust who I was selling them to. I had all the money
put in foreign accounts that could not be traced. We built
the community that you now live in, we owned every

house in it, and kept it filled with our people. Everything was working like a charm, then the kids we had started to grow up, nobody wanted them anymore, the kids were to old, too beat down, the public didn't pay half as much for adult porno. Then the Johnson's hooked up with some dirty cops and they were able to get some fresh kids. The kids we got with the cops were the last ones." I looked up at Mr. Brinson and asked, "Sugar?" He didn't answer as he leaned over Amy and kissed her gently on her forehead, "We all stopped making the films after they got too old and we went our separate ways. Then one night out of the blue Bill called with another plan to start up the movies, at first I wasn't interested, but his idea held some merit and we set up a meeting. Bill showed up with his freak show of a brother Robert and they told me that they had been trying to get kids from the homeless shelter unsuccessfully now for several months. Bill then told me that Danielle had a daughter and his plan was to use Danielle's child. They told me she was still pretty young, but she was being shown the way. Bill told me that Susie and Rose were still around and both were still being used. Bill also stated that Susie had a younger brother and Rose had given birth at 13 to baby boy and Bill was certain that he could get them to work. Bill told me that he did not need me anymore to ship the films overseas that he had a plan to sell this film here in the states. I was very well off, I had invested my money and really didn't need to take a chance on selling any films in the states. Bill and Robert had foolishly spent all of their money on drugs and other foolish shit, so they needed me to be the money to get this started back up. They wanted a loan, not a partner." I looked over at Amy and asked him how he could let them use his great granddaughter? Mr. Brinson quickly turned to stare at me. He then said, "Money, and fear of being ass raped the rest of my life in jail. Bill told me that they have the whole town in their pockets, and if they were unable to keep paying them, someone might talk, and that talk could implicate me." He then told me that Robert who sat quietly for most of the meeting became upset when he stated that he still wasn't interested, Robert yelled at him saying he was a god and that Mr. Brinson would end up in jail or dead if he didn't help before he stormed off. Bill stayed behind and told him that he was certain that his plan was safe and he already had over twenty thousand requests, not just for the new film, but the old ones also. Mr. Brinson stated he thought this was very dangerous and told Bill that even if one in the twenty thousand were to be a snitch, all of them would end up in prison. He then said that Bill then looked around the room, and that he made him feel like he was being set up. Mr. Brinson then sat on the cot next to Amy and said, "Bill then leaned in very close and whispered, I got the list from the government, I printed it right up off the fucking internet, every town has a listing of all child predators in their neighborhoods, right there in a little package, it list their names, addresses, and charges, we sell one time and move out of the country." Mr. Brinson then looked down at Amy as his wife checked on her, and then back at me, "Joe it was fucking brilliant, when I pulled up all these lists, even if we only sold one copy to ten percent of the people on those lists, we would make millions and millions of dollars, how could I not get involved." Mr. Brinson then stood up and lit a cigarette. "Only problem was that Amy's father came back, the father was one of the kids the police brought around, Johnny Downs. He was much older now and had gotten married, he had his own kids and he just became a cop himself. Then Danielle's brother got involved, claiming Amy was his. He claimed that Danielle had a boy that died and that he was paid by John to allow them to switch Danielle's baby with his baby. Dan's drugged out girlfriend Judy was just about to give birth. So on the night Judy went into labor Dan and Danielle staged a fight in public. Danielle had to be beat enough to be sent to the hospital and if Judy had a girl she was going to be told that her child died and Danielle was going to leave with her baby. Judy gave birth on February 11th to twins, but before she even knew she had twins, Fucking Dan told her that the baby died. Danielle left the hospital with Judy's baby girl, Amy, and if Dan didn't jump the gun, Judy would have left with Amy's twin brother and most of our problems would not have happened. So we took her twin brother Timmy and he was raised between here and Johnny Downs house. Judy didn't believe her baby died and hired a private investigator.

Robert Johnson worked in the hospital's record room and he was the one that the investigator contacted. Robert then had the investigator killed. He then burned the record room and half the hospital down, the guy was always a nut bag. So you see Joe, Amy is not my great granddaughter, my great grandchild died. So I told Bill I was in. As we got ready to do this movie, Bill started to become more and more paranoid, he kept talking about all this evidence that someone had hidden that would expose all of us. Bill started to drift from the plan that was to get as many orders as possible, make the film with both Amy and Danielle and then leave the country. Then Bill brother was brought back to town, and he ended up at Danielle's hospital until he died. Then shortly after Bill's brother death, Bill suddenly changed and started telling everyone that everything would work out, and when I asked him how he could be so sure, Bill told me that he had started to see what happens, that he was being guided by his dreams. Now a normal person would think that he was just fucking nuts, but you know Joe, I too was starting to have dreams, dreams that told me to make this film. As we got closer to making this film more problems started to come at us, first there was the nosey doctor, who tried to blackmail Danielle, then John's compulsion to force the girls to have sex with him jeopardized our plan. He ended up with a bullet between his nuts, not because of his lust for the girls, but he was also about to talk to the Feds. But none of this seemed to bother Bill. Then my fucking dreams started to intensify and I saw that Susie was killed because she was a snitch. I then had a dream where I called Judy and told her that I would reunite her with her child, give her and Dan money so they could start a new life" Mr. Brinson then looked at the floor and said, "It was so real that I got her son Timmy and set up a meeting with her. I drove out to where I was supposed to meet her, but as I drove up I saw a car pulling away with out its lights on. I didn't stop, but I slowed down and saw Judy's dead body half buried lying in a ditch." He then looked up and wiped the sweat from his face, "A lot of people have died because of what Bill saw in his dreams, and I agreed with Bill and knew what he was going thru. I found Danielle thru my dreams, and when my dreams came back, you saved my wife and me when you ripped those bags from our heads, only in my dream it wasn't you that saved us, it was Dan. These dreams were becoming so fucking real, plus Bill was taking everyone out that he was dreaming was getting in the way. I have no idea how he did it or who he had do it, and I didn't want to know. I just know I never got a drop of blood on my hands, all I could ever be convicted of was money laundering. It was too late for me to get out, so I just sat back and let him make the movie, and I was going to bank what was going to be a truckload of fucking cash." I looked up and told him that his granddaughter Danielle was Bill's hit man, that Danielle killed all of those people so that he could get a truckload of cash. He stood up and said that I could not possibly know that. I then said thru clenched teeth, "I can dream too." I then sat silently waiting for his next move. Mr. Brinson then calmly said, "I was only going to kill Danielle and Bill after anyway." I then looked up and asked how he was going to do that without getting blood on his hands. Mr. Brinson calmly said, "I had a dream that you were going to do it for me, I was almost right, but you did let Danielle live and that is why I have to get out of town before she starts talking." I then whispered, "You may want to wash that blood off your hands before you go." He knelt down face to face with me and angrily asked, "What blood?" I quietly said, "When Sugar killed Bill, when she took your gun and shot him, you became an assessor to murder." Mr. Brinson got up and checked on Amy as she started to move around on the bed. "Other then Sugar, who will be dead before noon, you are the only one that can could prove that", he then leaned down pulled the duct tape from Amy's mouth and kissed her on the lips, "Isn't she beautiful, she would have made me millions." He then turned back towards me and said, "Let me finish this". He then picked up the needle and held it up to the light, "You know those two dimwitted fuck job bank robbers only got thirty seven dollars from the bank they robbed? If not for knowing from my dreams that we would be saved, I might have done something stupid and we all would have wound up dead, and that is why this decision is so hard for me. You see Joe, you saved us, but then I saved you so we were even." I looked over at his wife as she left the shed but did not lock the door. I looked back over at Mr. Brinson and said, "I didn't only save you, I also saved your wife and child so maybe you could find it in your heart to just let Amy go." Mr. Brinson stood up and placed the needle on the bed next to Amy, he pulled his gun from his hip, "What do you think I am, don't think for a fucking second that I am an idiot." He then opened and checked his gun. "You and that little bitch on the bed are the only two people left alive that can fuck me. I still have dreams, and I have seen in my dreams that this nightmare wont be over until I get my hands bloody." He then raised his gun and pointed it at my head, "I am truly sorry for what I am about to do". Just as he started to pull on the trigger I stood up and swung the metal chair up from between my legs hitting him square in the face, his nose seemed to break off his face as he fell to the floor struggling to see thru the blood and find his gun. I kicked the gun towards the shed door and continued to beat him with the chair until Amy screamed for me to stop. I then searched his body and found the cuff key, as I un-cuffed Amy I saw the phone that she must of called me from under the cot. It only had a little power left. I called Agent Brown and I was surprised when he told me that he was already on the way. Agent Brown then told me before the phone went dead that he had seen what has been happening in his dreams, and that he saw it thru my eyes. As I flipped the phone shut Mr. Brinson's wife came thru the shed door. She grabbed the needle that was on

the bed and held it against Amy's neck. She became
hysterical when she saw her husband lying in a puddle of
blood on the floor. She raised her arm and went to plunge
the needle into Amy's neck. As I jumped towards them,
Mr. Brinson who was still alive was able to grab at my leg
and I stumbled and fell. I heard a gunshot as my head hit
the floor. I looked up and saw Mrs. Brinson slowly fall to
her knees before slamming face first into the metal frame
of the cot before hitting the floor. Sugar was standing
behind her holding Mr. Brinson's gun, this time she wasn't
shaking. Amy ran to me as Sugar dropped the gun and
sat in the grass just outside the door. I could hear the
sirens getting closer. Amy hugged me and said, "I guess
he didn't have this dream." I held Amy until the police
arrived.

The end?

6-28-98 / 8:00 am

After all the questioning, the court appearances and all the dreamless nights, I looked up at the sky and said "I hope this will answers all your questions" as I dropped the letter I wrote to Susie's brother Pete in the mail. I then turned and walked back to my car. Amy came running out of the corner store. "Wait for me" she yelled as she jumped into the passenger side seat. "What's in the bag?" I asked. She looked in then up at me and smiled as she pulled out a candy bar. "I just knew you would want one". I ripped the wrapper open and didn't notice as I pulled out into traffic that a fly had landed on the exposed candy. We then turned at the corner pulling the trailer with all we wanted to take with us and started our move to Florida.

I didn't notice that Sugar had walked out from the same store Amy just came out of. Sugar's phone rang and she answered it as we drove past her. Sugar then quietly said into the phone, "I just talked to her, they both just left, Amy said they are headed to Florida". Sugar hung up and put her phone back in her pocket. The fly flew off my candy bar and flew towards Sugar, suddenly a man walked up to her putting his arm around her shoulders, it could have been, but was it Sogod? On the other end Danielle hung up the prison phone and smiled, and when the prison guard asked her what she was so happy about. Danielle simply said, "Sometimes dreams do come true".

THE END

Robert Johnson	Dead
Johnny Downs	Dead
Susie	Dead
Doctor Adams	Dead
Judy Johnson	Dead
Dan Williamson	Dead
Henry	Dead
Rose	Dead
Joy	Dead
Bill Johnson	Dead
Mrs. Brinson	Dead

Mr. Brinson is currently in protective custody at the Mental Hospital.

His suffered 211 broken bones from the beating.

Big Ron was killed in prison while awaiting his trial.
The guards found him hanging in his cell at 2:11 am

Joe Pratt adopted Amy.
They live in Miami Florida, Dream Free, for now.

Sugar is living in Joe's house, under FBI surveillance.

Timmy Johnson is in foster care

Danielle is awaiting sentencing; her only visitor is
Timmy Johnson,
He visits her every night in her sleep.

Book Two
Six Twenty Eight
Dream Wedding

Twelve years later, Amy has met a nice young man, he too is adopted and he is very sensitive and understanding of Amy past. He is about to propose.

Danielle has been haunted with dreams from Timmy Johnson, dreams similar to Joe's that at first she don't understand. Soon Timmy takes her away from prison and they both set out to find Amy.

Amy's quiet life is also soon disturbed by dreams, dreams she holds from Joe. As Amy tries to cope with her own dreams, Joe too is visited again in his sleep; he is told once again that he must save her.